Come Home With Me

Come Home With Me

SUSAN FOX

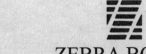

ZEBRA BOOKS
KENSINGTON PUBLISHING CORP.
http://www.kensingtonbooks.com

ZEBRA BOOKS are published by

Kensington Publishing Corp.
119 West 40th Street
New York, NY 10018

All Kensington titles, imprints, and distributed lines are available at special quantity discounts for bulk purchases for sales promotion, premiums, fund-raising, educational, or institutional use.

Special book excerpts or customized printings can also be created to fit specific needs. For details, write or phone the office of the Kensington Sales Manager: Attn.: Sales Department. Kensington Publishing Corp., 119 West 40th Street, New York, NY 10018. Phone: 1-800-221-2647.

Zebra and the Z logo Reg. U.S. Pat. & TM Off.

First Printing: January 2018
ISBN-13: 978-1-4201-4326-3
ISBN-10: 1-4201-4326-3

eISBN-13: 978-1-4201-4327-0
eISBN-10: 1-4201-4327-1

10 9 8 7 6 5 4 3 2 1

Printed in the United States of America

Chapter One

"Guess what?" Miranda Gabriel's brother cried, raising his girlfriend's left hand like a boxing referee proclaiming the champ. "We're engaged!"

Diamonds sparkled on Eden's finger, and when Miranda stared from the ring to Aaron's face and his fiancée's, their excitement was no less dazzling.

Miranda's heart sank like a heavy, cold stone.

She had been peeling sweet potatoes in the big kitchen at SkySong when Aaron and Eden burst into the room. Tonight's dinner at the serenity retreat was planned as a celebration of Eden's tidying up all the details around the sale of her family's home in Ottawa now that she, her parents, and her sister were becoming Destiny Island residents. Aaron, owner of Blue Moon Air, had flown over to Vancouver in his Cessna seaplane on this chilly, early December day to pick Eden up after her Ottawa flight. Now it seemed the celebration would be a dual-purpose one.

"He proposed on the dock," Eden said, her voice bubbly, neither she nor Aaron seeming to notice that their wet jackets were dripping on the terra-cotta-tiled floor. "Right there in the middle of Blue Moon Harbor." She laughed up at him, her amber eyes glowing with happiness and love. "In the rain, and it was the most romantic thing in the world."

Engaged.

Eden's aunt and uncle, Di and Seal SkySong, who owned this rustically lovely retreat on four acres of waterfront, rushed over to the happy couple, offering hugs and congratulations. Miranda's two-year-old daughter remained in her booster chair at the kitchen table, still absorbed in the tea party game she and Di had been playing with one of Ariana's cloth fairy dolls. And Miranda herself stood rooted at the teal-topped kitchen counter, her feet as leaden as her heart.

Of course she'd known where Aaron and Eden's relationship was heading. In truth, the depressed, pessimistic, defeated spot in her soul, the one she hated to surrender to, had known ever since that day back in June. The day when her pride had hit an all-time low. Evicted from her tiny apartment, without the funds to rent another, she'd felt worthless and powerless. For the sake of her precious daughter, she had phoned Aaron and admitted she had no choice but to accept his offer of help. There she'd been, more pathetic than ever before in her life. She'd had no strength left, no option but to leave Vancouver and drag herself and Ariana to Destiny Island, a place she'd always hated, to shelter under her big brother's roof.

But Aaron, the one person who'd always been there for her, was away in Ottawa, visiting a woman he'd just met.

Sight unseen, Miranda—selfish bitch that she was—had hated Eden Blaine for threatening the one bit of stability in her and Ariana's lives. But then she'd met the smart, sensitive, beautiful Eden, seen her with Aaron, listened to what her brother said and didn't say. She'd seen that despite the huge problems the two lovers had faced, Eden made him happy. And Aaron's happiness was the second-most important thing in the world to Miranda. Only the welfare of her daughter ranked higher.

Now, realizing she'd been silent too long, she forced herself to walk across the kitchen. Normally she found this room so warm and welcoming, with its white-painted wood and brick walls and cabinets, accented by a hodgepodge of vividly colored chairs, kitchen accessories, and artwork. But today her heart was a frozen lump in her chest and it would take a lot more than Di and Seal's cheerful, eclectic décor to warm it.

Throwing her arms around the happy couple, she squeezed both of them, but Aaron a little harder. Her handsome, dark-haired brother, her best and only real friend for all their lives, now belonged to someone else. "I'm so happy for you guys."

It wasn't a lie. Honestly, it wasn't. It was just a truth that jostled uneasily side by side with her selfishness and her envy. The guy who'd been so cynical—or, as he called it, realistic—about love had had, for the very first time, the guts to throw his heart into the ring. And what did he get? A freaking happy ending. As compared to her. She truly did believe in love and she'd been brave enough to go for it, to love and lose and try again, over and over. She'd been doing it ever since she was a tiny child hoping against hope that one day her mom would love her and be there for her. And yet here she was, twenty-seven years old and still alone.

So many times, as the children of a cocaine-addicted prostitute, she and Aaron had been the kids left outside, looking in windows at happy families eating together, at stores full of shiny new toys and games, at grocery shelves stocked with more food than anyone could possibly eat in a lifetime. Wanting, always wanting, but not getting.

Now Aaron had crossed over and he was on the inside. And she was left outside, no longer shoulder to shoulder with her big brother but all by herself.

She drew in a long breath, trying to flush the sour gray tang of depression and self-pity from her mind and heart. The fact was, she wasn't alone; she had Ariana. Having a daughter made life so much richer and more wonderful but also created pressures so heavy that a few months back, Miranda had almost cracked under them. Because it was one thing to be strong and resourceful enough to look after yourself. It was quite another when you were responsible for a small, fragile human being who deserved so much more than you'd ever been able to give her.

Miranda went over to the table where her beloved black-haired fairy princess of a daughter had stopped playing with her doll and, it seemed, belatedly come to the realization that everyone's attention was focused elsewhere than on her. Her cute face had gone pouty, a warning that a TTT—terrible two tantrum, as Miranda called them—was threatening to explode, as so often happened when the toddler felt neglected or thwarted.

"Sweetie, this is so exciting," Miranda said, hoisting her mocha-skinned daughter, so unlike her own fair self, into her arms. The familiar weight and warmth, the delicate scent of the baby oil Di made from the petals of wild roses, soothed Miranda's nerves.

Forcing enthusiasm into her voice, she brought the little girl over to the newly engaged couple. "Uncle Aaron is getting married." She glanced at his fiancée, the walnut-haired lawyer who'd given up her entire life in Ottawa to move to Destiny Island. "I guess that's going to make you Aunt Eden?"

Eden beamed, her happiness so vivid that, if Miranda had been a normal woman rather than a seething mess of insecurities, she'd have found it contagious. "I can't think of a bigger honor." She took Ariana's small hand gently in hers. "What do you think, Fairy-ana?" The nickname had been bestowed by Aaron a few months before, when his niece became obsessed with fairies. "Will you let me be your aunt Eden?"

Now that the attention was back on her, Ariana was happy. "An-te-den?" she ventured.

"That sounds so good," Eden said, turning to put her arm around Aaron, as if she couldn't bear to go more than a moment without touching him.

"It sure does," he said.

Oh God, Miranda's big brother, the guy who'd taught her to shoplift and pick pockets as necessities of survival, had gone all schmaltzy. With a reluctant grin, she had to admit it was actually pretty adorable.

And it was high time she stopped being so freaking pathetic and looked on the bright side. Aaron's happiness proved he'd been wrong to say that love wasn't in the cards for either of them. She was right: they *could* find true love. They could beat their track record of being unloved by their mom, their two dads—because, in truth, she and Aaron were half siblings—and their grandparents.

But right now wasn't the time to muse about love. She had to think about her and Ariana's immediate future. They couldn't keep living in the guest room at Aaron's small log home. That arrangement wasn't fair to him and Eden.

Resting her right hand on her shirtsleeved left forearm, she summoned the power of the tattooed dragon that lay beneath the faded blue cotton. The dragon that symbolized her strength and ability to cope with whatever life tossed her way.

Eden's aunt and uncle got back to the dinner preparations, Seal taking over the sweet potatoes Miranda had abandoned. Eden and Aaron went into the mudroom to take off their jackets and boots, then returned, pulled out chairs at the table, and sat down side by side, hands linked.

Bouncing Ariana gently in her arms, Miranda listened to

the conversation with half an ear while she formulated a plan for finding a new home for herself and her daughter.

"Eden, you've told your mom and dad?" Di asked.

"Yes, we stopped at their cabin first." Eden's parents and younger sister were living in one of the eight scenic log cabins at SkySong, though Helen and Jim planned to buy a house on Destiny Island in the spring. "Mom and Dad are thrilled to bits. They'll be over for dinner shortly. Kelsey was out for a run, so she doesn't know yet."

Eden went on, gushing about how she couldn't believe how wonderful the past year had been, finding her long-lost aunt Di, discovering this wonderful island, and best of all meeting the love of her life.

Helen and Di had been separated since their teens, when Di, the older sister, had run away from their Ottawa home along with her new, secret boyfriend, a member of the Mi'kmaq First Nation in Nova Scotia, who was also a teen runaway. They'd traveled west, all the way to Destiny Island, where they'd joined the Enchantery commune. Last summer, a long-lost letter had provided a clue that brought Eden here, and the rest was history. A family reunion, not to mention a new love.

Di, who'd been emptying glass canning jars of chopped tomatoes into a large pot on the stove, glanced over her shoulder. "Have you two talked about a wedding date?" The serene woman in her mid-sixties looked a bit like the hippie she'd once been, wearing one of the woven Guatemalan tops she loved, with her walnut-and-silver hair gathered into a long braid.

"Soon," Aaron said.

"But Aaron," Eden said, "I start my new job at Arbutus Lodge after New Year's. There'll be so much to do, and I need to concentrate on that rather than giving them short shrift."

Yeah, that was Eden. Superresponsible and organized.

"Do *not* tell me we're going to wait a year," Aaron said, sounding a little panicky.

"No, no, of course not. It's just, this is such a surprise. I need to get my head around it, and planning a wedding does take some time and effort."

He groaned, and Miranda gave him a sympathetic smile. Just wait until the poor guy found himself being dragged into discussions about flowers, music, and catering.

The scent of cooking tomatoes and herbs drifted across from the stove, stirring guilt in Miranda. She always tried to pull her weight and really should be helping with the meal. But right now something else was more important. She plunked down on a sky-blue chair across from Aaron and Eden, with her daughter in her lap.

Eden, gazing at Aaron, said, "How about the spring? April or May?"

"I guess I can live with that. After all, we'll be living together anyhow."

And there was Miranda's cue. "Ariana and I will clear out of the house as soon as I can find a place." She'd been in denial, should have done this back when Eden decided to move to the island.

Cuddling her daughter, she said, "I'll talk to Iris at Dreamspinner. She and her family know everyone on the island." The Yakimuras' bookstore and coffee shop were the heart of Blue Moon Harbor village. "I bet some of the summer folks would be willing to rent their place at least until May or June, and by then I'll have found—"

"Whoa," Aaron said, casting a quick sideways glance at Eden.

"That's for sure," his fiancée said. "Miranda, Aaron's place is your home, yours and Ariana's, just as much as it's mine. We don't want you to leave."

Even as she appreciated Eden's generosity, Miranda's

heart gave a twinge at the *we*. Already, Aaron and Eden were a *we* who made decisions together.

"Besides," Aaron said, "if you pay rent somewhere, you'll have to increase your work hours, and that won't give you as much time for your studies."

For years he'd been urging her to further her education. As an eleventh-grade dropout who'd never done well in school, she'd had no desire to go back to the books. And she'd been busy, what with the waitressing and retail jobs she'd held, and her pre-Ariana active life as a young single woman in a dynamic city. But then she'd gotten pregnant and life had changed.

Last summer it had sunk in that, if she was going to give her daughter the kind of life she deserved, she needed higher-paying work. So she'd worked her butt off for the past few months and almost finished her GED online. Turned out, she wasn't all that bad at schoolwork if she applied herself. In the new year, she'd start the online courses to get certified as an early childhood educator. Even if she busted her butt on those, too, which she fully intended to do, it would take her more than a year. "I'll still study," she said grimly.

"Are you sure?" he asked.

She'd have snapped at him for his lack of faith, except he had plenty of reason to doubt her. But now she was committed to building a better future for herself and the precious girl whose weight and stillness now indicated she'd dozed off on her mom's lap. "Yes, I'm sure." Somehow she'd find the time.

"And you guys need privacy," she said firmly. "Stop being so nice and generous and all that good stuff and be realistic." She managed a one-sided grin for her brother. "Isn't that what you've been telling me all these years? To be realistic?"

"Yeah, but—" he started.

"I have an idea." The calm voice was Di's, reminding Miranda that she and her brother had an audience.

Miranda glanced over her shoulder to see that Eden's aunt had turned away from the stove, where a pot of spicy tomato sauce now simmered. "Stay here, Miranda," Di said warmly.

"Here? At SkySong?"

The teen runaways had been together forever now. Never married, they'd rechristened themselves, changing the first names their parents had given them and taking the surname SkySong, and over the years they'd created this retreat by the same name. In addition to the lovely old wooden two-story home where Di and Seal lived, the scenic property included log guest cabins and a huge organic garden.

"We'd be happy to have you," Seal agreed, looking up from spreading something on a loaf of homemade French bread. Garlic and herb butter, from the delicious smell of it. He, like his partner, showed his hippie roots, clad in faded tie-dye and wearing his graying black hair in a pony-tail secured by a leather thong. His deep brown eyes were sincere behind wire-framed glasses.

"I can't take your charity."

"It's not charity," Di said firmly. "Nor is having Helen, Jim, and Kelsey in a cabin."

"No, of course it's not, with them," Miranda said. "I mean, they're your family." Not to mention the SkySongs were assisting in Helen's recovery after surgery and treat-ment for a recurrence of breast cancer.

"You're family, too," Seal said.

"No, I'm not." Aaron and Ariana were her only family.

"Of course you are," Di said, coming over and resting a hand on her shoulder. "Aaron's about to be our . . . uh, nephew-in-law and you're his sister. Besides, you sure can't accuse Seal and me of being sticklers for convention, can you?" Her bright blue eyes danced.

Miranda's lips twitched. "I wouldn't dare."

"For us," Di said, "it's the family of our hearts that counts. You and Ariana most definitely have a place in our hearts."

"It's the truth," Seal said.

Miranda swallowed, trying to clear away the lump that had formed in her throat. If she could believe them, she might cry. It was more acceptance and support than she'd had from her own grandparents, not to mention the unknown father who'd knocked up her mother. Or the mom who'd put her next fix or her current boyfriend ahead of her children's welfare.

"We're never full up in winter," Di went on. "You and your sweet girl can have a cabin for the next four or five months at least. You'll have lots of able babysitters, so—"

"It's no problem for me to take Ariana to the store." Blowing Bubbles, where she worked part-time, sold children's toys, furniture, strollers, and so on. Kara, the owner, brought her own little one along with her and encouraged Miranda to do the same. There was a fenced playpen for their toddlers and the kids of customers, and Kara gave the children toys and stuffed animals to keep them happy. She said the best advertisement was to see a smiling child loving one of the store's products. Mind you, since Ariana had turned two at the end of July, the whole happy-child thing wasn't happening as often as it used to.

"You might want to go out in the evenings, though," Di said.

"Going out isn't on my list right now." She hadn't had time to make female friends here. As for dating, her history with men was a succession of screw-ups: from the musician she'd moved in with when she was fifteen; to the gorgeous African-American actor who'd hung around long enough to father Ariana but not to see her born; to the chef she'd fallen for last year before realizing he changed women as often as he changed his special of the week.

Aaron said she looked for love in all the wrong places. Maybe he was right. All she knew now was that this wasn't the time to be looking. And, though she had no affection for Destiny Island, she had to admit it was a good place to be if she wanted to avoid temptation. There weren't many eligible guys, and those she'd seen were way too wholesome and boring to appeal to her. "My spare time's for Ariana and for studying."

"Wise priorities," Aaron said.

She sent him an eye roll just as the kitchen door opened again. This time it was Kelsey, Eden's younger sister. She wore damp jogging clothes and with one hand flicked raindrops from her spiky, blond-streaked hair. "Eden, Aaron? Mom and Dad say you have big news."

A grinning Eden held up her left hand.

Kelsey squealed and threw her wet arms around her sister and Aaron. "I'm so happy for you! For all of us!"

The commotion woke Ariana, who let out a demanding screech.

Kelsey said, "Oh, sweetie, are you getting ignored?" She came over to scoop the child from Miranda's arms and made funny faces that worked magic in calming the incipient tantrum.

Eden repeated the proposal-on-the-dock story and then Di said, "Kelsey, Miranda wants to move out of Aaron's house and I've told her she and Ariana should take a cabin here."

"You totally should!" Kelsey said to Miranda, her eyes—the same blue as Di's—sparkling with excitement. "That would be so cool. More additions to our big, happy family." She gazed down at Ariana again. "You'd like that, wouldn't you? I'd see lots more of you. Mom and Dad would love it, too. They're just crazy about you, you little sugarplum."

Kelsey, at twenty-two, was seven years younger than her

sister and almost five years younger than Miranda. She was spontaneous, generous, and optimistic, and she was also completely devoted to her mom. So much so that she'd taken a year off from university at McGill to move here with her parents to help out.

A big, happy family. It was the one thing Miranda and Aaron had always wanted. He was getting it, but she couldn't truly accept that it was being offered to her. Or that she deserved it. She glanced at her brother, who sat with his arm around Eden. His gaze met hers. A quarter of a century ago, the two of them had learned how to communicate without words. Now she knew he'd read her unspoken question.

Sure enough, he said solemnly, "Eden's right, that our place is yours, too. Never think you need to leave. But if you want to, I think you should accept Di and Seal's generous offer." His tone lightened. "Ariana would love having all these people to spoil her."

Miranda looked around the kitchen. A few minutes ago, everyone's attention had been on Aaron and Eden and now it was on her as they waited for her answer. Her brother knew exactly how to manipulate her. She'd do anything if she believed it was good for her child.

But could she really move to SkySong and be part of all this? The idea was overwhelming. She was so used to living alone with Ariana and had barely gotten adjusted to being in Aaron's house. Could she be a good guest here, pull her weight, ensure that Di and Seal didn't regret having made the offer?

Of course, she and Ariana would have a separate cabin. It wasn't like they'd all be living on top of one another. A lot of the time, she and her daughter would have more privacy than they did at Aaron's.

She gazed at her child, so contented in Kelsey's arms. Ariana was her anchor. Her heart.

Slowly, she said, "Di and Seal, if you're really sure, I guess that's what we'll do. But you have to let me at least pay something or cook meals or garden or—"

"Miranda, shut up," Seal said with a smile that deepened the curved lines bracketing his nose and mouth.

In the next moment, Di's arms came around her. Almost like a mother's.

Which was a dangerous way to think, because if there was one thing Miranda knew, it was that she couldn't rely on a mom.

Chapter Two

With his twin boys' fourth birthday coming up this weekend, widower Luke Chandler was, for the millionth time, thankful for two particular Blue Moon Harbor businesses. He relied on Blowing Bubbles for stuffed animals, toys, and games, and on Dreamspinner for books.

Now, in the late afternoon of a gray January day, carrying a Dreamspinner-logoed bag with two picture books, he pushed open the door to the kids' store. Normally, he asked Kara McConachie, the owner, for advice, but a quick scan of the bright space with its cheerfully crowded shelving and displays told him she wasn't there. In fact, the store seemed deserted but for a stormy-faced little girl in the fenced hexagonal play area. Curly black hair framed a brown-skinned face that would probably be cute when it wasn't all scrunched up. She looked to be somewhere between two and three. Having suffered through that age with Caleb and Brandon, that storm-cloud face made him wince in anticipation of a howl or shriek.

Hoping to ward it off, he strolled over to the multi-colored plastic fence and squatted down to her level, giving a reassuring smile. "Hey there, sunshine. Are you minding the store?"

His veterinary practice clients and staff said he had a magic touch with animals. Sadly, it hadn't carried over to his own two-year-olds, and apparently, it hadn't improved since then because the child let out one of those piercing shrieks that could shatter glass.

"Ariana!" a woman's voice called from the back area, where he guessed the stockroom and office must be. The voice grew closer. "Honestly, I leave you alone for one second and—oh!" The owner of the voice stopped dead and he rose to his feet.

It wasn't Kara, but an attractive blonde who looked to be a year or two younger than his own twenty-eight. He recalled hearing that Kara had a new part-time employee, but this was the first time he'd run into her.

Her gaze darted from him to the red-faced Ariana, and then back again. With a touch of wariness, she said, "I didn't hear the doorbell."

"I don't think it rang." He walked over to the door, opened and closed it again, and there was no sound.

"I'll tell Kara we need to get it fixed." She reached down and hoisted the wailing child into her arms. The motion seemed effortless even though the woman's body, revealed by snug-fitting jeans and a pale gray sweater, was slender rather than sturdy.

"Sorry about the, uh, crying," he said. "She looked kind of thunder-cloudy and I tried to cheer her up, but it backfired. What is she? Two?"

For the first time, a smile lit the woman's pale face, making her even prettier. Rubbing Ariana's back as the screeches subsided to snuffles, she said, "Two years, seven months."

"Five months to go."

The smile brightened. "You know something about two-year-olds."

"I had a couple of my own. We survived. Somehow."

"Gee, thanks, that's so encouraging." Huge grayish-blue eyes the shade of well-washed denim danced, tweaking some association from long ago. "I call it the TTTs, the terrible two tantrums," she said.

"Fitting."

"Would you give me just a minute, and then I'll be right with you?"

"Do what you need to. I'll browse."

But when he perused the shelves, the sound of the woman's voice as she soothed the girl distracted him. He peeked through a menagerie of stuffed seals, kittens, puppies, and bears to watch her gently bounce her daughter in her arms. When Ariana settled down and was back in the playpen, offering pretend tea to two cloth dolls, the salesclerk came over to him. "Finding anything? Can I help?" She shoved up the sleeves of her sweater.

His gaze automatically followed the motion, to see a tattoo of a colorful dragon on her left forearm. Lots of women had dragon tattoos, especially since that Swedish bestseller. But this dragon, combined with those denim eyes—and he remembered hearing a rumor that Aaron Gabriel's sister had returned to Destiny Island a few months earlier. Some of his clients gossiped, but he paid little attention unless their chatter related to the animals he was treating.

He looked up at her face again, trying to recall images from . . . what would it be? A dozen years ago?

"What is it?" she asked, that hint of wariness back in her voice. With her left hand, she brushed her shoulder-length hair away from her face. The gesture revealed a delicate ear, double-pierced with a dangly blue earring in one hole and a small silver heart in the other.

No black hair with fluorescent streaks; no bizarre makeup. No Goth black leather and ripped clothing. No nostril studs or eyebrow piercings. No attitude. But still there was something familiar. And did he see tiny scars where silver studs and rings might once have been? There was also her daughter's name: Ariana, like a feminine version of Aaron. "You're not Miranda Gabriel, are you?"

Dark brown lashes flicked down and then up again. As far as he could see—and he knew a bit about makeup, having spent years watching his wife carefully apply hers—this woman wasn't wearing anything except maybe lip gloss.

"Yes." She frowned at him. "Did we go to school together or something?"

She'd been a year behind him at Blue Moon High, for the couple of years between the time she moved to the island and the time she dropped out of school and ran away to Vancouver. But he'd sure noticed her. Despite the genuineness of his love for Candace and the fact that he was a total straight arrow, bad-girl Miranda had held a weird kind of allure. Like the way you could crave an ice cream sundae even though you knew it was bad for you. No, that was a poor analogy, because there'd been nothing sweet about Miranda.

Thinking of how the grown woman had cooed to her little girl, he reflected that it was more than her appearance that had changed. "You don't remember me?" he asked. "Luke Chandler?" Why would she? She'd been a loner, a rebel, much like his stepbrother Julian. Rather than hang out with the local kids, she'd hopped the ferry over to Vancouver on weekends. She'd had nothing good to say about Destiny Island, so he'd pretty much discounted the half-heard rumor that she was back.

"Luke . . ." She scrutinized his face, and did a quick up-down of his body, not that his jeans and winter jacket would have told her much. "Wait a minute. Straight A student, dated that redheaded cheerleader?"

He swallowed at the mention of his wife. "There were a couple of Bs. And yes, I dated Candace Yuen-Byrne." His best friend had turned into his girlfriend and then the love of his life. They'd planned a bright future but instead he'd lost her in childbirth. Fighting back a surge of melancholy, he said, "You've changed some."

She snorted. "You think?"

"Ariana's yours? Named after your brother?"

"Yes. He's the best man I've ever known," she said solemnly, making him wonder about the father who'd given Ariana her dark coloring.

She went on. "And you have two of your own, you said? You and Candace?"

He swallowed. "Yes, but no. She died giving birth, so I'm raising the twins on my own." Before she could rush in with some platitude, he said, "They're turning four. Two boys, identical twins. I'm looking for gift ideas." He and the boys' grandparents tried hard to make the birthday a day of celebration despite their own sad memories of losing Candace.

Those grayish-blue eyes, sorrowful and sincere, held his as Miranda refused to accept his attempted diversion. "I'm so sorry about Candace. It's terrible to lose someone you love."

Though he'd hoped to avoid this conversation, he found that her simple words touched a chord. "Yeah, it is." He lowered his voice so her daughter wouldn't hear. "How about you? Ariana's dad is . . . ?"

"Isn't. Never was, not since I told him I was pregnant."

"Asshat." The word burst out loudly before he could stop it. He cast a quick glance over at the little girl, but she was still happily absorbed with her dolls. "I'm sorry he ran out on you," he told Miranda quietly.

"Yeah, well." She shrugged. "Sometimes life sucks, as you well know. Anyhow, the guy might've been bad judgment but the result was Ariana, and she's the best thing that's ever happened to me."

"I feel the same about the boys." For their own sakes, and for the constant reminders of Candace that he saw in their light gray eyes and infectious laughter.

He and Miranda shared a smile. "So," she said, "identical twins. What's your approach? The same stuff for each of them so they know you love them equally, or different stuff so they know you see them as individuals?"

"Oh, they're individuals all right. They insist on different hairstyles, different clothes. I'm not sure if it's their reaction to looking the same or if it's their intrinsic personalities. Maybe the latter, because Brandon's like Candace: outgoing, impulsive, always on the go. Caleb's more like me. He's quieter, more reflective, and I think he prefers animals to people."

She cocked her head, humor dancing in her eyes. "You prefer animals to people? I remember you as being a popular kid."

He shrugged. "That was the Candace effect. She had such a wide circle of friends, I got drawn in." He'd valued all those relationships because things at home had been weird. His dad got cancer and died, and after that his mom was kind of lost, deep in her own grief. Then she fell in love again, remarried, and Luke acquired a stepfather and a stepbrother. If it hadn't been for Candace and her friends, and Viola Cruickshank and the animals at her veterinary clinic, he'd have been one miserable kid—like his stepbrother Julian. "I don't prefer animals, it's just that sometimes they're easier to be around. They're so straightforward."

"I don't know much about animals, but I agree that people are complicated. But that's what makes them so intriguing."

"I suppose."

"Anyhow," she said, "we keep getting off track. You're here to buy presents." She moved closer, gesturing to the shelves of stuffed animals, and a faint scent drifted his way, reminding him of the lily of the valley that bloomed in his mom's garden in spring. He'd always liked that scent, and the simple, bell-like white flowers. He'd bet that Goth-girl Miranda hadn't smelled like lily of the valley.

Miranda said, "We should use this window of opportunity before Ms. TTT realizes she's no longer the center of attention."

He laughed. It was easy to get distracted, with this new Miranda. Though she looked so conventional compared to the old days, she was even more attractive. And easy to talk to. Back then, they'd had nothing in common. Now, as single parents, they did.

In his entire life, he'd only ever dated one woman. Despite the best efforts of several well-meaning islanders, including his mom and stepdad and even his in-laws, he'd had no interest in dating since Candace died. He'd always suspected he was a one-woman man, and the fact that for four years he'd felt no desire to be anything other than friends with attractive women had confirmed it for him. But now . . .

Oh, man, what was he thinking? Was it just barely possible that he might want to date Miranda Gabriel? That was a big—no, make that gigantic—leap.

But perhaps going for coffee one day . . . Getting to know each other better. He could find out if what he was feeling was just an odd residual attraction from the fascination he'd felt as a teen. Coffee was only a small step. He could do that, couldn't he?

"Luke? Where did you go?"

He blinked and saw Miranda gazing up at him with puzzlement.

"Sorry," he said. "What did you say?"

"I asked if Caleb's into stuffed animals. And, if so, what does he already have?"

"Oh, right." He'd gotten distracted again. "Is there a man in your life now?" The words blurted out. No wonder, since he'd never done this before. With him and Candace, their relationship had evolved organically.

No surprise that his clumsy approach resulted in the beginnings of a frown. "No," she said. "Why do you ask?"

"There's no woman in mine."

Definitely a frown now, sketching lines across her pale forehead. "I don't date," she said flatly. "It's not a good time in my life for that."

He scrubbed a finger up the bridge of his nose, wishing he had an ounce of finesse. "I'm not sure it's what I want either. But this is nice. Talking to you. I thought maybe we could, you know, have coffee one day. Keep talking." And he could keep enjoying those stunning eyes, and hoping to win another of her warm smiles.

She pressed her lips together, the frown lines easing only a little. "I'm really busy. Though I only work part-time here, I'm doing online courses to get a certificate in early childhood education, so I can get a better job when we move back to Vancouver."

"Cool." Not the moving back to Vancouver part, though. "I'm a veterinarian, by the way."

To his astonishment, he got what he'd wanted: one of those smiles. And he hadn't even been trying.

"Animals rather than people," she commented.

"Yeah, but I have to deal with the people, too. You almost need a psych degree to cope with owners of pets—or fur babies, or children, or whatever they call their critters. Even owners of livestock can be tricky."

"You handle livestock as well as pets?"

"I treat every animal on this island, from Mr. Pettigrew's prize-winning bull to Azalea's goats to Suzie Jack's newt."

"Newt?"

"She says it's her totem animal. Who am I to argue?"

She smiled again, and he really, really needed to have coffee with her. What the heck was going on with him?

Chapter Three

"Be sure and call me if she kicks up a fuss," Miranda told Kara, the owner of Blowing Bubbles. "I'll only be a few doors down at Dreamspinner."

"No worries," the plump fortysomething woman said, waving a casual hand. "After all, kids are my life, at home and at work."

Miranda admired, and envied, her so much. Happily married for almost twenty years, Kara had spun her love of children into a wonderful and profitable business, one where she could bring her own little ones to work. After giving birth to adorable blond Kaitlin, Kara had developed serious fibroids and had to have a hysterectomy, but that hadn't stopped her and Robbie. They'd adopted boy and girl siblings who'd been in the foster care system. Then last year, they'd taken on another addition to their family, adopting the baby of two island teens who remained involved in their child's life.

At least once every day, Miranda thought *I want to be like Kara when I grow up*. And she was trying to grow up. She really was.

Now, as the shop door closed behind her with a jangle of the now-fixed bell, and she wrapped her woolen scarf tighter around her neck against the chill ocean air, she wondered if this afternoon coffee meeting—*not* a date—with Luke Chandler was a step toward maturity or a step backward.

As Aaron often told her, she took after their mom. *Never* in neglecting her child or turning to alcohol or drugs. But yeah, okay, in falling in love neither wisely nor well. She led with her heart. But why was it wrong to believe in love? After all, look at Aaron, now happily engrossed in wedding planning along with Eden and her entire family. She sure didn't begrudge him his good luck, that his heart picked a winner the very first time. She just wished her own heart had sounder judgment.

The main street of Blue Moon Harbor village was all of about four blocks long. So backwoodsy compared to cosmopolitan Vancouver, though she had to admit some of the shops—like Blowing Bubbles—were cool. Dreamspinner bookstore was another. As she passed its window, her gaze skimmed the display and she lusted after those shiny covers.

When she and Aaron were little, a neighbor at one of the crappy places they'd lived had given them some old picture books, and her clever brother had taught himself to read. Then he read to her, and taught her to read, too. The library had become one of the siblings' favorite places. Free books! What could be better? That was another of her complaints about this island: the tiny library's collection was pitiful compared to that of the Vancouver Public Library system. Of course, Eden had been fabulously generous in giving her an e-reader for Christmas, and Miranda appreciated finding free books to download. Still, though she'd never tell Eden, there was something more magical about actual physical books, perhaps because it was those books that had over the years offered escape from her dismal life, as well as fueled the dream that things might get better.

Miranda had always managed to save enough to buy

Ariana a brand-new book or two for her birthday and for
Christmas, but this year the gifts coming from all the new
people who called themselves "family" had been almost
overwhelming. The attention directed to her daughter, and
to Miranda herself, was so unaccustomed. She was still
wary of trusting in it.

Dreamspinner Coffee Shop adjoined the bookstore.
Before opening the door, she glanced through the window.
The warmly lit shop had a counter with a display case
full of pastries and snacks, and eight or so wooden tables,
most of them occupied. Plants tucked into corners, racks
of magazines and newspapers, artwork by local painters,
and a bulletin board with posters of island events made the
room welcoming.

Luke Chandler sat at a table near the counter, his casually styled auburn hair gleaming like dark cherry wood in
the light. He was chatting to a slight man with short, gray-
streaked black hair who stood with a takeout cup in hand.
She decided to let the guys finish their conversation before
she went inside.

Luke's jacket was off, revealing broad shoulders in a
blue plaid flannel shirt. His expression was warm and animated, as it had been when he'd spoken to her at the shop.

He seemed like a good guy: a loving and conscientious
dad; a man who'd built a career doing something worthwhile
that he loved. He wasn't exactly hard on the eyes, but his was
a comfortable kind of handsome, not the more dramatic,
edgy looks that appealed to her. When they'd talked in the
store, she'd liked him, but it wasn't that spiky, adrenaline-
type of buzz she experienced when she was falling for a guy.

And that was good. Since she'd hit bottom and come to
Destiny Island, her focus was on educating herself so she
could provide a better life for her daughter. Still, it might
be nice to have a friend. She'd never had a man friend,

unless she counted her brother. Either she was in love with the guy, or the guy was chasing her and she wasn't interested. She hoped Luke didn't ruin things by pushing for more than she wanted to give. When he'd asked her for coffee, she'd seen the unmistakable gleam of male appreciation in his eyes. And he'd only said he wasn't sure he wanted to date, not that he completely ruled it out.

Maybe he felt her gaze, because as he continued to speak to the older man, he glanced toward the window. Seeing her, he gave a big smile and raised a hand to beckon her in.

She pushed open the door, unwinding her blue scarf and unbuttoning her navy fleece jacket in response to the warmth of the room.

The older man turned toward her, revealing a face with Asian features and sharp, intelligent brown eyes. She recognized him despite the gray that now threaded through his black hair. In that moment she felt like an unhappy, rebellious, dyed-and-streaked-haired teen again.

Any hope that her former eleventh-grade math teacher wouldn't recognize her fled as Luke said, "Miranda, you remember Dahn Nguyen, right? Dahn, Miranda Gabriel and her little girl have recently returned to Destiny Island."

She ducked her head in a nod of acknowledgment. "Hello, Mr. Nguyen."

She was a slender five feet seven and he wasn't a whole lot bigger, but he'd always had such an air of authority. That hadn't changed one bit as he appraised her. "Did you ever finish high school, Miranda?"

Her chin came up. Glad that she'd finally listened to her brother's advice and accepted his help, she said, "Yes, I did." No need to tell the man that she'd obtained her GED only a few weeks ago.

He smiled. "That's very good. Education is so important.

It's one of the many things I appreciated when I came to this country."

She vaguely recalled that he'd been one of what the older generation referred to as the Vietnamese boat people, refugees who'd fled their country when that crazy war happened way back in the 1960s.

"I'll leave you to talk," Mr. Nguyen said. "Luke, Elsa and I will be in soon for her shots." He smiled again at Miranda. "My cat has blue eyes and my granddaughter was in a *Frozen* phase when she named her."

Astonished by the smiles, and at finding common ground with this man, she said, "My daughter's only two so she doesn't really understand the movie, but she loves the princess clothes. And Sven, the reindeer, and Olaf, the snowman."

When her former teacher had gone, Miranda sank into a chair. "Whew. Back in eleventh grade, he was always scowling at me." She peeled off her jacket and shoved it over the back of her chair along with her scarf.

"Back then, you deserved it," Luke said, flecks of green and gold twinkling in his gray eyes. Those were intriguing eyes, an unusual combination of colors.

She stuck out her tongue, but grinned. "Okay, fair enough." She propped her elbows on the table and rested her chin on her folded hands. "I was acting out because I hated being here."

He shook his head, looking puzzled. "Acting out? And why did you hate Destiny Island?" Then he said, "Hang on to those answers. Let me get you something to drink. Maybe a muffin as well?"

"That's okay." She pulled her wallet out of her jacket pocket. "I'll just—"

"No. My treat. I invited you. What would you like?"

One of her first life lessons was that, on the occasions you did have money, you stretched it by picking the cheapest items. But now, seeing the bowl-shaped cup of foam-topped coffee in front of him, and the giant cranberry muffin, she gave herself permission to indulge. "I would absolutely love a hot chocolate and a Destiny bar." The rich chocolate squares were the island version of Nanaimo bars, using Baileys Irish Cream flavoring instead of vanilla in the custard layer.

He grinned. "What is it about women and chocolate?" Not waiting for an answer, he took a couple of long-legged strides over to the counter.

Objectively speaking, the man had a fine butt to go along with those long legs and broad shoulders. He was obviously fit, and carried himself with a confidence that seemed unconscious, so different from the eye-catching, always-on-stage movements of Sebastian, the actor. Ariana's father. A man who wouldn't be caught dead offstage in a plaid flannel shirt. Or, come to that, in a backwater like Destiny Island.

When Luke returned, placing her hot chocolate and Destiny bar in front of her, he said, "Why did you hate it here?"

Before answering, she lifted the mug, admiring the artistic drizzle of chocolate syrup that decorated the peaks of whipped cream, and inhaled, closing her eyes to better savor the scent. Then she sipped, and smiled. "Pure, decadent bliss," she said with satisfaction.

Luke's hand stopped halfway to his mouth with a chunk of muffin, and his eyes widened, the gold flecks gleaming.

Oops. She hadn't intended to be suggestive, but it seemed he'd interpreted her actions that way. Putting the mug down, she said briskly, "I'm a city girl. I grew up in Vancouver and I love it." Well, not the Downtown Eastside or most of the other places she'd lived as a child, but the city itself. "It's so vibrant. There are so many things to see and do, and a lot of them are free. The people are such a great mix of races, cultures, lifestyles, and—"

"Hey," he broke in, putting down his coffee cup and holding up his hand to stop her. "Destiny's diverse. Look at Dahn Nguyen. The Yakimuras who own this place. Aaron's friend Lionel. Rachelle and Celia who own C-Shell. And then there's—"

"Stop. I hear you." The Yakimuras, a long-time island family, were Japanese Canadian. Lionel, her brother's best friend, was an African-American Vietnam War draft dodger. Rachelle was black, too, and married to Celia. On an island with a population of not much more than 1,500, there was a lot of diversity. "And yeah, before you say it, there's some arts and culture going on here, too, but much less than in Vancouver." She forked up a bite of gooey Destiny bar and managed to suppress a moan of enjoyment.

"You're into arts and culture?" His tone was so carefully neutral that she guessed he didn't see her as a big culture buff.

She had to chuckle and admit, "Well, maybe not so much. I do like theater and music. There are lots of free musical events in the city. Or if you volunteer, you often get to attend. Though I don't do that now, since Ariana came along. But even if you stand outside a paid venue, like on the beach outside the Vancouver Folk Music Festival, you can still hear the music." She added, with a grin, "Ariana's developing eclectic taste."

"Do you like my stepbrother's music?"

"Your stepbrother?" She frowned and sipped hot chocolate as she tried to remember. "Did I know you had a stepbrother?"

"We didn't hang out together. He was in your class, but like you he skipped school more than he attended. He always had incredible musical talent, and he's done well for himself. Julian Blake?" He cocked his head.

"Oh. My. God." She almost dropped the mug, gaping at

him in amazement. "Julian Blake's your stepbrother?" He'd been a moody, sexy bad boy. She'd had a mad crush on him, but he'd shown no interest in the girls at school. She'd wondered if he was gay, but didn't get that vibe. Several years later, she'd been stunned to hear him on CBC Radio, an up-and-coming musician. Since then, she'd followed his career.

Julian was indeed incredible, and crazy good-looking. Superhot. In the way she most definitely was attracted to. And definitely not gay, given all the social media photos of him with various attractive women. "I'm a huge fan. I even saw him live once, before Ariana was born and my budget got so tight." Intense, passionate, edgy Julian—with his tousled, burnished-gold hair, ripped black clothing, and tattoo—was pretty much the opposite of the comfortably handsome, easygoing, chestnut-haired island veterinarian. "You don't share a parent?"

"No. My dad died when I was ten, and two years later Mom married Forbes Blake, Julian's father. Forbes and Julian's mom were divorced."

He'd spoken impersonally, which led her to say, "You and Julian don't get along so well?" She ate more of the Destiny bar, thinking that it tasted the way Julian looked and the way his music sounded: a mix of rough and smooth, of sweet and bitter. An irresistible blend.

"No, we do. I mean, there aren't any problems. But we're very different people. And he's made himself scarce. Dropped out of school not long after you did, went over to Vancouver. He wasn't in touch for a while, not even with his dad and they'd been close. But then suddenly he emailed to say he was okay, playing music. Since then we all keep in touch, but he only comes to the island a couple times a year. I think he hates Blue Moon Harbor as much as you used to."

Automatically, she opened her mouth to correct him and say she still hated the place, but then she closed her lips.

There were good things here. And good people, like Eden and her relatives who kept calling her family. Kara, who provided a perfect working environment. Iris at Dreamspinner who made sure she got first crack when kids' books went on sale. Miranda still wasn't exactly nature girl, all passionate about the ocean and trees and eagles and stuff the way her brother was, but she had to admit that Destiny Island had its merits.

It probably always had. A realization sank in. "I blamed the island for everything that had gone wrong in my life."

"Your mom died, didn't she?" Luke said quietly. "Her parents took in you and Aaron?"

Miranda gulped. How stupid to have said that out loud, to open the door to memories she tried not to revisit, much less share. She glanced at her watch, but didn't read the time. "I need to get back to the store." She stood and, not about to abandon the half-eaten Destiny bar, wrapped it in her napkin. Too bad Luke hadn't bought the delicious hot chocolate in a takeout cup. Shoving her arms into her jacket sleeves, she said, "Thanks for treating me."

He stood, too, frowning. "Did I say something wrong?"

"No, of course not. But this is my coffee break and I left Kara not only minding the store but also looking after Ariana."

As she turned toward the door, wrapping her scarf around her neck, he said, "Hold on a sec." He strode over to the counter, got a cardboard cup, and neatly poured the remains of her hot chocolate into it. "To keep you warm."

Oh yeah, this was a good guy. "Thanks again." She gazed at him, into those very cool multicolored eyes, and got lost there for a moment. It was like looking into a kaleidoscope, and those were her favorite toys of the entire Blowing Bubbles inventory.

"Let's do it again," he said.

She pulled herself back out of the kaleidoscope. "Oh, uh, I don't know." As she walked toward the door, he grabbed his jacket and kept pace. He was beside her, pulling on his jacket, as she hurried down the street.

At the door to the kids' store, he said, "What's wrong, Miranda? We were having a nice talk, and now you're blowing me off."

"Luke, I . . ." A guy like this deserved more than a cool brush-off, so she'd tell him the truth, even though it was hard to admit. "I'm going to say that cliché thing that it's not about you, it's about me. You're a great guy with a great job and I'm sure your kids are great, too. But I'm, well, at a weird place in my life. I've always been kind of messed up. You knew me back when, so you saw how screwed up I was, and—"

When he opened his mouth, she held up a hand. "Let me finish. I look different now, but inside I'm still kind of a mess. I'm trying to straighten myself out, but it's hard. And I don't want to inflict that on anyone else." The words were true and as far as she was prepared to go. She wasn't about to tell him that something about him called to her in a way she wasn't comfortable with, tempting her to reveal secrets and vulnerabilities.

Gripping the door handle, she added, "I'm sorry." Then she squared her shoulders and went into the shop, leaving him out on the street in the cold.

A couple of weeks after he'd had coffee with Miranda, Luke was still thinking about her.

Sitting at his desk in the office of his veterinary clinic on a Tuesday morning after dropping the twins at daycare, with half an hour free before the clinic opened, he was supposed to be researching acromegaly. He had diagnosed the rare disease, a growth hormone overproduction, in one of his feline patients and needed to update his knowledge of treatment options. But, staring at the computer screen, the image of Miranda's face filled his mind. Particularly, those sad, hurting, blue denim eyes as she'd told him she was sorry.

Wounded animals reacted in two very different ways. Some crawled away to suffer alone. He wondered if that was what Miranda was doing when she cut off conversations that edged too far into the personal.

Other animals struck out when they were in pain. As a teen, Miranda had been abrasive and rude. Her favorite word started with *F* and she used it in all its variations. Including the oft-expressed "fuck off and die." At the time he'd taken her for a bad girl rebelling against a too-conservative world. Now he guessed maybe he'd been wrong, and she'd been hurting.

Hurting back then. And today, perhaps still nursing those wounds along with fresh ones suffered over the past decade. Like those inflicted by Ariana's father.

Luke was a healer. The evidence of it surrounded him: files, research manuals, and drawings and photographs of animals presented to him by grateful island kids and adults.

When he was nine and his father was diagnosed with non-Hodgkin's lymphoma, Luke had done everything he could to help, from going to the library to get mystery novels for his dad to learning how to make what his father called "proper English tea." None of it worked, though. He couldn't cure his dad's cancer. Nor could he heal his mom's pain at losing her life partner at the age of forty. It had taken Forbes Blake to do that. But in the two years before Forbes came along, Luke's mother was a bit of a zombie, stumbling through life on antidepressant medication. She'd barely noticed her son's efforts to look after her and cheer her up.

When Luke was twelve, he stopped trying because she met and fell madly in love with Forbes. Luke had resented the interloper; no one could replace his dad. He'd also resented that his mom had time for Forbes but not for him. Thank heavens for Candace, her parents, and his other friends.

But then one day something amazing had happened. Riding his bike home from school, he'd come across a cat being attacked by a raccoon. He managed to chase off the raccoon, and then wrapped the wounded cat in his jacket, bundled it into his backpack, and bicycled as fast as he could to this very building, which had then housed Viola Cruickshank's veterinary practice. She'd asked him to stroke the cat while she treated it. She'd said he had a healing spirit, which was as important as any medicine.

It might have only been a kind thing to say to a distraught kid, though gruff Viola, who'd lived alone all her life, had always denied that. She said she was kind to animals, not to people. Whatever her motivation, when he'd asked her to let him help out at her practice, she'd agreed. She had never wanted to hear about his personal issues, but she'd mentored him so effectively that when he went to the Western College of Veterinary Medicine in Saskatchewan, he'd come out top of the class. Of course, it didn't hurt that he'd inherited his mom's interest in, and aptitude for, sciences. But academic honors didn't matter to Luke. What counted was that he healed countless living creatures. As he'd told Miranda, animals were easier than people. He didn't know how to heal people. It was merely a perk of his job that, often when he healed a sick or injured animal, he also helped its owner.

Miranda Gabriel was a wounded creature. She said she was messed up as a teen, and was messed up now.

He didn't do well at fixing human beings. Besides, he

didn't need a messed-up woman in his life, and he didn't need to reprise his crazy high-school infatuation. Particularly with a woman who had a less-than-stable lifestyle, and seemed determined to return to Vancouver.

He had enough on his hands with his sons and his busy practice. Miranda had blown him off. He should accept that. But for some reason Miranda, the old version with the piercings and the attitude and the new one with the wounded eyes and the TTT kid, got to him.

"Oh hell, man," he muttered. "It's not just the eyes and the kid. She's the sexiest woman I've seen in years." His twenty-eight-year old body had almost forgotten what sex was like, yet the thought of Miranda made it stir. "Which is not a good reason to see her again." He wasn't that kind of guy, one who got into a relationship for the sex. Not that he actually knew what kind of guy he was when it came to dating and sex, since there'd only ever been Candace.

Luke picked up the phone. And put it down. If he called, she'd turn him down. Which was her right. She was a grown woman. Twenty-seven, he figured. With a two-year-old, a job, and a career plan. He knew her brother, Aaron. He was a good guy. No doubt he offered his sister all the support she needed.

Except hadn't he heard that Aaron was engaged to a woman from Ontario, who'd moved here with her entire family? Which meant Aaron had other things on his mind than searching his sister's eyes to see if there was something more going on with her than the kid, job, and career plan.

Luke was no schemer. He was a straightforward guy, not the least bit devious. So why did he find himself searching for an excuse to see Miranda again? Aha! Wasn't there a birthday party coming up for one of the kids in Caleb and Brandon's daycare? He needed to go gift-shopping. Checking his schedule, he saw a break in the early afternoon.

Miranda only worked part-time at Blowing Bubbles. In the past months he'd been in the store several times and he'd never run into her until that afternoon three weeks ago. What were the chances?

Maybe this was the test. If she wasn't there, he'd leave her alone. If she was, it was a sign that . . . what?

The shriek that assaulted his ears as he opened the door of Blowing Bubbles made Luke smile. Ariana had a distinctive wail. And if she was here, likely so was Miranda.

Yes, she was at the counter, looking frazzled as she talked to Penelope Abercrombie, a woman in her late sixties who didn't have the sweetest of dispositions. Glancing around, Luke didn't see Kara, so it seemed Miranda was on her own.

He ambled toward the red-faced toddler who sat in the middle of the fenced play enclosure, ignoring the dolls and stuffed animals scattered around her, registering her displeasure in ear-piercing wails. He couldn't possibly make her screech any louder than she already was, so he squatted outside a green plastic-mesh panel and said, "Hey there, pretty girl. It's me. Remember? I came to visit you again, because you're so darned irresistible."

Dark eyes squinted at him and tear trails gleamed on her cheeks, but the wails receded to hiccupy sobs. It seemed that, like most females, she appreciated compliments.

"You like being the center of attention, don't you, princess?"

She clambered to her feet and plodded over. "Up," she demanded, lifting her arms.

Hoping Miranda wouldn't mind, Luke stood and reached over the two-foot-high panel to hoist her into his arms. "Hey, Ariana. My name's Luke. I went to school with your mommy." This reminded him of holding the boys when they were younger, except that this child smelled sweeter than the twins ever had, even after their baths. Her scent was flowery and innocent, a little like wild roses.

"School?" she said, her head tipped up toward him.

"A long time ago."

"Mommy go school. On puter."

Computer, he figured. "Yes, I know. She told me about that." Experience suggested that a two-year-old's interest in anyone but herself was limited, so he said, "But how about you? What do you like to do?" He gestured toward the discarded cloth dolls, which wore fancy costumes. "Do you like princesses?"

She babbled a string of syllables from which he recognized the words, "Fairies! With wings!"

Now he noticed the wings, more bedraggled than perky, telling him these were much-loved dolls. "Yeah, fairies are much better than princesses. They can fly!"

"Fly! Unc Aaron flies."

"I know he does. But he isn't a fairy, is he?"

The girl giggled. "He's pi-lot." She said the word carefully. "He flies air-planes. With wings!"

"Yes, planes sure do have wings."

The raised voice that now claimed his attention wasn't the child's but Mrs. Abercrombie's, saying, "Yes, the very first time Tedward played with it! The tail just came off in his hand."

He turned to see the woman glaring at Miranda, who said, "I told you we'd replace the dog, ma'am. But if I might suggest—"

"But it's wrong! You stupid girl, you're not listening to me. You shouldn't sell defective merchandise!"

Luke was an even-tempered guy, but anger stirred inside him. How dare she use that tone and call Miranda stupid? Not to mention, it was Kara who ordered merchandise. Still holding Ariana, he walked over to the women, noting the stuffed dog on the counter and wincing at the obviously yanked-off tail. His boys, particularly Brandon, could be tough on toys, too. "Mrs. Abercrombie, there's no need—"

"Luke," Miranda said sharply. "I'm serving this customer. I'll be with you in a minute." Her narrowed eyes, steely gray rather than blue, warned him not to interfere.

Clenching his teeth, he rubbed Ariana's back, hoping the girl didn't pick up on the tension in his body and in the atmosphere.

"Mrs. Abercrombie," Miranda said, all politeness now, "perhaps rather than another stuffed animal, Tedward might prefer a toy truck? They're very sturdy. Great toys for strong, active kids. What do you think?"

Luke thought of saying that his boys were big fans of toy trucks. But he figured Miranda had the situation under control and he'd obey her unspoken request that he butt out.

"Hmm." The older woman seemed to have calmed down, and was considering the suggestion. "Perhaps you're right. Stuffed animals are more a toy for little children, aren't they? And girls, of course."

"Why don't I show you what we have?" As Miranda led the woman away, she shot Luke a quick smile. "Thanks for looking after Ariana, Luke."

Her eyes were denim blue again and that smile, though brief, warmed him. The child in his arms was a cozy bundle, relaxed now in the boneless way that told him she was dozing off. He rocked her lightly, simulating the motion of a cradle, and listened with amusement as Miranda's sales efforts resulted in Mrs. Abercrombie not only getting a free truck to replace the returned stuffed dog, but also purchasing a second truck.

When the woman, toting a big bag, had left the shop, Miranda came over to him. In a scoop-necked blue cotton tee and nicely faded jeans, wearing dangly sea-glass earrings, she was beautiful in such a natural way. It was funny, but

Candace, who was crazy about clothes and makeup, had looked more city-girl than Miranda. Whether or not Miranda was ready to believe it, she belonged here in Blue Moon Harbor.

"Whew." She drew her hand across her brow, grinned at him, and reached out for her sleeping child.

He passed Ariana over, finding he missed the warm weight. Watching Miranda cuddle her daughter, he felt a pang of sorrow. Candace, with her loving nature, would have been a fabulous mom. Life could be so damned unfair.

After a final hug, Miranda carefully set her daughter back down in the play area.

Luke got control of his emotions and said, "That woman was awful. I'm surprised you kept your temper."

She rolled her eyes. "You know what I've done all my life? Waited tables and sales-clerked. I can be polite to anyone in any circumstance."

That was so unlike the old Miranda, who was blunt and abrasive. He wondered how tough it had been for her to learn to put on a polite face. He also hoped that, with him, she could be genuine. "You handled her really well. I gather Tedward ripped the tail off that poor stuffed dog?"

"It's not the first time we've had a return on something that was given to Tedward."

"That was a good idea, suggesting trucks. My boys have them, and they're almost indestructible."

"Maybe it'll keep Tedward from getting the idea that it's okay to torture animals," she said, her tone dead serious.

"That would be a very good thing."

She tilted her chin. "Working in this store has been enlightening. When you see how kids play, you get an idea of their personalities. When parents shop and talk about their children, you gain insights into how those children are being raised. Kara says she can make a good guess how most of the island kids are going to turn out when they grow up."

"Huh. That's perceptive." And made him wonder what Kara thought about Caleb and Brandon, and his own parenting skills.

"Anyhow, you've been waiting a while. What can I help you with?" She smiled. "You aren't carrying anything, so I take it you're not here to return one of those birthday gifts?"

"Nope, no returns. There's a birthday party for a four-year-old girl, Katie Dvorak. I have no idea what she likes but I bet Kara's magic computer system can tell me."

"I'd bet on it." She walked away, toward the desk.

The woman had a fantastic butt, he thought as he followed her. And once she gave Destiny Island more of a chance, there was no way she'd move back to Vancouver. Besides, while her lifestyle might have been unstable in the past, and she'd confessed to being kind of messed up, she was clearly on the path to pulling it all together. So it wasn't crazy for him to want to ask her out.

He stood on the customer side of the counter while she, on the other side, clicked away at the computer.

"At first, I thought this database was a bit scary," she said. "You know, all 'big brother is watching.' But it does make a lot of sense. We're the only kids' store on the island and we want to keep our customers happy." She added dryly, "And keep them from shopping online, or over in Victoria or Vancouver."

Watching her slender fingers deftly click keys, he imagined those fingers on his body, a healthy male body that hadn't felt a woman's caress in years. Yeah, his sex drive had reawakened with a vengeance. Trying to sound like a logical adult rather than a horny teen, he commented, "You're the only kids' store, but you don't carry books."

"No. Kara told me it's a longtime agreement with

Dreamspinner. They carry children's books and we carry
everything else."

"That's typical Blue Moon Harbor." He seized the opportunity for a low-key sales pitch. "Businesses cooperating
rather than competing."

She glanced up, her eyes twinkling. "Yeah, yeah, I get it.
It's not a bad place." Then she gazed at the screen. "Katie
collects the Maplelea Girls, a set of dolls from different
parts of Canada. They're great toys because they're fun for
little kids to play with, and they have backstories that interest the child as she gets older. Katie doesn't have Jenna
from the East Coast or Saila from Nunavut."

"Let's go with the Inuit one."

"Great. I'll log it into the computer so no one else will
buy her the same thing." She clicked a few more keys, and
then went to the shelves and selected a box containing a
brown-skinned, black-haired doll in outdoor clothing and
mukluks.

She processed the sale, he paid, and she said, "Gift-
wrap?"

"That'd be great." When he was operating on an animal,
his fingers knew exactly what to do. When it came to tasks
like wrapping presents, he tended toward clumsiness. He
guessed that, when it came to asking a woman out, he'd be
even more awkward.

From a rack with rolls of wrapping paper, she selected
one that had puppies and kittens scattered over it. "This?"

"Good guess. For me, anyhow. But does Katie . . . ?"
About to ask whether the girl liked animals, he remembered her last name and made the association. "Dvorak.
They have a two-year-old Persian cat named Emerald because of her big green eyes."

"If it had been Emerald's birthday, you'd have known
exactly what to buy," Miranda teased.

"Most cats and dogs are easy," he agreed. "The ones that

are finicky, I know about it. Sometimes it's due to allergies or other health conditions, but mostly it's because the owners spoil them. They think they're being nice to the animal, but in fact they're screwing with its health." And he was lecturing, which probably wasn't the way to persuade her to date him.

And yet mischief sparkled in her blue eyes and she teased, "You, of course, never spoil your boys, right?"

"Uh, well . . ." Mischief looked so much better on her than sadness. "Mostly I'm pretty good." Okay, this was an opportunity, so he seized it. "But there's a place in everyone's life for a little ice cream, don't you think?"

"Especially if it's chocolate," she agreed promptly.

"Bring Ariana over on Sunday afternoon. We'll build sundaes. I'll make sure there's chocolate ice cream and chocolate sauce, whipped cream, and some fruit and nuts just for some token healthy stuff."

She made herself busy wrapping the present, her head down, ignoring him.

"Sprinkles?" he offered. "Chocolate chips?"

As she fussed with a froth of curly, multi-colored ribbon that was so much prettier than the plain old bow he'd have tied, he said, "Miranda?"

She gazed up at him, biting her bottom lip in a way that had him wanting to kiss it.

"What's the problem?" he asked. When they'd gone for coffee, she'd said it wasn't about him, but her. Seemed to him, that meant she didn't trust him to understand that she was dealing with some issues, and to treat her right. What had he ever done to make her feel that way? Or was it, perhaps, men in general she mistrusted? "Look, I don't know what guys have done to you in the past. Like"—he lowered his voice—"Ariana's father. But I'm not them."

"I know you're not," she said promptly, sounding slightly annoyed. "In every way, you're not them."

She almost made it sound like a bad thing, so maybe his hunch was wrong. "But you don't trust me," he said, needing to know what was going on here.

"I do." She dragged the two small words out slowly. "As a person, I mean. But like I said, I'm kind of messed up right now and I'm not into dating. And I can see, well, not to be egotistical or anything, but I can see you're attracted to me." She squeezed her eyes shut and squinted up her face. "Aagh. That sounds terrible. I'm sorry."

"Don't apologize. It's true, I find you attractive. But Miranda, if you don't want to date, I get it. We could just be friends. I wouldn't push you." Craving a woman's caresses—*oh hell, be honest, craving down and dirty sex*—was the stuff of fantasies. Dating, though . . . Now that he really thought about it, it *was* big, for him as well as for her. "I'm honestly not sure I'm ready for dating myself. Candace and I—well, she was my only girlfriend. Ever."

"Ever?" Her eyes widened. "You've only ever . . . uh, dated, one woman?"

He figured what she was really asking was if he'd slept only with Candace. It didn't damage his male pride one single bit to say, "Yes. One." Still, he figured an explanation wouldn't hurt. "I loved her. As kids, she was my best friend, and her friendship kept me going through some rough times. Adolescence hit and we became boyfriend-girlfriend. We fell in love. I guess more accurately, we realized we'd loved one another all along, but when all the hormones kicked in the love became non-platonic."

Miranda was gazing at him as if he were an alien life form, but when she spoke he heard a trace of envy. "That sounds amazing. Kindred spirits, right?"

He hadn't heard the term before. "Different in some ways but yeah, when it came to the important stuff—what we valued, what we wanted out of life—I guess we were."

"But still, you never got curious? What it'd be like with someone else? You were never attracted to anyone else?"

Remembering the inexplicable appeal of the girl with her punky hair and piercings, he swallowed. "Never seriously attracted or curious. I was smart enough to know the value of what Candace and I had together." If his wife were alive, he'd probably still find the new Miranda attractive, but no way would he consider doing anything about it.

Her eyes clouded. "And lucky enough that she realized it, too."

Maybe his hunch hadn't been so wrong. "You fell for a guy you thought was a kindred spirit, but he didn't feel the same way?" Ariana's father?

She snorted. "*A* guy? It's happened more than once. I have the worst luck. Or, as Aaron says, taste or judgment. I'm just like my—" She broke off. "Never mind. It's a long story."

"A story I'd like to hear."

The shop bell jangled and Jillian Summers and her son, Cole, entered the store. Luke wondered, as he and Miranda both said hi to them, if Miranda was thinking "saved by the bell."

Jillian, a seaplane pilot, flew for Miranda's brother's Blue Moon Air. She and Cole, who was eight or so, had a Dalmatian-Labrador cross called Freckles, a dog they'd rescued from the shelter three years ago.

Miranda asked how the wedding plans were going, and Luke remembered hearing that Jillian was engaged to Cole's father, a man who'd reappeared in their lives at Christmas.

Luke could have left, probably should have, but he wasn't going to let Miranda blow him off again so he browsed while Jillian filled Miranda in on all the details that women found so interesting. Cole had disappeared among the shelves, and finally Jillian went to join him, saying that they'd poke around for a bit.

Luke rejoined Miranda and said quietly, "Sundaes on Sunday. Three little kids, lots of mess, sugar highs, and I promise there'll be chocolate. Not a date. Maybe the beginning of a friendship. You can handle that. Can't you?" Deliberately, he made it sound like a challenge.

The old Miranda wasn't the type to walk away from a dare.

The new one studied him for a long time, and he wasn't sure whether she was trying to read his mind or to figure out her own feelings. It didn't matter because in the end, she spoke one word. It wasn't as enthusiastic a response as he'd hoped for, but he'd take it.

"Fine," she said.

Chapter Four

As Miranda drove to the address Luke had given her, on Tsehum Drive which wound along the west side of Blue Moon Harbor, she thought how different everything was from a year ago. Though she'd had a driver's license when she lived in Vancouver, she'd used it only a few times a year—mostly to drive friends and their cars home when they'd had too much to drink. In the city, transit passes were her friend. She and Ariana traveled everywhere on the bus or SkyTrain: to parks, beaches, street fairs, and bargain shops. Miranda would hold her daughter as they watched city scenery go by outside the window, or read while Ariana snoozed.

Driving on Destiny, she'd initially found the scenery—agricultural fields with crops, sheep, cows, horses, even llamas; patches of forest; a few scattered farmhouses—boring after the cityscapes. It was growing on her, though, or maybe lulling her into an "island time" languidness. Here, the only excitement was when she had to brake suddenly for a squirrel, rabbit, or deer with "suicide by car" tendencies.

This Sunday afternoon, no animals had a death wish, so it was an uneventful twenty-minute drive from SkySong in her old Toyota—the one she'd had no choice but to let Aaron buy for her since public transit here sucked.

The sky was a pale, wintry blue, with a bank of gray clouds moving slowly in from the south. That was one thing this place had in common with Vancouver: it rained a lot. Not that it mattered today, as they'd be inside at a kitchen table.

She wondered what Luke's house was like, and whether it was the one he'd shared with Candace. Had he hung on to that home and the memories it contained, or had that proved to be too painful? She wouldn't have bet either way, but did guess that the house would be small, cozy, and cluttered with adult and kid stuff of the male variety.

When she pulled up in front of the address she'd tapped into her phone, she didn't know whether to be relieved or sorry, because clearly, she'd made a mistake.

"I must've input it wrong," she said to her daughter, who was strapped into her car seat in the back. "Luke can't live here. Even if he looks after all the bulls, goats, and newts on the island, he can't possibly make that much money."

"Luke!" Ariana said brightly. The man had made an impression on her daughter.

The house was what Miranda thought of as West Coast modern. The cedar walls and shake roof blended in with the surroundings, but this was no rustic cottage like the one her brother had built. This spectacular home had unusual angles, huge windows, and several skylights. That style did not come cheaply. Nor did the stretch of waterfront property it sat on.

"This is Tsehum Drive," she said. "Maybe there's a Tsehum Road or Street. I could look it up. Or I could call him. Or you and I could go home and play fairy castles." Which would be the safer choice, and since she'd worked late last night catching up on her online courses, she needn't feel guilty about spending the afternoon playing with her daughter. But accepting an invitation—though she still wasn't sure why she had—and failing to show up was rude.

"Luke?" her daughter said doubtfully, and then babbled something Miranda didn't understand.

The front door of the eye-catching house opened and two dogs bounded out, a big golden-colored one and a small mop of gray and white fur. The larger dog, she noticed as the pair ran toward the car, was missing a hind leg, but its tail wagged vigorously, as did the short, fluffy tail of the mop-dog.

She was about to reassure her daughter that the dogs looked friendly, when Ariana squealed in delight, "Doggies!"

"Sit!" a male voice yelled, and both dogs promptly planted their butts.

Miranda took a long breath and looked away from the dogs toward the door of the house. The moment she'd seen the three-legged dog, she had figured she'd come to the right place. Sure enough, Luke stood in the doorway. Somehow, his faded jeans and gray T-shirt, unprepossessing as they were, matched the house perfectly. Yes, this was his home, even though she had to wonder how he could afford it.

"There he is," she said. "There's Luke."

"Luke! And doggies!"

He came down the steps as Miranda opened the car door and slid out. By the time she'd opened the back door and freed Ariana from her car seat, he was standing beside her. "Want me to take her?" he asked. "I'm guessing you have a bag or two of stuff."

Ariana reached out to him, again saying his name.

No, this didn't feel like a date, Miranda thought as she carefully passed her precious daughter into his waiting arms. Dating meant dancing at a club, listening to music, going to a movie, having sex. Two adults; no children. Since her daughter's birth, she hadn't dated much. Cash was scarce and better spent on nourishing food and birthday books than on babysitters. In the past three years, she'd only fallen for one guy—and that was her ill-fated relationship with Chef Emile at a restaurant where she'd waitressed. She'd lost not only the man but also a job that paid good tips. That was over a year ago, and since then she'd only had a few casual dates.

Aaron didn't give her enough credit for having *some* common sense.

With her purse on one shoulder, a tote bag of supplies over the other, and a baking dish of apple crisp in her hands, she followed Luke to his front door, the two dogs trotting behind.

In the entranceway, still holding Ariana, Luke toe-heeled off the moccasins he wore, leaving him barefooted on a glossy floor of reddish-brown hardwood just a couple of shades lighter than his hair.

"Bare feet in February?" she commented as she put the dessert dish and her purse on a side table, and let the tote slide to the floor. "You must pay a fortune in heating costs." In cold weather, she always kept the heat on low and bundled herself and Ariana in multiple layers.

"Nope. This house was designed to be energy-efficient."

She bent to untie the red Converse she'd bought from a thrift store a couple years ago. This close to Luke's feet, she appreciated how masculine and well shaped they were. Rising, sock-footed now, she cast an eye over the rest of him, confirming what she'd noticed before: the man truly was built. Better built, in fact, than a lot of the guys she'd dated. She tended toward edgy, creative types, lean in build, not healthy-looking men like Luke.

Built he might be, but he was too wholesome for her taste.

A doggy tail brushed her jean-clad legs. Distracted from her perusal of her host, she leaned down again and stretched out a hand to the golden dog. "Hey there." As a child, she'd wished for a pet but it was never a serious wish. First came things like food, clothes, school supplies, and electricity that didn't keep getting shut off.

"Doggies!" Ariana demanded, windmilling her arms and legs as she struggled to get free.

"Can I put her down?" Luke asked. "Will she be okay with them?"

"As long as they're not too enthusiastic. She's used to Chester, Lionel's dog." When she and Ariana had lived in the spare room at Aaron's cottage, they'd gotten to know Chester. A total sweetheart, the aging dog belonged to Aaron's neighbor and best friend.

Carefully Luke lowered Ariana to the floor, but held on to her hand. Miranda would have done the same thing, offering her daughter reassurance and security while allowing her the freedom and space to explore. Without even having met his kids, she knew he was a good parent.

"Hi, doggy." Ariana reached her free hand toward the golden one.

"That's Honey," Luke said as the dog pressed its nose into her palm, tail beating a happy rhythm. "She's a girl. The small one is Pigpen, and he's a boy."

"Pig pen?" her daughter said doubtfully.

"He's named after a cartoon character."

Peanuts, Miranda realized, watching the dogs closely, reassured that they weren't the least bit aggressive.

"Honey no leg," Ariana announced, stroking the dog's head.

"That's right," Luke agreed. "She had an accident and lost one."

While Ariana got down on the floor to stroke the fluffy, wriggling Pigpen, Luke stepped slightly away from her and murmured to Miranda, "A hit-and-run. Honey was an off-island dog, not chipped or tagged, and the owners never showed up to claim her."

"And Pigpen?" she asked.

"He's old and so are his owners. Health issues forced them to move in with their son, whose wife is allergic. It'd be hard to find a home for a dog like Pigpen, so the boys and I took him in. His owners can still drive, so they come visit him. Their dearest wish is that they'll die before Pigpen, but I don't think it'll work out that way."

Watching her daughter giggle as the little mop-dog licked her face, Miranda whispered, "You took in a dog that'll die soon? Won't that be traumatic for your boys?"

"A little, but it's a life lesson. Every living creature dies one day." He swallowed. "Sometimes before their time."

She bit her lip, knowing he was thinking of his wife.

He went on. "Pigpen's lived a long, happy life and he's got another year or two to go. He'll enjoy the boys and Honey, and they'll enjoy him. I'll make sure that when the time comes, he goes easily. Painlessly."

"I guess." Though she hated to think of a child's grief, she kind of saw Luke's point. Loss was a part of life. Maybe it was better to come to terms with that early on. And of course his kids had already suffered one of the hugest losses possible. They'd grown up without a mother, and never even had a chance to know her and experience her love.

Was that better or worse than growing up with a mom who sold her body to feed her cocaine addiction?

Choosing to change the subject, she said, "Where are your kids? For a couple of four-year-old boys, they're being awfully quiet."

"They're in the yard, playing in the fort."

"Fort?"

"I'm not great with a hammer and nails, but I managed to throw something together. We can make it fancier as they get older and are able to help out."

Yeah, he was a good parent. She loved the expression on his face when he talked about his sons. There'd been moments when her mom had been functional enough to look at Miranda and Aaron with interest and affection, but those moments had been rare and never lasted.

She shoved away the memories, and commented, "You didn't shave this morning. Is that a Sunday thing?" A light scruff of brown whiskers covered his jaw and her fingers itched to reach out and feel that intriguing mix of softness and bristle. With a start, she realized that it must've been ten or eleven months since she'd stroked a man's face.

"Yup." His lips curved. "If I'd shaved, it might've given the wrong message. Like I thought this was a date or something."

She laughed, thinking that she felt comfortable with this man. No, it wasn't a date. When she dated, she always felt slightly on edge, like with an adrenaline buzz: lust, anticipation, uncertainty, excitement. Something way more thrilling than the desire to feel beard stubble under her fingertips.

"Hey, Ariana," Luke said, raising his voice. "How about you and your mom come into the kitchen. I'll call my boys. Then we'll see if we can find some ice cream in the freezer."

Ariana looked up from her doggy friend. "Ice cream? I like ice cream."

Miranda reached for her hand and tugged her to her feet. "Come on, sweetie." She hooked her purse over her shoulder.

Luke hefted the tote and gestured toward the baking dish. "What's this?"

"Apple crisp to put in your fridge." She didn't believe in accepting hospitality without reciprocating.

"Thanks. What a treat." He lifted the dish and started down the wide hallway.

Still holding her daughter's hand, Miranda followed, glancing into the rooms they passed. The architectural design was as spectacular as the outside of the house, but the furniture was comfortable, some of it a little beat-up, and scattered toys and books created a homey ambience. She'd been dead wrong about the type of home Luke lived in, but right about the coziness and clutter.

She also noted a few photographs of Candace, Candace and Luke, Candace with other people. Luke's wife had always been gorgeous and distinctive with that fiery hair, slightly exotic features, and light gray eyes accentuated by skillfully applied makeup. Clearly, Luke wasn't avoiding memories of his wife, which made Miranda guess that this probably was the home they'd lived in together.

When she stepped through the door into the kitchen, she gasped. It was huge, efficiently laid out, and her experience working in restaurants told her that the appliances were commercial grade. But, lest she be completely intimidated, there were homey touches here, too: kids' brightly colored artwork stuck on the walls, photos and lists tacked to the fridge, and a messy stack of papers and envelopes taking up part of the counter. Large windows on two sides provided lots of natural light, and she glimpsed a view of ocean and sky. The table was right by the window, with five chairs around it. One had a booster cushion.

Luke opened the outside door, hollered, "Boys! Ice cream!" and then came back in, leaving the door open a crack. A few moments later, what sounded like a herd of elephants thundered across a wooden porch or deck, the door crashed open, and two children in jeans and fleece jackets raced inside.

"Close the door," Luke ordered. "Gently."

"Boys," Ariana announced, not seeming daunted. She'd spent a fair amount of time with other children, back in Vancouver with their neighbor Mrs. Sharma's grandchildren, and in the playpen at Blowing Bubbles.

Though Brandon and Caleb were physically identical, cute kids with reddish hair and a light dusting of freckles, one boy's hair was cropped short and the other's was longer. Both wore jeans, but one had a brown jacket and the other a blue one. She remembered Luke saying that the kids liked to express their individuality.

When he made the introductions, she learned that the short-haired boy in the blue jacket was Brandon. She said hi to them, and Ariana babbled a greeting. Brandon looked up at Miranda, a challenge in his pale gray eyes. "You went to school with Daddy?"

"Yes, for a little while."

"Mommy went to school with Daddy."

"I know. They were high school sweethearts."

Caleb lined up beside his brother. His eyes looked more soulful and his voice was quieter when he asked, "Why are you here?"

Luke saved her from fumbling for an answer by saying, "I told you earlier. They're here for ice cream sundaes. Now, who wants ice cream?"

"I do!" Brandon cried, happily distracted, but Caleb gave Miranda another long, questioning gaze before saying in a more subdued tone, "Me too."

"Ice cream!" Ariana put in.

Miranda raised a hand. "Count me in." This wasn't a date and she wasn't going to try to ingratiate herself with the boys. Better to let the relationship evolve naturally.

She assisted Luke, and it took only a few minutes to get all the supplies onto the kitchen table. They all sat down, Luke at one end of the table, Miranda on his right with

Ariana beside her, and the boys across from her. She was facing the window, and through it saw a large wooden deck bordered with glass-paneled fencing. It had started to rain, but through the sprinkles she saw the steely gray ocean.

Luke banished the dogs to a shared basket in a corner of the kitchen and she was impressed that, despite accusing gazes, the animals stayed there. "Your dogs are well behaved."

"They're trained in the basic commands," he said. "It's for their safety."

The boys built their own sundaes, with judicious intervention from their dad to make sure they didn't upend the bottle of chocolate sauce or spray whipped cream at each other. Miranda made her daughter a small sundae of chocolate ice cream, chocolate sauce, a sprinkle of walnuts, and a fizz of whipped cream, and made herself an adult version. Luke was the only one to forgo chocolate ice cream and dig into the other carton on the table.

"Black cherry?" she asked.

"Goes great with chocolate sauce. Don't knock it until you've tried it."

"Sorry. I'm a purist. Nothing beats classic chocolate." She spooned into the decadent treat, loving the rich smell of chocolate and eating small mouthfuls so she could fully savor the taste and make the sundae last. But she was careful not to moan, lick the spoon, or do anything else that Luke might find suggestive.

The kids were engrossed in their own dessert, and she knew there'd be face- and hand-washing to come, but for now she relaxed and enjoyed the moment. "This is an amazing house you've got," she told Luke.

"Isn't it?" He got the pensive, slightly melancholy expression that suggested he was thinking of Candace, and his words confirmed it. "Best wedding gift ever."

"Wedding gift?" Her voice squeaked in astonishment. "Someone gave you a *house*?"

"Candace's parents. And yeah, they're rich. Seriously rich. Her mom, Annie Byrne, is a computer genius. In the early eighties she invented one of the first, most popular video games. *Clue-Tracer*?"

"Wow. That's still around, right? Isn't it a crime-solving game for wannabe detectives?" She'd never been into video games herself, preferring to read.

"Yeah, and she still owns it. She updates it with all the latest CSI-type stuff. But anyhow, when she invented it, it was a top seller, up there with *Pac-Man*, *Donkey Kong*, and *Super Mario Bros*. She made millions in the first two or three years. Billions by now. She's invented other games, too. Not, obviously, because she and Randall need the money but because she loves it."

"I never knew that, back in high school." Glancing at the kids, who seemed oblivious to the adult conversation, she lowered her voice. "Though I do remember Candace having some expensive-looking clothes and jewelry."

He spoke more quietly, too. "Yes, she loved clothes and all the girly stuff, but neither she nor her parents let wealth make them all high and mighty."

"Her parents are Destiny Islanders?"

"Her dad, Randall Yuen, is a native. He met her mom in Vancouver when she was getting her computer science degree and he was studying photography. He brought her home to meet his parents and kid sister, and she fell in love with the place. After the two of them married, they moved here. He supported her while she got *Clue-Tracer* going, then when the money started rolling in, they bought property, built a house, he set up a photography studio, and she kept designing games."

He stirred the remains of his sundae into a soupy pink-and-brown mess. "They were nice to me when I was a kid, and they approved of me and Candace as a couple. They liked that I was following my passion and becoming a vet,

even though I'll never make a lot of money at it. Candace
was into cooking. She took courses, worked at restaurants,
and then set up a catering business. That's the reason the
kitchen here is so amazing."

"I still can't believe they bought you a house. This
house. On the harbor."

"Yeah, it's pretty incredible. They live half a mile away,
wanted us close. Wanted our kids to be able to play on the
beach." He glanced at the boys, who were squirting more
whipped cream into their bowls. In a husky murmur, he
said, "We figured there'd be more than two kids, and Candace would be here to play with them."

She nodded sympathetically, thinking about what he'd
said. Her brother had a house on the ocean, too. Lionel had
subdivided his property and sold Aaron a section of it.
Even though the price was reasonable, Aaron would be
paying off the mortgage for the foreseeable future. Of
course, now there'd be Eden's income as well, which would
really help out.

When Aaron had built his cottage, he'd told Miranda
there was a room for her and Ariana. Pride and her dislike
of Destiny Island had made her refuse that offer. It wasn't
fair that she'd always been the one to lean on him, especially once she'd grown up. But then last summer she'd
faced the cold, hard truth. Unable to put a roof over her
child's head, she'd known she needed a better answer than
accepting another loan from her brother. And so she had
swallowed her pride and accepted that standing offer, so
she could build a better future for her daughter.

Carefully she asked, "You were okay with Candace's
parents giving you a house?"

He raised his eyebrows. "Why not? Don't tell me you
believe in that archaic stuff about how the man's supposed
to be the sole provider?"

"No way." And that was the truth. "I just . . . Look, don't

be offended, okay? This isn't meant as a criticism. But I've always figured, we each need to look out for ourselves."

He cocked his head, reflecting. "I think we need to be *able* to do that, as much as we can. But when you marry, you're a team. Like with Candace's parents. No one cares that her mom makes way more than her dad. They're both doing work they love. Same with Candace and me. If she happened to be rich and I wasn't, why should we turn down a terrific house?"

Because of pride. Something Miranda had always figured was a strength. "No good reason, I guess," she said, not wanting to insult or argue with the man who'd supplied the delicious sundae ingredients.

Over on the kitchen counter, his phone rang. As he jumped up and hurried over, Brandon looked up from his bowl and said, "Dad-dy," in a drawn-out, accusatory way.

Luke checked the display, and answered with a lazy "Hey." He listened a moment, then said, "Sounds good. See you later." Returning, he said to Brandon, "Relax, it was Grandma Sonia." He explained to Miranda, "My mom. Not an animal emergency."

"Oh." Now she understood Brandon's whine. "I guess you get those."

"He does," Brandon said emphatically.

"He's the only vet on the island," Caleb said. "The animals need him."

"Thanks, buddy." Luke reached over to ruffle his son's longish hair.

Seeing their faces side by side, she realized that the boys mostly had their dad's features, though their eyes were the same striking clear gray as Candace's rather than the intriguing color mix of Luke's. They would grow up handsome. She'd bet on that.

Luke was going on. "I have regular clinic hours. And times that I schedule visits, mostly for the large animal work but also for folks who have transportation issues. But animal injuries and illnesses don't pay heed to schedules. My clients have my cell number."

"What do you guys do when you get an emergency call?" she asked the boys.

"Sometimes we go with Daddy," Brandon said.

"Yes, sometimes," Luke said, smiling at his son. The man really did have an appealing smile. "In a pinch. But mostly we use a sitter."

"I like Gary," Brandon said. "Tiffie has too many rules."

"I like Mrs. Kent," Caleb contributed.

"Gary and Tiffie are neighborhood teens," Luke told Miranda. "Responsible ones. Mrs. Kent's kids and grandkids live off-island and she loves having children to dote on."

"She makes good cookies," Brandon said. "So do Grandma Sonia and Granddad Randall."

"Mommy made good cookies," Caleb said quietly. "I know she did. She was a really good cook." He tipped his head toward Miranda. "Are you a good cook?" It came out more as a subtle, solemn challenge than a genuine question.

No way would she try to compete with the mother he'd never met. "I'm an okay cook. Not a really good one." It was an honest answer. She chose not to mention the apple crisp.

Luke gave her an apologetic glance and stepped in. "Both sets of grandparents help out with the boys, too. They're happy for any chance to be with them. And like I said, Candace's parents live half a mile away. Mom and Forbes aren't far away either."

Miranda took a paper napkin and started to clean the worst of the chocolate off Ariana's face. "That's quite the support network."

He shrugged. "You know that old saying, it takes a village to raise a child."

"Uh, no, I don't think I've heard it."

"Boys," he said, "you go down the hall and wash up, okay?" After they'd run off, he asked her, "How about you? I guess your village starts with your brother?"

Thinking about Aaron made her smile. "Did you know we're only half sibs? We have different fathers."

"No, I didn't know. But I can see it, him being so much darker than you."

She nodded. Aaron's dad had been an indigenous man. "It's one of those things that on the one hand doesn't matter in the least but on the other hand is kind of strange. D'you know what I mean?"

"Haven't a clue," he said cheerfully. "Go on."

"If we'd had the same dad—if a guy had stuck with Mom long enough to have two kids—our lives might've been different. But that didn't happen. Mom was, well, already on a bad path by the time she had Aaron. She actually knew who his dad was, even though—"

Chapter Five

Luke didn't mean to interrupt her, but couldn't help sucking in a noisy breath. Her comment implied that her mom hadn't known who Miranda's father was. He also wondered about the "bad path" her mother'd been on before she died.

His sons might not have a mom but at least they did have a stable, loving family.

Miranda said, quickly and dismissively, "Anyhow, Aaron and I relied on each other. Or me on him, really. We're closer than a lot of full siblings."

He wanted to hear more, and was sorry his involuntary reaction had caused her to shut down. She did that, he'd noticed. Got started on a story, her words running ahead of her brain, then she realized where she was heading and put on the brakes. Still, this wasn't the time or place for the conversation. The boys would be back soon, and Ariana was looking mutinous.

Checking out the window, he saw that the rain had stopped and the sky was mostly cloudless. "What do you say we take the kids and dogs down to the beach?"

"Sure." Miranda jumped to her feet, seeming happy to end the conversation. "Is there a bathroom Ariana and I can use? She's toilet-trained, mostly." She moistened her finger and swiped a final smear of chocolate from the girl's dusky pink cheek. "Aren't you, sweetie?"

"Yes! I big girl."

Luke began to collect the dirty bowls. "The bathroom's down the hall. The boys should be out in a sec."

It took several minutes to get organized. Miranda insisted on getting the dishes into the dishwasher, though he'd happily have left them in the sink. Then they had to help the kids into their outdoor clothing. When the boys and dogs had gone outside, Luke put on his socks, shoes, and a jacket while Miranda retrieved her sneakers from by the front door. She pulled on the same navy fleece jacket and blue scarf she'd worn to the coffee shop, the color of the scarf bringing out the blue in her eyes.

Luke grabbed his phone, hoping it wouldn't ring, and ushered her and Ariana, who was bundled up in a pink, puffy coat, out to the deck.

Miranda went to the railing and gazed around at the fenced yard, the fort he'd built, and the beach below. He watched her, admiring the clean lines of her profile, her delicate skin, and the wavy blond hair that stirred in the gentle breeze. It was strange seeing another pretty young woman here, at the home that he'd shared with Candace. But his wife had been gone for four years, and though he'd likely always feel as if a part of his soul had been torn out, he'd more or less come to terms with the loss. There was no point in tying himself up in knots over enjoying some pleasant, attractive, female company.

Miranda hoisted Ariana into her arms and pointed to the beach. "Look, sweetie. Luke and the boys have the beach on their doorstep."

The house, on a jut of rocky land, was just up from a crescent of pebbly beach shared with three neighbors. The path down was an easy one and the beach, on the western shore of Blue Moon Harbor, was sheltered. The boys, who'd learned to swim before they were Ariana's age, were under strict instructions not to go there alone, but Luke hadn't put a lock on the gate.

Children needed to explore, to play and experiment rather than be overprotected and bound up with rules. Much as he feared having anything bad happen to the twins, he did believe that. So did the boys' grandparents and, even more important, so had Candace. Even though she hadn't lived to see their boys, she and Luke had had many, many talks about child-rearing. When he faced a child-related dilemma, he called on memories of those talks. Remembering his wife's voice and earnest expression helped him restrain his instinct to wrap the boys up in a protective cocoon.

He and Candace might have been different in a few ways—like her wealth, vivaciousness, and attention to her appearance—but in all the ways that mattered they'd been soul mates. It was so damned unfair that she'd been taken away from him, that she wasn't here to enjoy their two wonderful, if challenging, boys.

Okay, so maybe he hadn't entirely come to terms with her death.

"Luke?" Miranda's voice recalled him to the present. "Shouldn't we follow Brandon and Caleb? Make sure they don't get into any trouble?"

"Yeah, we should." The sight of Miranda and her cute, black-haired daughter soothed his grief and resentment. "Hey, Ariana, want a ride down to the beach?"

She gave him a big smile, her baby teeth gleaming, and raised her arms. "Up."

"You can sit on my shoulders and hold on to my head." Turning to Miranda, he asked, "That work okay?"

"She does it with Aaron, so she knows how." She helped settle her daughter, who couldn't be more than twenty-five pounds, on his shoulders. "Ariana, remember you can't put your hands over his eyes or he won't be able to see."

The girl giggled and promptly gave Luke a finger-mask.

"Oh no!" he cried, "I've gone blind. I'll never find the beach."

With more giggles, she peeled her hands away again.

"My vision's come back. It's magic!" Grinning, Luke gripped her legs firmly and, with Miranda following, took the path downhill. The boys were out on the rocks, peering into a tide pool, and the dogs were investigating a pile of kelp. If they rolled in something nasty, so be it. He often had to toss them under the outdoor shower after a trip to the beach.

Most of Destiny Island's beaches were the rugged Pacific Northwest type, not gleaming stretches of white sand. This one was typical, with a mix of pebbles, rocks, coarse sand, kelp, and well-worn logs and driftwood. The small rocky outcropping at their end of the beach nurtured several tide pools that filled with small sea creatures.

"Be careful, it's rough footing," he told Miranda, keeping Ariana on his shoulders as they walked over to the boys. "And slippery after the rain."

When he let the child down, her mom took her hand and squatted to look into the pool. "Oh look, Ariana. Look at all the things that live in that pool. Caleb, Brandon, can you guys tell us what they are?"

As was typical, Brandon leaped in to answer first, naming off starfish, crabs, barnacles, and sculpins. Caleb brought up the rear, adding sea anemones and periwinkle snails—creatures Brandon had either forgotten about or didn't want to try to pronounce. Luke worried a bit about this dynamic, but the boys had distinct personalities. All he could do was gently encourage Brandon to be a bit more thoughtful and considerate, and Caleb to be more outgoing.

When Ariana reached into the still water of the pool and

tried to catch a sculpin, it was Caleb who said solemnly, "No, don't do that. It hurts them if we touch them."

"Hurt fish?" She turned big dark brown eyes on him.

He nodded.

"I pet doggies," she said.

Luke noticed that Miranda had her phone out, taking pictures.

"Doggies like it," Brandon said. "Fish don't."

"Some doggies don't like it," Caleb corrected. "Some bite when they're mad or hurt. You have to be careful."

Luke smiled to hear his son parrot his own explanation and warning. "That's right," he agreed. "Ariana, you shouldn't pet a doggy unless you're with a grown-up who says it's okay."

Her face screwed up, perhaps in disappointment but more likely in puzzlement. Adult rules must be so confusing for kids, especially before their brains had the capability for analytical reasoning.

"I wonder if this beach has shells," Miranda said, stowing her phone in her pocket and shifting to a less complicated topic. "What do you think, sweetie? Want to see if we can find some shells?"

"I find shells," the girl agreed.

Her mom gave her a boost down from the rocky outcropping and the pair walked along the beach, just up from where the ocean, a dark greenish-indigo under the pale gray sky, lapped the shore. Periodically, one or the other bent to pick up something and show it to the other.

Ariana was a bright, sweet child, Luke thought, a testament to Miranda's parenting.

He spent some time with his sons, telling them a bit more about the ocean creatures, and then the boys tired of the lesson and ran off to find sticks to throw for the dogs.

Hiking his butt onto a large, smooth log, still damp from the rain, Luke watched the peaceful Sunday afternoon scene and clicked a few shots of his own. If it had been July rather than February, some of his neighbors, along with relatives and friends, would be on the beach, but today his little group had it to themselves. He was truly grateful to Annie and Randall for providing his family with such a wonderful place to live.

Miranda glanced over at him, said a few words to her daughter, and then, leaving Ariana to play in the pebbly sand, came to sit beside Luke. "Islanders are nature folks, aren't they?" she said. "It's all about the great outdoors." Her cheeks were pink and her eyes bright—results, he figured, of being in that very outdoors. He wanted to run his finger across one of those flushed cheeks and touch his lips to hers, find out if they were chilly or warm.

"Hard not to be," he said, "when it really is so great. And so present."

"There's nature in Vancouver," she said mildly. "The mountains, Stanley Park and the other parks, the beaches. Even in the heart of the city, there are flowers and trees."

"Uh-huh."

Her lips curved and she ducked her head. "Yes, Destiny's more outdoorsy. I'm getting used to it. Though . . . promise you won't tell Aaron this?"

Intrigued, he said, "Promise."

"I like your place better than his. His is so wildernessy. The cabin's in a forest, tall trees all around. It's wilder than here, kind of spooky, especially at night. You've got a nice big piece of property, but it's landscaped. It's in a neighborhood." Her gaze rested on her daughter as she spoke. "Aaron's only neighbor is Lionel, and there's just a trail through the woods connecting their houses."

"But Aaron likes it."

"Loves it. Eden seems to, too. And that's what matters."

"Are you and Ariana living there with them?"

She shook her head. "At first, when they were dating

long distance. But not when she moved here and they got engaged. They needed their privacy."

"So where's home now?"

"A cabin at SkySong."

"SkySong? Di and Seal's place? Oh, that's right, Aaron's fiancée is related to them, isn't she?"

"Di is Eden's mom's long-lost sister. A hippie runaway who joined the commune on Destiny back in 1969, along with her runaway boyfriend, Seal. Di and Helen—Eden's mother—hadn't been in touch since their teens, then Helen found a letter from her sister that their parents had hidden away. It mentioned the commune on Destiny, and Eden came here to follow that clue."

"Huh. And she not only found Di and Seal, but met Aaron."

"Now she and her parents and sister have moved here. Her family is living in a cabin at SkySong, and Eden and Aaron are planning their wedding."

Watching his innocent little boys, Luke vowed to do everything in his power to raise them to be happy and secure, not teens who'd want to run away from home. Still, from what he understood, the sixties had been a kind of magical, if crazy, time in history. Musing, he said, "That old commune must've been quite a place. I think my stepdad spent a little time there, though he doesn't talk much about it."

"Nor do Di and Seal." She frowned slightly. "Which seems odd. I guess maybe they're embarrassed about all the drugs and free love and stuff that must've gone on. But I can see the appeal of a place where young people could take their dreams, be free of society's rules."

"Still the rebel at heart, are you?" he teased.

She gave her head a quick shake. "Not now, with a daughter to raise."

That was what he'd figured, and her answer reassured

him. Returning to the original topic, he said, "So you're in one of those cabins at SkySong?"

"Yes. Di and Seal offered and I didn't feel right about it, but they kind of insisted. Everyone pretty much insisted."

"Why didn't you feel right about it?"

"They're not charging me rent. It's charity."

"Is there such a thing as charity within a family?" That wasn't how things worked in his family. Money, time, and other resources were shared with a generous spirit.

"They're not my family. They're Aaron's."

"And you and Ariana are his family. His only family?"

"Unless you count grandparents in Florida who we haven't communicated with in more than a decade."

"Oh, too bad," he murmured. Clearly, things hadn't gone well when Miranda and Aaron's grandparents had taken them in after their mom's death. He was getting a better idea why Miranda had hated this island, and it wasn't all about missing city life.

She shrugged. "It's better that way."

He was about to pursue the topic, but she said, "Know what that elaborate structure is?" She pointed to a sandy part of the beach where her daughter was building something out of damp sand, pebbles, and sticks, so self-sufficient in her play this afternoon. The little girl's lips moved as if she was chattering to invisible companions.

Again, Miranda was changing the subject. Not wanting to make her uncomfortable, he accepted the distraction and guessed, "A castle?"

"A fairy castle."

He chuckled. "The boys build castles, too, but the kind with moats and battlements." Right now, though, the twins were throwing sticks into the ocean for the two dogs. The boys were haphazard pitchers. The dogs had worked things out so Honey chased the sticks that flew for yards into the cold sea, leaving the ones that went only a short distance for tiny, elderly Pigpen.

The dogs faithfully returned each stick to the twins, shaking vigorously so that droplets flew out in a blizzard. Then, panting, tails wagging, they waited for the next toss.

"Those are the happiest dogs in the world," Miranda said.

"Yeah. Give dogs a beach, a good meal, or a chew toy and they're in heaven." He felt a pang of envy. Not that his life was unhappy, but it sure hadn't turned out the way he'd once believed it would. "Wish it was that easy for us humans," he said quietly. "I suppose it could be, but we're too complicated. We make things complicated, don't we?"

Miranda gave a wry smile. "Oh yeah, human beings make things complicated." She watched her daughter happily chattering away to herself—or to the fairies—as she worked. Life had been easier before Ariana, but she wouldn't trade her daughter for anything in the world.

She went on. "But it's not always us making things complicated. It's the circumstances of life. Like . . ." She pressed her lips together. Should she say what she was thinking? But she'd seen the sadness in Luke's stunning eyes when he was speaking, and guessed he was already thinking of Candace. "Like losing your wife," she said quietly. "The boys growing up without a mom. You had no control over that, and you'd have done anything to prevent it."

He swallowed. "Yeah."

"I was in love with Ariana's father." She waved a hand dismissively. "Oh, it was nothing like you and Candace, kindred spirits from when you were kids. But I gave him my heart and he said he loved me. It turned out to be just words. He was an actor. He used words and body language as tools to get what he wanted."

"He sounds like a tool," Luke said.

She gave a surprised laugh. "Yeah, kind of. Anyhow, we used condoms, but something went wrong." Since then, she'd changed to a more reliable form of birth control, not that she'd had much chance to put it to the test.

Down the shore, Ariana's pink coat was trailing in the damp, seaweedy sand, but it was washable. Besides, what did dirty clothes matter when her daughter was having fun? "When I found out I was pregnant, I was thrilled. I had these crazy dreams of—" She stopped abruptly. What was it about this man that had her starting to open up about things she never shared? This was why she'd been wary about accepting his invitation. And maybe, if she was completely honest with herself, it was why she'd come. To explore this unusual and compelling bond that might be the beginning of a friendship.

"Dreams of?" he prompted.

"Oh, nothing." She dipped her head and studied her well-worn red shoes.

"Of love, a home, a family?" The sadness in his voice brought her head up again.

Perhaps that was why she found herself wanting to reveal things to him. Though he made her feel inadequate in comparison—he'd had a happy marriage to his kids' mom; he had a successful career; he'd always given his children a stable home—they had one thing in common. They'd both suffered. In the grand scheme of things, perhaps his sorrows were in fact bigger ones than hers. How did a dead wife and dead father stack up against an unknown father, a loser mom who OD'd on cocaine, sucky grandparents, and a string of failed romances?

She squared her shoulders and looked Luke straight in the eye. "Yes. That was my dream. That's always been my dream. I wonder what the Fates have against the two of us, that they didn't grant us the dream?"

He shook his head. "Beats the hell out of me."

"We have great kids, though," she said. "Healthy, happy ones. We do have love, even if it's not the full package we dreamed of."

"You're right." He stared down the beach.

Her gaze followed his. It was a gray day, still damp and chilly after the rain, but none of the kids minded a bit. Ariana was off in her imaginary fairy world, and the twins and dogs showed no signs of tiring of the stick game.

She brought her focus back to Luke's face, a handsome one with regular features, made special by his amazing eyes. And by the emotions that so often flickered close to the surface: his love for his kids, his caring for animals, his sorrow over the loss of his wife, and occasionally, as now, a pensiveness, like he was pondering deep issues.

He turned back to her and said, "I'm not the strongest person."

"What?" His words caught her off guard. "How do you mean?"

"It's a thing I learned about myself. When I was ten and my dad died, I couldn't handle it on my own."

"Your mom . . ."

"Was so shattered herself, she wasn't there for me. It wasn't her fault. She just wasn't strong enough either. Then Forbes came along, and she had their love to put her together again."

"And you had no one," she said sympathetically. She, at least, had always had Aaron.

"No, I did. I had Candace. Other friends too, but she was the special one. I could talk to her about anything. I could be sad with her, and I found that I could be happy. She helped me get through it all. My dad's death, then my mom falling for Forbes. Getting a new family. So many changes, but she was always there. She and her parents. I did homework at their kitchen table, ate Randall's cookies, listened to Annie's flights of fancy as she brainstormed video games."

"I'm glad you had them." And envious. "A home away from home."

He smiled affectionately. "I had another of those, too. With Viola."

"Viola?"

"Viola Cruickshank, the vet before me. I took an injured cat to her, and she basically took me in. She let me help out, and she taught me. I loved the animals. Loved helping heal them. In a way, I love her, too." He chuckled. "Though she'd hate it if I told her so. She's not exactly a people person."

"You became a vet because of her."

"Her and the animals." He did a quick visual check of his kids. He did that a lot, just as she did with Ariana.

This time he raised his hand in a wave, and she saw that another couple of adults had come down to the beach, a black-haired man in cargo pants and a Cowichan Indian sweater and a woman in jeans, a black jacket, and a purple hijab. They waved back.

"Neighbors?" she asked.

"Yes. Dr. Shakoor and her husband. I bet you'll be seeing them in the store soon. They're expecting their first baby later this year."

Miranda watched as the couple strolled along the beach, their arms around each other. Though envy nipped her, she truly hoped nothing got in the way of their hopes for the future.

"Diversity," Luke said.

When she turned to him, he winked.

She rolled her eyes. Yes, she'd realized that he was right, this island was almost as culturally diverse as Vancouver. He didn't need to keep hammering the point home. "Tell me more about Viola."

"When I graduated from vet school, she was almost

sixty. She wanted to volunteer with Veterinarians Without Borders while she was healthy enough to handle it. So I took over the practice. When she's not overseas, I sometimes consult with her and she comes in now and then to fill in for me if I have to do kid-related stuff. Feeding her addiction, she calls it." He grinned, that warm, engaging smile.

Usually it made her want to smile back, but the joking mention of addiction cut too close to home. Forcing away thoughts of her mom, she managed to say lightly, "I can see you doing the same, after you eventually retire."

"Retire? Who's planning to retire?" he joked. "But anyhow," he went on, sounding more serious, "I was saying about how I'm not strong enough to get through stuff on my own. After Candace died, I was shattered, grieving, and I had two babies. I needed help. From my parents, Candace's parents. From Candace, because, thank God, we'd talked about how we wanted to raise our children. I draw on those memories all the time."

He glanced at Miranda. "I'm fine with needing help. With not being all that strong and self-sufficient."

Lucky him, to have always had someone there to ask. What she'd learned was that people went missing. Physically or emotionally. Her mom had, and her grandparents. It wasn't fair to always keep asking Aaron for help. Besides, what if—horrible thought—one day he wasn't there either? "I'm not sure why you're telling me this."

He scratched his jaw, fingers rasping against his Sunday stubble. Would that scruff of beard abrade her skin if he kissed her, or would it feel soft?

She gave an internal head-shake. Luke wasn't her type, so why was she thinking about the slightly abrasive caress of his beard against her face? Or between her legs . . .

Hoping she wasn't blushing, she tuned in when he finally said, "Partly 'cause you're easy to talk to. But also, you have this thing about pride and being independent. I guess I wanted to let you know that I'm more about people supporting one another. Maybe I'm not as strong as you. But that's who I am."

"Okay," she said again. "So we're different. That's only one of the many, many ways."

"But I like you." He gazed at her, the gold and green flecks bright in his gray eyes. "I've enjoyed this afternoon."

"Me too." It had felt . . . honest. Except for not sharing her weird little fantasies about sex with him. She only hoped—or did she really?—that he wasn't also fantasizing about her. That wasn't what their relationship was supposed to be about. They were seeing if they might be friends. And that was how their conversation had gone. Friendly. Respectful. Luke might disagree with her on some things, but when he told her his opinion it didn't come across as if he was telling her what to do. They'd talked like equal adults.

Here, on the semiprivate beach adjoining his million-dollar mansion.

She huffed out air in a soft snort. Yeah, like she'd ever be Luke Chandler's equal.

"I'd invite you to stay for dinner," he said, "but—"

"No, of course not." She rose, brushing off the slightly damp backside of her jeans. "We've already overstayed our welcome."

"It's not that." He stood up, too, his gaze scanning the beach.

Quickly she pulled out her phone and clicked a shot of him, and then another when he turned to her with an amused smile. She had a feeling that whatever Luke was doing when she aimed a camera at him, the photo would turn out well.

"It's just," he said, "that I figured dinner could be a bit, uh, overwhelming. Mom and Forbes are coming over, and Annie and Randall. It's a Sunday night tradition. I host and provide some of the food, and they bring the rest. But if you'd like to stay—"

"God, no," she said fervently. "I mean, thanks, but yeah, that's not . . ." She shook her head. "Besides, we've got a Sunday dinner tradition at SkySong, too. And I need to get back to help out. And Ariana needs a nap." She only hoped her daughter could be persuaded to leave the fairy sand-castle without a major fuss.

"Let's do this again, though."

She studied him. A responsible dad, a responsible vet, a responsible son and son-in-law. A tall, undeniably hand-some man, solid and outdoorsy-looking, perfectly at home on this rugged beach. A man who listened to her, who treated her like an equal.

A friend?

A man with kaleidoscope eyes that changed with each emotion he felt. A woman could get lost in those eyes if she wasn't careful.

But Luke wasn't her type, and she wasn't looking for a boyfriend—even if her celibate body craved sex—so that wasn't going to happen.

"Just as friends," she said, to make sure he wasn't push-ing for something more.

"As friends," he repeated.

Maybe she could do this. Enjoy a man's company, even appreciate his attractiveness, without getting carried away and doing something stupid. "I'd like that," she told him.

Chapter Six

Miranda didn't seem to have noticed that he'd said "as friends" rather than "just as friends," Luke thought as he shaped ground beef into small patties. The truth was, he now knew he wanted more than friendship from her. The woman was complex, the opposite of Candace, who'd been utterly open, a "what you see is what I am" person. He'd loved that about her, yet Miranda intrigued and attracted him. She was a curled-up rosebud with lots of thorns, and he hoped that by the time the flower unfurled for him, he wouldn't be bleeding too badly.

Shrieks issued from the playroom next to the kitchen, where the kids and dogs, all washed and dried after playing on the beach, were having what sounded like a truck demolition derby. "Everything okay in there?" he called.

Happy shouts of acknowledgment reassured him.

His thoughts returned to Miranda. She was doing two steps forward and one back, but she was still heading in his direction. He'd seen a gleam of interest in her eyes now and then, whether she wanted to acknowledge it or not.

Hamburger patties finished, he washed his hands and checked his watch. His parents and in-laws should be here soon. He took salad ingredients from the fridge and started tearing the dark, leafy lettuce. Used to be, Candace was the chef and he happily played the role of *sous-chef*. It sure wasn't as much fun preparing meals on his own, and he'd already started training his sons to help out wherever they could. Not tonight, though, when they were running late thanks to the extended beach outing.

Some people swore there was such a thing as love at first sight. He guessed Miranda might be one of them. But the concept didn't make sense to him. Lust, sure. Or some kind of weird attraction/obsession thing like he'd felt for the Goth girl back in high school. But that wasn't love. You couldn't love someone unless you knew them, mind and heart and soul. At least not in his humble opinion.

Friendship was a good, solid start. It could grow deeper, through time together and sharing things—both trivial like ice cream, and substantial like views on child-rearing—until one day, you suddenly realized you were passionately in love with your friend. At least that's how it had been for him and Candace.

As for Miranda . . . Well, his mind was open to the possibilities.

The front doorbell chimed, and a moment later his mom called, "Hi, family. Where's everyone?"

"Grandma Sonia!" Brandon yelled, and Luke listened to his sons pelt down the hall and greet his mom and Forbes.

After that, he was too busy to think about Miranda. His in-laws followed on his parents' heels. Despite a sullen rain that had likely settled in for the night, Luke got busy grilling the mini burgers out on the deck, glad for the overhang of roof that sheltered the barbecue. In the kitchen, his mom and Randall, the cooks in their respective marriages, put the finishing touches to the rest of the food. Annie and Forbes were in the playroom with the boys and dogs, keeping them out from underfoot.

That morning, Luke and the boys had put placemats,

cutlery, and napkins on the big table in the dining room. Now the food was set out, smorgasbord style: the burgers and salad, his mom's baked stuffed mushrooms, and Randall's chicken casserole and cornmeal muffins. As usual it was a hodgepodge, but they'd long ago agreed they liked it that way, everyone free to contribute whatever they felt like.

They sat down in their usual places, Luke at the head of the table with one boy on either side. Separating them reduced the noise and mess. On the side of the table to his right were his mom and Forbes, and to his left were Randall and Annie, with the men seated across from the women. The other end of the table, Candace's spot, was as always vacant. Tonight, for some reason, maybe because he'd spent hours with Miranda, that chair opposite him seemed particularly empty.

Once they all had full plates, Annie said, "The boys told Forbes and me that you had company this afternoon." The youngest of the grandparents by a few years, her light gray eyes—Candace's eyes, and the twins'—were sharp behind navy-framed glasses, though all those hours of intent concentration at the computer had traced lines across her forehead and around her eyes. Her plaid flannel shirt and baggy jeans gave no hint that she was a bazillionaire, nor did the shaggy, silver-threaded red hair that was overdue for a cut.

"Oh?" His mom glanced at him, and then at his sons. "Who was your company, boys?" Sonia Russo was fifty-nine but didn't look it. The peach-colored top she wore over a long, casual skirt set off her Mediterranean coloring. Her olive skin still looked tanned though summer was long past, and her black, shoulder-length hair was free of gray. Luke looked nothing like her, being, as she said, "the spitting image" of his deceased father.

"*Dad's* company," Brandon said, talking through a mouthful of hamburger. "Not ours."

"Don't talk with your mouth full," Luke said before forking up another big bite of the delicious herbed chicken casserole.

Caleb gave an audible swallow, and said, "Her name is Miranda. Her daughter's name is Ari . . . Ari . . ." He turned to Luke for help.

"Ariana," he supplied.

"Ari-ana," his son repeated.

"She's a little, little kid," Brandon said dismissively. "And she's a *girl*."

"Girls can be excellent playmates," Forbes said with a twinkle in his blue eyes. "When you grow up a little, you'll find that out." He was the oldest of the grandparents, turning sixty-five this year. Like a few of the other "old hippies" on the island, he wore his thinning, graying hair in a ponytail, and favored tie-dye and denim.

Caleb leveled a thoughtful glance at his grandfather. "I'm growing up."

"Me too!" put in Brandon, after hastily swallowing what he was eating and thankfully not choking on it.

"It doesn't sound like it," Luke's mom said, "when you say boys are better than girls."

"Well put, Mom," Luke agreed.

"Who is this Miranda?" Annie asked. She was a straight-forward woman, rarely cloaking her words in a veil of social nicety.

"Miranda Gabriel. She's returned to the island."

"I'd heard that," his mom said.

"Returned?" Annie asked.

Luke was considering how to answer that question when his father-in-law spoke up. "Aaron Gabriel's younger sister." Randall Yuen, the same age as Luke's mom, was a native Destiny Islander like her, a perceptive guy and a brilliant photographer. Though he was a few years older than his wife, he looked younger than she, maybe thanks to his half-Chinese ancestry. His black hair hadn't a thread of gray and his skin was unlined. His clothes, a forest green jersey over jeans, fit better than his wife's.

"The siblings moved to the island as teens," Randall went on. "To live with their grandparents when—" He broke off and glanced at the twins. They were gobbling dinner, paying no heed to the conversation, but he lowered his voice. "When their mom passed away. Aaron ended up adjusting to island life, but Miranda didn't last long. Didn't she drop out of school and run away to Vancouver?" He glanced at Luke's mom, who was a high school sciences teacher.

"Yes. In eleventh grade, as I recall. She barely set foot on the island after that, but now she and her two-year-old daughter are back."

"A single mother?" Annie said.

"Honestly," his mom teased her, "you and Forbes miss all the gossip. Him absorbed in his music and you living in those fantasy worlds you create, rather than in the real one."

It was a small island with a small population, and most of the residents loved to gossip. Luke mostly ignored it. But the idea that people were talking behind Miranda's back irked him. It also made him wonder what his mother knew about Miranda that he didn't.

Brandon said, "What's for dessert?"

"I brought strawberry-rhubarb pie," Luke's mom said. "And Granddad Randall brought raisin oatmeal cookies. But we're not having dessert until the adults have finished their first course."

Luke had stowed Miranda's apple crisp in the fridge, saving it for himself and the boys to eat this week and not mentioning it to his relatives.

"May-I-please-be-excused?" Caleb ran the familiar words together.

The boys were quick eaters and fidgeted when forced to

sit at the table more than ten or fifteen minutes. "Not until you eat your salad," Luke said. "You too, Brandon."

They both heaved dramatic sighs and poked at the salad Luke had served them.

"I mean it," he said.

With pouty expressions, they gave in and polished off the veggies.

"Now you may be excused," he told them. "Take your plates with you and put them on the kitchen counter. We'll call you when it's time for dessert."

When they'd gone, his mother said, "Luke, you went to school with Aaron and Miranda, didn't you?"

"Aaron was a year ahead and Miranda a year behind. In Julian's class. I didn't really know her."

"I doubt anyone really knew her," she said. "She was, to put it charitably, a troubled teen. She didn't fit in with the Destiny kids, and I don't think she wanted to. She was forced to live here and she seemed angry. Or hurt, perhaps. Those kids had just lost their mother. Corinne."

"You knew Miranda's mother?" Luke asked.

"I taught her."

"Really? She was that much younger than you?"

"Ten years, give or take. I was twenty-six when I got a job at Blue Moon High. Randall, did you know Corinne?"

"I knew *of* her," he said. "I was taking the class photos. She showed up drunk, which made her fairly memorable. I also saw her hanging out with Dirk Jacobs and Harry Wong."

"Those two," his mom said with contempt. "The island's source of street drugs for a few years back in the eighties. Until Dirk got arrested and Harry moved his game to the mainland."

"Miranda's mom did drugs?" Luke asked. He didn't recall having heard that, back when the siblings moved to the island.

"Corinne drank and did drugs as a teen," his mom said. "She dropped out of school and ran away." Pointedly, she added, "The same as Miranda did. Corinne went to Vancouver, and years later died of an overdose."

Now he knew what Miranda had meant when she said her mother'd been on a bad path.

"Aaron and Miranda are half siblings, aren't they?" Randall asked.

"That's what she said," Luke replied. "But they're really close."

"With an addict mother, I bet they would be," Forbes commented. "They'd be relying on each other a lot."

"Not that it's ever a good thing to have a parent die," Annie said solemnly, "but it sounds like those kids were better off with their grandparents."

Yet Miranda had hated it here, and she and Aaron were estranged from their grandparents.

"Well, yes," his mom said, "but . . ." She exchanged glances with Randall. "The Gabriels were, hmm, how shall I put this? Strict and judgmental. Not kid-friendly. Corinne couldn't do the things other kids did, like go to parties or have friends over. Her parents tried to keep a tight leash on her. She rebelled." She gave a sad smile. "I felt sorry for Corinne. She seemed kind of . . . lost."

"And those are the grandparents Miranda and Aaron went to," Luke said, "just after losing their mom. Harsh. I can see why Miranda would act out." Just as her mom had.

"Aaron didn't start out so wonderfully either," his mother said. "But he somehow met Lionel Williams, who became a mentor and got him interested in flying. I don't think poor Miranda had anyone like that. I tried to get her to talk to me—I did that with her mom, too—but had no luck." She glanced at Luke. "I haven't seen her since she came back to the island. How did she turn out? Better than her mother, I hope."

"For sure." She didn't use drugs. Did she? Surely not; he'd seen no hint of it. "She seems like a responsible mom. She works at Blowing Bubbles and she's studying for a certificate in early childhood education."

"Good for her," his mom said.

"Yeah," Randall agreed. "It's always nice to see young people turn their lives around. The teen years are difficult for a lot of people, for a variety of reasons." He smiled at Forbes. "By the way, I heard Julian on CBC Radio, playing and doing an interview. His star keeps on rising, but he sounds balanced about how he's handling it."

"Yeah, I'm proud of him," Forbes said. He reached over to squeeze Luke's mom's hand. "Should say, Sonia and I are proud of him. I don't know what all was going on with him when we moved here. Well, I guess a whole bunch of things, really, and I admit I wasn't a very good dad. Too caught up in being a newlywed. But whatever it was, he grew up and got over it."

"Any idea when he'll be back on Destiny again?" Randall asked. "We enjoyed hearing him play with B-B-Zee last Christmas."

Forbes, a woodworker, had also been an amateur musician all his life. He and a couple of other guys his age had a band. B-B-Zee was Forbes Blake, Jonathan Barnes, who with his wife owned a B and B, and Christian Zabec, a drifter from California who'd ended up settling on Destiny. The band mostly only played on the island, at events like weddings and anniversaries, and sometimes on Friday nights at Quail Ridge Community Hall. Julian, who'd learned guitar from his dad when he was tiny, played with them on the rare occasions he came to visit.

Forbes's blue eyes lit. "My birthday's in May and Sonia's is in June. He usually tries to find a day or two break in his schedule to visit around then. Wish he could come more often, but his life's busy."

Luke's mom leaned over to give him a consoling hug.

Luke frowned, annoyed at his stepbrother. Forbes loved his son a lot, and missed him. Julian might not think much of the island, but he did seem to be really fond of his dad. Sure, he was busy touring and building a career, but family was important.

"Let's get back to Miranda," Annie said briskly. "Are you dating her, Luke?"

"Uh, not exactly. I met her when I was buying birthday presents for the twins, and found her easy to talk to. I think we're becoming friends. Neither of us is in a big rush to turn it into anything more serious." At least that was what his rational side told him, and it had to overrule his newly reawakened hormones.

His mom spoke up. "You know I'm not the judgmental type, but I am concerned about the boys. If you bring a woman into their lives, she should be, well, someone we all can trust."

"Mom—" he started.

She cut him off. "I'm not saying Miranda isn't trust-worthy. But, to put it bluntly, her mother wasn't. Her mother's parents were, well, not people one would warm to, shall we say. I know nothing about her father, or her grandparents on that side . . ." She paused.

"I don't think they're in the picture," he admitted. But he quickly added, "Aaron definitely is, though. She was living with him until Eden moved here, and now she's at SkySong with Eden's family."

"Meaning she doesn't want to live on her own, just her and her daughter?" Annie asked. "Or that she can't afford to pay rent? She's what, a year younger than you? And she doesn't have a place of her own?"

"I think she's had a tough time." He narrowed his eyes slightly. "Not everyone's genius enough to invent a game and make a million before they're twenty-five."

"No need to be defensive, son," Randall said. "Or to attack your mother-in-law."

He sighed. "Sorry. But someone needs to defend Miranda, since she's not here to do it herself."

"Next time, invite her," his mother said, making it sound more of a command than a suggestion.

Forbes gave a throaty chuckle. "Tell Miranda that four grandparents want to grill her and see if she's fit company for their grandsons. But we'll feed her while we're doing it. Who could resist that invitation?"

Luke's mother huffed. "If she has nothing to hide, she shouldn't be afraid to meet us."

"Mom, I'm not auditioning her for the role of wife, okay?" Exasperated, he spoke more loudly than he'd intended.

And now four startled faces were staring at him.

Candace had been his wife. He knew they were all thinking that, and mourning her loss. Quietly now, he said, "Candace was the love of my life. Right now, it's hard to imagine sharing my life and my boys with another woman. But that doesn't mean I don't enjoy female company."

"For the past couple of years we've all been urging you to date," his mother said. "We're happy you're considering it. But why not one of the island women? We know them. We know who's trustworthy."

He shook his head, exasperated again. "Our population barely tops fifteen hundred. Single women in the right age range . . . there aren't that many." Two or three of those had already hinted that they'd like to pursue a relationship, but he had no interest in dating them.

"What about Iris Yakimura?" Annie said. "I like her."

"I do, too," he said. Iris's family owned Dreamspinner, and she worked in the bookstore. Where Candace had been extroverted, Iris was reserved, maybe shy. She had not even hinted that she might be interested in going out with him.

"I don't think we have anything in common. All she talks about is books. Nothing against books, but that topic wears thin."

"She talks about books because you see her in the bookstore," Annie said. "When people visit your clinic, all you talk about is animals."

"If you took her for lunch," his mother suggested, "you might find you have lots in common."

"Ladies, I'm twenty-eight. If I want to ask a woman out, I'll do it."

"Aren't you sexually attracted to Iris?" Annie asked.

Luke dropped his head into his hands. He was used to his mother-in-law's frankness and usually appreciated it, but sometimes she could be way too blunt. "This topic is officially closed. Let's clear the table and organize dessert."

But, as he packaged up leftovers in the kitchen, he thought about Iris. She was beautiful and efficient, and seemed smart and nice. His mother was right, that he had no idea what interests and values they might share. If what he'd been reflecting on earlier was correct, that liking and friendship could over time grow into passionate love, why might that not happen with Iris? And yet he felt no desire to date her.

And yeah, though he had no intention of confessing it in this company, he was definitely sexually attracted to Miranda.

Still, as much as he hated to admit it, his mom and Annie might have a point. If a woman was going to hang out with his boys, he had to ensure she was totally trustworthy. Was Miranda?

Chapter Seven

It was the last day of February, and more than two weeks had passed since Miranda had last seen Luke. He'd said he had a good time and suggested they do it again. But he hadn't called.

True, Ariana had thrown a TTT when Miranda had told her she had to leave the sandcastle, which by then had been inhabited by a colony of fairies. But her daughter's tantrums hadn't discouraged Luke before, so what was the problem?

How ridiculous, Miranda thought as she restocked the shelves at Blowing Bubbles that Tuesday afternoon. Why was she obsessing over this? She, who had no interest in dating, much less in dating Luke, who wasn't her type. Although she had to admit that she'd spent far too much time gazing at pictures on the screen of her phone, especially one close-up with great lighting on his handsome face.

"I thought we were becoming friends," she murmured under her breath. "He said that. He wanted it." And he'd got her starting to believe it, he'd made her enjoy his company and feel close to him, and then he hadn't called.

Pissed off at herself, she gently put her armful of stuffed Bambis and orcas on the shelf, and gave herself a whack upside the head. "What century is this?" She was a feminist. She'd spent her life trying to be strong and independent. And now she was fluttering about all helpless and sad because some freaking guy hadn't phoned her. "Ridiculous! Pick up the damned phone!"

"Pardon?" her boss Kara called from behind the counter.

"Sorry. Talking to myself."

Miranda got back to restocking, and at the end of the work day drove herself and Ariana home to the cozy log cabin at SkySong and made them a chicken and veggie stir-fry. Then, when the dishes were done and Ariana was settled with a couple of favorite toys, Miranda picked up her phone and dialed Luke's number.

After the usual "hey, how are you" exchange, she said, "Thanks again for sundaes on Sunday, and sharing your beach. I wonder if I could return the favor and have you and the boys over for a pizza-building dinner one night."

He didn't respond, and she said breezily, "But if you'd rather not, I totally—"

He stopped her by saying, "It sounds good. Really. Thank you."

She refused to second-guess whether he meant it, or to ponder the little thrill that coursed through her. "Oh good. Great. What night works for you?"

"How about tomorrow? The boys and I were going to Mom and Forbes's place, but she's got a bad cold so that's off. And I don't feel like cooking."

"Tomorrow's good." Really good, because she wasn't working. She'd have plenty of time to clean and tidy, shop for ingredients, prepare pizza dough, and still do some coursework.

As she put down the phone, she pondered the fact that he'd chosen tomorrow. It suggested he was telling the truth about wanting to get together. Which was a good thing. Right?

* * *

This was the first time Miranda'd had anyone other than her brother, Eden, or Eden's relatives over to the one-bedroom cabin. Despite the fact that the entire place would almost fit into Luke's living room, and that she didn't own it or even pay rent, Miranda felt proud of her small home as she opened the door to greet Luke and his sons.

The boys roared inside, shedding raindrops, and Luke followed. "Nice place," he commented, handing her a paper bag and then grabbing his sons long enough to pull off their rain jackets, which he hung on the coat hooks by the door.

She glanced in the bag, to see a bottle of wine. "Thanks for this. And yes, we like the cabin." Except for Aaron's house, it was the nicest place she and her daughter had ever lived. The décor was rustic, and Di's deft, eclectic touch made it something distinctive. Most of the artwork, which featured ceramics, carvings, paintings, photographs, and weavings, had been created by island artists and artisans. And acquired through the island's barter system, with no money changing hands.

After hanging up his own jacket and flicking raindrops from his hair, Luke walked over to the coffee table, which was made of different kinds of wood put together in an attractive patchwork. "Hey, boys, look at this. It's one of Grandpa Forbes's pieces."

"Your stepdad made this?" she said to him. "It's lovely."

Luke had brought wine, which she appreciated, but he hadn't tried to kiss her when he came in, not even a peck on the cheek. That shouldn't irk her, but for some reason it did.

Ariana, who'd been playing in the bedroom, must have heard the voices because she came running out. She looked adorable in the long-sleeved tie-dyed tee Di and Seal had given her for Christmas. The front sported a peace sign and the back said, "Give peace a chance." Seal had said in a droll tone, "Get 'em when they're young."

The little girl came to a halt, casting a dubious look at Brandon and Caleb, who were exploring the living room. Then she ran over to Luke, raising her arms. "Luke! Up!"

Laughing, he obliged, hoisting her up so they were face-to-face. "Hey there, pretty girl. I like a woman who knows what she wants." He glanced over at Miranda.

If he was wondering whether she knew what she wanted, she'd have to say she wasn't one hundred percent sure. She'd thought it was only friendship, but there was something about seeing Luke today . . . He looked so tall and masculine in jeans and a black, soft-weave Henley that showcased his well-developed musculature. Maybe it was the black, making him look a bit more bad-boy than whole-some. But then again, she could hardly call him bad-boy when he was cuddling her child, who fit so comfortably and happily in his arms.

Whatever it was about him, she had to admit to a tug of attraction. Not mindless lust like she'd felt with Ariana's father or Chef Emile, but attraction. Partly physical but partly something else she couldn't identify.

There was no time to ponder all this, because the twins were messing with the screen in front of the natural gas fireplace. "Luke," she said, gesturing in their direction. "The glass window of the fireplace gets really hot. Ariana can't move that attached safety screen, but the boys might be able to."

"Kids," Luke said, "stop it. You could get hurt."

"We'll be careful," Brandon said, the words coming automatically, as if they'd been said many times before. He didn't stop playing with the screen. Caleb at least stopped tugging on it, to turn and look at his dad.

"If you break it," Luke said with a firmer, warning tone, "you have to pay for it. Out of your allowance."

Luke gave four-year-olds an allowance? Apparently so, because the threat proved effective. Both kids abandoned the fireplace and Brandon said, "Where's the pizza?"

"It's not ready yet," she told him and his brother, "because we're going to make our own. Like we did with those ice cream sundaes."

"Cool," Caleb said.

She started toward the kitchen, the boys racing past her, and Luke following her with Ariana in his arms.

Miranda had moved the chairs away from the four-top table to give easy access. On the table sat platters of toppings and a large pizza pan filled with oil-brushed dough. "Everyone like tomato sauce?" she asked.

"Yes!" Brandon yelled, and Caleb agreed.

Ariana added her decisive "Yes" as Luke pulled up the chair with the booster cushion and settled her at one end of the table where she could watch the proceedings.

Miranda spread the lightly chunky, aromatic sauce. "It's Di's, made with SkySong tomatoes. The best I've ever tasted."

When the pizza had a layer of sauce, she marked off a slice that was one-sixth of the total and put some mushrooms and cheese on it. "This slice is for Ariana. Boys, you get the rest of this pizza. Put what you want on it. There's salami, pepperoni, mozzarella, Parmesan, onions, mushrooms, green pepper, and olives."

"Cool," Caleb said again.

"Boys, wash your hands first," Luke said.

They obeyed, doing a sketchy wash at the sink, and then began to toss slices of salami onto the crust.

"That one's for us?" Luke asked, gesturing toward the other pizza pan, the one she'd borrowed from Di, which sat on the kitchen counter with another round of dough in it.

"Yes. Go ahead, add whatever toppings you want. I'm good with all of it." Eyeing his enthusiastic twins, she said,

"If you want any salami or pepperoni, you'd better grab it before your sons take it all."

He did exactly that, saying to her, "Can you spread tomato sauce on the crust?"

She obliged, and he distributed the sliced meat, then together they spread vegetables. Standing this close to him, their fingers occasionally brushing as they topped the pizza, she felt warmer than the heat of the oven justified. He really was very masculine, in his laid-back way. Rather than having the powerful immediate reaction she'd felt with Sebastian or Emile, Luke's impact snuck up on her in a disconcerting manner.

She was glad when Brandon loudly announced, "We're done. Let's cook it," and she and Luke stepped away from each other.

"I don't see any veggies on that pizza," he said, eyeing the sloppy pile of sausage and cheese. He evened out the toppings, cleared extras from Ariana's slice, and added a handful of sliced mushrooms and another of green pepper to the boys' five-sixths, ignoring their protest that he was ruining it.

"They used to eat vegetables," he told Miranda. "But then some kids at daycare said veggies were icky."

"Icky!" Brandon affirmed.

"What? Those kids sound pretty stupid," she said, speaking to Luke as she slid the children's pizza into the oven. "I thought Brandon and Caleb were smarter than that." She set the timer for ten minutes.

He shot her an amused grin. "One can only hope."

"We're smart," came Caleb's quiet little voice.

Miranda went over to where he stood by the table, and bent down to meet his gaze. "You see? I thought you were. Do me a favor and don't listen to what the stupid kids say."

Caleb frowned slightly and Miranda went on. "Your daddy's smart, right? He went to university for years and years, and he's an animal doctor. Everyone on the island who has an animal depends on him."

The boy was nodding vigorously, and Brandon said, "Daddy's smarter than anyone!" Then he qualified it with, "Except maybe Granny Annie."

"You got that right," Luke said dryly.

"There you go," Miranda said. "That's what I thought. So when other kids say something you're not sure about, you ask your daddy and he'll tell you if they're right. Because he knows ev-rything." She exaggerated her pronunciation and tossed a saucy grin in Luke's direction.

"A fact that all of you should remember," he joked back.

"Luke?" Ariana said, looking puzzled and not too happy.

Luke said, "Miranda, why don't you toss the rest of these toppings on our pizza?" He pulled up a chair and sat down beside her daughter. "Hey, I like that T-shirt. That's very cool."

"Cool!" she repeated. "Is peace."

"Peace is a very good thing," he said, no doubt realizing she was too young to understand the concept.

Finished preparing the pizza, Miranda took plates from the cupboard. "Caleb, Brandon, would you please put these on the table?" She didn't worry because the brightly colored dishes were virtually indestructible. "Then pull up chairs and sit down."

To Luke, she said, "Milk or apple juice for the boys? And I take it you're good with wine?"

"Milk for the twins, please. And yeah, a glass of red wine sounds good. But I'll only have one. Driving, you know."

"That means more left over for me," she said as she poured milk. She never had more than one drink. No way was she going to turn into her mom. But she looked forward to enjoying the rest of the bottle over the next two or three evenings.

The timer dinged and she removed the kids' pizza. After

sliding the adult one into the oven, she brought the cooked pizza to the table and gave it pride of place in the center. "Well done, guys. It looks terrific. Be careful, it's hot." She sliced the pie and put pieces on each of the boys' plates and then put on Ariana's bib. After blowing on the non-sausage slice to cool it, she gave it to her daughter along with some strips of raw green pepper.

With the children now all happily eating, she uncorked the bottle of Destiny Cellars Shiraz Luke had brought, and poured two glasses. Giving him one, she leaned back against the counter and said, "So, how've you been over the past week or so?" It wasn't exactly a "why didn't you call me?" but she hoped he'd offer an explanation.

He shrugged. "Oh, you know, busy. Lambing season's starting so I'm doing pre-lambing vaccinations and checking the ewes' health."

That was probably true, but the way he shifted position and gazed at the kids rather than looking at her made her think there was more than a busy workload behind his failure to call. But she wouldn't probe. It wasn't like he was her boyfriend. He was a casual friend and he'd chosen to be here tonight.

"How about you?" he asked. His tone relaxed and a mischievous sparkle lit his eyes when he said, "Any more returns from Mrs. Abercrombie?"

"No, thank heavens. That woman's a real challenge to the 'customer is always right' philosophy. She—"

Two things interrupted her: the ding of the timer and a knock at her door.

"Could you check the pizza?" she asked Luke as she headed for the door, squaring her shoulders. No one dropped by except Aaron and members of Eden's family. Normally, she enjoyed those visits, but why tonight?

She checked the peephole, groaned, and opened the door to her brother.

Aaron rested a hand on the doorframe, leaning through the opening, dripping on the floor. "Eden and I came to have dinner with her parents and Kelsey, and I saw Luke Chandler's vet SUV outside."

If only she could move the calendar forward two weeks. By then Eden's parents and sister would have moved out of the cabin three doors along. They'd be in the house they'd bought, only a few miles down the road from SkySong.

"What's going on?" her brother asked. "Did you and Ariana get a pet?"

"No, Aaron." She was trying to figure out what to say when Luke called, "It's done. Want me to slice it?"

She sighed, and called, "Sure, I'll be there in a sec." To Aaron, she said, "We're having pizza."

"Oh yeah?" Without being invited, he came through the door, nudging her aside.

"Do come in," she said sarcastically as he hung up his jacket and headed for the kitchen. She heard, "Hey, Luke," and "Hey, Aaron," and hurried after her annoying, overprotective brother.

Luke, who'd turned from the table, was standing facing Aaron, who'd stopped just inside the kitchen door. The two men were roughly the same size and build, both strong and fit, and dressed similarly. Luke's chestnut hair and winter-pale skin contrasted with the near-black hair and brownish skin that were legacies of Aaron's indigenous heritage on his father's side.

It was almost as if the two guys were squaring off, staring at each other and waiting to see who'd speak next.

It turned out to be Ariana, who cried, "Unc Aaron!" An excited smile beamed on her sauce-smeared little face.

He stared at Luke a moment longer before his posture relaxed and he turned to his niece, grinning. "Hey, Fairy-ana. I see you've been eating pizza."

"Pee-za!" she said.

Aaron dropped a kiss on top of her head, swiped a finger down her cheek, and then popped his finger in his mouth. "Mmm. Good pizza."

"Pee-za with Luke." She glanced across the table at Brandon and Caleb, who were ignoring everything but their dinner. Pouty-faced, she added, "And boys."

"So I see," Aaron said. He turned to Miranda, putting his back to Luke and the kids. "I didn't know you knew Luke."

"Well, I do." She crossed her arms over her chest.

"How long has this been going on?" he demanded. "And why didn't you tell me?"

She gazed pointedly in the direction of the three children, and beckoned him into the living room, aware that Luke was following. Ignoring him, she glared at her brother. "I don't know what you think *this* is, but if you're asking how long Luke and I have been friends, I guess it's a few weeks now. As for telling you, I didn't know I was required to report all my friendships to you."

Luke made a sound but she didn't look at him to see if he was sighing or stifling a laugh. Instead, she kept her challenging gaze fixed on her brother's face.

Aaron turned to Luke. "Friends? Miranda doesn't have friendships with men."

"Aaron!" she said angrily.

"It's true." He said it without glancing at her. To Luke, he went on. "My sister's trying to get an education while she's holding down a job and raising a two-year-old. She's got enough on her plate. Romance is the last thing she needs right now."

"Aaron!" She grabbed his arm. "This is none of your business."

Luke spoke, his voice calmer than either hers or Aaron's. "I know you care about your sister, but she's a grown woman. Seems to me, she's quite capable of deciding what she needs."

"Thank you for that." The way he kept his cool and defended her was pretty sexy.

"You don't know her," her brother said. "Not if you say that."

"Ooh!" She tightened her grip, wishing she had long nails to stab through Aaron's shirt and into his flesh. "Luke's my guest and my friend. Stop being rude to him and to me."

He turned to her, grasping her hand and prying it from his arm. "When I started dating Eden, you were damned rude to her. You kept telling her how awful Destiny Island was, trying to get her to dump me and stay in Ottawa."

Of course he'd bring that up. She screwed up her mouth. "Yeah, okay," she admitted. "But I was a pathetic bitch."

Luke snorted and a grin split Aaron's face. "Your words, little sister. And yeah, you were."

"Okay, fine. So take the high road and be better than that, *big brother*. And butt out of my life."

His grin faded. "You know I'll never do that. Just like you'll never butt out of mine."

It was true. The way they'd grown up, it had felt like the two of them against the world. She stepped forward and wrapped her arms around him, feeling his bigger, stronger arms close around her shoulders. "You know I didn't mean that," she said.

She gave him a squeeze and then stepped away. "But please, Aaron, dial it back. You've known Luke since we were teens. You know he's a good guy."

His brow knitted. After a moment, he said, "Yeah, he is." He glanced at Luke and then back to her. "A good guy. A stable, responsible guy. So maybe I do believe you, that you're just friends. Or maybe you really have grown up."

He walked over to the door and shrugged into his jacket. "I'll leave you to your pizza."

"Night, Aaron," Luke said calmly, as if the whole embarrassing incident hadn't happened.

When the door closed behind Aaron, she said, "Sorry about the interruption. Let's go eat that pizza before it's stone cold. And see if the kids have managed to destroy the kitchen yet."

Luke had to smile at the rueful expression on Miranda's face as she sat down across from him at the freshly wiped kitchen table, saying, "This isn't how I'd wanted things to go."

"Hey, we have hot pizza, red wine, and happily occupied kids." Not to mention, he was sitting across from a beautiful woman, feeling an attraction he'd never expected to feel again in his life. It was his birthday and, no offense to his mom or Forbes—he certainly wasn't happy that his poor mother had a cold—but this beat having the usual birthday dinner at their place. When Miranda had invited him, he'd thought twice about accepting, wondering if it was safer to stay away from her. He'd decided that wasn't fair to her, or to him, and now he was glad.

In the twenty minutes since Aaron had left, he and Miranda had cleaned up their respective children as well as the kitchen, got the kids settled in front of the TV watching *Ratatouille* on DVD, and reheated the pizza. He figured that was twenty well-spent minutes, because now he was alone with Miranda and they could relax and have an adult conversation.

He had a bite of pizza and said, "Di's tomato sauce really is amazing."

"I know, right? She said that if I'm on the island this summer, she'll teach me how to make it." The enthusiasm faded from her face. "Not that there's much point, I guess. She says the secret's in using fresh-picked organic tomatoes, and I won't be doing any tomato-picking when I move back to Vancouver."

"You still plan to move back?"

"That's the whole point of getting the early childhood education certificate. So I can get a decent job in Vancouver."

"You might be able to get a job at the daycare or preschool here. Hey," he added with a wink, "if you worked at Sunny Days you'd have the joy of looking after Brandon and Caleb."

She gave him a smile, but said, "I'm a Vancouver girl."

No, she wasn't. Why couldn't she see that she was turning into an island girl? He was tempted to launch into another sales pitch for Destiny, but figured she wouldn't welcome having another male try to tell her what to do. So, instead of speaking, he had a sip of wine.

Miranda put second slices of pizza on both their plates. "Earlier, when the boys were messing with the fireplace screen, you mentioned their allowance. Do you really give them an allowance?"

"Uh-huh. And they have piggy banks."

"What age did you start? I think Ariana's too young to understand."

He nodded. "I started when they turned four and I made it one of those 'now that you're a big boy' things. They still don't fully understand what money's all about, but I figure they'll grasp it more quickly when they're dealing with actual quarters and loonies. My mom and dad started early with me, and so did Candace's parents. We're all about learning responsibility in this family."

"Yeah, that's important. I mean, being able to manage your own life."

"Something Aaron doesn't seem to give you credit for."

She chuckled ruefully. "Yeah. He's very big brothery.

Don't get me wrong, I love him to pieces and it means everything to know he's there for me. But he can be a know-it-all, telling me how to run my life." She sighed. "The toughest thing for me is that, though I do believe strongly in responsibility and independence, there've been times I've had to turn to Aaron for help. Like when I came back to the island last summer."

"That's what family's about. I mean, yeah, try to be responsible, but know there's someone to lean on when you need to."

"But it's always gone one way. Me leaning on him."

She'd said things like that before, and they didn't fit his view of her, so he said so. "You've never come across as a leaner to me. Not now, and not back when you attended Blue Moon High."

"I worked hard on that tough-girl image," she said with a rueful smile. "I'd have hated it if anyone saw me as vulnerable." She rubbed her left forearm where, beneath her long-sleeved gray sweater, she had the dragon tattoo. As far as he'd seen, it was the only remaining outward symbol of her tough teen image. With a sigh, she went on. "But the truth was, I did depend on Aaron. That was rough on my pride."

Why couldn't she see that, within family, even among close friends, concepts like dependency and charity shouldn't exist? "You did things for him, too, I bet."

She gave a dismissive shrug. "Tiny, inconsequential stuff."

"Such as?"

A memory reflected on her face, but she blinked as if closing the door on it. Her eyes narrowed and then mischief brightened their blue tones and twitched her lips. "Well . . ."

He leaned forward, loving that sparkle, and curious. "Go on."

"There was the rat. Not a cute rat like Ratatouille, but a

nasty dead rat. Aaron took this girl out—this was back in Vancouver—but he didn't have money for a fancy date so he took her to Mickey D's and she told her friends that he was a cheapskate. The bitch. So I snuck the rat into her school backpack. On Friday afternoon. She wasn't exactly big on doing homework and it took her a couple days to find it."

"Oh, man." He snorted out a laugh.

She wrinkled her nose. "It was childish, but I was twelve. Aaron couldn't stop laughing. He thanked me for having his back." Miranda was so beautiful, her expression caught halfway between impishness and affection.

He wanted to reach over and hold her hand, but feared she wasn't ready for that. Besides, if he was going to get any more involved, he needed to know that his instincts about her were right. As his mom and Annie had said, he could only be with Miranda if he could trust her. "You'll always have his back, right?"

"For all the good it'll do him."

"Where on earth did you find a dead rat?"

Her jaw tightened. "We didn't exactly live in a fancy neighborhood."

Her eyes had turned steely gray, warning him against crossing the invisible line that, for whatever reason, was so important to her. So instead he made a point that she seemed to have missed entirely. "You keep suggesting that he does all the giving in your relationship. But you gave him a niece. Seems to me he adores Ariana."

The blue resurfaced in her eyes and her grim jaw softened. "Yeah, he does. Totally."

"He calls her Fairy-ana because she's so crazy about fairies?"

"Yes. It's his special nickname, though Eden's picked it up as well."

When the twins had been born and he'd realized he'd be raising them alone, he'd been glad they were both boys. He and Candace had known from the ultrasounds that they would be, which wasn't a surprise because on his dad's side it had been boys for generations. His wife had said that if after the first three children she'd yet to produce a girl, then they were going to adopt one. He'd agreed, because how could he deny her something like that? But now he was beginning to get it, the appeal of having a sweet-smelling child who built castles for fairies.

"There's something else I've done," Miranda said slowly. "For me, but kind of also for Aaron. I listened to his advice. I admitted that he was right about what I needed to do to be a better mom."

Luke smiled ruefully. "When you have kids, pride has to take a back seat. You can't do it alone. You have to admit you need help, for your kids' sake."

She sighed. "It took me way too long to realize that. I thought I was doing okay, looking after Ariana pretty well. But these past few months, since I accepted Aaron's help and came to Destiny, even though I miss a lot of things about Vancouver, I have to admit that her life—our lives—are better."

"Don't sound so dismal about that. See, it was your *destiny* to come here."

Her mouth twisted rather than smiled. "It pisses me off that I couldn't sort things out all by myself."

She wasn't abrasive, the way she'd been as a teen, but the woman did have prickles. Secrets, sensitivities, defensiveness, stubbornness, too much pride . . . and the list could go on. She was so unlike Candace, who'd been such easy company. Pursuing a relationship with Miranda would offer its share of challenges, that was for sure.

He wanted to. He was drawn to her in so many ways.

Physically, of course, with a craving that got stronger each time he was with her. Let's face it, he was a young, healthy guy who used to get a lot of great sex, and for four years he hadn't even been attracted to a woman. Now that he was, his body urged him to get on with it. Or, rather, to get it on.

The healer in him was drawn to her, too. He saw the fragility that lurked beneath her stubborn pride and he wanted to help her feel strong and confident—so she could accept assistance without feeling it was a sign of weakness.

He also wanted to share with her: to hear her tell his sons that he was smart; to help her calm Ariana's tantrums; to maybe even tell her more about the sorrows he'd suffered throughout his life. But he couldn't pursue a relationship with Miranda if it wasn't in his sons' best interests. What kind of woman was she, this rosebud, behind all the thorns?

Hoping she wouldn't shut him down, he ventured a question. "Neither your nor Aaron's father was ever in the picture?"

"No. Mom, well, she had some issues. She was in love with Aaron's dad, a First Nations guy, which is where Aaron gets that 'tall, dark, and handsome' thing. When she got pregnant, he didn't stick around. As for my father . . ." Miranda had a slice of pizza in her hand and took a tiny nibble.

Luke kept quiet, hoping she'd open up more than she had before.

She put the slice down and picked up her wineglass. Holding it by the stem, she said, "Mom drank too much." She put the glass down again. "And she did drugs. She became addicted. Got jobs, lost jobs. And so . . ." Her shoulders rose and she rotated them like she was trying to ease out tension.

"I'm way past thinking I owe her any loyalty" she said. "As a kid, I tried to be loyal. To keep her secrets so that teachers and social workers didn't find out. I was hanging on to some stupid hope that she'd get it together and provide Aaron and me with real love, with a real home." She rolled her shoulders again. "Sometimes she was nice to us, but mostly she was too fucked up, using drugs and trying to get the money for drugs. She was a crappy mother. We got taken away from her more than once."

"I'm sorry."

"On the day she OD'd in an alley in the Downtown Eastside, all my loyalty died with her."

And her hope, too, he knew.

Her chin came up and her eyes were gray and stormy. "She was a whore, Luke."

He couldn't suppress an involuntary shudder at the harsh word, and the harsh reality.

"A prostitute," she went on. "A sex trade worker. There's no pretty way of glossing over it. She had boyfriends, thought she was in love with guys, but she also sold her body to get money to support her habit. To lots of men. So she never knew who my father was."

"God, Miranda." His mom had been right about Corinne, and it was even worse than he'd imagined. Now no power on earth could have stopped him from reaching for her hand.

To his surprise, she let him take it. "Yeah," she said. "No kid should grow up that way. But I had Aaron. I don't know if I'd even have survived but for him. He's my half sib, but he's my true brother and he's been, well, everything to me."

Luke knew exactly what she meant. From when he first got to know her, Candace had been everything to him. "Aaron feels the same way," he said. "That's why he worries so much about you. Especially with him being the older sibling. He protected you then, and he can't stop."

Gently, she freed her hand and picked up her glass again.

This time, she did sip wine. Then she got up and walked on silent, slipper-clad feet to the living room.

He wondered if this was her way of ending the conversation, but she was back in a minute, saying, "Ariana's asleep. The boys are engrossed in the movie."

She sat down across from him again. "Aaron and I did some bad things. You say you want to be my friend, but you don't know me. It's only fair that you should know." Her mouth twisted. "And if you have any common sense, you'll say a polite good-bye."

He sure didn't feel like walking out of her life, but he had the boys to think about. So he said, "What bad things?"

Her glass went down and her chin came up. "Stole. We shoplifted, picked pockets. Mostly to get enough food to eat. But not always. You know when you said earlier that I'd probably done things for Aaron, too?" At his nod, her lashes flicked down, stayed there for a moment, and then came back up. "I stole a computer."

"What?" That was way more than pinching snack bars when the cupboards were bare.

"For Aaron. He was in sixth grade and starting to really need one, to keep up with schoolwork. Mom didn't have one, of course. She couldn't even keep the power bills paid. He used a computer at the library, but it was only available for short periods of time." She ducked her head and after a moment looked up again. "Or maybe that's just an excuse, and it was my pride, me wanting to do something for Aaron for once."

He nodded his understanding, encouraging her to go on.

"Anyhow, one of the johns that Mom brought to this tiny apartment we lived in at the time, he had a briefcase and I saw a laptop in it. Obviously, I couldn't steal it when he was at the apartment, or he'd know, but I followed him. He stopped to buy a newspaper from a box on the street, and put his briefcase down. Something in the paper caught his attention and he started to read. He was focused on that, and I slipped up and nicked his briefcase."

Wow. Luke couldn't imagine doing anything like that. But nor could he imagine living the way Miranda had as a child.

She swallowed. "He wasn't nice to Mom. And he didn't pay her hardly anything. So I told myself he deserved it. It wasn't fair that an asshole like him would have all this nice stuff and Aaron didn't even have a computer."

Nothing about her and her brother's childhood had been fair. "Did you tell Aaron where you got it?"

She shook her head vigorously. "He knew I'd stolen it and said we couldn't keep it, but I refused to tell him where I got it. I guess he figured it out from the files on it, but in the end he kept it." Her shoulders rose and fell as she sighed. "I do feel guilty about that computer. More than about the other, smaller stuff. That was more, like, necessity."

"Social assistance . . ." he murmured.

"Doesn't exactly work when the person who cashes the check takes the money straight to her dealer," she said bitterly.

"No, I guess not." Part of him wanted to reach for her hand again, yet part of him was appalled. He admitted, "I'm having trouble getting my head around all this. It's so different from the way I grew up."

"Lucky you," she muttered.

"Yes." He'd never considered his childhood to be particularly lucky. Not with his dad getting cancer and dying, and his mom suffering from depression. Not with acquiring a stepfather who monopolized Luke's mother's attention, and getting an unwanted stepbrother. But never had he wanted for food, shelter, school supplies, or even the small luxuries of life. "Yes, I was lucky."

He studied her, sitting back in her chair as if to maintain distance. The half-finished pizza sat on the table between them, growing cold again. "Miranda, the last times we were together, you let slip a few hints about your past. But when I asked questions, you shut down. Tonight you're opening up to me. Why now?"

She crossed her arms. "I didn't like how Aaron interfered."

"By basically saying that we shouldn't date, he made you want to do it?" Luke would be happy about that if he wasn't feeling so confused right now.

"Kind of. But also . . ." She dropped her head, staring down at her plate with a nibbled slice of pizza on it. "This is hard to say without sounding . . ."

"Just say it."

Her head lifted and she shot him a glance. "You're not my type, yet tonight I'm feeling kind of, well, attracted to you."

Yes! He managed to restrain himself from doing a fist pump. The thing he couldn't control was the swell of hot blood to his groin. But he had to be rational, and so he reflected for a moment.

Though her past shocked him, her honesty in sharing it impressed him. She and Aaron had done their best to cope with horrific circumstances, and Miranda was no longer that person. She knew she had issues and she was working on them. So, though she wasn't perfect, who was he to judge? The important thing was, he was coming to believe that she was trustworthy.

"Luke?"

He smiled and said, "I'm attracted to you, too. So, what are we going to do about it?"

Her return smile was an uncertain one. "I don't know. This is new for me. Spending time with a guy and our kids."

When they'd first met, she had said she wasn't dating. "You haven't dated anyone since you had Ariana?"

She snorted. "Oh, I did. Most memorably a chef named Emile. But a couple of other guys as well. Ariana wasn't part of any of that. There was a great older lady who lived down the hall. Mrs. Sharma. She's a grandmother, and she looked after Ariana when I went out." A smile flickered. "Every kid should have a grandma like Mrs. Sharma."

"You dated guys and didn't want them to meet your daughter?" That seemed inconceivable to him.

"Yeah. And they didn't show any particular interest. Which should've told me something, right?"

"Seems to me it should have told you everything you needed to know. Sorry if that sounds judgmental, but . . . You're a mother, Miranda."

"Gee, I keep forgetting that," she said sarcastically. Then she sighed. "No, sorry, you're right. But with Emile, I thought I loved him and so I figured things would work out somehow. And no, don't say it, I've already heard it enough times from Aaron. I was stupid. But with the other guys, it was purely casual. I just wanted, once in a while, to do something young and fun. Like go out dancing." Or have sex, he guessed, but was glad she didn't say it. "Is that so bad?"

"No, it's not. Sometimes I leave the boys with my in-laws or a sitter when Forbes's band is playing at Quail Ridge Community Hall." On the rare occasions that Julian was in town and playing with the band, Luke always tried to go. But he wasn't about to bring up the guy Miranda got all fan-girl over. Not tonight, when she'd admitted to being attracted to Luke. "It's fun to have a beer with friends, dance to some tunes."

"Who do you dance with?" Her question came so quickly that he wondered if jealousy was stirring.

"Whoever's there," he responded. Seeking a reaction, he said, "One of my favorite partners is Jane Nelson."

"Oh?" She toyed with her half-eaten slice of pizza. "I don't think I know her."

"No? I bet she's been in Blowing Bubbles, since she and her hubby have grandkids and a couple of great-grands."

"Mrs. Nelson? The eighty-something-year-old?"

"That's the one. Though it's hard prying her away from her husband. He may be in a wheelchair but that doesn't keep him off the dance floor."

"That's pretty cool."

He nodded. "They've been married more than sixty years." Candace and he used to bet that their marriage would outlast the Nelsons'. Good thing they hadn't put money on it.

"You've got that look."

"Hmm?"

"That sad, reflective one. You're thinking about your wife. About how things were supposed to go."

He shrugged.

"If you ever want to talk more about it . . ." Her eyes were soft now, the gentle grayish-blue of autumn wood-smoke.

"I may take you up on that one day."

She nodded, not pushing. "Want me to nuke the pizza again? Or should we make popcorn and share it with the boys?"

"Popcorn sounds like a good idea." But there was a concern he had yet to deal with, he realized. Was she, like her mother, too fond of alcohol and drugs? He thought he knew the answer, but he had to be sure. Rising from the table, he picked up the bottle of wine on the counter. "Want another glass?"

"No, thanks. Since Ariana was born, I have a one-drink limit." She rose too and began to clear the table. "Not that I ever drank a lot, because I don't want to turn out like Mom."

"So, no drugs either?" he asked, hoping she wouldn't be offended.

"God, no," she said vehemently. "That's just plain crazy."

"Agreed," he said, convinced she meant it. Relieved that his fears had been alleviated, he said, "Where do you keep the popcorn?"

"In that cupboard." She pointed. "Give me a few minutes to get the leftovers packaged and do the dishes." Deftly she moved around the kitchen. There was no dishwasher and, since she showed no inclination to leave the dishes soaking in the sink, he wielded a dish towel.

It wasn't until the room was spick-and-span that she put the popcorn in the microwave.

He wondered what the kitchen had looked like in that tiny apartment where her mother had turned tricks and shot up.

When they took two bowls of popcorn and a roll of paper towels into the living room, Ariana was curled up in a ball at one end of the couch, sound asleep, with a blanket tucked around her. The boys were still awake, sprawled on the floor in front of the TV.

"Popcorn!" Brandon cried happily, barely glancing away from *Ratatouille* to dip into the bowl Luke put in front of him.

Caleb looked at his father. "Is it a good birthday, Daddy?"

"It is, Caleb." He tousled his son's longish locks. "A very good one."

Miranda had seated herself on the couch beside her sleeping daughter. When he went to sit on Miranda's other side, she glared at him. "It's your birthday?"

"Yeah. Twenty-ninth. Only a year until the big three-oh."

"You accepted my dinner invitation and didn't tell me it was your birthday?" She sounded outraged, but he wasn't sure why.

"The boys and I were supposed to go to Mom and Forbes's, like every year. But he called yesterday to say she had a nasty cold and wasn't up to it. So I was feeling sorry for myself, having to cook dinner on my birthday, and you phoned and saved me. Which was a great present, by the way."

"I would've at least made cake," she grumbled.

"Cake!" Brandon almost yelled. Luke hadn't realized the boys were listening.

"Sorry, Brandon," Miranda said. "There's no cake tonight. It's your daddy's fault."

The conversation, or maybe just the word *cake*, woke Ariana. She stirred and knuckled her eyes. "Mommy?"

"Hi, sweetie. Want some popcorn?" Miranda balanced the bowl on her lap. She fed a few puffy kernels to her daughter, who soon drifted back to sleep.

The next time she dipped into the bowl, Luke did, too, letting his hand brush hers as if by accident. Neither of them spoke.

The time for personal conversation had passed, and there'd be no opportunity for anything any more physically intimate than hand-brushing, but Luke didn't mind. It had been a terrific birthday. He'd learned that Miranda didn't have her mother's addict tendencies and, though she'd made some mistakes in her life, who hadn't? She was trying hard, she was responsible, and she was a great mom. Those were the things that mattered.

Not to mention, she was attracted to him. Luke grinned, and it wasn't at the rat's antics on the screen.

Chapter Eight

The morning after the pizza and popcorn night, Miranda drove into Blue Moon Harbor, the windshield wipers flicking like a metronome against a steady drizzle. She was working today, but going to the village half an hour early. Dreamspinner bookstore opened before Blowing Bubbles, and Iris Yakimura had emailed last night to tell her about a sale on kids' books.

The radio was on but she paid scant attention to the morning chatter and songs. Her brain kept mulling over Luke's dinner invitation—the one she'd told him she needed to think about—and replaying memories from last night.

She couldn't believe he'd come for the evening and never told her it was his birthday. She'd felt blindsided when Caleb mentioned it.

She also couldn't believe the way she'd opened up to Luke. Her mom and her past were painful subjects, ones she tried to not think about. Ones she'd never shared with anyone except Aaron, who'd lived through all of it, too.

She couldn't believe that she'd told Luke she was attracted to him. Actually, she had trouble believing she *was* attracted. His stepbrother, yeah. She'd always had the hots for Julian Blake. He was her type. Luke wasn't. Except she was changing. Now that she had Ariana, her life had a different focus. She had new priorities, centered around the precious girl behind her who was, at the moment, contentedly babbling in what might have been a conversation with her fairy friends or might have been a commentary on the radio program or the passing scenery.

They were driving past a small farm now, where a couple dozen sheep dotted a green field, their woolly coats making them oblivious to the rain. Near the fence by the road, pale pink blossoms unfurled on an early flowering tree. They didn't seem discouraged by the rain either. Across the road, on a wooded stretch of property, a deer emerged from the trees. "Deer," Miranda told her daughter, slowing the car. She was ready to brake if it leaped out on the road, but it simply stood watching as she drove by.

Miranda returned to her musings. Used to be, when she fell for a guy, she kind of gave herself over to him. Oh, not her financial independence or stuff like that; her pride and feminism wouldn't allow it. But the men who attracted her were so passionate about their pursuits—music, acting, cooking, whatever—that she loved riding the wave of that passion. Being drawn into their new, exciting worlds.

Now it was sinking in that, if she was ever going to be serious about a man again, he would have to fit into her and Ariana's world. He'd have to love her daughter, be good to her, make time for her.

Luke would do that.

Was that at the root of her attraction to him? The notion that he might be a good father to her little girl? Was she daddy-shopping?

If so, she needed to be sensible about her choice. For once in her life, as Aaron would say. Luke seemed perfect in many ways, but he had baggage. She'd seen shadows cross his face when he thought of Candace. He'd been with one woman, only one woman. His soul mate. How could another woman ever compete with that, much less a flawed one like Miranda? Besides, he had two boys. Looking after one two-year-old girl was a daily challenge. Miranda might be studying to be an early childhood educator, but how could she possibly think she'd be able to be mom to boisterous Brandon and reflective Caleb?

Arriving in town, she parked in the free lot and extracted Ariana from her car seat, pulling up and securing the hood of her daughter's pink coat. The rain was really coming down now, and it was windy here by the harbor. She struggled against a gust as she raised the big umbrella to shelter the two of them and, hand in hand, they made their way down Driftwood Road, the main street.

As she passed the office of the *Destiny Gazette*, the door opened and Mr. Newall, the editor, stepped out, opening his own umbrella.

"Good morning," she greeted him, looking forward to his response.

His thin face serious, he said, "Temperature nine degrees Celsius, two millimeters of rain since midnight, probability of precipitation this morning ninety-five percent. Wind southeast at thirty kilometers per hour, gusting to fifty. Umbrellas are endangered."

"Thank you," she said as he strode away, his umbrella raised like a shield in front of a soldier. With anyone else, she'd have told him to have a nice day, but social comments like that didn't compute in his literal mind.

Grinning at the notion of umbrellas as an endangered species, she tugged Ariana's hand and they continued on to Dreamspinner. When Miranda had first heard one of Mr. Newall's weather forecasts, she'd asked Kara if he was a meteorologist. Kara'd said, "No, he's the editor of the island paper, and has Asperger's syndrome. He handles the business side and the detail stuff, and his wife and brother handle the people end."

Destiny Island, Miranda was coming to learn, harbored lots of interesting characters. Iris's aunt, a fabric artist as well as a bookseller, described the island's population as a "crazy quilt": the colors, patterns, and textures shouldn't have gone together, and yet blended amazingly to create a thing of beauty.

Miranda had also noticed that, though Destiny's temperate climate did, as with Vancouver, attract a number of transients, homeless people, and addicts, there were more community resources to help them. Here, it was rare to see a homeless person sleeping in a doorway or shooting up in an alley. Of course, Blue Moon Harbor didn't have many alleys.

Avoiding the coffee shop side of Dreamspinner, where the smells were too enticing for her perennially cash-strapped wallet, she stowed her wet umbrella in a rack by the door of the bookstore side. At this early hour, the coffee shop hummed with business but here in the bookstore, Miranda saw only one customer, deep in conversation with Iris.

As always, Iris was slim and trim, today clad in a tailored, long-sleeved mauve shirt over black pants, with a silk scarf in shades of purple looped around her neck. The scarf, Miranda knew, would be her aunt's creation, and a work of art. The customer wore an attractive burgundy hijab and a trench coat, and when Miranda saw her face she realized it was Luke's neighbor, Dr. Shakoor. She wondered if the book in the woman's hand was on pregnancy.

"Books, Mommy!" Ariana tugged impatiently at her hand.

Iris glanced over and smiled.

Miranda smiled back, and then guided Ariana toward the

children's book section. As they arrived at the back corner of the store where a low table and a few kiddie-sized chairs were surrounded by low bookshelves, Iris caught up with them. "I wondered if you two would be in this morning," she said.

Two or three years younger than Miranda, she was attractive in a classic, unobtrusive way. She wore no makeup, not even colored lip gloss, yet her beauty shone through in her perfect skin, gorgeous dark brown eyes, and wings of glossy black hair parted in the middle.

Bending down, Iris said, "Miss Ariana. I'm so glad to see you."

Ariana was no more in the mood for social conventions than Mr. Newall. "Want books!" she demanded.

"A girl with solid priorities," Iris commented as she rose in a graceful, flowing motion that made Miranda wonder if she did yoga or tai chi. "Here are the books that are on sale." The bookseller put a few brightly colored board books on the table and got Ariana settled on a chair to browse. "You will be careful with these books," she said quietly, making it a statement of expectation rather than an order.

"I promise," Ariana said.

Miranda smiled at Iris. "You have a way with her." She knew from Eden, who was friends with Iris, that the young woman was single. "Are you planning to have kids?"

"I do hope so," Iris said softly.

Keeping an eye on her daughter, who was turning the sturdy pages with appropriate respect, she said, "Then I wish you luck. You seem like a sensible woman. You'll probably do it the right way, with a loving guy to help raise them."

She gave a wistful smile. "Ah, yes, that's the dream."

The dream. There it was again. How many people had

that same dream—and for how many did it come true? "Anytime I've chased that dream," Miranda said wryly, "and thought I'd found Mr. Right, he turned out to be a toad."

"I think you mean Prince Charming, not Mr. Right. And it was a frog, not a toad."

"What? Oh, right. I remember." Aaron had read her that story when she was a kid. There was another book to add to the wish list, for when Ariana was a bit older.

The other woman's expression went serious. "I envy you, Miranda."

The comment surprised her, because until now Iris, while being efficient and kind, had also been reserved. Venturing a personal comment wasn't typical of her. Eden said she was shy.

"Seriously?" Miranda said. "What do you envy? My infallible knack for finding frogs?"

"I envy you having the courage to chase the dream, to go after what you want. I could never be so brave."

"Brave?" Aaron thought she was stupid, the way she flung her heart in the ring. "That's nice of you to say, Iris." She studied the woman, so classically lovely with her oval face and long, shiny hair. "I'd guess you haven't found the right guy yet. When you do, when you truly fall in love, then I bet you'll find that you're braver than you think."

"I'd like to believe that. The romance novels I read give me hope that all things are possible." And then, as if she'd shared more than she intended, she turned away, hair swinging to hide her face, and knelt by Ariana. "Which book do you like best, little one?"

"This one. This one. This one." Ariana pointed in turn to three of the half dozen books.

"You can only have one," Miranda said, hoping the announcement wouldn't trigger a TTT. "But maybe next time I get paid, we can buy another. Which one is your very favorite?"

Ariana's bottom lip pooched out as she deliberated, and then she selected one with a birthday cake on the cover. "Cake!"

"Cake it is." Relieved that her daughter hadn't kicked up a fuss, Miranda helped her off the chair and picked up the book as Iris put the others back on the shelf.

She owed Luke a birthday cake, Miranda thought as they all walked over to the sales desk. If they kept seeing each other.

He had upped the ante when he'd asked her out for dinner. He'd suggested they find sitters for their kids and go to C-Shell, a seafood restaurant on the harbor. It was moderately expensive and reputed to be excellent, and she'd never eaten there.

If she went out with him, it would be a date. She would be dating Luke Chandler.

She retrieved her umbrella at the door and unfurled it as she and her daughter went outside. Iris Yakimura thought she was brave. Iris thought she went after what she wanted.

The question was, did she want Luke? And, if so, was he a Prince Charming or a frog?

No, not a frog, she was sure of that. And if he did prove to be a Prince Charming, was there any possible way that she was good enough for him?

It was a relief to go into Blowing Bubbles, settle Ariana in the play enclosure with a few toys, and get into the familiar routine. Kara wasn't working today, and Miranda still got a thrill out of being trusted to run this wonderful store.

A quarter hour after opening, the doorbell jingled, announcing the first customer of the day. Miranda went to greet a petite, attractive woman about her own age, who

was putting a dripping umbrella into the basket by the door.
She was clad in a puffy purple jacket and jeans, and her
black hair was cut in a pixie style that suited her delicate
Chinese features. Beside her stood a cute little girl, a bit
smaller than Ariana. She looked like a miniature version of
her mom, with the same haircut and a similar jacket.

The pair had been in once before when she'd been working, and she thought she remembered their names. "Glory
McKenna?" she ventured. "And Gala?"

"Right you are," the woman said with a smile, pulling
off her gloves. She wasn't wearing a wedding ring and
Miranda wondered if she was a single mom, too.

"It's my day off," Glory said, "it's foul weather, and we
need a new toy or game to play with. Okay if I put Gala in
the playpen while I browse?"

"Of course." Miranda squatted down and said to the
little girl, "Hi, Gala. I'm Miranda."

The child turned away and buried her face against her
mom's pant leg. But a moment later, she peeped at Miranda.

"You look like you're close to my daughter's age," Miranda said.

"She's two and a half," Glory said.

"Just a little younger than Ariana," Miranda said to the
child. "The two of you can have some fun together."
Straightening, she said to Glory, "Fingers crossed. I warn
you, Ariana's prone to tantrums."

"So's Gala," the other woman said cheerfully. "Let's
hope they don't set each other off." She led her daughter
over to the play enclosure and unlatched the gate. "Hi,
Ariana," she said to Miranda's child, who was watching
closely.

Miranda joined them and said, "Sweetie, this is Gala
and she's going to hang out with you for a while."

Glory nudged her daughter so that she took a couple of

steps into the pen. There were a few stuffed animals lying around and Gala glanced at them and then at Ariana, frowning.

Ariana stared at her a moment, and then held up her cloth doll. "I has fairy!"

It was more of a boast than an offer to share. Fortunately, Gala didn't reach for the doll. Instead, she picked up a stuffed puppy. "I has doggy!"

A minute later, the two of them were settled on the mat floor, playing separately with the fairy and the dog, chattering happily though maybe not to each other.

"That went well," Miranda said. "Now, Glory, let's see what we can find to give you two a fun day inside."

As they considered options, she asked her customer, "Where do you work?" By now, she'd been into most of Blue Moon Harbor's businesses and hadn't seen the brunette with her pixie haircut at any of them.

"Arbutus Lodge, the seniors' residential facility."

"Really? My brother's fiancée, Eden Blaine, works there."

"Eden? So you're Aaron's sister?" She cocked her head. "Were we in school together? Aaron and I were in the same class, but I don't remember you."

"I was two grades back. I don't remember you either."

"I had really long hair then, and Coke-bottle glasses. Hurray for laser eye surgery."

Miranda shrugged, still not remembering. She didn't want to admit to being Goth girl, but in this tiny community someone was bound to mention it to Glory, so she bit the bullet. "I was the one with dyed black hair, Goth clothing, and lots of piercings."

Glory tilted her head. "Seriously? That's so not you."

"Thank you for that. I guess it was back then, though."

"Teens go through phases, right?"

Happy that the other woman had dismissed Miranda's

questionable past so easily, she agreed, "That's for sure. So, anyhow, you know Eden?"

"Of course. She's new, but she seems terrific."

"She is. And she loves her job. How about you? Do you enjoy working with seniors?"

"I do. I'm very close to my grandparents."

"Must be nice," Miranda said dryly.

Glory either ignored or saw beneath her flippancy, giving a gentle smile and continuing. "My parents adopted me from a Chinese orphanage after I was abandoned as a newborn. They and both sets of their parents made me feel so wanted and loved." Another smile. "I had been given a Chinese name and Glory is one of the translations for it. My adoptive family chose it because they said they gloried in being lucky enough to find me."

"Wow." It was awful that Glory's birth parents had abandoned her, but how nice to have parents and grandparents who loved you and enjoyed being with you.

"I try to forget I wasn't born in Canada, and usually succeed. Listening to my grandparents' stories makes me feel like my roots are here." She shrugged. "Anyhow, my relationship with my grandparents gave me the idea of working with seniors. I'm not a nurse or anything, but I handle the reception desk and I spend a lot of time talking to the residents. They're such amazing people, with so much experience and such interesting opinions."

Though Miranda hadn't had the same kind of grandparents as Glory, the other woman's comment did resonate. "That reminds me of our neighbor in Vancouver. She babysat Ariana, and we'd often share a cup of chai and talk. She'd come from India as a teenager, in an arranged marriage to a man she'd never met. Can you imagine all the things she went through? But they ended up loving each other and raising four kids, though sadly he died a few years ago. She's very close to her kids and grandkids, though." Miranda kept in touch with Mrs. Sharma, the two of them exchanging news and photos of the children in their lives.

"Grandchildren who love her stories, I hope." Glory glanced over at the play enclosure. "The kids still seem happy but I'd better not push my luck. I think I'll go with *Monster Bowling*. Glory and I can both work out our frustrations."

"Great." Miranda wondered if that was just a figure of speech, or if this petite woman had frustrations of her own. As she rang up the purchase, Miranda remembered something. "By the way, Dreamspinner has a sale on kids' books. You might want to check them out."

"Thanks for the tip, Miranda. I'll do that. While Gala's still in a non-tantrum mood."

The two moms walked over to the play enclosure, where now the fairy doll was riding the stuffed puppy, with noisy encouragement from both children. "The girls get along well," Miranda commented.

"Gala goes to daycare on the days that her dad and I are both working, but I've never seen her hit it off so well with another child."

So the lack of a ring didn't mean there wasn't a man in the picture. Lucky Glory, to be parenting with a partner.

"Hey," Glory said, "why don't the two of you come over for a playdate? Just us girls."

"Oh, that's really nice of you, but I'm . . ." Wait. Yes, she was busy with her studies, but it would be good for Ariana to have a playmate. And nice for Miranda, too, to have some girlfriend-type company. Even though Eden and her younger sister, Kelsey, were great, they weren't exactly girlfriends.

"I make amazing biscotti," Glory said. "We can indulge

and get to know each other while the little ones do their thing."

"That sounds tempting," Miranda admitted. "Yes, let's do it."

"Perfect. The next time we both have a day off."

After Glory and Gala left the store, Miranda went over to pick up her daughter. "You know what this means, sweetie? It seems we're actually kind of starting to build a life here. I was so sure we'd go back to Vancouver, but now . . ." She held her daughter up in front of her so she could peer into her cute little face. Putting on a serious tone, she asked, "What's your considered opinion on the merits of Blue Moon Harbor versus Vancouver?"

Her daughter considered her with apparent seriousness and then broke into a smile. "Luke!"

Miranda laughed softly. "Yes, that's an excellent point. Okay, I'm going to call and say I'll go out for dinner with him. It'll give me a chance to wear one of my Vancouver outfits that's been sitting in the closet gathering dust."

Chapter Nine

Luke's "Hi" died in his throat when Miranda opened the door of her log cabin at SkySong. After swallowing hard, he managed to croak, "You look amazing."

Her wavy blond hair was up in a fancy hairdo with a few loose, curly tendrils. It drew attention to her face, and she was wearing more makeup than usual. Not the exaggerated stuff she'd worn as a teen, but the kind Candace had favored, that made her eyes look even larger and brighter, and called attention to her high cheekbones and full lips. Silver and abalone earrings dangled from delicate earlobes.

As if that weren't enough, she wore a scoop-necked, long-sleeved top that hugged her slim curves. The fabric was silky and the blue-green colors rippled and shifted like the ocean. With it she wore a black skirt that ended well above her knees, revealing amazing legs in sheer black hose and pretty feet in strappy, high-heeled shoes.

"You're so beautiful," he breathed. "I didn't realize . . . I mean, I knew you were attractive, but wow."

She was grinning, seeming to take pleasure in his stunned reaction. "You clean up okay yourself, Dr. Chandler."

You rarely saw a suit on Destiny, not even at weddings or funerals, and he saw no reason to own one. Tonight he'd gone with tailored black wool pants, a green cotton shirt—sage green, his mom had said when he'd opened it at Christmas—and the green-and-gold striped tie she'd paired it with. "You can thank my mom. She's the only one in the family"—at least now that Candace was gone—"who gives a damn about clothes."

"Not Candace's mother? Candace was always so well dressed."

"In reaction to her mom, who lives in denim and flannel."

"I guess if you're that rich, you can do whatever you like."

"Ready to go? Is Ariana in good hands?"

"I hope so. Eden's sister is looking after her." Miranda took a black leather coat from a hook by the door. "She's been going 'please, please, please let me babysit' for months, but I've almost never gone out."

He took the coat and held it so she could slide her arms into it.

That lily of the valley scent drifted toward him and he leaned closer, inhaling and enjoying.

Miranda hooked the strap of her purse over her shoulder and called, "Bye, bye."

"Bye! Have fun!" came a light feminine voice.

"I'm fighting the urge to issue the reminders again," Miranda admitted as she closed the door behind them.

"To call you if she has any concerns?" He tucked her hand through his arm because SkySong, a rural retreat by the ocean, had limited lighting and the sun, such as it had been on this early March day, had already set. Or maybe just because he wanted to be closer to her.

"And to remember that Di and Seal are close by." She sighed. "I'd have had Aaron and Eden babysit, but they're off at Jillian's wedding. You know her, right?"

"Sure. She's another island native." Jillian was a pilot and flew for Aaron part-time.

She nodded. "It's a small ceremony, just their families and Aaron and Eden. Jillian says she's eternally grateful to Aaron because he introduced her to flying."

"It's her passion?" he asked as he opened the passenger door of his SUV and helped her up. The vehicle wasn't built for a woman in high heels, though it was perfect for his needs: comfortable seating for him and the boys, plus a large back area for the family pets, his vet equipment, and any smallish animals he needed to transport. He could also tow a horse trailer.

She waited while he went around and climbed in the driver's side. "Seems so. Just like with Aaron, who in turn was inspired by Lionel."

"And I wouldn't be a vet if it weren't for Viola." He turned on the engine and adjusted the heater. "It's great to have that kind of inspiration and mentorship." He guessed that Miranda'd never had a person like that, so he didn't ask. Instead, as he carefully drove the unlit road through the SkySong property, he said, "Is working with little kids your passion?"

"I think it might be. I love kids and I'm enjoying the coursework, though some of it's tough." Wryly, she added, "I don't exactly have the best track record when it comes to school. But it helps when I'm interested in what I'm studying."

"That's for sure. But you can work at some daycares without being licensed, so why put yourself through the course?"

"Because children are important," she said solemnly. "They're the most important thing, I think. And they deserve to be properly looked after."

"I sure won't argue with that." Yeah, she'd be good at her job, and her studies would help her be an even more knowledgeable mom. "I hope it does turn out to be your passion.

It's so much easier to get up on a cold, dark morning when that alarm rings, knowing you're going to a job you love."

"It would be. Waitressing and retail were okay, depending on where I worked, but they sure never made me feel that way."

It was nice having her beside him in the big cab as he drove through the night toward the village of Blue Moon Harbor, the radio on low, providing background music. He could get used to this.

After a minute or two, she said, "You said your in-laws liked it that you were following your passion. They are as well, right?"

"Yeah. Her with her video games and him with photography."

"How about your parents?" Miranda asked. "And your stepdad? You said he made the coffee table in my cabin?"

"Yes. Forbes is a woodworker and has a real sense of the wood. He does enjoy it but his other passion is music. He's always played."

"He taught Julian? And inspired him?"

"Guess so. Julian was already really good by the time Forbes and Mom married. As for my own dad, he was a chiropractor and yes, he loved it." How ironic that his father, who'd happily devoted his life to healing, had been defeated by cancer. "Mom's always been a teacher—except for a couple of years when she was on leave, when Dad was really sick and then he died and she was so depressed. But yeah, she does enjoy it, so much she may never quit."

"What and where does she teach?"

"You'd have had her in school, for sciences. Sonia Russo."

"Oh gosh, Ms. Russo! I'd never have guessed. Your name's Chandler, and you don't look much like her."

"No, I don't. She looks like her Italian parents and I take after my Anglo dad."

"She didn't change her name when she married. Nor did your mother-in-law."

"Nope."

"I totally agree with them. So does Eden. The notion of a woman taking her spouse's name is archaic and paternalistic," she stated firmly. "Unless you do what Di and Seal did when they had their commitment ceremony, and share a new last name."

"I'm with you. So was Candace." He gave a little smile. "Good thing. Annie'd have had a heart attack if her daughter, Candace Yuen-Byrne, became Mrs. Luke Chandler."

Miranda snorted, and then said, "To get back to your mom, have you told her you're seeing me? She'd think you're crazy."

"I told her. And Miranda, you were a kid. A kid who'd had some crappy stuff happen to you. Mom knows that people can change. Look at Julian. He was as messed up as you in high school. And he's made a success of himself."

"I am so *not* Julian Blake. I'm just a salesclerk single mom who wants to work in a daycare or preschool."

He hated the way she put herself down. "Where you'd care for children, which we agree is one of the most important jobs in the world."

"Oh." Her surprised tone suggested she'd never thought of it that way.

They were driving down Driftwood Road, passing the first village shops. He found a parking spot at the curb and went around to help Miranda out. Remembering the thinness of that leather coat when he'd held it for her, he said, "You going to be warm enough in that?"

"I'm not wearing fleece out for dinner."

"That's not an answer."

"I'll be fine. It's the only nice coat I own. Can you believe it was only forty dollars at a thrift shop, and it had barely been worn?"

"Well, it looks great. You look great."

He reached for her hand as they walked down the sidewalk, and her slim fingers slipped easily between his larger ones. "Downtown" was quiet on this Saturday night, with only Dreamspinner and the half dozen restaurants and pubs open.

"Have you been to C-Shell before?" he asked.

"No, but I've drooled over the menu. You've eaten there, I'm sure."

"Candace and I used to come every month or so." Then, so she wouldn't think he'd be depressed, remembering dinners with his wife, he added, "Since then, it's been my go-to place for parental birthdays and anniversaries."

She nodded. "What's up with the name, by the way?"

"It's owned by Celia and Rachelle. Rachelle is a native Destiny Islander. Her dad is descended from very early settlers of the island, freed slaves from the States who came north to Victoria and then scattered around the area. Anyhow, she runs the front of the house and her wife Celia, who grew up in Vancouver, is the chef."

"Cool combo on their names. Obviously, it was meant to be, them getting together and opening a seafood restaurant."

"Like it was their destiny, right?" He winked.

She groaned. "I really wish this island had a different name."

He chuckled. "Before C-Shell, this was a fish and chips place, but not a very good one. Rachelle and Celia renovated it outside and in." They'd reached the front door now.

"I like the cedar shakes."

"They probably wouldn't look so good in Vancouver," he teased as he ushered her inside.

Rachelle, all brown and black as usual, with her chocolate skin and black, long-sleeved shirt and pants, glanced up with a smile. "Luke! It's so good to see you." She came toward them, her only touch of color in the bright beads that decorated her ears and were woven into her intricate black braids.

"You too, Rachelle. This is Miranda Gabriel. You may remember—"

Miranda jumped in. "You were in Aaron's class, weren't you, Rachelle? Your name didn't ring a bell but I do remember admiring that stunning hair."

"And you're his little sister, all grown up and beautiful. Have to say, I wouldn't have recognized you."

Miranda laughed as she let Luke take her coat. "And that's a good thing." She glanced around. "What a great job you've done here. I can't believe you and your wife own a restaurant. And Luke's a vet, and Aaron has Blue Moon Air. It makes me feel like we're all so old."

Rachelle gave a rich laugh. "Older and wiser, if we're lucky. Come on, I'll show you to your table." She turned, straight and sleek and gorgeous. She could have been a model. And yet Miranda's less dramatic looks appealed to him more.

Crossing the room, he exchanged nods with several islanders, and noted that Miranda smiled at a couple herself, probably customers of Blowing Bubbles. By later tonight, the gossip mill would be churning and an expanding circle of islanders would know he and Miranda were dating.

When Rachelle had seated them at a window table looking out on the harbor, she said, "Luke, I can't thank you enough for making that emergency call when Fairley got attacked by that dog. Mom was crazy worried and if she'd had to drive she could've crashed the car."

"No problem. It comes with the job."

To Miranda, Rachelle said, "Fairley's my mom's ferret. And best friend, I think. My dad was out fishing—he supplies the restaurant, by the way—when a crazy dog lit into Fairley."

"I'm glad Fairley's okay," she said. "And I'm looking

forward to the seafood. This is a real treat for me. I've been wanting to eat here." She gently touched the sprigs of purple heather in a small pottery vase and then gestured around. "I love the décor. The nautical touches are just right, adding authenticity without making it kitschy."

Luke agreed, and knew that the fishing nets and old floats, the rusted anchor, and other items were genuine, provided by Rachelle's dad.

Miranda went on. "I've worked in a lot of restaurants over the years, and it takes real talent to hit the right note."

"Thanks, Miranda. I appreciate that." She winked. "And I'll tell the staff to be on their toes, since they're looking after one of our own. Speaking of which, your server will be along in a sec to see what you'd like to drink, so I'll let you peruse the cocktail menu and wine list. First drink's on me, as a thanks to Luke, so make it a special one."

After she'd gone, he and Miranda both put their phones on the table and exchanged smiles. He only hoped that neither phone vibrated for the next couple of hours.

Miranda picked up her menu and made a humming sound. "Oh, this is nice. Being in a fine restaurant as a customer rather than as waitstaff or busgirl." She gazed out the window at the harbor view. "It's so dark at night at SkySong and at Aaron's place, but here you can see the lights on the boats down on the docks. Like stars that shine even when it's cloudy out."

When she pulled her gaze from the view and turned it on him, he saw sparkly stars in her blue eyes, though maybe it was a reflection from the candle on the table.

"Thank you for this, Luke. It makes me feel special."

"You are special, Miranda." And so beautiful, with that fancier hairdo and the touch of makeup. Her bare neck and upper chest looked creamy and feminine against the greenish-blue top. The abalone earrings danced and caught the light, calling attention to her delicate ears and long neck. He'd noticed that whatever pair of earrings she wore, the silver heart remained in her left ear.

She glanced down at the menu. "Not so special. I'm just a hardworking single mom who's made more than her share of mistakes in her life."

"And haven't we all done that? We learn from them, we keep trying. That's what you're doing. Don't put yourself down, okay? You're special. Don't ever let anyone tell you otherwise. Especially yourself."

Her head was still down and he said, "Miranda?"

When she finally looked up, her eyes were moist and gleaming. "I hear you. Thanks. But please stop talking now, okay?"

Smiling, he ducked his own head and perused the menu. "I'm not much for cocktails or hard liquor. Think I'll have a craft beer from Blue Moonshine. How about you?"

"I'm a woman," she announced, some sass back in her voice.

"I kinda noticed that." He matched her teasing tone and tried to keep his eyes from the scooped neckline of her top, which bared a lot of skin but stopped short of revealing cleavage. "But the significance of it escapes me at the moment."

"I like girly drinks." She read the beverage menu, with a lot of, "Oh, listen to this" and "Doesn't this sound amazing?" comments.

Their server, a middle-aged woman in black pants and shirt, with a neat blond braid, came over to the table. He knew most of the locals, but didn't recognize her. "I'm Ellen," she said, "and Rachelle asked me to take special care of you two. What can I bring you to drink? And how about some appetizers to start with? Celia's lobster ravioli and the crispy crab bites are my personal favorites, especially on a chilly night like this."

"Tell me more about the C-Shell cocktail," Miranda requested. "I've never heard of guavaberry rum."

"It's a special liqueur made on the island of Sint Maarten, from berries that grow there," Ellen said. "Rachelle has relatives there and she and Celia discovered it on a visit. Now they import it for that cocktail and a couple of dessert specials. The flavor's kind of fruity, kind of herbal. It goes beautifully with the orange juice, pineapple juice, and cream in that cocktail."

"Sold. It sounds delicious. Can you give us a minute to think about appies?"

"Of course. Sir?"

He ordered his beer and he and Miranda studied the menus. She put hers down and plunked her elbows on it, leaning forward and saying dramatically, "I want everything!"

Her eager expression and the desire in her voice had him thinking about an entirely different "everything" than what he knew she meant. What would it be like to have Miranda in his bed, making that enthusiastic pronouncement? His body tightened with arousal.

"How can I possibly choose?" she went on.

In bed, he'd take the pins out of her hair, one by one. And then he would slowly, thoroughly, and erotically give her *everything*. Happily. And then he'd do it all over again. He cleared his throat and suggested, "Want to pick a few things and share?"

"Yes, please." She sat back, the silky sea-colored top rippling across her breasts. "What about starting with those two appetizers? If a server recommends a dish, it's because either the kitchen wants to get rid of it or she genuinely loves it. At this place, I'd bet it's the latter."

"Where's the business sense in pushing something that's maybe subpar?"

"Depends on your clientele. If it's tourists who'll eat

there once and never come back, why not use up leftovers and stuff like that on them? Though I do think it's dumb, because some of them go online and leave bad reviews. Most good restaurants don't do it." She grinned. "The staff get to take home the crappy leftovers."

"There's lots to think about when you run a business."

"For sure. I'm happy leaving that to someone else and just doing my work and earning my paycheck. Running your own business is too risky for me. Though"—she gave him a smile—"if you're the only vet on an island, I guess the risk factor is low. As long as those bulls and newts keep on breeding."

He was laughing as Ellen delivered their drinks. Miranda's was a frothy, peach-colored concoction in a martini glass. The server carefully poured Luke's beer into a glass mug and departed with their order for appetizers.

Miranda took a sip and said, "Oh, my. This might even beat chocolate."

Rachelle dropped by to ask, "How do you like the C-Shell, Miranda?"

"It's orgasmic."

Luke almost choked on a swallow of beer and Rachelle gave him an amused glance. "Glad you're enjoying it." She winked. "A girl can never have too many orgasms."

Okay, now he was officially choking and, he guessed, beet red. Not to mention battling an erection.

After Rachelle departed, Miranda turned an impish grin on him and then her expression grew thoughtful. "So if— no, never mind."

He was almost afraid to find out what she'd started to ask, but he said, "If we're going to date, I want us to be honest. Miranda, this is maybe rude or insensitive, but here's the thing. We're two independent grown-ups, but that's not all we are. We're parents. Whatever we do, we have to think how it'll affect our kids." Even if his aroused body, so frustrated after years without intimacy, urged him to make sex his priority.

"Yes. Totally." She swallowed. "I'm not exactly the best influence, given my past."

"Your past is . . . well, of course it's relevant, because it's part of what made you the person you are today. But that's what's important to me: who you are now. I need to be able to trust you. And you need to be able to trust me. Right?"

She nodded. "Yes."

"So I think you should be able to ask me anything. Even if it's about something that might be painful for me to talk about. To think about. And vice versa. Okay?"

She thought about that and then gave him a half-hearted, "I guess."

Ellen served the two appetizers and they divided them and tasted them. Luke thought they were delicious, but the best part was Miranda's obvious enjoyment. He ate quietly, letting her concentrate on the food. But when the appetizers were finished, and they'd ordered the shrimp and sausage jambalaya and the miso-maple glazed sablefish, he said, "You were going to ask me something earlier, after you were raving to Rachelle about your drink."

"Was I?"

"Yeah. You started, and then said, 'Never mind.'"

"Oh, that." Her lashes lowered, darker than usual with a touch of mascara, and he noticed the bluish-green makeup that accented her eyelids.

"Go ahead and ask."

"It involved Candace. And it was, uh, intrusive. It's not something I need to know."

"Ask, and if it is too intrusive, I'll tell you." He braced himself.

Toying with the straw in her fancy drink, not looking at him, she muttered something he didn't catch.

"What?"

She glanced up and whispered, "Sex."

Thank God he wasn't drinking beer this time, or he might have spewed it across the table. "What about it?" His erection was painful now.

Cursing her own curiosity and impulsiveness, Miranda wished she'd never started this. It was too embarrassing and far, far too personal. But now that she had, and that Luke had insisted they be open with each other, she pretty much had to go ahead and ask. "You've only been with one woman. And she was only ever with you?"

He nodded.

She knew she was blushing, and there was a flush of pink on Luke's cheekbones. The man sure did look good tonight. His dark chestnut hair gleamed like satiny wood, making her want to run her fingers through it. The muted sage green shirt and green-and-gold striped tie brought out the green and gold flecks in his amazing eyes. Luke was the kind of handsome that didn't whack you in the face with an "OMG, he's hot!" reaction, but grew on you the more you looked at him and spent time with him.

She took a breath and came out with her question. "So how did you, you know, learn? About sex."

"Uh, the good old-fashioned way, I guess," he said. "Experimenting. Playing. Figuring out what felt best for each of us." As he spoke, she could see him relaxing, even smiling as if he enjoyed the memories. "Laughing. With sex, you have to have a sense of humor, right?"

"Uh . . . I haven't done a whole lot of laughing in bed." If she wanted to chuckle, she read a humorous book or watched a comedy on TV. "I mean, sex should be, well, arousing and satisfying. I don't think of it as funny."

Those colored flecks in his eyes danced as he gave a teasing grin. "Not even when you try some weird position in the *Kama Sutra* and get all tangled up and fall off the bed?"

Oh my God. If he was trying to get her back for that tease about her drink being orgasmic—which had been another impulse she maybe should have resisted—he'd certainly done it with a vengeance. "The *Kama Sutra*? Seriously?" Luke? The handsome, responsible dad, the island vet, knew the *Kama Sutra*? She'd only ever glanced at it herself, finding it too foreign to relate to.

What kind of erotic sex tricks did the man seated across from her know? Sexual awareness hummed through her, centering between her legs, and she tried not to squirm.

"Can you believe, it was a gift from my mother-in-law? She's very frank."

"Frank?"

He nodded. "She's a wonderful, loving person, but, well, the social niceties often escape her. She's in your face. It takes an effort for her to think about censoring herself before she blurts out whatever she's thinking. Sometimes it's amusing, sometimes it's painful. Often, she's spot on, insightful, but she can miss subtleties that are obvious to the rest of us."

"Huh. Candace must have taken after her dad then. She was definitely socially skilled."

"Yes, and you're right that her father is, too, though he's quieter than Candace was. She was just naturally bubbly and sociable."

Yes, she had been. Personable, beautiful, and pretty much perfect. How could Miranda ever compete with Luke's memories of Candace?

Fortunately, Ellen's arrival distracted her from that depressing thought. The server set out a platter of fish and veggies and a covered cast-iron skillet. Earlier, she'd placed empty dinner plates in front of each of them. "Since you're sharing," Ellen said, "I'd suggest you start with the sablefish. The flavor's milder than the jambalaya. The jambalaya will stay warm in the covered pan. Enjoy."

Taking her advice, Miranda and Luke served themselves portions of miso-maple glazed fish along with the accompanying sautéed sugar snap peas and mashed potatoes. Miranda tasted everything. The fish melted in her mouth, the peas crunched, and the potatoes—"Oh, my, those are the tastiest potatoes I've ever eaten." As best she could tell, the creamy mash combined white potatoes, sweet potatoes, a touch of ginger, and a tang of sour cream or cream cheese.

The food even went well with the final sips of her stillfrothy C-Shell cocktail.

Between bites, she returned to the subject that intrigued her. "Your mother-in-law really gave you guys the *Kama Sutra*?"

"She said that in a long-term relationship that involves fidelity, sex can become routine and it's important that you not let that happen. So she gave us the book." He smiled. "At first Candace wouldn't touch it. She said that if she looked at the pictures, she'd imagine her mom and dad doing that stuff."

Miranda laughed, spontaneously and loudly, and then clapped a hand over her mouth. "Sorry. I take it she got over that?"

"Yeah, we had some fun with that book."

"And here I thought you might be less experienced than me. You probably know way more than I do." And didn't that notion keep her body buzzing? How had she ever thought that Luke wasn't a particularly sexy man?

He frowned and then said, "Sticking with my honesty thing, I have to admit it bothers me to think of you with a bunch of other guys."

She swallowed. "Because it makes you think I'm slutty?"

"No. I'm sure it's more typical of twenty-somethings than the faithful-to-your-first-love thing Candace and I had. It's more that I hate to think of other men's hands on you. I don't like the idea of you caressing other guys, being intimate with them." He shrugged. "It's some kind of primitive male reaction, I guess. 'My woman. Hands off.'"

His woman? She leaned forward. "That makes no sense. You didn't even know me until a few weeks ago."

"Did you hear me say 'primitive male'? It's instinct. There's nothing rational about it." He lifted the lid from the cast-iron skillet of jambalaya, and dished out portions for both of them.

"Well, as long as you admit you're irrational," she teased. After all, it was irrational of her, the feminist, to feel pleased by his caveman reaction.

She tasted the rich, spicy mixture of shrimp, sausage, rice, and tomatoes. "Oh my God, that's even better than the sablefish. And so perfect for a cold winter night."

"Chef Celia's a genius," he affirmed.

Ellen dropped by and asked if everything was to their liking, and they both gave her raves. On her heels, a man approached their table. He looked familiar, so perhaps he'd been in the store once or twice. He was dressed up, for an islander, wearing a nice sports jacket and tie. He looked to be in his mid-fifties, kind of handsome in a distinguished way. His hair was a mix of gray and blond, he wore glasses with tortoiseshell frames, and as he extended his hand, he flashed a big, white-toothed smile.

The smile did it. This was the Destiny Island Realty guy; his photo was on all their signs.

Luke half rose to shake his hand. "Hey, Bart. Good to see you. I noticed you and Cathy having dinner." He waved in the direction of a window table a little ways away, and Miranda saw a dark-haired woman in a navy dress with a matching jacket. She'd definitely seen her before, working in the credit union as some kind of manager.

"It's been a while since we've seen you," the older man said, "so I figured I'd come say hi and meet your lovely companion."

"Miranda, this is Bart Jelinek, owner of Destiny Island Realty and an old friend of the family. Bart, this is Miranda Gabriel, Aaron's sister."

"Miranda, I'm so glad to meet you." Jelinek extended his hand.

"I'm pleased to meet you, too." Unsure whether to call him Bart or Mr. Jelinek, she omitted his name. She put down her fork and took his hand. He gave her a warm, hearty shake.

"A belated welcome to Blue Moon Harbor," Jelinek said. "I hope you'll be with us for a long time."

She gave a polite smile. "We'll see how things go." Right now, she just wanted to enjoy this fabulous meal and Luke's company.

The man returned his attention to Luke. "Cathy and I ran into your mother and Forbes at Destiny Cellars a week or two ago. It was nice to catch up with them. I told them we needed to get together for dinner soon." He pressed a finger against the bridge of his glasses, like he was pushing them up except they were already in place. "Haven't seen that stepbrother of yours on the island for a while. He's making a name for himself, isn't he?"

"Yes, Julian's doing great," Luke said. "His career keeps him busy."

"It's always nice to see a Destiny Island boy doing so well."

"To the extent that Julian's an island boy. He only lived here for a few years and he's never seemed that fond of the place."

"Oh. Well . . ." Jelinek shifted his weight, looking restless.

"I'd best get back to Cathy. She's always saying that when we go out, I spend more time socializing than talking to her. But that's what it's like on a small island, isn't it? I know almost everyone who lives here, and it's the friendly thing to say hi."

But not at the expense of leaving your wife alone, Miranda thought. Or interrupting someone else's meal while their food grew cold.

"We won't keep you any longer," Luke said.

Jelinek took a couple of steps away from the table and then turned back. "By the way, don't know if you heard, but Walter Franklin's planning on retiring when his term ends. Some folks have been after me to run for his spot. If I did, could I count on your vote, Luke?"

Luke smiled. "I'd think you could count on my whole family's votes, Bart. You'd make a great trustee."

The man rubbed his hands together and beamed. "That's what I like to hear. With support like that, how could I not run?"

As he made his way back toward his wife, shaking hands with other people along the way, Miranda grabbed her fork and took a large bite of jambalaya. After swallowing she said, "He's going to run for office?"

"It seems, if Walter Franklin does retire. The man holds one of the island's two trustee positions with the Islands Trust, and he's had it for a long time. Do you know much about local government?"

"Only that it's complicated. Some things are federal, some are provincial, there's the Capital Regional District, too, and then the Islands Trust. And local commissions and committees and so on. But I don't really know which body is responsible for which stuff."

"A lot of people don't. And, oddly, it mostly all works out. Anyhow, the Islands Trust is responsible for preserving the special ecosystems on the Gulf Islands. Land zoning and community planning fall under its jurisdiction. Each Gulf Island elects two trustees for three-year terms."

She cocked her head. "So the Trust is basically anti-development, or at least it makes sure that development is properly controlled?"

He nodded.

"That's a wonderful concept." She frowned. "But Bart Jelinek owns a realty company. Mightn't he be pushing for development, because that'd bring him more income?"

"He's not like that. I mean, yeah, of course he wants to make a decent income, but he's not in favor of big development. He's a great guy. He's been president of the Rotary Club forever, and they've raised funds for a bunch of community projects. The medical clinic, parks, playgrounds, equipment for the volunteer fire department. And Bart's the one who spearheaded the efforts to bring the Al-Khouri family here, and help them get settled."

The Al-Khouris were a family of Syrian refugees who'd been sponsored by the island. Blowing Bubbles had donated a number of items to the cause, from children's furniture to stuffed animals.

Luke was going on, reciting Jelinek's virtues. "And he's coached softball, sponsored the school band, mentored a number of island kids."

"Wow. He does sound like a terrific guy." Yet she didn't find herself liking him much. Maybe it was just one of those weird things that happened now and then, when you inexplicably were drawn to or repelled by someone. Pheromones or whatever. "He's a friend of your family?"

"Yeah. Dad was in the Rotary as well. When he got sick, Bart was there for us. Mom leaned on him, and his wife, Cathy, as well. After Dad died, Bart tried to help me, invited me to hang out with him sometimes. We'd toss around a softball. He had turned an outbuilding on their property into his 'man cave' and we'd watch sports movies and eat popcorn. I appreciate what he was trying to do, but it didn't sit right. I preferred being with Candace and our friends, or with Viola and the animals. I couldn't let a man get close to me because it felt like I'd be replacing my dad. Same thing when Mom married Forbes."

She and Luke had finished their first servings of the entrées, and they went back for seconds. "How does Forbes get along with him?" She could imagine some jostling for position between the two men.

"Okay. They're kind of opposite people. Bart's 'establishment' and Forbes isn't. But Forbes respects Mom's friendship with the Jelineks, and appreciates what Bart does for the community."

"And Julian? Does he like Jelinek?"

Luke shrugged. "Haven't a clue. Why?"

She mirrored his shrug. "Just curious." There was no reason to tell Luke that she hadn't warmed to his friend, and was wondering if she was the only one.

Watching Ellen serve dinner to the elderly couple at the next table, Miranda said, "A bunch of islanders have seen us here. Word's going to spread that we're . . . you know."

"Dating? You can say it. Dinner at C-Shell definitely constitutes dating. Are you okay with that?"

"If I wasn't, I wouldn't have come." He was handsome and sexy. He was a great father, he did worthwhile work, and he was popular in the community. A woman would be crazy to not want to date him. Why hadn't she realized that from the beginning? "I wouldn't have asked Eden's sister to babysit, thereby notifying Eden and her family, not to mention my brother."

She put down her fork, knowing she had to stop nibbling in order to leave room for dessert. "It was kind of hard," she admitted. "I'd told Aaron and the others that I wasn't going to date. That I was totally focused on Ariana, my job, and my studies."

"This doesn't take away from those priorities."

"No, I suppose it doesn't. Eden's family's been after me to have more of a social life, so they're happy. Di and Seal think you're wonderful."

"The feeling's mutual. But I notice you didn't say that Aaron feels the same."

"Oh, he has only good things to say about *you*." Except that he'd expressed doubt whether Luke would ever get over loving Candace. That might be true, but starting to date was at least a step in the direction of moving on. "But you heard him the other night. It's me he's skeptical about. It's taken me forever to even get my GED, and he doesn't want me to lose focus."

Looking concerned, Luke asked, "Are you in danger of doing that? I don't want to get in the way of you pursuing your career."

She pressed her lips together, giving his question serious consideration. "I feel focused. It's the first time in my life that it's actually felt achievable, me getting a great job with a reliable paycheck." Toying with an abalone earring—a Christmas gift from Eden's sister—she said, "It does hurt my pride that I've only gotten here by letting people help me. I do what I can to pay them back, but it doesn't even out."

"I bet they're not keeping score."

"No, I'm sure they're not," she admitted. "But that doesn't mean I don't."

"People like to help. It makes them feel good."

She studied him, this man who on the surface seemed to have it all together, but who'd admitted to accepting lots of help: from Candace, from the old vet, from his family. "It truly doesn't bother you, having to accept help from others?"

He didn't answer for a moment, and then Ellen was there to clear their empty plates. "Room for dessert?" She held up two menus.

"Do I look crazy?" Miranda asked.

Ellen laughed and put the menus down.

After she'd gone, Luke said, "No, it doesn't bother me. I think maybe it's because of my dad. He was a strong guy. A healer. I looked up to him and we were close. Closer than Mom and I were, in some ways. We did stuff together, hiking and boating, things Mom wasn't into. Anyhow, then he got sick." The flecks in his eyes were subdued now, gray clouds supressing the sunshiny sparkles.

"He needed help," he said. "From doctors and other caregivers, Mom and me, other family members, friends like Bart. But that didn't make him any less a strong person. He taught me that it's a strength to be able to know when you need help and to ask for and accept it." He gave a wry smile. "You're frowning. You don't agree, right?"

"No, I . . . I don't know. I'd never thought of it that way. But it kind of makes sense."

"You'd have liked Dad. He'd have liked you."

"Seriously? Why would he have liked me?"

"Because your heart's in the right place and you're interesting." He leaned across the table. "Want to hear a secret?"

"Always." Intrigued, she leaned forward, too.

"Bart Jelinek?" he murmured. "He and my father were good friends because they shared lots of activities and a vision of what was right for Destiny, but Dad confessed to me that he got tired of all that heartiness. He said Bart didn't have much depth."

She grinned. "I do think I'd have liked your dad. But really, you think I have depth?"

He gave a snort of laughter. "Says the rosebud with thorns."

"Huh? What does that mean?"

"It's kind of like saying you're an onion, but more flattering."

"An onion?"

He raised his eyebrows. "Layers? Lots and lots of layers, like a rosebud. And peeling them makes a person cry, as does pricking yourself on a rose's thorns."

"You're saying I make people cry? Luke, I—"

"Not intentionally. Just that you're complicated and you're prickly. You've had some crappy things happen to you. You've got strong views about being independent. And you've got a ton of defenses."

She wrinkled her nose, considering what he'd said. "I guess I can't argue with any of that. Which leads me to wonder why on earth you'd want to spend time with me."

Chapter Ten

Miranda's question took him aback. Stalling, he said, "For all sorts of reasons."

"I'm really different from Candace," she said softly.

"True." Candace had been a thornless rose from the day he met her. A sunny yellow rose, all her petals open. It wasn't that she hadn't had depth, but she'd been warm and generous from the surface to her core, with no dark corners or secrets. If he'd fallen in love with Candace, why would he be attracted to a woman like Miranda? Surely it wasn't just a holdover from his teen fascination with the bad girl.

Miranda ducked her head and studied the dessert menu. She didn't pursue her question, and that made him want to give her a genuine answer.

"You're intriguing," he said. "Attractive, of course, and sexy. I like how you are with Ariana. I like how hard you try."

She was looking at him again. "Try?"

"To create a better life for your daughter and yourself. I even kind of like the thorns," he admitted. "You're a challenge." Whereas Candace had always been easy. Easy to hang out with, easy to like, easy to love. As a kid, with all the changes he'd been going through with his family, easy had been a wonderful thing. Now, though, he felt ready for a challenge.

"A challenge, eh?" A spark ignited in her eyes, and her lips curved a tiny bit. "So I shouldn't make things too easy for you?"

Funny how she'd echoed the word he'd been thinking. "I know I'll regret this, but no, maybe you shouldn't."

She laughed. "Good. Because I don't think it's in me." She pointed to the dessert menu. "Have you looked at this?"

"I take it you want dessert?"

"They have a sampler for two."

Obviously, that's what they'd be getting. He caught Ellen's eye and placed the order, with both of them ordering coffee as well.

And then the thing he'd been dreading happened. His phone pulsed with an incoming call. Checking the display, he saw that it wasn't the babysitter, thank God. The name showing was Mrs. Goldfarb, the neurotic owner of a Chihuahua named Zeke. "A work call that I need to take," he told Miranda. "Hopefully, I can deal with it over the phone."

Responding to the call with a quiet, "Hello, this is Dr. Chandler," he rose. "Hang on a minute, until I get to somewhere I can talk." But of course she ignored his request, and as he walked toward the entrance of the restaurant, a moderately hysterical babble hit his ears. From it, Luke distilled the essence: Zeke's dry eye was acting up despite the antibiotic eye drops Luke had prescribed. Not an emergency, even if Mrs. Goldfarb might think so.

After Luke had advised the worried owner what to do and asked her to bring Zeke by in the morning, he went back to the table.

"Do you have to go?" Miranda asked.

Seating himself, he shook his head. "No, it wasn't an

emergency. Sorry, but you're not going to have that dessert platter all to yourself."

Her nose wrinkled as she grinned. "Somehow, I'll manage to survive."

Studying the golden-haired rosebud sitting across from him and wondering if he was risking pricking himself, he asked a question that had been on his mind. "Aaron kind of implied that you don't date good guys."

She raised her eyebrows. It wasn't exactly an invitation to go on, but nor had she shut him down.

"I wondered what that meant. And if it's true, what does it say about us?"

She buried her face in her hands, shook her head, and then looked at him. "You really want to go there?"

"Wouldn't have asked if I didn't. Seems to me, if we're starting a relationship, this would be good information for me to know."

"I suppose it would," she said wryly. "Okay, here goes. I have a thing for what Aaron calls bad boys. Guys who are edgy, unconventional, creative, passionate about something like acting or cooking. When I left the island as a teen, it was partly because I was miserable here but also because I'd met this guy in Vancouver, a musician with a band that was getting a few gigs. He was ten years older than me, all tats and ripped clothing, and I thought he was superhot."

Another Julian. Oh, great.

"I was head over heels for him and flattered that he was interested in me. It lasted a few weeks, until I found out he was screwing three or four other groupies."

"You didn't come home then," he commented.

"This island wasn't home. Vancouver was my home. I knew how to survive on the streets. I got fake ID, got a job in a sleazy bar that didn't look too closely, found a room with some other kids. I survived. Over the years, there were other guys from the same mold."

"Ariana's father being one of them, I take it."

"Ah, Sebastian. He was an actor, in town for the summer Bard on the Beach season."

"Bard on the Beach?"

"You really don't get out much, do you?" she teased. "They perform Shakespeare in tents by the ocean. It's really cool."

"You like Shakespeare?"

"Don't sound so surprised. I may only have a GED, but I read a lot. And if I volunteered to help, like as an usher, I got to see the shows. Anyhow, Sebastian was gorgeous, this utterly stunning black guy, and he had a posh British accent. He was talented and seemed really classy. And again I was flattered that a guy like him would choose me."

"He doesn't sound much like a bad boy."

"He was the fancy version, and all he cared about was his career and sex. I got caught up in the façade and didn't look below the surface."

"When you mentioned him before, you said he told you he loved you. That doesn't sound so superficial."

"Yeah, well, he was a good actor. Turned out I meant zero to him. He left at the end of the season, and then I found out I was pregnant." Her mouth twisted. "I messaged him on Facebook and he freaking blew me off."

"Did you think of, uh, options other than having a child and raising it?"

"Oh, yeah." She sighed, looking weary. "Maybe I had no right to have a kid. Not having a proper job, a stable lifestyle."

"No," he said quickly, "that's not what I meant."

"Well, anyhow, when I thought about having an abortion, I couldn't do it. I figured I'd give the baby up for adoption. She'd have had a more secure home. But when I had an ultrasound, she became a *she* rather than an *it* and I started to fall in love with her. I couldn't give her away. I guess that's selfish." Her eyes were huge and sad.

He shook his head. "It's maternal. And maybe someone else would have given her a more secure home, but you give her so much love. The two of you belong together."

She gave a wobbly smile. "Thanks for that. I only wish I'd done better by her."

"Seems to me, she's a healthy, happy, intelligent kid."

Now her smile brightened. "She is, isn't she?"

"You said you've dated a few guys since she was born? The chef and a couple others?"

"The only serious one was Emile." She rolled her eyes. "A brilliant, creative chef and a fascinating man. All muscle and sinew. Fiery red hair and a temperament to match. The energy he gave off sucked me in. Of course, how much of that energy and creativity was due to cocaine, I'll never know."

"He did cocaine?"

"Restaurant kitchens are strange places. High pressure, close quarters. Drugs aren't uncommon." She added quickly, "Not that I ever got into that. It's stupid. And yeah, it was stupid of me to get involved with a man who did drugs, but unlike my mom he seemed to be handling it." She shrugged. "Bottom line: whether it was sensible or stupid, I felt powerless. He was like a magnet. When he smiled at me, I couldn't resist him."

"What happened?" Aside from the guy apparently having no interest in her daughter, from what she'd said before.

"Turned out I was a seasonal special. He got tired of me, found someone new." She scowled. "And he got me fired, the bastard. Not that I'd have enjoyed working there and seeing him with next season's *dish*, but it was a good restaurant. Good tips."

He'd listened carefully to everything she said. "You talk

about being attracted to these bad boy types. Being flattered, unable to resist them. But were you actually in love?"

"I thought so at the time. Luke, I—" She broke off to smile at their server, who was delivering coffee and a plate with four desserts ranging from fluffy and pink to dense, dark chocolate. "Oh my, those look fabulous, Ellen."

"Try the pink one first. It has guavaberry rum in it. And work your way to the chocolate, because it'll kill your taste buds for anything else."

Luke waited patiently while Miranda tasted and moaned. If she'd been deliberately trying to arouse him, she couldn't have done a much better job, yet she seemed oblivious to him. He took some tastes of his own, enjoying everything though he'd have been quite content with black cherry ice cream topped with chocolate sauce.

When she finally rested her fork and drank some coffee, he said, "You thought you were in love with those guys?"

She blinked and her dreamy, dessert-satiated expression sharpened. "I've always led with my heart. I believe in true love, that it's out there for everyone. You know I'm right, because you and Candace found it. I keep thinking it's in front of me, but so far I've been proved wrong. Aaron always told me I was crazy, that love wasn't for people like us, but hah! Look at him and Eden."

"Yes, I do think almost everyone can find love. And that you will." Was it possible the two of them might fall in love? Being with him broke her usual pattern. He was nothing like the men she'd fallen for, and clearly she wasn't madly infatuated with him. "But Miranda, your relationships with those guys seemed so fast and intense."

She nodded. "Passionate. All-consuming."

"Uh, okay." *All-consuming* sounded scary. "But how can you love someone when you barely know them? Don't you need to know their values, their beliefs, their strengths and weaknesses, all that kind of stuff?" He wondered if she'd been overly eager to find love because her mother had never made her feel loved and secure.

"I suppose that would be nice. But you feel what you feel. Right?"

"Okay, so you felt attraction and passion. What else?"

"How d'you mean?"

"Did you truly like these men? Did you have conversations like we're having? Did you respect them? Trust them? Did you enjoy spending time with them doing normal stuff, like washing dishes or going for a walk?"

"There wasn't a whole lot of normal stuff," she said slowly. "Or a lot of conversation. Not this kind, anyhow. We talked about, well, their interests mostly. I learned a lot about music, theater, cooking, whatever. There was a guy who wrote graphic novels. Another who created works of art out of the weirdest stuff." She paused, her eyes narrowed in thought. "As for liking and respect, I guess that was maybe more about their talent and energy than those other things you said. Beliefs and values. And trust? Well, I guess I did trust them, but obviously there was no foundation for it because they betrayed me in the end."

Bitterly, she added, "Story of my life," and he figured she was thinking of her mom, too, and maybe her grandparents.

"Did the men really betray you?" he asked gently. "Or was it miscommunication?"

She sighed, looking tired again despite the sugar and caffeine she'd ingested. "Miscommunication? Are you saying it was partly my fault?"

"I'm saying maybe you wanted one thing and they wanted another, and the two of you never really discussed it. Even if you used the word 'love,' that can mean different things to different people. These guys sound like men who were used to going from one woman to the next, but you didn't see that, or you thought it would be different with you. But it wasn't, and they didn't really betray you, just did what they always did. If you see what I mean."

She was frowning, so obviously she didn't.

He tried to clarify. "It was about them, not about you. They weren't rejecting you as a person. They weren't even seeing the real you. They just wanted a fun, sexy, beautiful woman to enjoy for a while, and you fit the bill."

"Hmm. Maybe."

Warming to this concept, he went on. "And you didn't see the real them either. You saw these talented, sexy, exciting guys. They seemed, oh, larger than life, to use that trite expression. They fascinated you." Just as the Goth girl in high school had fascinated him, but he'd had the sense not to confuse that feeling with love. "And they noticed you, were attracted to you, brought you into their glamorous worlds. You were seduced by all of that. You wanted to find love, and you were ready to see it but you didn't look below the surface."

She groaned and dropped her face into her hands again. Speaking from behind her hands, she said, "Am I really that pathetic?"

"No." He reached across the table and tugged at her hands until she dropped them. He kept one, threading his fingers through her slender, warm ones. "Not at all. Just . . . hopeful."

"Needy," she muttered.

"Everyone needs love. That's being human, not needy."

She gazed at him, her eyes a soft blue. "You're sure you're a vet, not a shrink?"

"Positive." He squeezed her fingers, which felt so good interwoven with his.

"You seem pretty wise to me. How come you know this stuff and I'm such a dimwit?"

"To tell you the truth, I'd never thought much about all of this."

"So this is just on-the-fly insight? That's even more impressive."

"I want to understand you. I want *you* to understand you." He gave a self-deprecating smile. "Maybe I don't want you rushing off, falling madly in love with some—" The thought of Julian crossed his mind and he stopped smiling. "Rock musician or something."

"There aren't a lot of those in Blue Moon Harbor," she said dryly. Turning her gaze out the window, she said, "It's lovely out there, but it's still so chilly. I wish it was summer. It would be nice to go for a walk on the docks."

He shouldn't be surprised that, after a conversation this intense, she wanted to change the subject. "It would be," he agreed. "But spring's in the air and it won't be long."

She looked back at him. "My mom did the same thing, you know. Kept falling for the wrong guy, thinking she was in love." And then she made a quick, dismissive gesture. "No, I don't want to talk about her tonight."

Rising, she unhooked her purse from the back of the chair beside her. "I'm going to freshen up, then I'd love to hear some stories about your boys."

If she wanted to distract him, she couldn't have picked a better topic. Besides, he didn't want to come across like he was psychoanalyzing her.

She walked away from him in a slow, easy saunter, shapely butt swaying gently, long legs showcased by the sheer black hose and high-heeled shoes. Sexy as hell. He wanted her. His body was making that clear. His fingers tensed with the desire to curve around that delectable ass and he imagined those slim legs wrapping around his hips as he thrust deep inside her.

Luke clenched his hands together and bit back a groan. Even if she might be receptive, he didn't want them to leap into sex the way she'd done with other guys. He wasn't like those men. He'd never disrespect her. He didn't, despite his body's urgings, want a hookup. For him, it had to be a relationship. For him, and for the sake of his sons. And her daughter. So he'd take this slowly and make sure they were both serious about where things might head.

Ellen approached purposefully. "Are you done with the dessert?"

Three of the selections had been finished, but not the chocolate one. "I'm pretty sure Miranda'd kill me if I let you take that."

"I hear you. A top-up on your coffees?"

"Thanks."

She complied, then said, "Your date's on her way back," and left him.

He turned to watch Miranda approach. There was a natural, attractive rhythm to her walk. So different from the jerky way she'd moved as a teen, her every movement expressing anger and, he knew now, unhappiness. As she sat down, he shoved the platter over to her side of the table. She smiled and dug into the remaining dessert, enjoyment obvious on her face.

He wondered what that lovely face would look like if he teased her nipple between his thumb and index finger. If he stroked between her legs until she writhed. Oh yeah, he wanted her. But he was a patient man.

"Stories about your boys," she prompted between bites.

Now there was the perfect topic to distract him from craving sex. Always happy to talk about Caleb and Brandon, he launched into a story. Then, encouraged by her obvious interest and the questions she asked, he carried on.

Suddenly, half an hour had passed, and they both needed to get back to their sitters. He paid the bill, adding a sizable tip, and he and Miranda both gave Ellen and Rachelle their compliments on the food and the service.

Outside, it had passed chilly and turned damned cold. Using that as an excuse, Luke put his arm around Miranda's shoulders. When she snuggled close and tucked her arm around his waist, he wished they could walk for hours. But, aware of her thin coat and their waiting sitters, he escorted her straight to the SUV.

When they were on the road, heater blasting, Michael Bublé crooning in the background, Luke said, "Let's go dancing next Friday. Forbes's band will be playing at the community hall." Should he mention that his mom, her old teacher, would be there? No, she should realize it was likely. Besides, she was bound to meet his relatives at some point, and a casual venue full of islanders would be less pressure than a Sunday dinner. "Have you been there yet?"

"No. Aaron and Eden have invited me, but I hadn't left Ariana for the evening until now. And I wasn't in the mood." She glanced over. "I think I'm in the mood now."

For dancing, or did her words have a double meaning?

"Then it's a date."

He was content to drive without further conversation and it seemed she was, too. She hummed along, in tune, to the songs playing on the radio.

When he pulled up in front of her cabin at SkySong, light glowed from behind a curtained window. He flicked off the headlights and turned off the engine. "I'll walk you to the door."

"Don't be silly. It's ten feet away."

"Twenty. And it's dark out." He got out and went around to open her door. When she started to clamber out of the high seat, awkward in her heels and short skirt, he put his hands on her waist and lifted her to the ground.

She stood in front of him and he didn't remove his hands. "I had a good time, Luke. Thank you."

"I did, too. Thanks, Miranda." He bent slowly, watching her reaction.

The moon was shining through wisps of cloud, and her face and hair looked pale and almost mysterious. But her smile gave him an unmistakable go-ahead.

He touched his lips to hers, finding them full and soft. She didn't respond, but didn't pull away either. He sensed she was waiting to see where he'd take this. So he didn't settle for a good-night peck, he pressed more firmly, angling his mouth, asking her, daring her, to answer him. Heat surged through him, an almost irresistible drive to thrust into her mouth, to pull her to him and grind against her, but he fought the urge.

She sighed, one of those utterly feminine actions he had missed so much. Moving closer, her arms came up to loop around his neck and pull him toward her as her lips moved under his.

Different lips than he was used to. He was kissing a woman for the first time in four years. He was kissing a woman other than Candace for the first time in his life. But then those thoughts dropped out of his brain and there was nothing but Miranda and this kiss.

The tip of her tongue flicked the seam between his lips and he opened gladly, liking that now she was taking the initiative.

He wrapped his arms around her, holding her close but not so close that she might feel his erection through the layers of their coats. And for long, sweet minutes they explored each other's mouths. Though he smelled her lily of the valley scent, her lips didn't taste delicate and flowery, but like dark, rich chocolate and coffee. Now, this was a dessert that beat black cherry ice cream all to hell.

The sensations, the experience, it was almost too much. He felt like a dried-out seed in parched earth, sucking in drops of life-giving rain that filled his veins until they were ready to burst. It was delicious, but too painful to sustain.

He pulled away, breath rasping. "God, Miranda. That was . . . You're . . . Wow."

She looked a little dazed. "Yeah." But then she recovered and grinned. "That's one question answered."

"Dare I ask?"

"You're hot." And with that, she turned and sauntered up the dirt-and-gravel path to the cabin door.

Leaving him staring after her with a foolish grin and a hard-on that wasn't likely to quit anytime soon.

Chapter Eleven

When she'd accepted Luke's invitation to go dancing, this wasn't what she'd had in mind—which made Miranda realize that her brain hadn't completely adjusted to life on Destiny Island.

To her, "dancing" meant a dark club, pounding music, lighting that was almost psychedelic. Anonymity, the crush of writhing, overheated bodies in trendy clothes, the scent of perfume, sweat, and booze.

Not a wooden barn of a community hall, with a steeple on one side indicating it had started life as a church. Not the country-twangy song B-B-Zee was playing, and the twenty or so line dancers out on the floor in cowboy boots, denim, and a couple of long, boho skirts.

Nor had she expected to be sitting at two shoved-together tables with not only her brother, Eden, Di, and Seal, but also Luke's mom and in-laws. In retrospect, she probably should have. She knew B-B-Zee was a popular island band, that Aaron and Eden loved them, and that Di and Seal were friends of the band members. She knew Luke's stepdad was one of those band members.

But, silly her, she'd been fussing over what to wear, not over making a good impression on Luke's family. Or having her big brother scrutinize her every interaction with Luke from across the wooden four-top. Maybe that was a good thing, or she might've canceled.

And really, this wasn't so bad. The islanders had started with "haven't seen you in a while" chatter and then segued into Aaron and Eden's wedding, scheduled for the end of April. Miranda had mostly stayed quiet. At this table, there were she and Luke, Aaron and Eden. Eden wore a long skirt and casual top, and Aaron was in jeans and a navy Henley. At the adjoining table, on Miranda's right was Randall Yuen, Luke's father-in-law, and beside him his wife, Annie Byrne. Her wealth and success sure didn't show in her plaid flannel shirt and well-worn jeans. Her unstyled paprika-and-salt hair showed fading tones of the same blazing red as her daughter's had been, and her eyes behind navy-framed glasses were the same striking light gray as her grandsons'. Black-haired Randall was more put-together than his wife, in khakis and a cream-colored shirt with a First Nation eagle design on the pocket.

Across from the two of them sat Di and Seal, in their usual modified hippie garb, and at the end of that four-top was Luke's mom. Ms. Russo hadn't aged much, with her shiny black hair and olive skin, and looked attractive in a cranberry-colored sweater over fancy jeans and tooled boots. All the same, Miranda was quite happy that Luke's mom was too far away for easy conversation. Not that she figured the conversation would flow all that "easily" anyhow.

The three jean-clad men on stage were all of parental vintage, gray-haired or balding. Luke had pointed out his stepdad, ponytailed like Seal though Forbes's hair was thinner, the only one wearing a tie-dyed tee as opposed to a casual shirt.

The band, which was actually very good, switched to a

slower song, and now couples were on the floor in each other's arms. Having listened to a lot of Canadian music on the radio, she recognized the old Gordon Lightfoot tune. Forbes was at the mic, singing poignantly about being lonely, away from home, in the early morning rain. Personally, she figured the guy in the song wasn't all that bad off. At least he had a home to miss. It was more than she and Aaron had ever had as children.

Of course now Aaron did. He had a home, would soon have a wife, and Eden's family had become his as well. Everyone wanted, maybe expected, Miranda to make this island her home, too. Luke kept saying how great it was compared to Vancouver. While she didn't agree that it was better, each place had merits. Just like Quail Ridge Community Hall versus a trendy Granville Street club.

Could she and Ariana belong on Destiny Island?

She glanced at the phone lying on the table in front of her, beside a bottle of Blue Moonshine honey lager. Eden's younger sister, Kelsey, was back at the cabin with Ariana. She had met Luke tonight, when he picked up Miranda, and given them both a wink, saying, "Stay out as late as you want. This woman at work loaned me the first two seasons of a nineties TV show called *Sex and the City*, and I'm addicted." Kelsey had a part-time job at the school board office, and was building up her art portfolio with the idea of applying to art school.

Luke touched Miranda's forearm. "Worrying about Ariana?" he asked softly.

She glanced at him, looking so handsome and fitting in perfectly here in his blue denim shirt and jeans. Better than her in her slinky black top, rhinestone-bedazzled skinny jeans, and mid-heel shoes.

"Not really," she said. "Just suffering a touch of separation anxiety."

He nodded understandingly. "Even though I'm a dad not a mom, I feel like there's an emotional umbilical cord tying me to the boys. I said that to my mother one day, and she says it never goes away. Even when I was in vet school in Saskatchewan, she felt it."

She nodded. "I believe that. But not all parents have it. Or if my mother did, it got destroyed by all the drugs."

He squeezed her forearm, his touch conveying as much as words ever could.

She smiled to reassure him. "I'm not depressed, honest. Tonight I'm going to have fun." Her lips curved higher. "Or at least as much fun as I can, given all the watchful eyes." Though, on balance, she was glad to have her brother, Eden, Di, and Seal there, like a support network buffering her contact with Luke's relations.

He gave a rueful laugh. "Yeah, we do have a chaperone or two. That tends to be the story when you go out on Destiny. Privacy's hard to come by."

"Tell me about it," she said ruefully.

He leaned closer and whispered, "So you're safe, at least while we're at the community hall."

A warm thrill tingled through her. What did he have in mind for later? That first kiss had knocked her socks off—or, to be more accurate, made her want to strip off her sheer black panty hose. But Luke wasn't the same kind of man she'd dated before, and she had no experience with this kind of relationship. She really didn't have a clue how things would go. But maybe that was part of the fun of it. That, and the anticipation. The man knew the *Kama Sutra*!

Before she could decide whether to offer a sexy retort, he'd leaned away and reached for his beer.

She had a sip of hers and listened as Eden responded to Sonia Russo's question about how she enjoyed working at

Arbutus Lodge. She had started in January, as the facility's legal counsel and program director.

"By the way," Miranda said, "I ran into someone else who works there. Glory McKenna."

"Oh, yes." Eden smiled at her and then at Aaron. "An old classmate of Aaron's. You must've been in school with her, too, Miranda."

"Yeah, though I didn't recognize her. She seems nice."

"She's great. The seniors adore her. She may even be here tonight. She loves to dance and gets Brent out as often as she can."

"She has a two-and-a-half-year-old named Gala. We talked about doing a playdate."

"Good idea," Eden said. Then she said, "Oh, Aunt Di, before I forget . . ." She turned to the older woman.

"What is it, my dear?" Tonight, Di's silver and brown hair was pulled back in a long, thick braid, showing off her classic bone structure and vivid blue eyes. She wore a lovely embroidered top over jeans and boots.

"Gertie Montgomery was particularly lucid today. She said something else about Starshine."

It seemed to Miranda that Di's face tightened, and there was a rare impatience in her voice when she said, "Eden, I thought you'd let that go. It does the soul good to concede defeat now and then."

The hint of discord was unusual. Usually Eden and her aunt were a mutual fan club. Miranda had heard about Gertie before, but who was Starshine?

"Ha," Aaron said. "It's not in my fiancée's nature to quit without solving a puzzle."

"Who's Gertie Montgomery?" Annie asked. "And who's Starshine?"

Miranda was beginning to see what Luke had meant,

about his mother-in-law being blunt and not always so attuned to the social niceties.

"Gertie's one of the residents at Arbutus Lodge," Eden responded. "A real sweetheart, though sadly she has Alzheimer's. She's a painter, and my mom and sister visit her sometimes and they all paint together. But anyhow, she used to be a public health nurse. Starshine was one of the hippies at the old commune. You know that in the late sixties and early seventies there was a commune on Destiny?"

"I've heard it mentioned," Annie responded. "Go on."

"Di brought Starshine to the clinic for a medical emergency, and Gertie treated her because the visiting doctor wasn't there at the time."

"We've come a long way since those days," Randall said. "With a properly staffed and equipped medical clinic."

"Anyhow," Eden said, "today, Gertie remembered seeing Starshine again."

"Oh?" Di said, the single syllable sounding a little strained. Miranda noticed that she and Seal, who sat beside her, had clasped hands.

"Yes, at the ferry dock, in the foot passenger departure line. So it seems she left the commune safely."

"Didn't I tell you that?" Di said, and at the same time Annie said, "Safely? The girl was in danger?" Both their tones were sharp.

Eden addressed her aunt. "You said she left and you said Merlin did, too, but you were vague about it."

"Forgive us for not being so good with the details," Seal said laconically, "but back then we were stoned most of the time."

Everyone chuckled except Annie, who repeated, "This Starshine was in danger?"

"Eden, you're going to have to tell the whole story,"

Randall said with amusement. "She'll never be satisfied until you do."

Miranda was still watching Seal, and saw his brown eyes narrow behind his wire-framed glasses. He exchanged a look with Di, who opened her mouth.

But before she could speak, Luke was leaning forward, his sleeve brushing Miranda's arm and giving her a warm shiver. "You've got me intrigued, too, Eden," he said. "Miranda told me it was the commune that first brought you to the island?"

"That's right," her future sister-in-law said.

Knowing this part of the story quite well, Miranda sat back with a smile, happy that everyone's attention was focused elsewhere than on her.

"It brought her to me, too," Aaron teased. "Don't forget that part."

"Not for a moment, darling." Eden squeezed his arm, the diamonds in her engagement ring sparkling. "Anyhow, Mom's older sister ran away in 1969, after major battles with their strict parents. Mom never knew where she'd gone and, though she tried to trace her over the years, she never found her. But then, after my grandmother died, Mom found a letter indicating that Lucy and her boyfriend Barry"—her lips curved and she pulled them straight—"had joined the commune here. Mom was too weak from cancer treatments to come look for clues, so she sent me."

"Di was Lucy?" Annie said. "And Seal, were you Barry?"

"He was," Di answered. "We were both running from unhappy homes and we chose new names. I was Diamond, for the Beatles' song, 'Lucy in the Sky with Diamonds.'" She nodded at Seal to continue the story.

"One day when I was out with a local fisherman, a seal offered itself to me as my totem animal," Seal said. "I honored it by taking its name."

"How fascinating," Randall said. "I knew the commune was there, but I was too young to care much about it." He glanced at Luke's mom. "How about you, Sonia?"

"I was curious, but my parents wouldn't let me anywhere near it. The hippies didn't come into the village much, did they, Di? Seal?"

The way the SkySongs were sitting, shoulders close and hands clasped, Miranda had a sense of "the two of them against the world." But Seal sounded casual enough when he said, "No. The commune was in a remote location and we were quite self-sufficient. Someone made a grocery run into town every couple weeks. And like I said, I did go out with a fisherman sometimes, me and a couple of the other hippies. We traded labor for fish. Other than that, there wasn't a lot of mingling."

"But this Starshine," Annie persisted. "She wasn't safe?"

Seal and Di exchanged glances. Di said, "Hippies, drugs, rock music, free love. It could be a crazy scene."

Miranda had noticed in the past that, while the two of them still wore hippie-influenced clothing and had retained a lot of their sixties beliefs and values, they didn't seem keen on revisiting their commune days. Whenever the family conversation turned in that direction, the SkySongs changed the subject. It seemed that for them, as for her, there were things in the past that weren't exactly fond memories.

Eden, seated across from Luke, twisted sideways to study her aunt and uncle. "It was more than that." She turned her gaze on Annie. "The leader, Merlin, abused his power. Some of the girls were infatuated with him and he used that. Used them." She frowned at Di. "I don't know why the former members of the commune seem so determined to gloss over that. Abuse is a serious matter."

Miranda caught her breath. This part of the story, she hadn't heard before.

"Damned right," Annie said, her forehead creased in a frown. "So this Merlin guy hurt Starshine?"

"Someone did," Eden said. "She was pregnant and someone beat her, maybe kicked her. She miscarried and was bleeding badly, which was why Di took her to the nurse."

"Starshine didn't say it was Merlin who did it," Di said quietly.

Aaron, who had listened in silence, spoke now. "Eden and I talked to a number of former commune members when we were trying to find Lucy." He glanced at Sonia. "Forbes being one."

She nodded. "I didn't meet him back then. He's a few years older than me. He came over from Vancouver, joined the commune, but didn't stay long. From there, he went down to San Francisco, and a few years later ended up in Victoria."

Eden picked up the tale again. "No other names came up as possible abusers. Can you think of anyone else it might have been, Di?"

"It was a long time ago," she responded. "And as Seal said, most of us were pretty stoned."

"No one reported this to the police?" Annie asked. "Merlin got away with this stuff? And, by the way, I gather that's not his real name?"

"Hippies weren't big fans of the police, or vice versa," Seal said. "And no, I'm sure it's a made-up name. It was a time of rechristenings."

"Starshine as well," Annie said. "Did you ever know their real names? Merlin's and Starshine's?"

With an edge to his voice, Seal said, "The whole point of rechristening was to be new people. The ones we wanted to be. We didn't talk much about our pasts."

"That's not an answer to my question," Annie pointed out.

Miranda couldn't help a quick grin. The billionaire video

game designer didn't let anyone get away with anything. She was sure glad the woman's attention was on someone other than herself.

Beneath the table, Luke's big, warm hand settled on her jean-clad thigh. Without looking at him, she rested hers on top. No, this wasn't the night she'd anticipated, but it was interesting; his relatives weren't grilling or judging her; and having him beside her made it special. She'd never before been with a man who could fire her up with passionate kisses, yet make her feel comfortable in a situation like this. Not, of course, that she'd even met family members of any other men she'd dated, nor introduced her boyfriends to Aaron.

"Merlin's name might have been Otto Kruger," Eden said. "I talked to Bart Jelinek. Being in real estate, he's been interested in the commune land—which, by the way, is tied up in a trust for people in Germany who don't seem interested in it. Anyhow, the land had been owned by an elderly German man, a hermit who died without a will, and it was hard to trace relatives. Merlin claimed to be related, which was his rationale for setting up the commune there. Bart said that this Otto Kruger person turned out to be the closest relative, but he couldn't be traced. Which ties in with Merlin disappearing, if he really was Otto. But it's hard to imagine why he wouldn't want to get legal title to a big chunk of land."

"Hippies weren't into ownership," Seal said.

"It's quite fascinating," Annie said, her gray eyes gleaming behind the lenses of her glasses.

"She's wondering if she could turn it into a game," Randall said.

"No!" The exclamation burst from Di's lips. She took a breath and said, more calmly, "Who would be interested in a game that harks back to the sixties and the flower children?"

"Baby boomer flower children," Annie said. "And others, I'd bet. As Randall said, we were too young to really get caught up in it the way you did, but we weren't immune. The times were exciting. Paradigms were not just shifting, they were being shattered."

"I don't think it'd sell," Seal said slowly, "but if you do it, you should set it in the States. Things were more dramatic there. The draft, protests against the Vietnam War. Police in riot gear and hippie girls sticking flowers in their guns. Lots more racial tension than here."

Annie's eyes narrowed. "Excellent points. Besides, an American setting would have wider appeal." She grabbed her phone and began to thumb-type at a furious pace.

"And we've lost her for the rest of the evening," Randall said with amused resignation.

"Seal," Di said, "let's dance." The two rose and left the table.

"Good idea," Eden said, and she and Aaron joined them.

"Miranda?" Luke said.

"Yes, please." As interesting as the conversation had been, she hadn't come here to listen to commune stories. Besides, now that her buffers had gone, Luke's mother's gaze had fixed on her. She could stay and possibly be grilled, or she could check out Luke's moves on the dance floor. Not to mention, feel his arms around her. Fortunately, the current number wasn't a line dance, though it was more "country" than the music she was used to hearing in Vancouver clubs.

As she rose and put her hand in his, he said, "You know the two-step?"

"No, but you'll teach me." She had a good sense of rhythm and trusted her ability to pick it up.

"It's two steps quick then two steps slow. That's all there is to it." Finding a space on the crowded floor, he took her in a dance hold. "We'll start with the simple stuff, which is just walking. Me forward, left foot first. You—"

"Backward, right foot first. Got it."

He led, and he did it well. Confidently, firmly, but not shoving her around. After they'd repeated the pattern a few times, going counterclockwise around the dance floor, he started to mix things up, twirling her out and back, or doing the steps side by side. It was easy and fun, not as sexy as she'd like, but they couldn't exactly dance sexy with all those watching eyes. Even so, there was something distinctly sensual about it. Luke seemed so at ease, his shoulders square and strong, muscles flexing under her hand. Their bodies brushed in a tantalizing way as he swung her out and brought her back, and she gave her hair a toss and smiled up at him.

"Having fun?" he asked.

"Yes, though it's not what I expected. When you invited me, did you know all your relatives would be here?"

"Not Annie and Randall, but Mom. After all these years, she still calls herself Forbes's number one groupie. That's how they met, you know."

The song ended and they paused along with the other dancers, still in their dance hold, waiting to see what B-B-Zee would play next. "Fox-trot?" Luke queried as the music started, some dancers leaving the floor and others coming on.

"I think I've done it once or twice, but remind me."

He set them in motion again, equally assured with the steps of this dance.

"You were saying," she prompted, "about how your mother met Forbes?"

"He was with a band from Victoria and they came over to play at this hall. Mom was still depressed, two years after Dad died, and she never went out. I mean, except for work and buying groceries. Anyhow, this one night a couple of her girlfriends came over to the house and said it was an intervention. They fixed her hair and makeup, picked out clothes for her to wear, and dragged her off to the community hall. Sat her down, gave her a beer, the band came on. Forbes—who had a full head of hair back then, and the ponytail—played the guitar and sang, and Mom said her life changed in that instant."

"Ms. Russo fell in love with a musician in a band?" She'd never have guessed that about her sciences teacher. "I don't believe it! That's the kind of thing I do." She quickly amended that to "Used to do."

"I'd sure never seen that side of her. She and Dad were always so practical. But they did both like music, especially folk music and rock. There was always sixties and seventies stuff playing in the house."

"I guess there's a part of every woman that wants the sexy guy on the stage. Wants him to strum his guitar and sing just to her." And wasn't that exactly how she'd fallen for the band member when she was fifteen?

"It's a wonder the rest of us regular guys ever find a woman," he said dryly. "Anyhow, Forbes fell for her, too. Mom had family and friends here, and a good job. I had friends, school. Mom didn't want to uproot us. And Forbes really liked the island. Being a craftsman and a musician, he fit in great here."

"Lucky them."

"Yeah. Though Julian and I weren't impressed at the time."

She nodded sympathetically. After that, she and Luke were quiet, dancing to two or three more songs. This felt strangely right, even though the mood wasn't exactly romantic what with the family members all around them. Aaron and Eden were dancing, and Di and Seal. She'd seen Sonia and her brother-in-law Randall on the floor for a number or two, but now they were back at the table. Annie had finally lifted her head from her phone and she and

Sonia were talking intently while Randall gazed toward the stage.

The band started another number, a line dance. "Up for it?" Luke asked.

"Not in these shoes. Next time I'll have to borrow a pair of boots."

As they threaded their way off the dance floor, hand in hand, Luke said, "I need something cold to drink. Want anything?"

"I've still got half a beer, but a club soda with lime and lots of ice would be wonderful."

"Back in a minute."

He headed for the bar, and she made her way, on pinched-toe feet, toward their table. Used to be, she could wear pointy toes for hours on end, but this was only the second or third time she'd worn them since she'd moved to the island.

As she approached the table, Luke's father-in-law rose and walked toward the hallway where the restrooms were located.

Leaving her alone with Sonia and Annie. She was tempted to redirect her steps toward the bathroom, but didn't want to look as if she was running away. So she rested her hand on her dragon, hidden below the tight sleeve of her black top, summoned her courage, and went to sit with the older women. Drawing a dramatic hand across her damp brow, she said, "Whew. It's a while since I've been dancing. This is fun. Ms. Russo, your husband's band is terrific."

As she'd hoped, the woman's face lit. "It is, isn't it?" But then her expression turned serious. "Call me Sonia. I'm no longer your teacher."

"You remember me from high school," Miranda said resignedly. "I guess it's hard to forget the only Goth girl. I probably should have tried to blend in. But I was acting out."

"Acting out of pain."

Surprised at the woman's insightfulness, she said, "I guess. And anger."

"Life cut you a raw deal. You were unhappy."

Well, duh. She shrugged.

"I taught your mother, too," Sonia Russo said evenly.

"Oh my God. I had no idea." She studied the older woman more carefully, seeing that her glossy black hair and smooth olive skin looked more like nature than artifice. "You don't look old enough."

"It was my first year."

Afraid to ask, but too curious not to, Miranda said, "Was she really messed up even then?"

Sonia nodded. "Alcohol and drugs. More than just teen experimentation. I tried to help, but I was young. Inexperienced. She was having none of it."

"Thank you for trying." She swallowed, remembering a brief conversation after class one day. "You did that with me, too. Invited me to talk to you about what was going on in my life. But you were a grown-up and I didn't trust grown-ups, so I blew you off. I'm sorry about that."

The older woman gave her a sympathetic smile. "You're not the first teen to do that, and you won't be the last."

"To get back to the point," Annie said. "Did you—"

"Annie," Sonia silenced her with the word and a head jerk.

The last thing Miranda would have expected right now was to feel a smile rising, but she did, and pressed her lips together to hold it back. It seemed the two women had strategized this chat, agreeing that the more tactful Sonia would take the lead.

"Yes, to return to the point," Sonia said. "You weren't happy as a teen, Miranda. Are you happy now?"

"I . . ." Any impulse to smile died. Happy? What did that even mean?

"It's not that tough a question," Sonia said quietly.

"I just . . . Happy isn't something I've thought about much."

"Here's the thing," Annie said, scraping her shaggy paprika-and-salt hair back from her face with both hands and leaning forward. "We—"

"Annie," Sonia broke in warningly.

"No," Luke's mother-in-law said to her. "It's my turn. This time, it's better to say things my way." She stared at Miranda, not with hostility but clinically, like a scientist examining a specimen. "We love Luke. We love Brandon and Caleb. We were all shattered when my daughter died. My grandsons and son-in-law deserve the best. Another woman like Candace. A woman who knows what it's like to be happy, to be fulfilled, to love and give herself freely. If you're going to date Luke, we need to know that you're that kind of woman." She turned her stare on Sonia. "There, I've said it my way and I'm done. Your turn."

"I'd have phrased it a little differently," Luke's mother said, "but I have nothing to add."

And then both women turned narrowed-eyed gazes toward Miranda.

She didn't have the faintest clue how to respond. Because they were right. Luke and his boys deserved a woman like Candace. And Miranda wasn't that woman. She didn't know what happiness and fulfilment felt like. It didn't matter that she'd had a crappy childhood. She was who she was, and it wasn't good enough. It never had been.

"Hey," Luke said, coming up behind her and setting a glass of fizzy water on the table. "What's everyone talking about?"

She picked up the glass, ice cubes clinking, and took a long slug while Sonia not so subtly elbowed Annie and said, "Oh, just girl talk. Nothing you'd be interested in."

Chapter Twelve

Luke finished vaccinating a sixteen-week-old calico kitten named Patchwork. He told the owner, Ms. Fitzpatrick, the head librarian at their tiny island library, "That's the last set of shots. She's good to go for now. You'll want to bring her back at six months to get her spayed, unless you're planning on kittens."

"I don't think I could handle kittens in the plural," the woman, stick-thin with short-cropped gray hair, said wryly. "I'll make that appointment before I leave. By the way, we're starting a spring story hour for preschoolers. I'm emailing a notice this afternoon. Your boys might be interested."

"If the reader could make Brandon sit still long enough to listen, it would be a miracle. But we'll give it a try. Thanks, Ms. Fitzpatrick."

He glanced at his watch, confirming that it was almost noon. Today he was having lunch with Viola Cruickshank, who lived just down the road from the clinic. She was back from her Veterinarians Without Borders assignment in Tanzania, and they planned to catch up over soup and sandwiches.

"Luke." It was Crystal, his assistant, at the door, her

chunky body clad in the same kind of blue scrubs he wore, and her medium-brown hair in its usual stubby ponytail. In a calm voice, she said, "We have an emergency. A rabbit that was hit by a car."

"We're just finished here," he told her. "But would you please call Viola and tell her I've been delayed?"

Ms. Fitzpatrick cuddled her kitten, its furriness a contrast to her stark, tailored lines. "That poor creature. People should drive more carefully."

He nodded in agreement.

"At least it wasn't a hit-and-run," Crystal said as the three of them walked down the hall. "The driver brought the rabbit in and she's really distraught."

"I hope you can save the creature's life, Dr. Chandler," Ms. Fitzpatrick said.

"I hope so, too."

The waiting room was empty but for a blond-haired woman perched on the edge of a chair, huddled over a fluffy purple bundle on her lap. Her shoulders were bare but for the thin straps of a tank top, skimpy clothing for a crisp March day. No doubt she'd been wearing the sweater she'd used to wrap up the rabbit.

As Ms. Fitzpatrick slipped out the front door, Luke's gaze fixed on the dragon tattoo on the blonde's bare forearm, and he realized it was Miranda. He hadn't seen her in a couple weeks, not since the night they'd gone dancing. The night that had ended early, with her pleading tiredness and avoiding his attempt at a good-night kiss.

He'd texted twice to ask if she and Ariana would like to get together with him and the boys, but each time she'd replied that she was too busy. There'd been a curtness to those texts that sent a clear signal. Either he'd done something wrong, or she'd decided she wasn't interested in him. Maybe both. Taking her to a dance where the whole community, not to mention his mom, stepdad, and in-laws, were watching probably hadn't been the smartest move. Or maybe she'd decided he wasn't sexy or exciting enough. When he'd told her about how his mom and Forbes got together, perhaps Miranda had decided that a happy ending was possible for a groupie who was attracted to a band member, and she was going to hold out for that.

But now here she was, and it seemed she was the driver who'd hit a rabbit. "Miranda?"

Her head lifted and she jumped to her feet, white-faced and wide-eyed. "Luke, it's a bunny. It leaped out in front of the car and there was no way I could stop. I swerved but I still clipped it. It was trying to run away but it couldn't, and it was all bloody, just staring up at me." She held out the fluffy purple bundle, with a terrified rabbit face and two long ears sticking out.

Gently he transferred the wrapped-up creature to his own arms, feeling its trembling through the wool sweater. Chattering teeth confirmed that it was afraid and in pain. He had enough clients with pet rabbits, and had treated enough injured wild ones, to be attuned to rabbit body language.

"Where's Ariana?" he asked. "Is she in the car?" If so, he only hoped the child seat had supported her when the car braked and swerved.

"No, thank heavens." Her body trembled as badly as the rabbit's, and she wrapped her arms around herself like she was holding herself together. She looked fragile, vulnerable, and he felt a powerful urge to put his arms around her and offer warmth and comfort. He resisted as she went on. "Di sent me to the hardware store and she and Seal are babysitting."

"Good. Okay, I'll take a look at this little guy. Or gal. Crystal, can you find something warmer for Miranda?

Long-sleeved scrubs, or there's an old flannel shirt in my office."

"I have a nice cozy cardigan," his always-efficient assistant said.

"Luke, can I come in with you?" Miranda asked.

A good idea. He could keep an eye on her, since she was exhibiting symptoms of shock. "Once you put that sweater on." He smiled at Crystal. "Thanks for that. I'll call you if I need you."

Then he hurried into the examination room where he washed his hands, put on gloves, and carefully unwrapped the sweater from around the rabbit.

Miranda slipped into the room, draped in a heavy grayish-brown cardigan that was about six sizes too big for her. Her skin looked, if such a thing was possible, even paler than before, her eyes seemed unfocused, and she was still shaking.

"You were wearing a seat belt?" he asked.

"Y-yes."

"The airbag didn't deploy? You didn't hit your head?"

"No, I'm f-fine. It's the . . . the bunny."

Reassured that she wasn't concussed, he said, "Sit down and drop your head between your knees. Leave it there until you stop feeling cold and shaky."

"What?" She sounded dazed.

"You're suffering from shock. Don't want you passing out on me."

Silently she obeyed.

He began his examination of the rabbit, and after a few minutes she came to stand beside him. A quick glance told him she no longer seemed to be in danger of keeling over, and she didn't seem nauseous at the sight of all the blood. So he ignored her and carried on.

Finally he said, "We're in luck. This little guy—he's a boy—is going to make it. He's got a broken leg and some nasty lacerations, but I don't think he's suffered any internal injuries. I'll have to set the leg and put a cast on, and stitch up the cuts. Would you mind going out and telling Crystal I need her to assist?"

"Could I do it?" she asked in a small voice.

It would go quicker with Crystal, but he could see this was important to Miranda. "Sure. Wash up and put on a pair of gloves. Then I'll need you to hold down Junior, gently but firmly, until I get him sedated. Avoid getting too close to his mouth. He's scared and hurting and might bite you."

She obeyed, and then as she held the rabbit, Luke readied his supplies.

He put the rabbit to sleep with a low dose of sedative, not telling Miranda that rabbits were more sensitive, and responded less predictably, to sedatives than dogs and cats. Monitoring the creature carefully, he went to work on the leg, occasionally asking Miranda to hand him something or hold something for him.

She was quiet beside him, not interrupting to ask questions and, when he darted an occasional glance at her face, she looked intent rather than upset.

When the leg had been cast, he went to work on the cuts, gently moving the rabbit a couple of times to reach everything. It wasn't long before all the gashes had been cleaned thoroughly, treated with antibiotic ointment, sutured as needed, and dressed.

"What happens now?" Miranda asked. "He can't go back out in nature."

"We'll keep him here. Monitor his progress, make sure he gets proper nutrition and exercise until he's ready to return home. Where did this happen, Miranda? I'd like to take him back to where you, uh, found him."

"Hit him," she said flatly, staring at the unconscious

rabbit as it lay on the table. "Don't gloss over it. It was across from the llama farm. I feel terrible, Luke. I do watch out for rabbits and squirrels and deer, because they're always darting onto the road. I wasn't speeding, I swear."

"Hey." He waited until she looked up at him. "I believe you. Sometimes there's no avoiding it. I'm just glad you didn't go off the road, and glad Ariana wasn't with you. And also that you stopped and rescued this little guy and brought him here."

"Of course I would." Her eyes widened in surprise. "I couldn't leave him lying there."

A lot of people would have. He was really glad she wasn't one of them.

The rabbit was stirring, coming out from the anesthetic. "He's not going to be happy when he discovers he won't be able to hop for a while," Luke said.

"Poor bunny. But he will be able to, won't he? After he heals? He won't be crippled and more vulnerable to predators?"

"No, he should be as good as new."

He should call Crystal and have her take the rabbit to a recovery cage and keep an eye on it. He'd have to phone Viola to apologize and reschedule lunch. And he needed to grab a snack from the clinic's fridge, because the first afternoon patient would arrive any minute.

But here was Miranda, in this small room with him, looking so damned appealing in that huge, dirt-colored sweater, her blue eyes full of concern for the injured rabbit. He couldn't let her go before asking for clarification. "I got the feeling from your texts that you don't want to go out with me again. Is that true?"

She ducked her head, looking young and vulnerable. "I don't think it's a good idea."

"Why not?" She'd seemed to be having a good time, dancing with him. Then he'd gone to get drinks, and when he brought them back to the table, she'd said she was tired and wanted to leave. It didn't make sense. Except . . . An image formed in his mind and he remembered she'd been talking to his mother and mother-in-law. Girl talk, supposedly. "Did Mom or Annie say something?"

"They . . . they just care about you and the boys." Her shoulders shrugged. "They want to make sure you're happy."

That didn't give them the right to judge Miranda, or try to scare her off. Damn it, his relatives were reasonable, caring people and he'd trusted them to be polite. No, more than that, to be nice to his friend, to make her feel welcome. "I'm really sorry," he said grimly. "And, for the record, being with you made me happy." Surely his mom and mother-in-law had seen that. "Didn't it make you happy?"

Slowly she looked up at him. The dingy cardigan made her faded-denim eyes look even bluer. "Happy? There's that word again."

He had no clue what she meant. "You didn't like being with me?"

"I did, Luke. I really did."

And that didn't translate, in her mind, to happiness? It must be a woman thing. He was more proficient in reading rabbit body language than in understanding the female brain. Rather than ask her to explain some esoteric distinction he likely wouldn't grasp anyhow, he got to the point. "Then go out with me again. See if you like it."

Her lips curved at the corners. "Is it really that easy?"

"Why shouldn't it be? Don't let Mom and Annie get to you. They were out of line and I'm damned well going to tell them."

"No!" Her smile vanished. "Please don't. That'll only reflect badly on me."

He frowned, not understanding.

She pulled off Crystal's sweater. "I need to get back to SkySong."

"Okay, but will you go out with me again? Me and the kids, or just me. Whatever you want."

"I . . . I'll think about it." She cast a glance at the now-restless rabbit, which he was gently restraining with both hands. Her gaze lingered, and then she sighed and turned on heel. "I'll pay the bill for the bunny's treatment on my way out."

"No, Miranda, there's no need to—"

But she was gone, closing the door to the examining room behind her. He sighed and buzzed Crystal, telling her to give Miranda a discounted rate but not let on that she was doing it. He'd have happily done the work for free, but he guessed that would annoy Miranda, with her stubborn pride.

This, Miranda thought, was exactly what she needed. A playdate. A couple of hours with a nice woman her own age, sipping lattés and eating Glory's orange-almond biscotti and the chocolate chip cookies Miranda had brought. Their two black-haired girls happily chattered and screeched over *Monster Bowling* on the playroom floor at Glory's house. The children seemed to have bonded, and Miranda hoped the same would happen with her and the petite Chinese Canadian woman sitting beside her at the bar-stooled island that faced into the playroom.

It was a day off for both of them, this Monday, a few days after Miranda had taken the injured bunny to the vet clinic. Although she'd checked a couple of times on the rabbit's progress, she had yet to give Luke a "yes" or "no" on going out with him again. Maybe this morning's coffee chat would help her come up with the right answer.

But it was too soon to dump her man problems on Glory,

so instead she focused on the girls. "I never thought of trying this game out on Ariana. I'm not much of a bowler."

Glory made a face, her fine features scrunching up, which, combined with her short cap of black hair, made her look even more pixie-like. "I'm pathetic at bowling myself, though Brent loves it. But this game's fun."

"I'm not sure Ariana grasps the concept of bowling, but she loves whacking down the monsters." Not that the term really applied to the brightly colored plush toys, which were anything but scary.

Glory laughed. "Same with Gala. It's driving Brent nuts. He's all about, 'You have to use the ball to knock them over,' and Gala's just as happy to use one monster to bash another. She's either a slow learner or a rule breaker. Or has violent tendencies." She frowned. "None of which is good."

"You're not seriously worried, are you?" Miranda had thought she was the only one who obsessed over things like this.

"Not so much, but it's hard, right? I mean, you want your child to be everything. Healthy, happy, smart."

Miranda nodded.

"But really, they're just kids," Glory said. "My parents and grandparents help me keep perspective. And so do the seniors at the lodge. Some have the greatest advice."

"I get advice, too, from Eden's parents and her aunt and uncle. And Kara at the store. I appreciate it, but, well, they're all older than me. It's really nice to talk to you, to someone my age, going through this for the first time like I am."

Glory nodded. "I hear you. So we'll share. Stupid worries and smart tips."

Miranda smiled, knowing she was making a friend. "If I ever come up with a smart tip, I'll be sure to tell you."

The other woman put down her coffee cup and rested

her chin on her hands as she stared at the children. "Do you feel like you're being watched all the time?"

"Watched?" Miranda studied her profile. Was this seemingly normal woman maybe suffering from paranoia? "You mean, like, stalked?"

A laugh burst from Glory's lips and when she turned to Miranda, her brown eyes gleamed. "Oh man, yeah, it is kind of like that. By everyone. Everyone in this teeny little community. They're all watching. Waiting for you to screw up. Wondering stuff about you."

"Stuff?"

Her mouth twisted. "Like wondering if Brent's ever going to"—she made air quotes—"'put a ring on it.' And don't you just hate that expression?"

"Oh my God, on so many levels! Like hello, feminism has happened. This isn't the dark ages."

"Exactly," Glory said. "And anyhow, it's up to each couple to decide how they want to structure their relationship, right? It's no one else's business."

"It sure isn't. Lots of couples are happy and committed but don't believe in marriage. Like Di and Seal."

She meant to be supportive but Glory didn't look entirely reassured as she muttered, "That's true."

Miranda returned to the original subject. "Anyhow, yeah, I sure know what you mean about feeling watched. It's impossible for me to even just start clean with most people, so they don't have any preconceptions. You, for example. You work with Eden, you were in Aaron's class in high school, you and I even were in school together. There's stuff you know about me and have heard about me." She huffed out a breath. "I'm amazed you invited me over." Glancing at the two little ones expending their energy on plush monsters rather than in tantrums, she smiled. "Glad, but amazed."

"Miranda, our teens are when we try things out. Figure out

who we really are." She grinned, her good mood restored. "You obviously decided that Goth wasn't the real you."

"No, but I haven't exactly toed the straight and narrow either. Even after my Goth phase, I was a drifter. Fell for a bunch of guys, had a bunch of jobs. God knows, I'd probably still be doing it if Ariana hadn't come along."

"But she did, and you're not, and from what I can see you're a great mom." Glory bit into a chocolate-chip cookie and made an approving sound. "And you've lived an exciting life. Whereas me, I've just been on this island doing same old, same old." She shrugged. "Which actually, for me, works really well."

"I'm not sure 'exciting' is the term I'd use for my life."

"One day you can tell me stories. When you know me better and trust me."

"I'll do that," Miranda agreed. She dipped a biscotti in her coffee and then savored the mixed flavors as it dissolved in her mouth.

"I heard you and Luke Chandler were dancing at the community center a couple of weeks ago," Glory said. At Miranda's raised brows, she added, "What can I say? Being watched, right?"

"Yeah, we were there. Along with my brother and Eden, Di and Seal, Luke's mom, his stepdad up on stage, and his in-laws. And half the rest of the island. Not you, though. Eden says you like to dance, so I thought I might see you."

"My parents were busy and couldn't babysit."

"If you ever get stuck for a sitter, let me know. Most evenings, I'm working on my computer, taking courses online. I could bring over Ariana and the computer and watch Gala. Or you could drop her off at my place."

"That's supersweet of you." She cocked her head. "Dare I ask? I mean, tell me if I'm being pushy."

"To ask me to babysit?"

"No, I mean about you and Luke."

"Ah." Here was an opportunity, and from what she'd seen, Glory was perceptive and not judgmental. Her perspective could be helpful. "We've hung out a couple of times, him with his kids and me with Ariana. And been on two dates. He seems like a nice guy."

Glory nodded. "Everyone likes him. This woman I work with thinks he walks on water. He found this cutting-edge treatment for her sick dog and saved his life."

"I've seen him work." She told Glory about the bunny. "He was so gentle with it. He has these big hands, right? So masculine. But the confident, delicate way he treated that little creature, it was amazing." The truth, one she wasn't ready to share with anyone, was that, watching Luke treat that rabbit, she'd fallen a little bit in love with him. It seemed that veterinary medicine could be just as exciting and sexy as music or acting, at least when Luke was the practitioner.

"Very sexy." Glory winked. "You have to love a man with good hands."

"You're so bad." But yes, Miranda had imagined those hands exploring her body, not to heal but to arouse. "So anyhow, he asked me out again and I do like him, but I'm not sure."

"You small-*L* like him or large-*L* like him?"

"Large," she admitted.

"Then why wouldn't you go out with him?" Brown eyes gleaming, she added, "And find out exactly how good those hands can be."

Despite her concerns about dating Luke, Miranda cracked up at that comment. But then she sighed. "His mom and mother-in-law told me that he and his boys deserve another Candace. And they're right."

She frowned. "What does that even mean? There was only one Candace. Yeah, he loved her since forever, and it's tragic that she died, but the fact is that she's gone."

"They mean someone perfect, like her."

Glory snorted. "Okay, for one thing she wasn't perfect."

"No? Really? Everyone seems to think so."

"Admittedly, she was great. But everyone has some weaknesses, some flaws."

Miranda narrowed her eyes. "Would it be really rude to ask if you know any of Candace's?"

Glory shrugged. "Look, I liked her a lot, okay? But she was a little too obsessed with how she looked. I get it, because her mom's a superstrong feminist and against anything girly. Like, when Candace was little, she wasn't allowed to wear pink. Her toys had to be gender-neutral. Once Candace had a decent allowance and was allowed to choose her own clothes and stuff, she indulged her girly side."

"That's kind of understandable," Miranda said a little grudgingly. "Any other flaws?"

"This is going to sound petty, but is being too nice a flaw? She was just, well, never *petty* or mean. She was friendly to everyone, generous, always sunny and sweet. If she ever had PMS or was in a bad mood, she didn't show it." Glory wrinkled her nose. "I sound like a total bitch, don't I?"

"No, I get it. Well, at least you won't have that problem with me. No one's ever accused me of being too nice. But it does make me wonder why Luke wants to date me."

"You're not competing, Miranda," Glory said firmly. "You're you. Don't try to compare yourself to her."

"Even if I don't, Luke's mom and mother-in-law will. Probably he will, too," she added gloomily. "And believe me, I have lots of flaws."

"Being human is good," Glory asserted. "If you big-*L* like Luke, give him a chance. Give yourself a chance. See where it goes." Her eyes narrowed. "Or are you jumping ahead, thinking about getting married and blending families?"

"God, no. No, but . . ." She sighed. "This is all so different

for me. It's the first time I've had a relationship where kids
were involved. What if his boys don't like me? They
haven't exactly warmed to me so far. They've never had a
mother, but there are photos of Candace in the house and
I'm sure Luke and the grandparents talk about her. The
boys know she's their mom, and they've had their dad to
themselves. Luke hasn't been dating, so this is new to them.
I'm sure they wonder who I am and why Ariana and I are
being thrust into their lives."

"Give it time. Don't push, just let it come naturally."

"Ariana's already nuts about Luke." She studied her
daughter, who was bashing one monster with another, giggling madly. "If the twins do come to like me, and then
Luke and I end up breaking up"—which, let's face it,
seemed likely given her track record with guys—"what'll
it do to the three kids?"

Glory slid off her stool and topped up their cups with
plain coffee. When she sat down again, she picked up a biscotti and said, "I hear you. Once you're a mom, you always
have to put the kids first." Her dark eyes got a sad, distant
expression.

Miranda remembered how Glory had said that her birth
parents had abandoned her. Was that what she was thinking
about now? Should Miranda say something?

Before she could decide, Glory shrugged. "Life has no
guarantees. We hope for happy endings. Sometimes we get
them, but sometimes we don't. I think you probably know
that better than a lot of people our age."

"Yes." What was the other woman saying?

"And we cope," Glory said firmly. "We may feel awful,
but we cope. You can't . . . not *live*, just because you're
afraid life may hurt." She dipped the biscotti and bit into
the soggy end.

Miranda had always coped. Even last summer, when
she'd hit an all-time low, she hadn't given up. She'd swallowed her pride, admitted to being totally pathetic, and

come crawling to Aaron for help. Because of Ariana. If she'd been on her own with no money for rent, Miranda would have found a couch here and there to camp on. But no way would she inflict that life on her daughter. So she'd coped in the only way she could—and as a result, her life had slowly turned around. "When it's just me, I'll take risks. But I don't want Ariana to get hurt."

"Of course you don't." Glory gently touched Miranda's hand. "But here's the thing, the really scary thing. Our daughters will get hurt. Life will hurt them. It's inevitable. You know that."

"I do. But I don't want to be the instrument of that hurt." It was the thing she'd most tried to avoid. There were times she'd subsisted on generic ramen noodle soup, but she'd always made sure Ariana had decent food. Even if she'd had to go to the food bank. Or even, once or twice, resort to tricks learned in childhood and shoplift.

"So you plan never to date, because the relationship might not work out? You'll cut Ariana off from getting to know a great guy like Luke? You'll nix the possibility of her ever having a father who loves her?"

"Oh God." Miranda buried her face in her hands. "I didn't think of it that way."

"So stop being so angsty. You like the guy, he's one of the good ones, and he wants to date you. Go. Have fun, talk." Her tone lightened. "See what those big *hands* are capable of." She wiggled the biscotti suggestively, indicating that hands weren't all she meant. "See where things go. If it works, that'll be awesome for you and Ariana, and for Luke and his boys. If it doesn't, trust in your ability to cope and your ability to help Ariana deal with it."

"You make it sound so reasonable." Which gave Miranda hope, and she managed a small smile. "Could you now please have the same talk with Sonia and Annie?" She added a quick "Just kidding, of course."

Chapter Thirteen

Luke drove his white SUV slowly through the grounds at SkySong, with the boys in their booster seats in back. The forecast had for once been right and the sun shone with surprising warmth for this time of year. April had just begun and spring was literally springing out all around him. Pink blossoms festooned the magnolias and ornamental fruit trees, daffodils were giving way to tulips and hyacinths, and a pale green haze of buds and unfurling leaves skimmed the deciduous trees. In the vegetable and herb garden, Seal and several others were at work. Miranda had told Luke that many of the retreat's guests enjoyed tending the organic garden and the grounds. Down on the lawn by the ocean, he saw Di, graceful in a flowing top and leggings, leading others through moves he guessed were tai chi.

He pulled up in front of Miranda's cabin, where she and Ariana sat side by side on the top step. With a warning, "Be nice, guys," he turned off the engine and climbed out.

Brandon and Caleb were less than thrilled about having two girls come along on their Sunday outing. Luke wasn't sure whether it was the gender of their guests that most bothered them, or having to share their dad's attention.

Miranda smiled and stood as he approached, as fresh

and springlike as the flowering trees in her pink T-shirt and tan capris. But it was Ariana who gave him the warmest welcome. "Luke!" she cried excitedly, bouncing to her feet and stretching her arms up to him.

He hoisted her. "Hey, Ariana. I've missed you." Shifting her to one arm, he reached out his free hand to touch Miranda's shoulder but, mindful of her prickliness and his sons' gazes, didn't lean in for a kiss. "You too. I'm glad you decided to come."

"So am I." Her faded-denim eyes twinkled. "It's Sunday and you shaved."

He winked. "Because this is a date. You okay with that?"

She smiled again, a slow-spreading one. "I guess I am." She slipped one strap of a small backpack over her shoulder. "Are you finally going to reveal where we're headed? I'm thinking the kayaks on the roof are a clue."

"Can't fool you for a minute, can I?" He owned one kayak and had borrowed another kid-friendly one from neighbors. "We're going to Thuqulshunum Lake," he said as they went down the steps, him carrying Ariana. "Do you know how to kayak?"

"I went out a couple of times with Aaron last summer. But Luke, the kids are too young for kayaking."

"Too young to do it on their own, but it's never too early to get them comfortable on the water. Does Ariana swim?"

"Swim?" Ariana picked up on the word. "I swim!" Her big brown eyes were so bright and pretty.

"You do?" he said. "That's wonderful. What a smart girl you are."

"She splashes and paddles, wearing water wings, with me right beside her," Miranda clarified.

"I has wings!" Ariana said.

"Just like a fairy," Luke said. "I guess that makes you a water fairy." When she looked puzzled, he tried again. "A swim fairy?"

She nodded vigorously. "I swim fairy."

They'd reached his SUV and Miranda said, "I'll go get her car seat out of my Toyota."

"Before you do, take a look in back. I brought one of the boys' old seats. See if it'll work."

She opened the door to the back seat, where his boys sat in their front-facing boosters and he'd installed the smaller rear-facing one for Ariana. "Hey Caleb, Brandon," she said.

"Hey," Brandon said in an unfriendly tone, while Caleb didn't reply at all. If the boys didn't smarten up, he'd be having words with them.

The dogs were enthusiastic, though. Three-legged Honey and fluffy little Pigpen barked tail-wagging greetings from the back of the SUV.

"Nice to see all of you," Miranda said. "All set to go kayaking, boys?"

"We kayak with Dad," Brandon asserted.

Luke winced. "What do you think of the car seat, Miranda?"

"It looks good. I'm glad it's rear-facing. At the store, we recommend keeping kids in them as long as possible, even up to age four."

"It's a little kid seat," Brandon said dismissively.

"Well, Ariana's a lot smaller and younger than you," Miranda said in a friendly tone. "When she's a big kid like you two, she'll get a different seat."

"We're big kids," Caleb said proudly.

"Good," Luke said. "Because big kids are polite to their guests."

Brandon's gaze fixed on Miranda's bare left forearm and his eyes widened. "You have a tattoo! It's a dragon!"

"Yes, it is." She held her arm out and both boys stared at it, fascinated. He waited for Caleb to say that his mommy hadn't had any tattoos, but both boys seemed for once to be struck dumb.

Miranda moved away, shooting Luke an amused glance, and he put Ariana in the booster seat. She squealed, "Doggies!" and reached toward Honey and Pigpen.

"You can play with them later," he told her, securing the fastenings and hoping she wouldn't pick now to have a tantrum. Fortunately, she kept quiet.

Miranda climbed into the front with her backpack. "Your vehicle's versatile," she commented as he got in beside her and started the engine.

"Yeah. It's old, but it's solid and it meets our needs. I bought it when Candace and I moved back to the island after I finished my vet training."

"How many years of school did that take?"

"Six years of post-secondary."

"Wow, I'm impressed."

"The first three were tough, because Candace stayed here. I came back for holidays and worked for Viola. But when Candace and I turned twenty-one, we got married that summer and then she came with me. She took cooking classes, worked for caterers, and developed ideas for the business she wanted to run back here."

He turned on some music, which he'd found was the best way of keeping the kids happy while he was driving. As soon as the boys heard "The Wheels on the Bus," they began to sing. Ariana sang, or at least babbled, along as well.

Under the screen of the music, he said quietly to Miranda, "I've told them a lot about Candace. I want them to know their mom."

"Of course."

He wondered what, if anything, she'd told Ariana about her absent father. "After I graduated, we came back to Destiny and Annie and Randall gave us that house, a belated wedding gift. They offered to buy me a vehicle as well, because I was taking over Viola's practice, but I drew the line at that. Bought this one, which was a few years old, from a guy who was leaving the island and gave me a good price."

He'd felt like life was unfurling perfectly in front of him. "Candace was pregnant. We knew she was carrying twin boys. The SUV would meet our needs—the family ones and my work ones." In the world he'd envisioned, Candace would have been sitting in the seat beside him. By now, there might well have been another child. Given his family history, it would likely have been another boy. If so, he and Candace would've been talking about adopting a cute little girl like Ariana.

After a minute or two of silence between him and Miranda, listening to the kids now singing "Itsy-Bitsy Spider," she said, "You took over the vet practice as soon as you graduated?"

"Yes. I'd been working for Viola since I was twelve. Half my life. I knew all the patients and their owners. She was excited about working with Veterinarians Without Borders." He always loved hearing her stories about her animal adventures in foreign countries, like her most recent trip to Tanzania.

He glanced over. "Viola wouldn't take any money for the practice. She said all she cared about was knowing that the island's critters were in good hands."

"And they are," she said with certainty.

"That's nice of you."

"I saw you with that bunny. He's still doing okay, right?"

"He's a quick healer. His injuries were straightforward. I've treated far more serious things than that. And"—he glanced in the rearview mirror to ensure the kids were absorbed in their song and not paying any attention—"I've lost some, I'm sad to say."

"If they could have been saved, you'd have done it. You're good, Luke. You have a gift."

A pretty woman was complimenting him on a career

that was way more than just a job to him. He wasn't going to argue; he'd simply bask in the warm glow.

One nice thing about Destiny Island, it was never far from point A to point B. Soon he was pulling into the parking lot at Thuqulshunum Lake Park, finding a spot among shade trees and rolling down the windows a few inches so the dogs would be comfortable.

"The lake has an unusual name," Miranda commented.

"It's an anglicized version of the First Nations word for 'rainbow.'" The forest-fringed lake was undeveloped but for this park and the Rainbow Days resort down the road. The park was simple but nicely maintained with its coarse sand beach, scattered shade trees, dozen picnic tables and barbecues, and restrooms with showers as well as toilets. There were a number of vehicles in the lot already, people at a couple of the picnic tables, and more on the beach and playing in the shallows. At the boat launch area, two men in fishing vests were putting a rowboat in the water.

"One of the nice things about this lake," he told Miranda, "is that they don't allow power boats. It's not only safe here, it's quieter and more peaceful than Montague Lake."

As they extracted their children from the back seat, she asked, "What about the dogs? Surely they don't come kayaking."

"No, they can nap in the SUV. Then we'll liberate them and they can play while we have a picnic lunch."

She set her daughter down and straightened, hands on her hips. "You didn't say anything about lunch."

"Sorry. Did you have other plans?"

"No, but if you'd told me, I would have brought something."

"It's our treat." He corralled his kids, a hand on each one's shoulders. "We have PB&J sandwiches, carrot sticks, cheese, crackers, apples, lots of good stuff. Oh, and there might be cookies." He shook each shoulder gently. "But only if everyone's good."

Releasing his sons, he said, "Okay, boys, you can play on the beach but don't get wet. You know how icky it is if you have to sit in wet jeans."

"Tell me how to help with the kayaks," Miranda offered.

"I've got it. They're light." His and his neighbor's were cheap plastic tandem kayaks for beginners. In a year or two, Luke would buy the boys their own mini kayaks. "You look after Ariana. Oh, and bring warm sweaters. It's often cooler on the water."

"Yes, sir," she said with a mock salute.

"Sorry. Guess I'm used to bossing the kids around."

"Don't worry. If you get too bossy, I'll tell you."

He opened the back of the SUV and reached for the life vests, holding the eager dogs back so they couldn't escape. "Later, guys. Right now it's nap time."

He dumped the vests on the ground and reached up to untie the ropes securing the kayaks to the roof rack. After lowering the first kayak, he piled the two adult vests in it, hooked a hand into the side of it, and hefted it down to the water. By the time he'd locked the SUV and brought the second kayak and the kiddie vests, everyone was assembled.

Down the beach, a family with kids and a golden retriever was wading close to shore and a couple of teenage paddleboarders were setting out.

"How are we going to do this?" Miranda asked, a tinge of nervousness in her voice. "I'm not that experienced."

"That's why I'm putting you with the boys."

"Daddy!" Brandon protested. "We kayak with you!"

He squatted down to be on eye level with his sons. "I need you guys to look after Miranda. She's pretty new to this, and you've been kayaking since you were smaller than Ariana."

"Want to go with you," Caleb said softly.

Miranda squatted down too. "I really hope you two can help me. Ariana's too small, and like your daddy said, I'm not very experienced at kayaking. If I had a couple of big boys helping me, I'd feel a lot better about it."

Caleb studied her with huge, solemn eyes, and then pronounced, "I'll help."

Not to be out-big-boyed by his brother, Brandon promptly said, "I paddle really good. I'll help you."

"Thank you," she said, her voice not betraying any of the amusement Luke guessed she was feeling. "I'm grateful to you. I imagine this is going to be worth at least one cookie each. If," she added in a warning tone, "we get back safely." She rose and turned to Luke. "You'll be careful with Ariana?"

"Of course. We don't want the swim fairy going for an unscheduled dip."

"I swim!" Ariana said.

"You swim in warmer weather," Miranda said. "And from the beach, not the middle of the lake."

"Okay," Luke said, "now that we've got all of that settled. Vest up, everyone."

He helped Miranda put a small vest on Ariana and then checked that his sons had secured theirs properly. He cast an eye on Miranda and saw that she knew what she was doing with the vest, but he said, "Give me your phone." She'd been taking pictures, and had stowed the phone in the pocket of her capris.

"Not because I think you're going to tip," he clarified as she handed it over. "But water can drip off the paddles. I have a dry bag for the important stuff." He put her phone, his, and his wallet and keys in a waterproof orange bag, sealed it, and stowed it, along with a couple of old towels, in the storage compartment of the borrowed kayak. Then he pulled on his own vest. Having grown up by the ocean, he never used to wear one, not unless he was out on a rough sea, but now he had to set an example for his kids.

"Boys," he said, "you and Miranda take our kayak, since you know how it works." To Miranda he added, "That's the orange one. Let's get you launched and then Ariana and I will climb into the blue one."

Both kayaks were sit-in ones rather than sit-on-top, chosen because the design kept the paddlers dryer—and the water here, be it lake or ocean, was cold. He hauled the orange kayak into the water and steadied it. "Miranda, you climb into the back seat." As she obeyed, he was reassured that she seemed comfortable as she got settled.

"Caleb, you start out in the front seat, with Brandon in the bow ahead of you."

He braced the boat as the boys clambered in, rocking it far more than Miranda had. Then he handed her a paddle, and gave Caleb a smaller, lighter one. "He'll paddle," Luke told Miranda, using the term loosely, "and Brandon's your scout. We'll stop partway through our outing and the boys will switch." This was the way he resolved the twins' argument over which was the preferred position. "All set?"

Was she all set? Miranda wasn't particularly nervous about kayaking with the boys, but her maternal instinct protested at being separated from Ariana. It wasn't that she didn't trust Luke, but this was a new experience for her daughter. Who knew how she'd react? And it was a big, cold lake.

Miranda gazed up at Luke as he held on to the edge of the orange kayak, ready to shove her and the boys away from shore.

Maybe he read uncertainty in her eyes, because he said, "Don't worry about Ariana. I won't put her up front. I'll start her out sitting between my legs. She'll be secure and be able to get accustomed to the feel of the kayak. The chances of her falling out are really slim, but it's possible. Absolute worst case scenario, she gets to play swim fairy and I rescue her and we dry her out."

She liked that he hadn't said there was absolutely no risk. She wouldn't have believed him. Instead, he'd acknowledged it and reassured her. "Okay, then. Boys, what do you say? Brandon, are you ready to scout? Caleb, are you ready to paddle?"

They gave hearty affirmatives, their excitement over the adventure clearly outweighing any doubts they had about her presence.

Luke pushed the kayak away from shore. Caleb's paddle was already flailing, sometimes even getting into the water. Miranda grinned as she paddled forward, getting a feel for the long paddle and for how the craft responded.

Backstroking on one side and forward stroking on the other, she turned the kayak back toward shore and saw Luke paddling toward her, with Ariana beaming. "Mommy! I kay-ak!"

Oh, how she'd love a picture of that. So would Aaron and Eden, and Mrs. Sharma in Vancouver. "You sure are kayaking, sweetie. You look great. So, guys, where are we heading?"

"Down to Rainbow Days resort," Luke said. "There aren't many spots on the lake where you can go ashore, and it's one. It gives us a chance to stretch and the boys can swap seats. It's about a kilometer and a half away."

"That shouldn't take long."

"Figure on half an hour."

"Really? I could walk it faster than that."

"The point of kayaking, at least the way we do it, isn't to cover distance but to enjoy what we're doing and seeing. Besides, since you're a beginner, we don't want to tire you out. Right, boys?"

Caleb was "paddling" now with great intent, a few cold drops flicking back on Miranda's legs. She began to stroke as well. The turquoise kayak pulled up beside them and then a little ahead, where it held position.

"Hi, Mommy!" Ariana said.

"Hi, sweetie. Isn't this fun?"

"Fun!"

For the first few minutes Miranda was kept busy finding her rhythm and figuring out how to adjust to Caleb's frenetic paddling and Brandon's occasional lurches as he saw something and cried out. "Paddleboarders!" "Fish!" But soon she grew comfortable enough to gaze around.

As they left the park behind, the shoreline changed from beach to reeds and rushes. Very wildernessy, as was typical of this island. As a teen, she'd shunned Destiny's lack of development, but now she was learning to value it.

A distinctive trilling birdsong made her search the rushes, finding a red-winged blackbird perched on one. In Vancouver, her bird identification had consisted of robins, pigeons, gulls, ducks, and Canada geese. Here, there were so many nature lovers that she'd absorbed knowledge as if by osmosis and had added a dozen or more species to her list.

Other kayakers were out, and someone was casting a fly line from a red canoe. A couple of rowboats held more fishermen. And, as Brandon had observed, there were paddleboarders.

"Ducks!" Brandon yelled, and she saw a pair of birds swimming swiftly away from the kayaks. Not mallards, the most commonly seen ducks, but the sleeker, more elegant pintails with their lovely cinnamon-brown heads.

"Let's stop paddling," Luke said, "and all be really, really quiet. I see more ducks up ahead and we don't want to scare them away."

She rested the paddle on the sides of the kayak and

rotated her shoulders. Though they'd only been paddling for fifteen minutes or so, she didn't mind the break. She was strong from toting Ariana and handling stock at the store, but kayaking used her muscles in a different way.

The boat drifted and the surface of the water settled to stillness, reflecting the few clouds in the blue sky. Sunshine warmed her shoulders through her sweater. The only sound was the chirping and twittering of birds in the reeds and scraggly bushes along the shore, and an occasional call or laugh drifting across the water from the teen paddle-boarders.

A cluster of half a dozen ducks swam lazily past, their webbed orange feet visible through the clear water. These were mallards, and the flashy green heads of the males were dazzling in the sun. The boys pointed and grinned, but kept their mouths shut. They were darned cute.

She glanced over at the other kayak, to see their dad leaning forward to whisper something to Ariana. The sight of his chestnut head so close to her black-haired one tugged at something in Miranda's heart.

It was a perfect moment, one she'd happily have held on to forever.

I'm happy, she realized with surprise. *This is what happy feels like.*

Luke paddled closer to shore and reached up to tug a twig off one of the bushes. The ducks had gone by now, the ban on speech over, and when he held up the twig, he said, "Pussy willow," and gave it to her daughter.

Ariana stroked it and said, "Soft."

Miranda steered the kayak closer. "What's that?"

"You don't know pussy willow?" He gave his head a brief shake. "No, I guess nature was never a big part of your life." Reaching again, he separated another twig from a branch, and extended it toward her.

She put the paddle down again and reached for it. The

twig had no leaves yet, just furry gray buds. Gently she stroked one. It felt like the fur of a tiny, smoke-colored kitten. She smiled at her daughter. "Soft like a kitty, Ariana."

In front of her, the boys had turned around, curious. She extended the twig to Caleb, who put down his paddle and touched a bud with a cautious fingertip. "That's cool."

"Very cool," Luke said. "Right, Brandon?"

"I guess. Can I paddle now?"

"In a few more minutes," his dad said. "We need to get to Rainbow Days, where we can go ashore."

They resumed paddling, and perhaps ten minutes later rounded a small point and entered a cove with another beach, the sand brownish and coarse like at the park. On a slope of rough grass was a string of ten or twelve log cabins, each with a picnic table and barbecue in front. A wooden dock extended into the lake, and nearby she saw colored kayaks, canoes, and rowboats. On the beach, children played and a number of adults lay on deck chairs or towels.

"Tourist season's already starting," Luke said. "This place is always full from May through the Labor Day weekend."

"That's the story of the island, isn't it?" She'd learned that the islanders had a love-hate relationship with the tourists. While residents felt proprietary about Destiny and hated having to share it with transients, many local businesses and artists only survived because of those tourists.

"Let me go ashore first," Luke said, "and get Ariana safe on the beach, then you and Caleb can paddle in and I'll help you get out."

"The kayak tips," Caleb said. "You can fall when you get in or out."

"Thanks for telling me," she said. "Let's stop paddling,

Caleb, and we'll drift. Brandon, you keep a watch and let us know when your dad's ready for us to come in."

"Okay," he agreed.

Luke was quick about getting himself and her daughter out of their kayak and tugging the craft a few feet up the beach. He took the orange bag from the storage compartment. When he gestured to them, Brandon said, "Paddle now!" and she obeyed, with Caleb contributing his best efforts.

On shore, Luke was taking pictures with one of their phones, but he put the phone in his pocket as they reached shore. He caught the bow of the kayak and used the attached rope to pull the boat in a bit, and then he assisted first Brandon and then Caleb to climb out. He then pulled the boat even higher so she wouldn't get her feet wet, and even though she didn't need the hand he offered, she took it anyhow.

"This is fun," she said, letting her eyes tell him that she was referring to his company, not just the outing.

When she noticed Brandon eyeing their linked hands, she casually let go, claimed her camera, and walked a few feet along the beach, shaking out her arms and shoulders. "Paddling is harder work than it looks." She snapped pictures of her daughter, who looked adorable in her little orange life vest. "Having fun, sweetie?"

Ariana's brown eyes were dazzly with sunshine and excitement. "Fun. I kay-ak!"

After Miranda had taken pictures of Luke and the boys, they climbed back into the boats. Caleb and Brandon swapped positions, and this time Luke put Ariana in the front seat of his kayak. "Now remember," he said, "that you have to sit. You can't stand up."

Miranda was glad that he didn't go on and tell her that if she did, the kayak might tip them into the water. Ariana wasn't big on cause and effect yet, but if she did manage to grasp his point, she just might want to tip the boat so she could go swimming.

Fortunately, her daughter behaved herself as they paddled back, and when they arrived they found that the park was busier than before. Luke carried the kayaks and vests back to his SUV and returned carrying a cooler and Miranda's backpack. The dogs bounded ahead of him, delighted to be released from confinement.

For a few minutes, it was a jumble of kids and dogs, but Miranda didn't mind one bit. All up and down the beach, and in the park by the picnic tables, the same thing was happening.

This was what real families did on weekends. Parents didn't leave their kids alone in dingy apartments with empty cupboards. They didn't bring back men with rough voices and needles full of drugs.

She shook away the past, noticed a group leaving one of the picnic tables, and hurried over to claim it. Luke herded the kids and dogs in her direction.

A squirrel scampered over, probably anticipating handouts. Ariana cried out in delight, "Skir-rel!" She ran toward it, and the squirrel darted away and scrambled up the trunk of a tree and out on a limb, where it perched and scolded them.

"Skir-rel!" This time her daughter's cry was a frustrated one. Her face scrunched up and Miranda had that just-before-a-thunderstorm feeling of apprehension.

She went over to Ariana, hoping to forestall a TTT, but it was too late. With a sense of inevitability, she picked up her now-shrieking daughter. The calm had been too good to last. The adventures of the day had overstimulated Ariana, so no wonder she was now unraveling. "It's okay, sweetie," she murmured. "The squirrel just got scared.

Settle down now so we can enjoy our lunch. We've got all sorts of goodies."

"We do," Luke affirmed, beginning to lay out food on the picnic table. "Look, Ariana, we have peanut butter and jam."

But the little girl continued to wail.

Miranda said, calmly but more firmly, "Stop crying now, Ariana. There's nothing to cry about." Her daughter was getting old enough to understand that TTTs weren't acceptable, and that she could control her behavior.

Brandon pitched in, saying in a disparaging tone, "Big kids don't cry."

"Ethan cried," Caleb said more objectively. "He broke his arm. He's twelve! And Jang-mi cried when her mommy was sick." He turned to his dad, whose back was turned as he put paper plates on the table. "Daddy? Did you cry when Mommy died?"

Luke's back stiffened, and Miranda's heart went out to him. Slowly he turned, then he squatted and put a hand on his son's shoulder. "Yes, Caleb. I cried a lot. You're right, everyone cries sometimes. But I think what Brandon means"—Luke reached out with his free arm to draw his other son close—"is that big kids don't cry unless something really bad happens."

Swallowing a lump in her throat, Miranda realized that Ariana had stopped howling to listen. Seizing the opportunity, she told her daughter, "Listen to Luke, sweetie. You saw a cute squirrel, and that's a good thing. Not a bad one. We went kayaking and saw fish and ducks. That was a good thing. And now we're going to have peanut butter and jam sandwiches. It's all good, Ariana."

Glancing past her daughter, she saw Luke smiling at her, and she smiled back. Yes, it really was all good.

Soon they were seated at the table, the boys on one side and she and Luke on the other with Ariana between them.

Everyone had a can—or sippy cup in Ariana's case—with his or her preferred cold drink, and a paper plate with a collection of snacks. Honey and Pigpen sat in the shade under the table with a bowl of water and whatever scraps the boys could manage to sneak them without Luke noticing.

"Caleb has lipstick," Brandon said, pointing at his brother. "Just like Grandma Sonia."

"Do not," the boy protested.

Seeing a smudge of red above Caleb's lip, Miranda reached across the table and removed it with her thumb. Smiling at him, she said, "Brandon can't tell lipstick from strawberry jam. And speaking of which, these are excellent sandwiches somebody made." They did taste good, oozing messily with an overabundance of peanut butter and jam. The slices of cheddar and mozzarella and the veggie sticks, in contrast, had been cut with surgical precision.

"We did, we did!" Brandon crowed. "Me and Caleb."

She pretended surprise. "Wow, you guys are really good cooks."

Caleb studied her and then said, "You could come for dinner tonight."

"For dinner?" Wow again. Was she winning one of the twins over?

"We have hot dogs," Brandon chimed in.

She wasn't sure whether he really wanted her to come, or was just trying to outdo his brother. Nor was she sure she wanted to go. She could always plead the family dinner at SkySong as an excuse, but really, there'd be no problem missing it. She had spent lots of time with Eden's family over the past month, as they all helped Helen, Jim, and Kelsey get settled in their new house.

"And salad," Caleb said. "Our grannies like salad."

"I like salad, too," Miranda confirmed. Ah yes, the grannies. The women who thought Luke deserved better than her. She touched her dragon, on proud display below the short sleeve of her pink T-shirt. She hadn't let Sonia's and Annie's opinions stop her from coming today—and she'd had a wonderful time.

"And cake," Brandon said. "Or pie. Sometimes cake *and* pie."

"Cake!" Ariana contributed.

"I definitely like cake and pie," Miranda said, smiling, letting herself be tempted.

"It's the family Sunday night dinner," Luke said, and she gazed at him, trying to determine if he was warning her off or if he wanted her there.

"Mom and Grandpa Randall are both great with desserts," he said. "You should come, Miranda."

She met his warm gaze and thought, with that same unexpected realization as earlier, *I'm happy.* When Sonia and Annie had asked if she was happy, she hadn't known how to answer because she'd never let herself think much about happiness. But now she knew she was a person who could be happy. That knowledge, combined with her dragon courage and Luke's support, told her she could face the two older women with at least some measure of confidence.

"I'd like that." She smiled at Luke and then across the table to his sons. "Thanks, guys."

Chapter Fourteen

Luke was glad the boys had started warming to Miranda. Now if only his parents and in-laws would behave.

Three hours after he'd dropped Miranda and her daughter back at SkySong, he was ushering the pair into the kitchen at his house. It was a bit of a chaos zone since everyone had arrived at more or less the same time.

Miranda certainly looked good, in a long-sleeved blue top that matched her eyes, worn with tan pants. Sea glass earrings danced like miniature wind chimes when she moved her head. They'd shared a hug at the door, which was all that seemed appropriate in the circumstances, but each time he was with her, he felt a growing need to touch her in increasingly intimate ways.

Inside the kitchen door, Ariana glued herself to her mother's side and stared at everyone as he made the introductions. Then he said, "Boys, how about you take the dogs and hang out in the playroom?"

After their noisy departure, Annie, a gleam in her pale gray eyes, addressed Miranda. "So you didn't let Sonia and me scare you off."

"Mom. Annie." Luke glanced from one to the other with a hint of warning. He had respected Miranda's wishes and not asked what they'd said to her at the community hall. But when he'd told them she was coming tonight, he'd said he expected them to be courteous.

Before either responded, Miranda said, "Maybe for a moment or two. But you made me think. And here's what I realized. I'm not perfect."

"No one's perfect," he said, because it was true.

"No, they're not," Miranda said. She looked at his mom. "As for me, I'm a much better person than I used to be, and I'm a person who can be happy." She turned to Annie. "I know how to love with all my heart and if you have any doubts about that, just ask my daughter or my brother."

Luke was proud of Miranda for standing up to them. Whatever insecurities plagued her, she seemed to be getting past them.

"So, I'm here," she said evenly. "I've come for dinner." Holding up a cloth tote bag, she added, "And I've brought cheese puffs. Or *gougères*, if you want to be fancy about it."

"Mmm," Forbes said, stepping forward to take the bag from her. "Sounds delicious. Welcome, Miranda."

Was Luke the only one who noticed that Miranda's shoulders sagged a little, as if a burden had been lifted? He stepped closer and said, "*Gougères*? Did you make those?"

"They're a bread basket specialty at a restaurant where I once worked." She spoke loudly enough so everyone could hear. Then she tipped her head up to him and whispered, "When Chef Emile dumped me and got me fired, I stole his recipe. I don't feel an iota of guilt."

He grinned. "Nor should you."

Fingers tugged at the leg of his jeans and he looked down to see Ariana staring up at him, looking unhappy. He bent and hoisted her up, and announced to the group, "Ariana went kayaking for the first time. She did great."

Now she smiled, confirming, "I kay-ak."

"Tell them what you saw," he prompted.

"I see fish! I see ducks. I see kitty . . . kitty . . ." She gazed up at him for help.

"Pussy willows," he supplied.

"Yes! Soft."

Miranda smiled at her daughter and then turned to Luke's stepfather. "Forbes, I really enjoyed B-B-Zee the other night. Your music was great. And you have a terrific voice."

Sonia linked her arm through her husband's and teased him, "Looks like you have a new groupie." The smile she gave Miranda was warm and Luke realized that he should have told Miranda that the way to his mom's heart was through praising her husband.

She grasped the point quickly because she raved a little longer and then said, "I love Julian's music, too. I've been a big fan ever since I first heard him years ago."

And there was the way to Forbes's heart—even more than complimenting his own music.

Luke bounced Ariana in his arms, sensing it was time to find her something more fun to do than listen to adults. His mom must have the same idea because she came over and said, "Hi, Ariana. Aren't you the prettiest little girl?"

"I pretty," the child agreed, smiling at her.

"My name is Sonia and I'm Luke's mommy."

"Luke!"

His mom glanced at Miranda. "I could take her to the playroom, if you don't mind trusting me with your adorable little one."

"Of course. That would be great."

Sonia touched Ariana's hand. "How would you like to come with me, honey? I bet we can find a stuffed animal to play with."

"Kitty?"

"Maybe not a kitty, but I know there's a doggy and a—"

"Pig-pen! I play Pig-pen," she said happily as Luke put her down.

After confirming that Miranda was good with that, his mom took Ariana's hand and the pair left the kitchen.

It didn't take the rest of them long to organize the food and get the serving dishes for the main course onto the dining room table. Earlier, when he and the boys had set the table, he'd had to think about where to seat Miranda and Ariana. Everyone else had a customary seat, and the only vacant chair was at the other end of the table, where his pregnant wife had once sat. But life went on, and he tried not to give too much meaning to putting Miranda there, with a booster-seated chair for Ariana beside her.

He was both sorry and glad that she was so far away. There'd be no inadvertent or not-so-inadvertent brushes of hands as they passed food, or of elbows as they ate. Given how attracted he was to her, that was probably a good thing, with all the older generation eagle eyes watching.

When everyone was seated, they dished out the food, with the twins even accepting servings of veggies. As usual, there was an eclectic assortment: lasagna, a green bean and almond casserole, Waldorf salad, Miranda's *gougères*, and the promised hot dogs.

They all dug in, and when he tasted the light, tasty cheese puffs, he told Miranda how great they were. Others echoed the compliment, and then his mother said, "Well, Miranda, I'd sure never have recognized you as that same high school student I taught. I must say, I do like the changes."

To Luke, that sounded like a bit of a backhanded compliment, and maybe Miranda felt the same way because her chin came up and her eyes narrowed, but all she said was a calm "Thank you, Sonia."

"What have you been doing in the years you've been off island?"

Luke saw tightness in Miranda's shoulders, but she didn't avoid the question. "Until I got pregnant, I was enjoying being single in Vancouver. Oh," she hurried to add, "nothing too wild and crazy. But it's a great city with so much to offer. Lots of places to walk, free events on the streets, art galleries and stores you can browse through, lots of music and theater. And of course a fantastic library. That was my favorite place."

"What work did you do?" Annie asked.

Miranda turned to her. "Mostly I worked in retail or in restaurants. The salesclerk jobs usually had better hours but waitressing had better tips. Plus I'd often get a meal, and leftovers to bring home. That was especially important since I had Ariana." She glanced back at Sonia. "I know that dropping out of high school wasn't the brightest move. Aaron was always after me to get my GED, but I wasn't motivated because no particular career appealed to me."

She leaned toward her daughter and broke a chunk of lasagna into smaller, more manageable portions for her to spoon up.

"But now you do have your GED," his mom said. "Luke tells me you're taking courses online in early childhood education?"

"Yes. Last year, I realized that I needed a better job, one with regular hours and a regular paycheck, to provide properly for Ariana. And I'd learned from being with her, and with our sitter's grandchildren, that I really love kids. I know daycare and preschool work doesn't pay a lot, but I'd enjoy doing it. Besides, I'd be able to take Ariana to work with me until she's ready for kindergarten."

Luke smiled at her, glad she'd found a career direction that suited her. He only hoped that once she got her certificate, she'd look for a job on Destiny.

"Loving your job is more important than how much money you make," Annie said.

Miranda straightened her shoulders and Luke could almost see her deliberating, and then she said evenly, "Sorry, but I disagree. The most important thing about a job is making enough to support your child."

His smile widened. Points to her for having the guts to differ with his strong-minded mother-in-law.

Annie blinked. "You're absolutely right. I of all people should have added that qualifier. I grew up poor. My parents always managed to keep us fed and clothed, but the clothes came from thrift shops and sometimes dinner was from a food bank."

Luke knew that Annie still grabbed much of her clothing from the island's thrift store but, thanks to Randall's love of cooking, their meals verged on gourmet.

"I had no idea," Miranda said.

"I was lucky. Neither of my parents are particularly bright, nor are my two siblings. But some genetic quirk made me a genius." She stated it as a fact without a hint of arrogance. "I whipped through school, got scholarships, started developing video games. A couple of supportive professors helped me make the right connections and, almost overnight, I had more money than I or my family had a clue what to do with. So you see, I realize how much luck plays into things. I had the luck to be born brilliant."

"And I had the luck to fall in love with Annie," Randall said, "and have her fall in love with me." He leaned toward his wife, clearly intending to kiss her cheek, but she intercepted the move and met his lips with hers. Chuckling, he said, "Yeah, I'm definitely lucky. But as I was saying, when I was a teen who wanted to be a photographer, research told me it was a tough way to make a living. As it happens, I've done okay, but Annie's income took the pressure off my shoulders."

Luke had considered himself the luckiest guy in the
world to be Candace's best friend, and then for the two of
them to fall in love. But that luck had turned out to be a
mixed blessing. Yes, he had two wonderful boys, and generous and supportive in-laws. But when you had loved so
long and so well, it left such a hole in your life and your
heart when you lost that person.

And now there was Miranda. Pretty and warmhearted
and sexy, yet prickly and damaged. She wasn't Candace.
No one could replace Candace. But she was special in her
own right, and she came with a bonus package: a little girl
who made his heart lift each time she crowed a delighted
"Luke!"

He was vaguely aware that his mom and Forbes were
talking about how lucky they'd been to meet. Now, catching Miranda's gaze on his face, he saw her raise her eyebrows in a question. Had she noticed that his mind had
wandered?

She seemed attuned to him, or was that his imagination?
He really wished now that, despite the curiosity of the older
adults, the two of them were sitting closer. It would be so
nice to touch her arm or rest his hand on her thigh. And
why shouldn't he? Everyone knew they were dating. Casual
touches were normal when a couple was dating.

Dating. Yes, that's what they were doing. He needed to
remember, as he'd told his mom once, that he wasn't auditioning Miranda for the role of wife. Not every dating relationship turned into a lifelong commitment. Yes, children
were involved, but what was wrong with kids seeing their
parents date? It would help them learn that there were different kinds of relationships, and that when ultimately you
fell in love and married, that was something truly special.

He was so damned inexperienced. For a moment he
resented the way he and Candace had bonded from the

beginning. It had meant neither of them had ever dated anyone else.

"Daddy? Daddy!" It was Brandon, hollering at him.

"Sorry. What?"

"We want to be 'scused."

"Please," Caleb added.

They had cleaned their plates, including their vegetables and Miranda's *gougères*. "You may be excused. We'll call you when it's time for dessert." He gazed down the table to see how Ariana was doing. She seemed contented as she nibbled a hot dog. Miranda caught his eye and gave him a questioning "Is everything okay?" smile.

He nodded and smiled back, wondering if they should have a talk. What was she looking for with him? From what she'd said about past relationships, she either fell irrationally in love with a guy or she dated purely casually. Obviously, she wasn't crazy in love with him, so she must think of this as casual. Yet she'd never involved Ariana in one of her casual relationships before.

He blew out a breath and stared down at his plate. Yeah, when it came to dating, he was way out of his depth. So for now, he'd eat and try not to worry about it.

Luke was so far away, down at the other end of the table, and Miranda almost felt like the people in between them— his parents to her left and his in-laws to her right—were a barrier guarding him from her. Not that the older people were being actively hostile, but *comfortable* wasn't the word that best described how she felt at this dinner table.

Okay, fine, she'd known it wouldn't be all warm, welcoming arms. Slowly she'd begun to win over Luke's boys, and maybe she could do the same with the rest of his family.

"Annie," she said, "I'd never played *Clue-Tracer*, but

when Luke told me you'd created it, I had to give it a try.
It's amazing."

"Yes, it is."

Coming from anyone else, the comment would have
sounded egotistical, but Miranda filtered it through the
insight Luke had given her, that Annie's bluntness wasn't
intended to be rude. "I know you're a genius, but it amazes
me that one mind can come up with something so imagina-
tive, yet also so intricate and detailed. Creativity and logic
don't always go together."

"That's for sure," Forbes said. "Thank God I have Sonia
for the logic part." He gave his wife a one-armed hug.

She rested her black-haired head on his shoulder. "And
I'm grateful for your wonderful musical talent and your
artistic creativity working with wood. They make my life
so much richer."

Miranda envied their easy affection and appreciation for
each other. Was it possible that she and Luke might some-
day be like that? Realizing she was gazing at him with an
unguarded expression that might well express longing, she
looked quickly away and checked on her daughter. Ariana
had stopped eating and was toying with what was left on
her plate, muttering to herself. Miranda moved the plate
away and took a napkin to her daughter's smeared face.

Forbes went on. "My mom says that, even back before I
can remember, I drove her crazy trying to make music with
whatever was at hand."

"Apparently," Sonia said, "I was a born teacher. Before
I even knew what a teacher was, I was making my dolls do
the same things I was learning myself." She laughed.
"Guess I was born with the instinct to boss people around."

"To instruct," Annie corrected, clearly not getting the
joke. "There's a difference. As for childhood hobbies, yes,
I was a nerd. Science, math, games, sci-fi books."

"When I was a kid," Randall said, "I was fascinated by the pictures my family took, and believe me, they took a lot. My uncle noticed my interest, and gave me a camera for my sixth birthday. Thereby sealing my fate." He turned to Miranda. "How about you? As a child, did you have any hobbies that indicated you'd end up wanting to work with little kids?"

The man seemed well-intentioned, no doubt wanting to make sure she didn't feel left out. But seriously, hobbies? If she told him her childhood obsession was having enough to eat, and her spare time was spent shoplifting, it wouldn't go over well. This conversation only reinforced how different she was from these people. But she hunted for something to say, and came up with, "My biggest hobby was, and still is, reading. We got books from the library, and when I was tiny, Aaron read to me. He taught me, and I must've gone through hundreds of books. But no one's going to pay me to read books—and if they did, that might take the fun out of it."

"You could review books," Annie said. "That would exercise your critical skills."

"Which I'd bet is exactly what she doesn't want to do," Luke said. "For some of us, hobbies are supposed to be about pure relaxation. Right, Miranda?"

She sent a grateful look down the long table, wishing he was beside her and she could squeeze his hand. "Exactly."

Ariana was wriggling. For once, Miranda was glad of the threat of a TTT. "I think it's time for my little one to excuse herself. Her quota of good behavior is nearing its end."

"Why don't you take her into the playroom?" Luke suggested. "And while you're there, make sure the boys aren't destroying anything." He glanced around the table, saying, "Everyone done? Let's clean up, and get dessert going." He smiled at Miranda. "We'll be sure to call you when it's ready."

"I should help," she protested.

"No need."

"Or you could," Sonia said, "and I'll entertain your daughter in the playroom. Nothing against my wonderful grandsons, but it's fun playing with a girl for a change."

"That would be great. But if she gets too fussy, come and get me."

"Gender is intriguing when it comes to child-rearing," Annie said. "No matter how you try to avoid instilling any of the antiquated sexist views about gender roles, it's almost impossible to prevent it. I think I'll come with you."

Barely managing to suppress an eye-roll, Miranda glanced at Luke. He made no effort to hide his amused grin.

It occurred to her that if she and Luke ever really got together, Ariana would have a very interesting upbringing with Sonia and Annie as grandmothers.

If. It was a gigantic "if" for so many reasons, she thought as she watched Sonia bear Ariana away in her arms, with Annie right beside them. The two women were such a contrast, not only in personality but in appearance: Sonia with her sleek black hair and cherry-red top, and Annie looking as if she still frequented thrift shops and only went to the hairdresser if someone dragged her there.

This evening, being a guest at someone else's family's Sunday dinner, reminded her of the first days at SkySong. She'd felt like such an outsider, only there because of Aaron's relationship with Eden. Now, after months of getting to know Eden and her family, she felt more comfortable, though always slightly removed. Here at Luke's house, it was hard to believe she could ever belong.

Ariana could. Loving a child was easy, and Ariana was generous in returning affection. Miranda could imagine Luke's parents and in-laws accepting her daughter into the fold. But when it came to an adult, an adult with her own unimpressive history and emotional baggage . . . No, it was almost impossible to imagine these people, who had loved the wonderful Candace so deeply, ever truly accepting Miranda.

Nor would they accept her if she sat staring at her empty plate, feeling sorry for herself. She sprang to her feet and began to gather dishes. If there was one thing she was good at, it was cleaning a kitchen.

She was in the middle of rinsing dishes and putting them into the dishwasher when a high-pitched shriek, distinctively her daughter's, almost made her drop a plate. "Damn. A tantrum. I'll go and—"

"Hang on a minute." Randall, who'd been putting packaged leftovers in the fridge, stopped and held up a hand. "Annie's good at dealing with tantrums."

"Yeah, she gives the kid a lecture on why they're not logical," Forbes said.

When Miranda chuckled, Forbes said, "No, seriously. She does. And it usually works."

Sure enough, in less than a minute the screaming ended. "I'm filing that trick away for future reference," Miranda said, going back to the dishes.

Their team worked efficiently, and soon dessert was on the table. She went down the hall to the playroom and stopped in the doorway, surprised to see Ariana on the floor with the boys, playing with trucks, while Sonia and Annie sat on a brown leather couch, watching.

"How did you stop her tantrum?" she asked the women.

"It wasn't us," Sonia said. "It was Caleb. He offered her a truck."

Ariana called out, "I play trucks, Mommy!"

"She likes to crash trucks," Brandon said approvingly.

"Uh, that's nice," Miranda said. "Thanks for letting her play with you, boys."

To the women, she added, "It seems my daughter has a savage streak. She and a friend's little girl were knocking over toys playing *Monster Bowling* the other day."

"Just because a child enjoys games that, on the surface, involve violence," Annie started, "it doesn't mean—"

"Sorry to interrupt," Sonia said, "but did you come to tell us that dessert's on the table, Miranda?"

"I did."

The boys jumped up and raced down the hall, and Sonia said, "We don't want to keep everyone waiting."

Miranda collected Ariana, who was still happily smashing one truck into another, and everyone took their same seats at the table. Mostly she avoided giving Ariana sugar, especially in the evening, so she'd brought a plastic container of fruit salad. "You get a special dessert, sweetie," she told her as she added a tiny portion of German chocolate cake.

Fortunately, her child bought it. "I special!"

As everyone else served themselves chocolate cake and strawberry cheesecake, Annie said, "Miranda, you can tell Di SkySong that she doesn't need to worry about Starshine."

"Starshine?" Sonia queried. "The girl who left the commune?"

"Correct. Now, I don't know whether she did suffer abuse at the commune, but there's a high probability that she did leave the island safely and is now living in Sedona, Arizona. Married, no children."

"Good heavens," Sonia said. "How did you find that out?"

Randall said, "It's best not to inquire about her methods. Trust me on this."

"Ha ha," Annie said without humor. "Most people have no idea how much information is out there, and how accessible it is."

"But you didn't even know her name," Miranda said.

"I knew what she looked like, so—"

"How?" Luke asked.

"I went to see Gertie Montgomery."

Miranda gaped at her. She'd thought Eden was the tiniest bit obsessive about needing answers to unsolved puzzles, but Annie had her beat. Fascinated, she listened as Luke's mother-in-law went on.

"In lucid moments, she told me about the girl's distinctive white-blond hair, worn very long and parted in the middle as was the hippie style. I checked the *Destiny Gazette* archives, but had no luck. The hippies were reclusive and there were almost no pictures, and none with a girl of that description. However, I could estimate Starshine's age, and the probability was that she was a runaway."

She straightened her glasses and went on. "I had a time frame, as the commune only existed for around three years. Although not all runaways would have been reported, nor all records from that time period digitized, I found one young woman with that same distinctive hair color. Frida Larsson, from Washington. She did return home to her parents, but only briefly. She moved to Sedona and married some years later. Her name is now Frida Jones. There's a high probability that she's Starshine. I was going to contact her to verify, but Randall said that might be seen as intrusive."

Miranda's mouth had fallen open as she listened to Annie's recital. Working on her crime-solving video game had clearly given her lots of resource tools, and Miranda had to wonder if all of them were strictly legal. She wasn't about to ask.

"I'm sure Di and Seal will be happy to hear the news," she said. And Eden would love to have the mystery solved. "And yes, I think it's best to leave any follow-up to them." If the two old hippies preferred not to revisit their commune days, Frida/Starshine might feel the same way. "By the way, Annie, did you find any trace of Merlin?"

"No. I admit to failure there. I'm quite sure he was Otto Kruger, but I can't find a trace of him after the commune days."

"Poof, he vanished like magic," Forbes said. "As befits his name."

"Of course he didn't," Annie said. "I believe he must have died at the commune."

"What?" Miranda's shocked question was echoed all around the table.

"It's the only logical conclusion. Otherwise, my research would have located him. I'm very skilled."

"I'd tend to believe her," Randall said.

"But," Luke said, a frown tugging at his handsome features, "how could he have died and none of the commune members known about it?"

"Of course someone knew about it," Annie said. "The first possibility is that he died of an overdose or natural causes, and some or all of them disposed of his body. Which they well might do because as I said the commune members were reclusive."

"I knew Merlin," Forbes said. "Only briefly, because I didn't like him and I left the commune. But I believe he would have preferred a nature-oriented spiritual ceremony. Not the formalities society would impose."

"But his family should have been notified," Sonia said.

"A number of hippies had cut ties with their families," her husband pointed out. "That seemed to be the case with Merlin. Otto Kruger. Whatever."

She shook her head, clearly having trouble relating to that.

"Annie," Luke said, "if that's the first possibility, what's the second?"

"That he was killed and his killer disposed of his body

and no one else knew, or a group of them were in on either the murder and/or the disposal." She frowned around the table. "Why do you all look so stunned?"

Miranda felt like her eyes had widened so far that they might pop out of her head. Luke looked equally shocked as he exchanged glances with her.

"Uh, because we are," Randall said. "Why didn't you tell me this before?"

"I was going to, but I got caught up in developing my new commune game and forgot until now." She turned to Miranda. "You'll tell Di and Seal?"

"And Eden and Aaron. They're interested in the mystery, too."

"What do we do now?" Sonia said. "If there was a death at the commune, should we report it to the police?"

"Technically, yes," Annie said, "but what's the point? Otto Kruger has no living relatives except extremely distant ones, and they've believed him to be dead all these years anyhow."

"Isn't justice the point?" Sonia asked.

"If a few hippies buried or cremated a body in a spiritual ceremony and didn't notify the authorities," Forbes said, "I don't see that as a huge crime. But if it was murder . . ." He turned to look at Miranda.

She realized that the other adults' eyes were on her, while the children, in happy oblivion, ate their dessert. "Di and Seal," she said slowly, realizing what everyone was thinking. The couple weren't her relatives, and yet she felt defensive on their behalf. "They told Eden that Merlin disappeared. They didn't know anything more than that." She glanced around. "You all know them. They have integrity, right?"

"I did say that only one person or a few people might have been involved," Annie said.

"They have integrity," Forbes said, measuring out his

words. "But they have that same thing I do, and a number of other Destiny Islanders. We aren't fans of many of society's rules. We've learned to get along in our fashion, not rock the boat too much, but back in the sixties and seventies we were really antiestablishment and we made more waves. We protested, marched, and practiced civil disobedience."

"What are you saying?" Miranda asked.

"Di and Seal never opted into the institution of marriage, right?"

"No, they did a personal thing, a commitment ceremony." She'd seen pictures of the two of them, young and beautiful with their long hair and glowing faces. "You're saying that if someone died . . ."

"If someone who chose to live on—to lead—a commune died, wouldn't it be the moral act to honor him with a spiritual ritual at that commune? Not to turn his body over to the establishment to deal with in its coldhearted fashion?"

Di and Seal would no doubt still prefer it. She nodded. "And if that happened, then the commune members would have a pact of silence, so none of them got in trouble."

"That's what I'm thinking," Forbes said.

She was just coming to terms with that, understanding that it wasn't such a bad thing, when Annie said, "Or of course, as I said, maybe someone killed Merlin."

Chapter Fifteen

It was shortly after eight when Luke came downstairs from checking on the twins. His parents and in-laws had gone through the Sunday night ritual of tucking in the boys and reading them bedtime stories, and had taken their departure five minutes earlier.

"Sound asleep," he reported to Miranda as he entered the playroom. She was sitting at one end of the leather couch, her sock-clad feet curled up under her. "Fresh air and exercise are the best way of getting them to bed on time."

"Works on her, too," she said with a nod toward Ariana, who'd dozed off during dessert and was now sleeping wrapped in a blanket on the seat of a recliner chair.

Luke held out his hand. "Let's go to the front room where we can talk without disturbing Ariana." Miranda let him pull her up, and he kept her hand as they walked down the hall.

In the large front room, he chose a sofa with an ocean view and they seated themselves side by side. He rested his hand on her knee, happy to be touching her even if it was through the cotton of her tan pants, but wanting so much more than that. "The others often stay and talk for another hour or so," he said. Tonight, though, they'd somehow all had other things they needed to do.

"I chased them off?"

He shook his head. "I think they wanted to give us a chance to be alone."

This was his perfect opening for discussing the nature of their relationship, but before he could find the right words, she said reflectively, "That was weird, eh?"

"Uh, that they seem to approve?"

"No, sorry, that's not what I meant. Though"—she gave a soft laugh—"it would be kind of weird if they approved of me, and I'm not sure they do yet. But no, I meant what Annie said about Merlin."

His brain shifted gears. "I know. Coming from anyone else, I'd say it was pure fantasy. But Annie's credible. Are you going to talk to Di and Seal?"

"I'm sure they'd like to hear that Starshine seems to be okay. But the Merlin thing . . ." She shook her head. "I think I'll talk to Eden first. They're her aunt and uncle. She should decide if she wants to ask them about it."

"Makes sense."

"Annie's interesting, isn't she?"

"That's for sure. Can you imagine being married to her?"

"Not so much. But she and Randall seem to have a genuine connection."

"They're both creative."

"Idiot." She whacked his hand gently with hers, and then left it resting atop his. "I meant emotionally."

"Oh, yeah. Right. Yes, they do. He says she keeps him on his toes." And the gentle pressure of Miranda's hand was warming him down to his toes. "She says he keeps her grounded. She also says the sex is hot, which is not something I really needed to know but as you've seen, she doesn't have many filters."

"She's big on honesty, that's for sure."

And there was another opening. This time, he leaped in before it could close. "On the subject of honesty . . ."

Her hand twitched. "Uh-oh. I noticed you were kind of quiet at dinner. A few times it looked as if you were miles away. It must have been odd for you, having me there." She dropped her head, studying her hand resting on top of his. "Were you thinking of Candace?"

"Yes. And us. I like being with you, having you in my house, seeing you and the boys getting along. Having Ariana around, too. But I'm not sure what we're doing."

"And you need to know?" she asked wryly.

He gave a half-hearted laugh. "I want to make sure we're on the same page. You know this is a first for me. And you've said you've never, uh, brought a man home to meet your daughter, so this is a first for you."

She chuckled at his phrasing. "For what it's worth, she clearly approves."

"So what I'm thinking is, can we just date?"

Her eyebrows pulled together. "I thought we were. Oh, d'you mean without the kids?" Her frown deepened.

"No. Well, yeah, sometimes, because I like being alone with you. But I also like doing family stuff like going kayaking. No, what I mean is, can we just date and see where it goes? Not put a lot of pressure or expectations on it."

Her frown had dissolved and now she smiled. "That's exactly what Glory said."

He and Candace had gone to school with Glory McKenna, and he'd always liked her. "You talked to Glory about us?" The idea of girl talk fascinated and kind of horrified him. What had Miranda said about him?

"A little. It's what girlfriends do, and she's becoming my friend. I even babysat on Friday, so she and her partner, Brent, could go dancing at the community hall."

Luke was glad she was making friends. Anything that tied her to Destiny Island was good by him. "What advice did she give?"

"She said we should have fun and see where things go." A mischievous smile curved her lips. "The subject of big hands came up."

"Big hands?" He glanced down at his. "You've lost me."

"I might have mentioned that you have big hands."

"O-kay . . ."

"She might have suggested that I find out what those big hands are capable of."

And now he got it. So suddenly, so intensely, that blood pounded through his veins and he was instantly aroused. He swallowed hard before he could speak. "What do you think of that suggestion?"

Her dark brown lashes slowly fluttered down and then back up. "Watching when you were treating that bunny, your hands fascinated me. They're so big and masculine but they're so gentle and . . . deft." Another blink. "Are they like that when you touch a woman?"

The only woman he'd touched that way was Candace, from their first teen fumblings through to their experimentation with *Kama Sutra* positions. She'd always seemed satisfied, but then she'd never been with another guy. Performance anxiety dried his mouth and he had to swallow before he could say, "I don't know."

Her flirtatious expression turned to surprise. "Wow. That's honest."

"I'm not going to lie to you." He hoped she got the subtext: that he wasn't like those other guys she'd been with.

"Hmm." A twinkle lit her blue eyes. "So, since you don't know and I'd love to know, we'll just have to find out." She uncurled her legs, rose, and sat down again—on his lap, straddling him. Not close enough to press against his erection, which was probably a good thing if he was going to retain an ounce of sanity. He and Candace had often made love with her on his lap, and his body ached for the sensation of bare skin against bare skin, of his hot hardness slipping inside a tight, moist sheath.

Miranda touched a hand to the side of his face, running warm, featherlight fingers from his brow past the outer corner of his eye. She fanned them so that she brushed his cheek and his ear, then she explored his jaw, and then a finger traced the outline of his mouth.

Everywhere she touched, he felt tingly pulses of sensation. There was nothing overtly erotic in what she was doing, but that was how his body interpreted it.

She lowered her hand and said, "Very nice."

"Now I get to touch you?" When he thought about the parts of Miranda he most wanted to caress, her face, much as he liked it, didn't top the list. But with an open door, and her little girl and his two boys sleeping in the house, things couldn't get too hot and heavy.

"Close your eyes," she said.

"What?"

"You heard me."

He and Candace had always gazed into each other's eyes, sharing their souls. That was as intimate as you could get, so why did the idea of closing his eyes make him feel vulnerable? But whatever Miranda might do, or make him do, he figured it would involve more pleasure than pain. So he obeyed, forcing his reluctant lids to stay closed until the tiny muscles relaxed.

"Now"—she took his hand—"touch my face."

He knew her face, the teen version and the adult one. In school, he'd spent too much time sneaking peeks at her— fascinated and to his shame a little turned on. Her Goth style mightn't have caused second looks in Vancouver, but in Blue Moon Harbor it had made a statement. Stark black, weirdly streaked hair contrasted with near-white skin; either she'd worn pale makeup or, like a vampire, avoided the sun. Exaggerated, sultry eye makeup, near-black lipstick, and piercings everywhere had made him wonder why she was so dissatisfied with what she saw when she got up in the morning and looked in the mirror.

The adult, natural version was much more appealing because it didn't conceal, it revealed her pretty features and her expressions. This face, he'd spent a lot of time looking at, openly and without guilt. What more could he possibly learn about it?

But of course he would give her what she'd asked for, and when she raised his hand and pressed it to the side of her face, he smiled at how soft and warm her skin felt. She took her own hand away, and cautiously, keeping his eyes shut, he spread his fingers. "Close your eyes, too," he suggested, scared he'd poke her in the eye.

"Mmm, good idea. Then I can concentrate better on the sensations."

Okay, that was a sexier interpretation. He traced her hairline upward to her forehead, his fingertips transmitting information: silky skin over firm bone; fine hairs springing from her scalp and tickling his fingers. Smooth forehead, the arch of her eyebrows, the angle of her cheekbones. He followed one to her left ear and skimmed the shell, then rested a finger on the silver heart earring. "You always wear this one."

"I bought it when Ariana was born."

"Nice." His fingers tracked back to her face and explored her cute little nose, which ended in a slight upward curve. And then the shape of her mouth, a puff of breath warming his fingers as she parted her lips. The tip of her tongue touched his finger and his body tightened.

"Nice," he said again, and with his eyes still closed he leaned forward to place his lips where his fingers had been. Miranda gave a sigh of welcome and shaped her mouth to his. And now, rather than using their fingers, it was their lips that explored, familiarized themselves, and created erotic pleasure. As the kiss heated, they opened for each other and their tongues joined the party.

With a soft moan, she slid forward so the crotch of her pants rubbed against the fly of his jeans. When she wriggled against him, he grew so hard he was afraid he'd burst.

He cast a glance toward the door, ensuring they had no visitors. Then he slid a hand under the bottom of Miranda's long-sleeved top and stroked her back, from the long swoop of her shoulder and upper back down to the tender dip at her waist, skimming the back of her bra along the way.

He wanted the top off, the bra, everything else she was wearing. He wanted her naked, spread out on top of him like a blanket while he thrust inside her in long, slow strokes. Not that he could likely manage long and slow this time. He was so aroused that round one wouldn't last long. But Candace had always said there was nothing wrong with gulping down the appetizer, all the better to savor a lengthy, drawn-out feast.

Was it wrong to think about his wife when he was with Miranda? Was it disloyal to one or both of them? Even if it was, he couldn't turn off the thoughts, the memories, the comparisons. He wondered if Miranda was comparing him to Chef Emile, or to Ariana's father.

Her lips separated from his. "What's wrong? You tensed up."

"Sorry. It's just strange. I mean, it's great, but my brain doesn't want to turn off. I guess I'm nervous. And with the kids in the house, we shouldn't go too far."

She shifted her weight back. "But you want to? You want me?"

"Pretty desperately," he admitted. "I had some idea that we should go slow with this dating thing. I didn't want to be like those other guys you hooked up with so quickly. But I think I'm over that."

Humor glinted in her eyes. "Good to know. Because I don't want to wait much longer."

"Then we'll find a time when we can be alone. Soon."

Chapter Sixteen

The next night, Miranda was at another family dinner, this time at Aaron and Eden's log cottage in the woods. She had called Eden first thing this morning and told her about Annie's research. When she said that Starshine appeared to be living in Sedona, Eden said, on a note of surprise, "Sedona? Really? What else did Annie find out?"

Miranda said that Annie had researched Merlin, a.k.a. Otto Kruger, and shared the conclusions she'd drawn. Eden remained silent. "I'm not sure whether we should tell Di and Seal," Miranda finished. "Like, what if some kind of crime really was committed, and they knew?" Eden was a lawyer; she'd understand the implications way better than Miranda.

Eden had been quiet for a long moment, and then said, "Maybe this is selfish, but I can't stand not knowing. And I have a lot of trouble believing that Aunt Di and Uncle Seal would be involved with anything criminal."

"They might not have seen it that way." She told Eden what Forbes had said, about the antiestablishment views of a lot of the hippies.

"That makes sense," Eden had said thoughtfully. "Well, I think we need to find out the truth, and then we'll all decide how to handle it." In her typical businesslike fashion, she had arranged to host a family dinner. Of course she had to do it immediately, because unsolved problems drove her nuts. Miranda had said she didn't need to be there, it was a family thing, but Eden was having none of it. "You're the one who heard what Annie said. That's hearsay, but it's better evidence than me telling them what she told you. If you get what I'm saying."

She hadn't, exactly, but it was hard to refuse a determined Eden. So now here they all were, crammed into Aaron's living room, juggling bowls of chili and their drinks of choice. When he'd built the cottage with help from Lionel and other friends, Aaron had designed it to accommodate himself, plus a room for Miranda and Ariana—in hopes that, as had finally happened, she'd come to her senses and accept his help. He'd never envisioned falling in love, much less with a woman whose entire family now resided on the island. His kitchen table accommodated four. His living room was at least larger than the kitchen.

Seal was in a comfy chair with Di sitting in front of him lotus-fashion on a cushion on the floor. Eden's parents sat on the two-seater sofa, Helen Blaine juggling her chili bowl while Ariana, who'd eaten earlier, cuddled up with her head on Helen's lap, half asleep. It was wonderful to see Eden's mom looking healthy, her chemo-destroyed hair now a thick, stylish cap of gleaming silver, her cheeks brushed with color from the spring sunshine.

Kelsey sprawled by her mom's feet on another floor cushion. Aaron was in a second upholstered chair with Eden perched on the arm. She looked businesslike in a tailored shirt and pants with her walnut hair pulled back in a low ponytail. Likely she'd come home late from her job at Arbutus Lodge and not had time to change.

Miranda, with the choice of dragging in a kitchen chair

or sitting on the floor, had opted for a cushion on the floor. She'd placed it off to the side, hoping she wouldn't have to participate and hoping that no one minded her being here. Earlier, she'd had a private word with Aaron, who told her Eden had filled him in. Looking uncomfortable, he'd said he was there to support his fiancée, but would otherwise stay out of things, it being a Blaine family issue. Miranda had nodded in agreement.

For the first ten minutes, the chatter was general. Eden was eating quickly, not seeming to taste the chili Aaron had prepared. It was a significantly upscale version of one of his and Miranda's standard childhood meals, which had usually been meatless.

Eden spoke quietly to Aaron, who nodded. She rose and put her bowl on the hearth of the rock fireplace where on this unusually warm, early April evening no fire burned. "I invited you all here for a reason," she said, her voice strong and sure, slicing through the threads of chatter and silencing everyone. "Annie Byrne has been doing some research. The conversation we had at the community hall aroused her curiosity."

Miranda's gaze was on Di and Seal, so she saw how the relaxed lines of their bodies stiffened. She put down her own half-empty bowl, the better to focus on their reactions.

"There's good news," Eden said. "It's likely that Starshine is alive."

"That's hardly news," Di said in a tight voice. "We always assumed she was. And Gertie Montgomery, if her long-term memory can be trusted in the least, verified that Starshine left the island."

"Her real name," Eden went on, "was probably Frida Larsson. If so, she's married now and is Frida Jones. They live in Sedona."

Di had glanced up at Seal when Eden started out, and now said casually, "Probably?"

"Sedona?" Helen said. "Arizona? Isn't that where . . . ?" She broke off, looking confused.

"Isn't that where," Eden took it up, "you go each June, Aunt Di and Uncle Seal?"

What? Miranda managed to keep her mouth shut, but Kelsey cried, "What? Seriously?"

Jim Blaine took his wife's chili bowl from her and put it and his own on a side table. He wrapped his arm around Helen's shoulders as Eden went on. Ariana dozed, oblivious to the tension in the room.

"When I was here last summer," Eden said, "trying to find Lucy and interviewing everyone who'd lived at the commune, Aaron said you were off island. Everyone knows that you go every year, at the height of tourist season when SkySong could be fully booked. And that you never say where you've gone. Except, one night I happened to overhear you telling Mom about the energy vortexes in Sedona. That's where you go, isn't it? To visit Frida Larsson."

As Eden spoke, Di shifted position, reaching up to put her bowl on a table and ending up with her cushion beside Seal's legs rather than in front of him. She and Seal exchanged glances again, communicating in the nonverbal way of two people who know each other very well. And then, putting his bowl down, too, and resting his hand on Di's shoulder, Seal said, "Yeah, we visit her. What's the big deal?"

"I don't know," Eden said. "You two are the ones who're so secretive."

Di moistened her lips. "Frida is a private person. She's built a new life for herself in Sedona and she regrets her commune days."

"Seeing the two of you would be a reminder," Eden pointed out.

"We meditate together," Di snapped. "Sedona's a healing place with all the energy vortexes."

Miranda wasn't sure what energy vortexes were, but at the moment Di sounded anything but her usual serene self. As for Eden, her lawyer side was coming out.

"Annie also researched Otto Kruger," Eden said.

Seal and Di sat as if frozen. Helen said, "Who's Otto Kruger?"

"The original heir to the land the commune was located on," Eden said, not turning her gaze toward her mom. "And, most probably, Merlin."

"Are you saying Annie found proof that Merlin was—or is—this Kruger person?" Di asked. She rested her hand on top of Seal's where it lay on her shoulder, and said, with a casualness that struck Miranda as contrived, "Did Annie locate him, too? Is he still alive?"

On the sofa, Helen and Jim Blaine both looked intrigued. Kelsey, leaning against her mother's pant-clad legs, caught Miranda's gaze and shot her a "What's going on here?" look. Miranda shrugged, feeling a little guilty for having told Eden about Annie's research.

"Annie didn't locate him," Eden said.

Tension seemed to seep from Seal's shoulders as he said, "Guess he was more successful at disappearing than Frida was."

"That's not the conclusion Annie came to," Eden said. "Right, Miranda?"

Miranda would have preferred to remain a silent observer. Reluctantly she said, "Annie's confident of her abilities. I haven't a clue how she does her research, but she figures that if she couldn't find him, he, uh, isn't there to be found."

There was silence in the room. Finally Jim, who still had his arm around his wife, spoke. "Do you mean he successfully assumed a new identity?"

Miranda shot Eden a narrow-eyed gaze and kept her mouth shut. Di and Seal had been good to her. She didn't want to be the one to present Annie's hypothesis.

After a moment, Di said, "He liked his aura of mystery. And he was smart. If Otto Kruger became Merlin of the Enchantery, he could easily have become someone else, somewhere else."

Eden said, "That's not what Annie thinks. She believes Merlin never left the commune. That he died there and was buried or cremated."

"Died?" Kelsey said. "Like, seriously?"

"But people would have known," Helen said, stroking Ariana's shoulder, perhaps as much to calm herself as to soothe Miranda's sleeping daughter. "If he'd overdosed or had a heart attack or something, the commune members would have called a doctor. Wouldn't they?" She turned to her sister.

"But remember what Gertie said," Eden told her mom, who'd become friends with the elderly Alzheimer's patient. "Back then, there wasn't a doctor on the island. Gertie was the nurse at the two-room medical clinic, and a doctor visited the island for a couple of days a week."

"If a commune member was really sick," Di said slowly, "and the others weren't so stoned out of their minds that they didn't realize it, someone might have tried to get help."

"What if they *were* too stoned?" Helen asked, an edge to her voice. Miranda had learned, from the sisters' occasional discussions of the past, that while Di had been a rebellious hippie, her younger sister had been more of a "good girl." Helen's voice softened a bit and she added, "Or if the person died before anyone realized he was in trouble?"

When neither Di nor Seal answered immediately, Eden said, in a quiet voice that resonated with tension, "Or if

Merlin finally went too far and the girl he was abusing killed him?"

Miranda gasped, hearing the same sound echo around the room in feminine and masculine versions. Her gaze flew questioningly to Aaron's face, and he shrugged and gave her an apologetic look.

She scowled at him. He'd known about Eden's theory and not shared it with her.

No one was speaking. Eden's slim body almost vibrated with tension. So did Di's and Seal's, linked now by tightly clasped hands. Kelsey was leaning forward, bright-eyed with curiosity. Her mother, on the other hand, had shrunk into the shelter of her husband's arm, looking more like the frail woman who'd come to the island last fall, recovering after her cancer recurrence. All the same, it was she who spoke first. "Di? Did Merlin disappear and assume a new identity, or did Starshine kill him? Have you and Seal been protecting her all these years?"

Miranda happened to be looking at Di's and Seal's linked hands, and she saw the squeeze Seal gave his partner. Di gave him a rueful half smile. But, surprisingly, the tension faded from their faces.

"He was an evil man," Seal said.

Oh my God. Miranda let out a long breath.

"He kicked her in the belly," Di said. "Knowing she was pregnant with his child. She loved him, but he caused her miscarriage and she could have died. She hadn't even recovered when he was at her again. Not just sex, but violently abusive sex." She gazed at Eden, her blue eyes bright as a sunny sky. "What's that phrase defense lawyers always use? She snapped. Temporary insanity. Or self-defense. Take your pick."

"Starshine didn't commit a crime," Seal affirmed. "She

protected herself and she saved other women from his abuse."

"Uncle Seal's right," Kelsey said vehemently. "The asshole deserved to die."

"You knew," Helen said softly to Di and Seal. "Did everyone at the commune know?"

"Only a handful of us," he said. "The rest truly believed that he'd abandoned us."

What had they done with the body? Miranda knew that the question had to be on everyone's mind. She wasn't going to be the one to ask it.

Kelsey did. "So where's the body?"

"We buried him," Seal said. "He believed in cremation. He said it released the spirit into the world. We didn't want his spirit released, so we stuck him in the earth with the worms."

Aaron finally spoke, for the first time since Eden had started all this. "His body's still there?"

"As far as we know," Seal said.

Miranda had another, less grisly question and decided to ask it. "Why do you visit Starshine—Frida—each year?"

Di turned to her with a gentle smile. "She's fragile. She feels guilty and has never truly come to terms with what she did. She told her husband everything, and he's supportive but he doesn't really understand. No one can, who wasn't at the Enchantery." She glanced at Eden. "Merlin died in early June. It's a hard time for Frida. We go to offer support, to heal together, to help her get past it for another year."

Seal, too, fixed his gaze on Eden. "Now you know. It actually feels good to let go of the secret. But what are you going to do about it?" His mouth twisted in a grim smile that was unlike him. "Are you going to send us all to jail, Niece?"

"Eden!" Helen cried. "No, you can't. I don't really agree

with any of it, but in the context of the times, a defenseless girl being abused in a community that shunned the law— and, as I remember, was often condemned by the police without good reason . . ."

Now, finally, Ariana woke and wriggled around on the couch, her little fists and elbows poking Helen. Miranda rose and went over as Eden sighed and said, "I hear you, Mom. No, I'm not going to report anything to the authorities. Aaron and I talked about it and that's what we decided. But I wanted to know. I couldn't let it go until I knew the truth."

Miranda lifted her daughter into her arms and rocked her.

Eden studied her parents and sister. "If we told anyone, it would only hurt Aunt Di and Uncle Seal, and poor Frida."

"Lips zipped," Kelsey said, raising her fingers to reinforce her words with the gesture.

"Of course," Jim said, and Helen nodded.

Eden focused on Miranda. "How about you? Will you keep the family secret?"

It's not my family, she wanted to protest. But that fact wasn't relevant. "I will."

"What if Luke asks whether you passed on what Annie said?" Eden asked. "What if Annie persists in her research?"

Miranda blew out a puff of air as she considered. Slowly she said, "I wouldn't know how to discourage Annie from doing more research. But she seemed satisfied with her conclusions. Her energy's focused on a new game." Miranda only hoped the commune game didn't feature a murder.

Ariana was knuckling her eyes and wriggling in Miranda's arms, her face scrunching up like she was thinking about crying.

"And Luke?" Eden said. "You two are dating. When you care about someone, you should be honest with him. But this isn't your secret. It's Di's and Seal's and Frida's."

"I know. I understand the difference." Oh, how she hated being put in this position. Even though her curiosity had been satisfied, she'd rather not have known the truth.

The next evening, Miranda had tucked Ariana into bed and read the "cake" board book for the thousandth time. She was ready to turn on her computer and start on coursework when a knock sounded at her door. Figuring it would likely be Di or Seal, she was surprised to see Eden standing on the porch. Glancing past her guest, she saw Eden's car, but no Aaron.

"Hey there, I didn't expect to see you again so soon," Miranda said. "Come in. Uh, do you want a cup of tea or anything?"

"No, thanks." She stepped inside, kicked off her shoes, but didn't take off the light jacket she wore over jeans. Choosing an upholstered chair, she perched on the edge rather than sinking back into it.

"If you're worried about me sharing Di and Seal's secret, I really won't. I promise. You didn't have to drive over to persuade me."

"Thanks, I believe you. That's not why I came. There's something else I wanted to ask you about. I'm doing scheduling."

"Scheduling? Oh, d'you mean wedding stuff?" If so, why did Eden look so tense? Miranda took the couch across from her, pulling up her yoga-pant-clad legs to sit cross-legged.

"Do you realize, the wedding's in three weeks and I haven't bought a dress?"

"Haven't you?" Now her anxious expression made sense. "I'd have thought that was a priority."

"I've been busy. New job, other stuff to plan." She waved

a hand. "Besides, I'm a standard size so I shouldn't need fittings."

"What do you need me to do?" Joking, she added, "I may be a whiz at shortening pants and mending rips, but that's where my sewing skills end. I won't offer to make your dress."

A smile lightened Eden's tense expression, but only temporarily. "You can come shopping with me. Aaron or Jillian will fly us all over to Vancouver on Thursday or Friday, if you can get the day off. There's a bridal salon that, from what I've seen online, looks perfect. But I've lined up a couple of others just in case. And we can have a lovely lunch, drink some wine, have a fabulous day." Her words came out faster than usual.

"Us all?"

"Mom, Kelsey, Aunt Di, you, and me. You all need dresses, too, since you're part of the wedding party."

"Oh, uh . . ." Eden's mother, along with her dad, would walk her down the aisle—which, if the weather cooperated, would be a petal-strewn grass one on the grounds of SkySong. Di was the matron of honor, Kelsey was a bridesmaid, and Eden had asked Miranda to be her other bridesmaid. That was sweet of her, as was inviting Miranda along on the dress-shopping expedition, but she had to know Miranda and Ariana didn't really belong. "If you want the bridesmaids' dresses to match, pick out something that Kelsey's happy with, and it'll be fine with me. I'm a standard size six."

"You don't want to come?" Miranda would have expected her to look relieved, but instead she looked almost hurt.

"Look," Miranda said, "you guys are all family. You'll have a great time together. You don't need me, and besides, with Ariana throwing TTTs on a whim, you don't want her at some fancy bridal salon, so—"

Eden shrugged off her jacket. "Sorry, I should have said. Dad and Uncle Seal are happy to look after her for the day. You trust them, right? Between them, they've helped raise five kids."

"Yes, I trust them, but . . ."

"You don't want to go," Eden said flatly.

"It's not that. Not exactly." She took a breath. This woman was going to be her sister-in-law. She was a good person and Aaron loved her to pieces. Miranda had to be honest with her. "Eden, it sounds like an amazing day. I've never had that kind of day in my life. But it's *your* day. Those are all your people. Your relatives. I don't belong there."

Eden leaped to her feet, rushed over, and dropped down in front of Miranda. Staring earnestly at her, she said, "You do. Or at least we all think you do. I wouldn't have had you there last night, Di and Seal wouldn't have trusted you with the truth, if we didn't all think of you as family. So why don't *you* think so? You're nice to all of us, but you never really want to be part of our family. Why not, Miranda? Is it us, or is it—"

"No, God no." Miranda hugged her arms around herself. "No, you're all great. But you're . . . a unit."

Miranda knew her words had been less than clear, but somehow Eden picked up on what she was trying to get at, because she responded, "Aunt Di and Uncle Seal weren't part of that unit until last summer. Yet they fit so naturally, and so could you. If you wanted to."

"It's not that I don't want to . . ." Or was it?

"Then why do you keep holding back?"

She wasn't sure of the answer herself, so how could she possibly explain it? "I'm sorry, Eden. I'd be happy to go on your shopping expedition. I have Thursday off, if that works for everyone else."

Eden's shoulders squared and she rose. Only to sit down on the couch beside Miranda. She curled her legs up so that one knee touched Miranda's. "It's because of how you grew up, isn't it?"

Miranda's muscles locked. After a long moment, she realized she wasn't breathing, and forced air into her lungs.

"Aaron told me all about your mom," Eden said quietly, her tone sympathetic. "I know that you and he only had each other to rely on. And then after she OD'd, her parents took you in, but they were horrible."

"Yeah, well. Sometimes life sucks." Miranda stared down at her thighs, not wanting to see Eden's expression or to have the perceptive woman read her own face. "We survived and we're fine."

"Better than fine in many ways. But Aaron was emotionally damaged. He didn't believe he'd ever find love. I mean, other than the love that's so strong between the two of you, and him and Ariana."

"I'm not like that," Miranda said wryly. "I always believe I'll find love. It just never happens."

"Do you really, really believe you'll find love?"

Finally Miranda glanced up. "Of course. Look at how many men I've fallen for."

"I don't know much about those relationships. I know Aaron thinks you're attracted to, uh, unsuitable men."

Though this conversation was anything but humorous, that phrasing startled a laugh from Miranda. "Unsuitable men? Oh man, what century do you come from?"

"I was trying to be polite. Okay, losers. Bad boys."

"Those aren't synonymous. Ariana's father is quite a successful actor. A chef I dated is getting rave reviews."

"But they're relationship losers, aren't they? Not the kind of men who are looking for anything serious."

"That turned out to be true," she admitted.

"So you fell in love with men who didn't want to fall in love back."

"Uh, not to be rude, but isn't that exactly what you did with my brother? But he changed his mind. Because of you. Because of what the two of you had together."

"We walked the path in parallel. In the beginning, we both only wanted a fling. But after that first week together, when I went back to Ottawa, we both realized it was more than that. He came out to see me, we talked, and we kept on talking. I'm guessing you didn't have a lot of relationship-type talk with the men you fell for."

"No, you're right. So that's a lesson learned. And, by the way, I haven't done the stupid-relationship thing in almost two years. Yes, I'm seeing Luke, but it's not like with those other guys. We *are* talking. Mostly, we're being friends and getting to know each other." And planning to have sex Friday night, which was a secret she wasn't about to share.

"That sounds really good. From what everyone says, he's a great guy. And that's what you and Ariana deserve. But it seems to me that, in past relationships, you were maybe, well, self-sabotaging."

"Huh? What's that mean?"

"Picking men who were emotionally unavailable."

"I didn't *pick* them. I met them and fell for them. I led with my heart, not some checklist in my brain."

"You led with a wounded heart. A heart that had been disappointed over and over by your mother and by your grandparents. A heart that maybe didn't truly believe that it deserved love, or that love would stick around and be trustworthy."

"I . . ." She would have been annoyed with Eden for

being so pushy and preachy if she hadn't seen honest concern and distress on the other woman's face.

"And since this is my night for being totally presumptuous, I'm going to go on and say that I wonder if that's what you're doing with me and my family. We want to welcome you in with open arms, but you can't let yourself trust in that because at heart you're still the little girl whose mom kept letting her down."

Was that what she'd been doing? "I've always tried to be independent," Miranda said in barely more than a whisper. "I don't think that's wrong."

"Of course it's not. But, excuse me for saying this, it seems to me you didn't do that with men. You've kind of got it backward. In my humble opinion. You trusted guys you barely knew, you gave your heart to men who didn't want the same thing you did. But when it comes to me and my family, you go all independent, not wanting to trust that we'll really be there for you. And we will. We're family, the right kind of family."

Eden gave a short, wry laugh. "Okay, except for maybe covering up manslaughter, but you know that's with the best of intentions. And we're not family that's messed up with drugs or that's cold and resentful and hurtful. We're good family, caring family. You saw that last night, didn't you?"

"I did. You are." Which made it even more difficult to imagine truly being one of them. And yet Eden didn't seem to have any trouble envisioning it.

Eden touched Miranda's arm. "And you're part of that family. Miranda, I want to be your sister. Not just the legal relationship we'll have when Aaron and I marry, but a sister of the heart. Will you let me?"

Eden's hand wasn't large but it felt so warm, resting

there like an offer of something amazing. An offer of love, steady and reliable.

Miranda blinked against a haze of tears. "I can see why Aaron fell in love with you. You're pretty special, Eden Blaine."

"And so are you, Miranda Gabriel. I want you for my sister."

Gazing through those tears, Miranda felt more naked than she'd ever felt in her life. And yet, somehow, stronger. "Then you've got me."

And then they were in each other's arms, both sobbing.

Chapter Seventeen

With relief, Luke saw Miranda's old silver Toyota drive down the street and pull into his driveway late Friday afternoon. She was twenty minutes late and he'd been afraid she'd had second thoughts. It had taken some planning on both their parts to organize this date—this sex date—and his anticipation level was through the roof.

He opened the front door as she jumped out of the car and hurried toward him, clad in a buttoned cotton shirt over a short denim skirt. "I'm sorry," she said as she came up the steps. "As I was leaving Glory's, Ariana decided to throw a TTT. There've been way fewer of them recently, but of course she had to pick that moment. I stayed to help settle her down."

"She's okay?" He ushered her inside and closed the door.

"Just doing her 'me-me-me' thing. Center of the universe, and not at all pleased that Mommy was deserting her." She put her purse on the table by the door and shook her head vigorously, sending blond curls flying. "But we got her distracted and I'm sure she'll be fine. And I'm here!" She beamed up at him and went up on her toes to press a quick kiss to his lips. Glancing around, she asked, "Everything went according to plan with the boys?"

"Yup. Mom and Forbes are feeding them and taking them to a movie. The theater's showing *Toy Story* and the boys haven't seen it on the big screen. We have at least three hours before they get back. Which is nowhere enough time for everything I'd like to do to you."

"Ooh, I want to hear about that." Her fingers went to the top button of her shirt. "But I also want to tell you about girls' day in Vancouver yesterday."

He'd much rather talk about sex—he'd much rather *have* sex—but women approached things in their own mysterious way. "Was the shopping trip a success?"

"We had so much fun." She was still unbuttoning, which was encouraging, but she didn't let the front of her shirt pull apart. "We all got great dresses, and we laughed so much. Drank too much wine, but who cares because no one was driving. Or flying. I mean, Aaron was flying, but he just dropped us off and picked us up again, he didn't spend the day with us."

She'd finished the buttons and held the shirt closed with one hand. "It wasn't just dress and shoe shopping, though. Eden needed fancy lingerie for her honeymoon. And the store we went to, wow, it was incredible." Now she let go of her shirt and in one slow, utterly feminine gesture, shrugged it off her shoulders.

She wore a semi-sheer, lacy black top with a built-in bra that molded her breasts and accentuated her cleavage. Tiny straps crossed her shoulders, tempting him to pull them down.

"Wow." Not brilliant, but his brain wasn't engaged.

"I blew my budget for the month, but I couldn't resist. Everyone bought something."

He could care less about "everyone." Just as he was going to suggest they adjourn to the bedroom, his attention was caught by her hands as they moved to her waist.

But again she surprised him, this time asking, "Where are the dogs?"

"Honey's out in the backyard. Pigpen's having a weekend sleepover with his owners." The elderly couple's son and his wife with the dog allergy had taken an anniversary trip to Victoria.

"Good." With tantalizing slowness, Miranda undid the button at the waist of her jeans-style skirt, and then eased down the zipper. With a hip shimmy, she sent the brief garment tumbling to the floor.

The black top was a camisole. With it she wore skimpy black lace panties that left just enough to the imagination to drive him crazy with lust.

"You like?" She raised her arms above her head and made a slow, seductive pivot—revealing that her undies were a thong that bared her creamy buttocks.

"I like," he croaked. "If I liked it any better, I'd . . ." Nope, he didn't have a clue where to go from there. With a sole thought in his brain—his little brain, which wasn't actually all that little right now—he grabbed her hand and said, "Let's go upstairs."

He had thought they might start with a glass of wine, but no way was that happening now, with her in that provocative outfit. It was going to take every minute of those three hours to properly appreciate her sexy beauty.

She didn't seem to mind a bit, holding back only to grab her bag. He wasn't insulted, knowing her phone would be in it, her lifeline to her daughter. His own cell was in his pocket.

Once they were in his bedroom, he quickly peeled his tee over his head and attacked the fastenings of his khaki shorts.

"Luke?"

Miranda's voice stopped him, and he saw she was glancing around, looking nervous now. "Was this your bedroom? With Candace, I mean?"

He shook his head. "It used to be the guest room. It was too hard being in the same room, after . . ."

She fiddled with a strand of hair. "And you're okay with this? With us?"

"I am." He'd spent some sleepless hours arriving at that conclusion, but he knew Candace would want him to move on. To be happy again. "Are you?"

"Now I am." She smiled and it lit her eyes.

"Good." He shoved his shorts down his hips, debated whether to take off his navy boxers as well, and then thought that might be rushing things. Not that the cotton concealed much, with the way the front was tented.

"Mmm," she purred. "Very nice, Luke."

He never thought much about his body, but he was glad she approved. His parents' genes had given him a decent physique and he'd always been active. Large vet work took even more strength and stamina than wrangling the twins, so he was in good shape.

He ran his hands down Miranda's arms in a long, gentle caress, caught her hands, and stepped forward until the fronts of their bodies brushed. With their clasped hands at their sides, he tilted his head and leaned down to kiss her.

She met him, the slight friction of her body against his making him even harder. Then they were kissing, at first with a touch of tentativeness, but that didn't last long.

He was hot, fiery hot, the blood rushing through his veins, but he controlled his body, only letting his tongue demonstrate his passion as it hungrily parried hers.

She whimpered and rose on her toes, pressing down on his hands for leverage, and then hooking one leg around him like she was trying to climb him. Swiveling her hips, she ground against his erection. "I want you," she panted. "I don't want foreplay."

"I'm not sure I'm capable of foreplay," he replied honestly. "Not this time."

"Good, because I'm so ready." Her blue eyes were open wide, the pupils dilated. "Fuck me, Luke."

That f-word, the first he'd heard from the grown-up Miranda, tipped him over the edge. He was powerless to do anything but obey her.

He thrust her away from him and pushed her onto the bed. She landed partway across it, on her back on the chocolate-brown comforter, her legs dangling over the side. He shoved his boxers down and took a condom from the drawer by the bed.

As he sheathed himself, she braced herself on her elbows, head raised watching him. "I'll take off my cami," she offered.

Damn, but she was stunning. It wasn't just the perfection of her body, but the contrasts: pale skin, black silk and lace, golden hair, and those eyes—dark denim now, with the huge pupils—all showcased against a deep brown background. She could have posed for an ad for lingerie or perfume, but instead she was his. All his.

"Leave it on. Leave everything on. This time." He stepped between her legs, driven to do the exact thing she'd demanded of him.

Trying to gentle his impatient fingers, he slid them inside the damp crotch of her thong and stroked her, opening folds that were slick and hot. She hadn't lied about being ready. He didn't yank off the flimsy garment but instead pulled the crotch aside and, holding his throbbing cock in his other hand, stepped closer. Glancing at her face to ensure she really wanted this, he was met by glittering eyes and the harsh command, "Now. Please, now."

As he guided himself to her entrance, her legs came up to wrap around his hips, and then he was sliding in, feeling the amazing pressure and heat all around him. My God but he'd missed this.

Miranda's arms braced her body, letting her raise her

butt and hips off the bed, aligning their bodies perfectly. His hands were free, though. As he pumped in and out of her, light-headed with how good it felt, he leaned forward to caress the buds of her nipples, which poked against the black silk of her cami.

He tried to slow his strokes, but it was almost impossible. The drive to let go, to thrust faster, to reach climax was close to irresistible. Especially when she thrashed her head back and forth on the comforter, her eyes slitted, her cheeks flushed.

Knowing he couldn't last much longer, needing to bring her with him, to give her the same release he craved, he touched the place where their bodies joined. Finding her swollen clit, he rubbed it gently.

"Yes," she cried. "Oh, yes. Yes, I . . . oh, God!" Her eyes flared, glittered, and she said, "Luke, yes!" She convulsed then, in wrenching spasms.

Those spasms—and the fact that she'd looked at him and spoken his name—were his undoing. With a groan, he surrendered to his body's need and reached his own climax. It was so forceful that it hurt, and yet it was the best kind of hurt. His four-year dry spell was over. He and Miranda were lovers.

Her legs loosened their grip on his hips and he eased out of her as her body dropped down to the bed, legs flopping over the side as if she'd lost all strength. He stepped away to deal with the condom. When he returned, she hadn't moved. Her eyes were closed and she looked boneless, like a discarded toy. And that was the very last thing she was. This was the first time in his life he'd made love to anyone other than Candace, and Miranda had made it so amazing. So natural.

He sat beside her, smoothed damp curls back from her face, and gently touched his lips to hers. "Hey. You okay?"

Her eyes drifted open, looking unfocused. "Okay," she

repeated. "Oh yeah, I'm most definitely okay." She spoke slowly, dreamily, and her chest heaved as she sucked in breath.

Did she mean *just* okay? He'd been so carried away, he hadn't felt a twinge of performance anxiety, but now he thought of the other men she'd been with. He knew she'd climaxed with him, but he'd been pretty selfish.

"Man, that was really something," she said.

Was she being generous or honest? "Given the total lack of finesse," he said ruefully.

"Finesse is overrated." She blinked. "No, wait, I take that back. Feel free to try finesse. I mean, there's a time for all of it, right? Finesse and, uh, lack of finesse." She groaned. "Sorry. Not feeling too articulate."

He took that as a good sign. But, eyeing her position, legs dangling off the bed, he said, "You can't be comfortable."

"Can't I? I can't even feel most of my body."

"I'll feel it for you." He skimmed his hand over the front of her camisole and her nipples perked to life again. Amazingly, considering how fiercely he'd just come, so did his cock.

How had she ever thought this man was anything but supremely sexy? Gazing up at Luke as he teased her body back to life, admiring the firmness of his muscles, watching his body stir with arousal again, Miranda thought she must have been crazy.

Though her well-satiated body felt as limp as over-cooked fettucine, she struggled to hike herself backward so her legs no longer hung off the bed. She reached for a pillow and slid it under her head.

Luke came down beside her, lying on his side, brushing the flat of his hand over her silk-clad nipples. "I wonder what these breasts look like?" he said, his gaze on the front of her cami.

"Why don't you find out?" she teased. Earlier, she'd worried that he might be all angsty about having sex with someone other than Candace, but thankfully he seemed fine, totally engaged with her and not suffering with memories or misplaced guilt.

"I'm enjoying the anticipation." He lifted his head and winked. "This time, there *will* be foreplay."

"You bet there will."

He frowned slightly. "I'm sorry about the first time. It had been so long and I got carried away. I promise, the next time will be better."

"Luke." She rolled her eyes. Was he insecure about his sexual prowess, this man who, allegedly, had experimented with the *Kama Sutra*? "It was perfect. I was in a hurry, too." But now the *Kama Sutra* was in her brain and she felt a tiny worry that he might find her inadequate in bed. She'd been with her fair share of guys, but the sex hadn't been especially adventuresome. "The *Kama Sutra* thing," she ventured, "I don't really know what that's all about."

His frown transformed to a grin. "Got you curious, did I?"

"It's a bunch of kinky positions, right? I'm not very experienced with that, but"—she tried out a wink of her own—"I'm ready and willing to learn."

"Ah, Miranda." He ran his finger along her collarbone, raising shivers of arousal. "The *Kama Sutra* and tantric sex are—"

"Tantric sex?" It came out as an embarrassing yelp. "You're into that, too?"

"Annie again. She's not your conventional mother-in-law. I hate to think what kind of books she'll give the boys when they approach puberty."

She had to laugh. "That *is* a little terrifying, isn't it? But as long as you're open with Caleb and Brandon, I'm sure they'll be just fine."

He grimaced. "Could we stop talking about the twins?"

"You're the one who mentioned them."

"Big mistake. They're not going to have sex until they're at least thirty, and that's a very long way off. So I'm not going to think about it."

She laughed again. "Believe me, I get it. But, to get back to present company, I turn twenty-eight in a few months and I'm hoping to have lots of sex before and after that."

"I like that idea."

His finger returned to her collarbone. His hands were everything she'd hoped they would be, deft and tender yet totally masculine.

"Tell me about tantric sex," she requested.

"Well, you, uh, attune yourselves to each other. Synchronize breathing, gaze into each other's eyes until you feel like your souls are merging. It's more about that than about orgasm."

"Not about orgasm? Luke, I guess I'm not very evolved because, you know—"

He cut her off, chuckling. "Yeah, I like the orgasms, too. The tantric thing is more for later in a relationship, when you know each other really well."

"And are bored with orgasms? Is that even possible?"

He laughed. "I doubt it. No, it's just something different. Variety. Annie says humans crave both stability and variety. In a long-term relationship, you have the stability. You can get variety from outside, like with different friends and—"

"Sex with other people?" she asked disbelievingly. Surely Annie didn't advocate that.

"No, that's not what I'm saying." His fingers traced the lacy top of her cami, dipping into her cleavage. "I mean, it's an option for some people but that's not how I'm built." His fingers stopped moving and he narrowed his eyes. "You?"

"If you're not in a relationship, I mean if you're just hooking up, then I don't care about fidelity. But if it's a real relationship, like you and me, then no. I'd hate the thought of you being with someone else."

"Me too." He caressed her again, sliding his fingers under the lace of her cami and over the upper curves of her breasts. "No, what I meant about variety outside the relationship is having some different friends and interests. Like you hanging out with Glory or going on that shopping day. Monday nights I get together with some friends and we shoot hoops. When it comes to sex, you can get variety within the relationship. Hence the books."

"Okay, now I get it."

"And yeah, the *Kama Sutra* has a bunch of different positions, all designed to find the best ways of giving both partners pleasure. But really, all you need to do is use your imagination, not be shy, and listen to your body."

"Right now my body wishes you'd pull off my camisole." Since she wasn't supposed to be shy, she went on. "And apply your lips to my breasts."

"That would be my pleasure." He caught the lacy hem in both hands and gently tugged the fabric upward. "Look at how perfect you are," he murmured as he bared her tummy, her rib cage, and finally her breasts.

She raised herself so he could slide the garment up farther, and lifted her arms as he pulled it over her head. In her opinion, her body was fine, decently slim and fit, but nothing special. The heated appreciation in his eyes told a different story. One she very much enjoyed reading.

His body was the perfect one. She wanted to touch him everywhere. Especially to clasp his now-sizable erection.

"I'm listening to your body now," she said, "and there's a hard-on that would love some attention."

"Very true." His big hand clasped her hip, holding her down so she couldn't reach for him. "But if it gets that attention, then the foreplay isn't going to last long."

"You're not saying I'll never be able to touch you?" she said with disbelief. Changing to a more seductive tone, she added, "Or suck you?" Her eyes were on his cock, and she noted how it twitched in response to her tease.

"God, no," he said fervently. "I'd never say that. Just not now. Right now, think of me as a horny teenager, ready to blow at the slightest provocation. I promise, I really am a grown-up and I can be patient, at least once the first two or three orgasms are out of the way."

A wicked notion hit her. He believed in equal relationships. So, in sex, he shouldn't always be the boss. Pushing against the strength of his hand on her hip, she sat up, twisted her body, and before he knew what had hit him, she fastened her lips around the head of his erection.

"Jesus, Miranda," he gasped. "Oh, man, that feels . . ." He tugged on her hair. "Stop it or I won't last."

She raised her head only enough to say, "Don't want you to," and then she went to work with her tongue, lips, and hands, getting to know every silky-smooth inch of him, all of it throbbing with need and power. Teasing swirls, firm strokes, pulsing suction, she gave it all to him.

His fingers remained woven through her hair, but he no longer tried to pull her away. Nor did he guide her action. It was more like he was hanging on for a wild ride.

Everything she did turned her on, too. Listening to her body, she knew she was selfish enough to want to climax, too, and with him inside her. When she could feel that he was right on the edge, she freed him long enough to demand, "Condom" and stretch out her hand.

He shifted position to reach for one, and she skimmed off her thong. She sheathed him, careful despite her impatience. Not wanting him to explode before she could come with him.

And then, her body trembling with arousal, she swung her leg over his hips. She saw his face, the feverish glazed eyes, the burning cheeks. Guessing she must look just as crazed, she held his gaze as she reached down to grasp and hold him as she lowered herself, taking him in.

Her body rippled, pulsed, and she began to rise and fall, riding him, grinding down against him, angling so that his erection rubbed her clit. He groaned and his hips rose, thrusting hard, and then he was coming and she was, too, explosions rocking her core.

Luke hadn't felt this good in a very long time. His body was so drained that he might never walk again, but as long as Miranda was here in bed with him, who cared?

They had been making love in various ways for more than two hours. Probably it was just as well that his mom and Forbes would be back with the boys in not much more than half an hour. If he and Miranda had sex one more time, it might kill him.

He was flat on his back with her curled against him, her head tucked between his chin and shoulder, her hair a soft tickle against his skin. She wasn't Candace and yet she fit just right, which was a relief, a blessing, and downright incredible.

Her scent was rich in his nostrils: sweaty sex intermingled with delicate flowers plus a hint of chocolate. "Have I sold you on black cherry ice cream?" he asked. Part of that long, drawn-out lovemaking had involved him doing his best to persuade her of the merits of his favorite ice cream, topped with chocolate sauce—especially when the treat was spread on assorted body parts. There'd been a lot of giggling, reminding him of when they'd first discussed sex, and how the concept of laughter during lovemaking had seemed foreign to her. He loved giving her experiences that other men hadn't.

"I may be coming around. But you know how it is when you're trying a new food," she teased. "Sometimes it takes more than once before you get hooked."

He chuckled. "That can definitely be arranged."

She made a satisfied "mmm" sound, pressed a kiss to his chest, and brought her left arm up across his ribs.

"That perfume you wear, is it lily of the valley?"

"Wow. Most guys can't tell one flower from another. Do you like it?"

"It grows in Mom's garden and I've always liked it. The smell, and those simple, bell-like white flowers."

"It's not perfume, it's an oil that Di makes from the real flowers."

"It suits you. Feminine but not cloying." He liked this, the intimacy of lying together and getting to know each other in a new way. Idly he traced the dragon tattoo that covered much of her forearm. "I remember this dragon from school. You must've been really young when you got it done."

"It was part of my tough girl image," she said flippantly. But then, a moment later, she went on. "Okay, that's true. But there's more to it, something no one else knows but Aaron."

Would she trust him with her secret? "I'd like to hear about it," he said quietly.

She pulled back a little so she could look at him, and serious blue-gray eyes searched his. Then she glanced down at her arm, drawing his gaze with hers, and turned her arm over to reveal the underside where the tail of the dragon whipped across her wrist. She caught his hand and guided his fingers to stroke over the colored pattern. He felt raised skin in a few places, like scar tissue.

"I used to cut myself."

A breath hissed out of him. "God, Miranda. I'm sorry." He circled her wrist with his fingers as if somehow he could soothe the old hurt that had driven her to do that.

"I did it because I needed to feel in control of something, and it made me feel so alive, that silver razor blade, the sharp slash of pain, and my red blood welling up. It was so clean, so simple."

That image choked him. "You never . . ."

"Tried to kill myself? No. The cutting helped, believe it or not. When I was feeling desperately unhappy—depressed, worthless, powerless—it took the edge off the pain. Physical pain and control, they trumped emotional pain and lack of control. At least for a while. Enough to get me through for a bit longer."

He'd heard about cutting, of course. Intellectually he could understand what she was saying. But it tore him up to think that she'd gone through that. "But you stopped?" Surely, she had. He'd made an intimate exploration of her lovely body, and noticed only a couple of silvery stretch marks on her abdomen.

"Aaron caught me. Made me talk about it, and that's how I figured out why I was doing it. He said there were other ways of feeling strong. Better ones. And he said I *was* strong already, for having survived our mother, our life. He said I was strong and fierce and smart, like a dragon." She smiled at Luke. "I got the tattoo so I'd never forget that."

He let out a breath he hadn't realized he'd been holding. But how had a kid who shoplifted in order to eat managed to afford this elaborate tattoo? Tentatively he said, "Tattoos are expensive, aren't they?"

"Yeah. The artist was a single dad, and he needed to

work some weekends and evenings. I babysat for his two little kids, and he paid me in ink."

"Nice." Reflecting on her story, he said, "I hope Caleb and Brandon will always be there for each other, like you and Aaron. Though I sure hope they never go through the kind of crap you did."

"You'll make sure they don't. So will their grandparents." She sighed. "I'm glad the twins have each other. I feel kind of bad about Ariana being an only child. Here on Destiny she now has lots of . . ." She paused, gave a gentle smile, and went on. "Of family who'll be there for her, but it's not the same as a sibling bond. And if we did go back to Vancouver . . ."

"You said 'if.'" He was convinced she would stay, and encouraged that she seemed to be more open to that possibility.

"All right, maybe the island is my *destiny*." Mischief twinkled in her eyes as she emphasized the last word. "I confess I'm getting won over. By the island. Eden's family. Glory and Gala."

"Obviously, I'm not trying hard enough," he teased back.

"If you tried any harder, I wouldn't be able to walk."

Smiling, he felt entirely content. If things worked out with him and Miranda the way he thought they might, one day down the road her little girl would have two big brothers. And with any luck, he and Miranda would add a fourth kid to the mix. Right now, anything seemed possible.

Except for lying here any longer. "I hate to say this, but we need to get up and dressed."

"And showered." She grinned. "*Eau de* sex smells good to me, but probably not so much to your mom and Forbes."

"Good point." He forced his drained body over to the side of the bed, sat up, and ran his hand through his hair. "It'll have to be a quick shower."

"No time for shower sex." She gave him a pouty, teasing look as she climbed out of bed.

As they walked on wobbly legs to the bathroom, he remembered something he'd meant to ask. "By the way, did you end up telling Eden and the others about the information Annie dug up on Starshine, and her theories about Merlin?"

Miranda stumbled, suggesting that her legs were even shakier than his, and he caught her arm to steady her.

"I just realized," she said, "that my shirt and skirt are lying on the hall floor. I should go down and get them, in case your family gets home early."

"I'll do it."

"No, that's okay. But do you think you could find a shower cap? I'd like to keep my hair dry."

"I'll look."

She scooted out of the bedroom, obviously recovering her strength, and he went into the bathroom and rummaged in the bottom of the cabinet under the sink. He'd kept some of Candace's odds and ends, and found a package labeled "Shower Cap."

When Miranda returned, she took it with an "Oh, good." Opening it, she said, "These things are ugly. Promise not to look," and then she piled her hair up and tucked it inside the cap.

"Nope. Cute." It was true. "You were going to tell me about the commune thing," he reminded her.

"Oh. Right. Yes, Di and Seal were happy to hear that Starshine seems to be okay," she said as she reached behind the shower curtain to turn on the water. "And not surprised Merlin had disappeared completely. They said he was a man of mystery, and smart. It would be like him to assume a new identity somewhere else, an identity that even Annie couldn't trace." She adjusted the temperature and stepped into the shower.

"So Di and Seal don't think he died at the commune, and was cremated or buried there?" he asked as he followed her.

"It's one theory." Her face was tilted up to the shower spray and her words came out muffled. "But it would have been really hard to cover up something like that."

"I guess."

Her back was wet and sleek, graceful and feminine. He'd thought he was physically incapable of arousal again so soon, but the curves of her hips and butt were a powerful motivator. Stepping up behind her, he put his arms around her and caressed her breasts. "A quick shower, eh? I can be quick."

She turned to him, smiling. "With you, so can I."

He wrapped his arms around her wet body and kissed her. Then he remembered. "Damn, the condoms are by the bed."

With drops dewing her lashes, she gazed at him. "I'm on birth control. And I'm clean, Luke. I always used condoms."

It would take only a few seconds to jump out of the shower and drip his way across the bedroom, but he trusted Miranda. And he hated condoms, hated having a barrier between their naked bodies. "That is really good news."

Chapter Eighteen

Back in early December, when Aaron and Eden had announced their engagement, Miranda had felt a sense of loss. But on this sunny April afternoon, as wedding guests assembled at SkySong on a stretch of lawn above the ocean, her heart was full to bursting with joy.

For months, Aaron, Eden, and Eden's relatives had been telling her—showing her—in a variety of ways that she wasn't losing a brother but gaining a family. Her stubborn brain and hard-shelled heart had finally come to believe it. And every single member of that family, from Eden's impulsive younger sister, Kelsey, through to her "aging hippie" aunt and uncle, was fabulous. That had been demonstrated, yet again, as they'd worked together today to make the last-minute preparations for the wedding.

Now the retreat's guests had been politely warned to keep their distance, everything was set up for the ceremony, and the wedding guests were arriving.

Harp music drifted gently through the air, played by a friend of Di and Seal's. Folding chairs faced a trellised arch, and the grassy aisle was strewn with white and pale pink hawthorn blossoms. White tents had been set up as a precaution against rain, but now it seemed they wouldn't be needed, except for the catering tent. Celia and Rachelle of C-Shell were handling the food. B-B-Zee would provide music for the reception, and a portable dance floor was set up.

"You're a beautiful bridesmaid," Luke said, squeezing her hand as they walked among lilacs and hawthorns that filled the air with their sweet scent, over to the rows of folding chairs. His fingers had been intertwined with hers ever since she'd met him in the parking lot at SkySong, where they'd shared a long kiss.

"Thank you," she said. In Vancouver, she, Eden, and Kelsey had easily agreed on the bridesmaids' outfits. The cornflower-colored sundresses were comfortable, and flattering to her and Kelsey's blue eyes. The short length, paired with the nude color of their strappy sandals, made their bare legs look long and shapely despite the fact that the sandals were flat-soled. Di had pointed out that you couldn't look graceful walking across grass in high-heeled shoes.

The sun was warm enough that the women of the bridal party shouldn't even need the blue-and-gold pashminas they'd bought. Miranda's dragon was on full display and she wore it proudly. Yes, she was strong and smart, and could be fierce when she needed to—but these days she was feeling mellow.

"I'm a happy bridesmaid, too," she told Luke. Happy about not only the wedding, but everything else in her life. Even the bunny story had turned out well, and she loved watching the video she'd shot on her phone: Luke opening the cage and that little guy poking out, sniffing the air, and then without a backward look hopping off into the trees.

She smiled up at Luke. He was the sexiest, most amazing man she'd ever met, and he looked wonderful this afternoon, in khaki-colored dress pants, a cream-colored cotton shirt with the collar open and the sleeves rolled up, and brown loafers. Aaron, who hated suits and ties, said he had no intention of being uncomfortable on the happiest day of his life, and Eden had told him he could wear whatever he pleased as long as she could do the same. Their wedding invitation had specified a "be comfortable" dress code.

Other wedding guests drifted by, and Luke said hello to them. Miranda added her own greetings to those she recognized. After a few months working in tiny Blue Moon Harbor on tiny Destiny Island, she'd met a lot of the residents.

"Do you miss Ariana?" Luke asked.

"Yes, but it's nice not to have to worry about her throwing a TTT." Miranda had talked to Aaron and Eden about whether the girl should attend. They'd all had mixed feelings, but in the end decided it would be better to have a serene wedding. Ariana was spending the day with her BFF Gala, first at Glory's house and then, since Glory and Brent were attending the wedding, at Glory's parents. Miranda had met the McKennas, a friendly, generous couple who, being big-boned and fair-skinned, looked completely unlike their petite Chinese daughter.

Glory and Brent hadn't arrived yet, but when Miranda glanced in the direction of the parking lot, she noticed Iris Yakimura approaching, slim and quietly elegant in a lilac sheath dress with another of her aunt's multicolored silk scarves tied around her neck. The two of them had gotten together for coffee a couple of times, and were becoming friends. Smiling, Miranda beckoned her over and they were all saying hi when a woman she didn't recognize rushed up to them.

A few years older than her, the brunette had big hair and a way-too-tight pink dress with a low neckline that showcased impressive cleavage. She caught Luke's elbow. "Luke, I'm so glad to see you. I think there's something wrong with that dog food you recommended. Candy just picks at it."

"Excuse me a minute," Luke said, releasing Miranda's hand and stepping away from her and Iris. Miranda heard him suggest, politely but firmly, that if the woman was still feeding scraps and treats to Candy, it was no wonder the dog wasn't interested in the diet that was intended to bring her down to a healthy weight.

Miranda and Iris exchanged smiles. "Such a happy day," Iris said, yet a shadow clouded her lovely brown eyes.

"You're here alone?"

The corners of her lips turned down. "That's the story of my life." Then she shook her head. "A pity party. How humiliating and entirely inappropriate. Truly, I'm thrilled for Eden and Aaron, and I'm sure my turn will come one day. And Miranda, I'm so happy for you, too." She glanced at Luke, who was still deep in discussion with the big-haired brunette, and lowered her voice. "You found a Prince Charming who won't turn into a frog."

"I'm happy for me, too." Luke was indeed a winner. Handsome and sexy, smart and successful, compassionate and gentle. Fantastic in bed. As wonderful with kids as he was with animals. "I feel so lucky. His boys and even his parents and in-laws seem to be coming to accept me." She'd been to family dinners a couple more times and, courtesy of Annie's bluntness, everyone now knew that she and Luke were sleeping together. The grandparents had even helped give them evenings alone together, babysitting the boys and sometimes even taking Ariana. Sonia and Annie insisted that they loved being able to play with a girl, and she sensed they were both missing Candace. After all, even though Annie'd been her mom, Candace had spent a lot of time at Luke's house, too, since they'd been best friends for so long.

"Could you pass some of that luck along to me?" Iris said, in a joking tone that was belied by the seriousness in her eyes.

Impulsively Miranda gave her a quick hug. "There you go. Consider it passed."

Iris looked startled, which made Miranda realize that the other woman tended not to be physically demonstrative, but then she smiled and said, "You're sweet, Miranda."

"No, honestly, I'm not. But since you're feeling charitably disposed toward me, may I venture a bit of none-of-my-business advice?"

"Um, I suppose so."

"Iris, you have so much going for you. If you were just a little more confident and outgoing, then men would see that."

"Easier to say than do. Besides, my shyness is a part of me, just as it is with my father and aunt. It has its pros as well as its cons. When I meet my own Prince Charming, he'll recognize that and love all of me, as happened with my mom and dad."

"Maybe so." She reflected. "After all, Luke seems to like, or at least accept, all of me, even though I'm far from perfect. Yes, I was so, so lucky to meet him."

Iris frowned slightly. "Well, I suppose it wasn't solely luck," she said almost reluctantly. "You were brave enough to put yourself out there, to take risks. I don't think I'd have the guts to do that."

"No guts, no glory?" Miranda suggested gently. Thinking about how her own relationship with Luke had developed, she went on. "Maybe it takes the right man to bring out that side of you. I'm different with Luke than I've ever been with anyone else. He brings out the best in me."

And so did Destiny Island, this second time around. When she'd come here as a teen, she'd hoped that her dreams of finding a home and love would finally be realized—but her grandparents had promptly shattered that illusion. Last summer, when she'd hit bottom and dragged her pathetic self back here, all she'd wanted was to get her life together and return to Vancouver. But the island and its people had wormed their way into her heart. For the first time in her life, when she hadn't even been looking, hadn't dared hope, had she found a home? And maybe even love? Had she really, as the locals liked to say, found her destiny here on Destiny Island?

A strong hand touched her elbow and Luke's body brushed hers as he returned to her side. "My ears are burning. Thank you for that, Miranda. And in return, I can honestly say that you brought me back to life. After Candace's death, I never imagined that I—" He broke off with a cough. To Iris, he said apologetically, "Sorry. I guess weddings bring out my mushy side."

So she wasn't the only one. Miranda leaned into him.

"It's charming that you have a mushy side," Iris said quietly. "Now I'll leave you two lovebirds alone."

But then shy Iris, who seemed to be feeling unsettled today, would be alone. Miranda reached out and caught her arm just as Luke said, "Don't go. Miranda's going to desert me any moment. Keep me company while she does wedding stuff."

Iris gave him a bashful smile. "I'd like that."

"Luke's right," Miranda said with a glance at her watch, "I've been away too long. We're almost due to start."

After stretching up to plant a kiss on Luke's cheek, she hurried back to Di and Seal's big house. There, everyone seemed organized and calm. Aaron, Eden, and her family stood chatting with Lionel Williams and Jonathan Barnes. Lionel, Aaron's old friend and mentor, was his best man. Jonathan, a marriage commissioner, would officiate and then serve double duty because he was a member of B-B-Zee.

Aaron and Eden had shunned the superstition about not seeing each other before the wedding, and stood hand in hand looking gorgeous. Aaron wore black pants and a smoky blue shirt, perfectly complementing his dark hair, brown skin, and grayish-blue eyes. Eden was a dream in cream-colored lace, her walnut-brown hair pulled up in an artfully casual style and dotted with white blossoms. Her amber eyes glowed golden, like the woven chain around her neck, a gift her father had given her mom on their wedding day. Dangling from her ears were stunning earrings made of gold threads and sparkly topaz stones. They were a gift from Aaron, custom-made by the same local jeweler who'd crafted Eden's engagement ring and their wedding rings.

"You two take my breath away," Miranda told them, happy tears hazing her eyes. Blinking them away with mascaraed lashes, she checked out the others.

Kelsey looked like a younger, short-haired version of herself, and Helen and Di were lovely in short-sleeved tops and long, patterned skirts in gentle shades of silver and gold that flattered their sixty-something beauty. Di had created a few narrow braids in her long hair, weaving them with gold and silver ribbons, and Helen had a couple of jeweled pins in her short silver hair.

Seal and Jonathan were both dressed in good jeans and shirts of unbleached cotton. Seal's long hair was ponytailed while Jonathan was bald, with a neat gray beard. Jim Blaine and Lionel both wore black pants and crisp white shirts, Lionel's making his dark chocolate skin look almost black.

"I think everyone's arrived," Miranda told the group. "They're just milling about, chatting."

"I'll round them up," Seal said. "Give me five minutes, and everyone will be in their seats."

Aaron let go of Eden's hand and stepped toward Miranda. With his hand on her shoulder, he steered her slightly away from the Blaine family. "Well, Little Sister, who'd have ever thought this day would come?"

She beamed at him. "Not me. Never. Thank God for Eden."

"You can say that again." He ducked his head to stare straight into her eyes. "It's all good, Miranda. You know that, right?"

Thankful that she could give him a wholehearted answer, she said, "I do, and it is. I'm so happy for all of us."

When he leaned down to drop a kiss on her forehead, she didn't even try to stop herself from grabbing him in a tight hug. She clung for one long moment and then gently shoved him away. "Let's get you married, Big Brother. You have your vows?"

He patted his shirt pocket. The bride and groom had decided to write their own vows, and he'd begged Miranda's help in finding the right words to express his emotions. Though he'd memorized the vows, he was carrying a paper copy for the sake of his peace of mind.

When he went back to Eden, Miranda walked over to Kelsey and took her hand.

"If everyone's ready," Jonathan said, "let's get this show on the road."

And then they were in motion. Jonathan, Lionel, and Aaron went first and a minute later Di, followed by Miranda and Kelsey. As they neared the assembled group, with everyone turned to watch them, the only sound was the strains of Pachelbel's Canon in D on the harp. Aaron stood under the trellised arch, with Lionel and Jonathan off to the side. Smiling at her brother, Miranda walked with Kelsey down the aisle.

When they reached the front, the harpist stopped playing. They stepped to the side and turned, and the harpist struck the first notes of "Ode to Joy."

And there was Eden, flanked by her parents, taking the first steps onto the petal-strewn aisle. She walked faster than at the rehearsal, as if she couldn't wait any longer to join her life with Aaron's. Miranda glanced at Luke, catching the moment when Eden passed the aisle where he and Iris sat side by side. When he turned to face forward, his gaze shifted from the bride to Miranda, and they exchanged smiles.

Was it just wedding-day emotion, or was it possible that one day the two of them would be doing this? If so, there would definitely be kids present, because their children would be part of the union.

Gazing at her handsome lover, she remembered how, when she'd come to Destiny, she had resolved to avoid relationships and figured she wouldn't be tempted because the single guys were too boring. How wrong she'd been. But honestly, she'd never have believed that an amazing man like Luke might care for her. A man who was as impressive in his own way as Chef Emile or Ariana's actor father, but such a better person.

She'd never have imagined any of this. Being part of a family and part of a community. Coming to be accepted by Luke's kids and his parents and in-laws.

It was all so *normal*, really. Which was the last thing that, until now, her life had ever been.

As Aaron and Eden gripped each other's hands, stared lovingly into each other's eyes, and recited their vows— Aaron not needing to pull the paper from his pocket—she wondered if she was totally crazy to think, *One day, this could be me.*

The reception was hopping. Miranda was with Luke, talking to Glory and Brent, and Jillian and Michael. Jillian, a pilot who flew for Aaron's Blue Moon Air, had recently wed Michael. An architect, he had now moved from Toronto and set up business in Blue Moon Harbor.

"Cole's not here today," Miranda commented. Jillian and Michael's son—who really was *their* son, due to a birth control misfire back in university—was eight. A regular customer at Blowing Bubbles, he was a smart, well-behaved boy.

"We offered him the choice," Michael said. His attractive brown-skinned face crinkled in a smile. "His reaction was, to quote, 'Eeewww.' He'd rather hang out with his best friend."

A male server in jeans and a blue tee offered them a tray of drinks. Glory and Brent both chose prosecco. Miranda, who'd reached her one-drink limit with the champagne used for the toasts, took the sparkling passionfruit punch. Luke, perennially on call, did the same. Michael took a glass of prosecco, but Jillian also chose the punch.

Miranda, thirsty after half an hour on the dance floor, drank a good portion of the delicious concoction. "I guess you didn't even get to drink the champagne, did you?" she asked Jillian. The young, blond-haired woman would shortly be flying Aaron and Eden to their honeymoon destination in Tofino, a town by the ocean on the west coast of Vancouver Island. A pilot couldn't have even one drink before a flight.

"No, no alcohol for me," Jillian confirmed. She glanced up at her husband with a smile. "But I can live with it."

"Good thing," he said in a soft, loving tone that had Miranda's eyes widening.

As the couple exchanged warm glances, Miranda skimmed her gaze down Jillian's body, slim and toned in a coral sundress. "You're not . . ." She gestured toward her tummy.

Jillian's pink cheeks turned a deeper color and her sky-blue eyes sparkled. "Shh. We only found out yesterday. And yes, this time we intended to get pregnant."

"Oh my God, that's fantastic."

After everyone else offered congratulations, Miranda asked, "Does Cole know yet?"

"Yes," Jillian said. "He's thrilled at the idea of being a big brother. But don't tell anyone else, okay? We've only told him and our parents. Not even Aaron, because I don't want anything to distract from his and Eden's celebration."

"Of course," Miranda said, and the others agreed.

Luke touched her shoulder. "How about another dance?"

"Thought you'd never ask." She drained her drink and they excused themselves and headed for the dance floor where several couples were two-stepping to a country song.

After a couple of dances, all the liquid she'd been drinking necessitated a trip to the ladies' room. A couple of deluxe porta-potties had been set up, but as a resident of SkySong she instead darted across the lawn to her own cabin. There, she took the opportunity to call Glory's parents and make sure the girls were fine, and to tidy her hair and refresh her light makeup.

Humming under her breath from sheer happiness, she made her way back across the lawn. She was crossing behind the tents where a smorgasbord of snacks was laid out, when a sandal strap came loose. As she bent to refasten it, a woman's voice drifted out from inside the tent. "I can't believe Luke is actually dating her. He deserves so much better than *that*."

Miranda froze, her breath catching. The voice sounded like that of the brunette in the tight pink dress, though the tone was waspish now.

Another female voice replied, "I've shopped at Blowing Bubbles and she seems okay."

Thanks for that, whoever you are. She couldn't identify that voice, so she doubted the woman was a regular customer.

"So she can be a semi-efficient salesclerk," Wasp Voice said. "That doesn't prove anything. Remember what she was like back in school? All weird and Gothy, totally not interested in being friends with any of us."

Who'd want to be friends with a bitch like you? Miranda hadn't recognized the woman as a former classmate; in fact, she'd taken her to be several years older.

"No doubt high all the time," Bitch-Woman went on. "Just like her mother. You know her mom OD'd, right?"

"Yeah, I heard." A pause, then Voice Two said, "Aaron turned out really well, though."

"And superhot, right? Too bad someone finally snagged him. But, obviously, the brother and sister were never anything alike. Did you see that dress she's wearing today? All young and flirty. It looks great on Eden's sister, but on Miranda . . . she's just old and trying too hard."

Talk about the pot insulting the kettle. Miranda smoothed her hands down the blue sundress. When she and Kelsey had picked them out, they'd both thought they were adorable. If the style was too young for Miranda, surely Eden, Helen, or Di would have told her so.

"I guess. And you're right, Luke deserves someone superspecial."

"If anyone could ever compete with the memory of Candace," Bitchy said. "He was so head over heels crazy for her, it's not funny. Seems to me, it would take someone, like, just incredible to take her place in his heart."

Hard to argue with that.

"Yeah, she was pretty much perfect, wasn't she?"

Bitchy huffed. "No one's perfect. Though Luke seemed to think she was."

"Men. They can be so blind. Give them great sex and they don't notice a girl's faults."

"Which is obviously why Luke's with Miranda. I bet she's a total slut, just like her mom." The last words were muffled, as if she was talking with her mouth full, but

Miranda still heard them. "But Luke'll figure it out before long, and dump her."

"I saw him sitting beside Iris at the wedding. She'd be a better match for him."

"Oh, please, she's boring. And now, for heaven's sake, tear me away from these incredible snacks. I swear, I'm going to split the seams of this dress if I keep eating this stuff."

Miranda darted farther behind the tent and waited, holding her breath. Cautiously she edged forward again, until she could see the pink-dressed bitch walking away, arm in arm with a skinny, brown-haired woman in a green dress.

How dare they say those things?

And how dare they be right?

She gazed across the lawn, looking for Luke. There he was, chatting with Iris. Something he said made her laugh, and hearing Iris laugh was a rare occurrence. Iris wasn't at all boring, not when you got to know her. She was smart and insightful, gentle and kind, and she loved children. She really would be ideal for Luke. Just look how elegant she was in that simple, classy dress. It wasn't too young for her; it wasn't "flirty." No one would ever accuse Iris of trying too hard and she was the polar opposite of slutty.

What had Miranda been thinking, that a woman with her background and her flaws could be a good match for Luke? That he might fall in love with her. That she might finally, after all the years of hoping, achieve the dream of love and a happy home. In the end, surely he would reject her, just like her mom, her grandparents, every man she'd fallen for in the past.

She was thinking of ducking back to her cabin again, but Iris saw her and beckoned her over. Reluctantly she joined them, but didn't take Luke's hand or touch his arm.

"Look," Iris said, gesturing across the lawn. "The bride and groom are heading off."

Miranda gazed in that direction. Aaron wore the same clothes, but Eden had changed into a fabulous blue-and-gold patterned top, worn over honey-colored linen pants. Miranda wondered if Aaron would even give his bride a chance to don the white lace negligée she'd purchased for her wedding night.

White lace. Classy and beautiful. Whereas Miranda had chosen black for her lingerie, and only rejected red because it wasn't the most flattering color on her. Red was slutty. Probably so was black.

"Want to go say good-bye?" Luke asked her.

She shook her head. Her brother and Eden were surrounded by family and friends. No one would notice her absence, and she was no longer in a celebratory mood.

Maybe Luke wasn't the most sensitive guy when it came to understanding women, but it seemed to him that something had changed. He'd been having a great time, happy for his old classmate Aaron and his new wife, and delighted to be spending the afternoon with a vibrant, glowing Miranda.

But now Miranda's mood had altered. And Iris, who'd been laughing only minutes earlier, was saying in a subdued tone, "It's time I headed home. Thanks for keeping me company."

"My pleasure," Luke said with complete honesty.

"Bye," Miranda said.

She gazed after Iris as she walked away. "She's gorgeous, isn't she? And smart and really nice." There was an odd tone to her voice, almost as if she was issuing a challenge.

Did she think he'd say that her friend was an ice queen? He'd heard a couple of guys use that term, but he didn't believe it. "True. But she's shy, right? At least unless you talk about books. Though today she loosened up a little."

"I saw her laughing at something you said."

"I was telling her how the boys have been acting out stories from books she recommended."

"She'd love to have kids. And she'll make some guy a great wife."

"Yeah, I'm sure."

"Right." His words of praise for her friend didn't seem to have improved her mood.

He put his arm around her shoulders. She stiffened for a moment and then relaxed against him with a sigh. "Are you upset about Aaron getting married?" he ventured.

She jerked away and scowled at him. "Of course not. What do you think I am? That I'd be, what? Resentful? Jealous? Luke, I'm thrilled for him and Eden."

"Okay, okay." He raised both hands in a gesture of disavowal. "I'm sorry. You just seemed a little . . . I don't know. Like you're not having fun anymore." Maybe she had PMS, but he'd learned from the women in his family that a guy should never suggest that. He remembered a particularly memorable lecture from Annie that ranged from sexism to Irritable Male Syndrome.

Miranda shook her head. "No, I'm sorry. I guess maybe I have had a little too much wedding. I should probably get changed and go pick up Ariana."

"Too bad you have to take off that pretty dress." She always looked great, but today she was especially beautiful. The blue of the dress set off her coloring: those stunning eyes, the golden curls that brushed her shoulders, and the hint of a tan on her nicely toned arms and knockout legs. All afternoon he'd been gazing at her with admiration as well as lust. "That is," he added with a wink, "unless you were taking it off for me. Is there time for a quickie before you need to leave and get Ariana?"

Her eyes narrowed. "A quickie? You want a quickie?"

"What I'd really like is a whole night of incredible sex." With plenty of time to figure out how to tell her the thing he'd realized earlier this afternoon. When he'd been saying that she'd brought him back to life after Candace's death, his tongue had run on and he'd barely managed to stop himself. He'd been about to blurt out that he'd never imagined he'd fall in love again and yet it seemed to be happening. That hadn't been the time or way to tell her, and certainly not in front of Iris. Now wasn't the right time either, not with Miranda needing to pick up her daughter soon.

Or was he looking for excuses? What if he said those words and she told him she didn't feel the same way? That he was a "friends with benefits" guy and lacked the special *whatever* that had made her fall for men like Ariana's father and that crazy chef? Could he handle hearing her say that? Sometimes it felt like his life had been a saga of loss, even though his dad, his mom, and Candace hadn't intentionally abandoned him.

Striving to keep things light, he said, "But since I know we don't have the night . . ."

"You want me to rip off this flirty little dress so we can have a quickie?" There was a challenging edge to her voice.

"Something wrong with that?" What was going on with her? "You've never had a problem with that before."

"No, that's me. Good old Miranda, ready to lie on her back and spread her legs at the snap of your fingers."

"What the hell?" He might be falling in love with her, and maybe she had PMS, but she was starting to piss him off.

"Let's face it. You hadn't had sex in years and now you can't get enough of it, but you know in your heart that I'll never replace Candace."

"No one can replace Candace," he snapped. "That's not—"

"Exactly! That's not where this is going, you and me."

Stunned, he took a step backward. Earlier, he'd thought that "this" might well be heading toward a marriage proposal and a blended family. But it seemed that was the last thing Miranda envisioned. Thank God he hadn't spoken up.

Hold on. Don't overreact. He took a deep breath and tried to calm down. She'd seemed fine. Great, even. They'd been dancing and then she'd gone to her cabin to use the bathroom, and it was when she came back that her mood had changed. This seemed like more than a sudden onset of PMS.

Cautiously he said, "Earlier, you seemed happy and now you're upset. Did something happen when you went back to your cabin?"

Her shoulders rose up, hunching, and she wrapped her arms around herself. She dropped her gaze. He tensed, too, having no idea what she might say.

Staring at the grassy lawn between their feet, she said, "I overheard a couple of women."

"Huh?"

"Gossiping. About me. And you."

Light dawned. Grimly he asked, "What did they say?"

Those hunched shoulders shrugged. "That I'm not good enough for you. That I'm slutty and you only want me for sex. That I could never replace Candace in your heart, and that you'll get tired of me and dump me soon."

No one could ever replace Candace in his heart, but if he said that when Miranda was in this mood, she wouldn't understand. It turned out that his heart had a pretty big capacity. There was room for his kids, his mom, Forbes, Annie, and Randall. Room for memories of Candace and the love he still felt for her. But also plenty of room for Miranda and Ariana.

"They said I'm not good enough for you," Miranda murmured, gazing up at him with soulful eyes that were now more gray than blue.

Luke opened his mouth, about to protest and to ask who those idiot women were. But then he realized that wasn't what truly mattered. "Do *you* think you're good enough for me?"

She glared at him. "Of course not." The words dropped heavily between them.

His heart sank along with them. He'd tried in every way he knew to show her that he thought she was special. Each time they made love, he told her with his words and his body how much he appreciated her. He'd brought her and her daughter into his and his boys' family time, and introduced her to the kids' grandparents. He told her about his work and asked her about her courses and her ideas on child-rearing and education. Occasionally he disagreed with her, but he respected her opinion and never belittled her. What more could he do?

Yes, he could tell her he was falling in love with her. But even if he got down on one knee and proposed, that wasn't the answer. If she didn't believe in herself and in their relationship now, an engagement wouldn't change things.

"Look," he said, disappointment and annoyance creeping into his voice, "I know you've had a lot of crap in your life. But isn't it time you grew up and got over it?"

"Excuse me?" More glaring.

Okay, maybe that wasn't the most tactful phrasing, but he was tired of tiptoeing around the eggshells of her insecurities. He mattered, too. He'd had true love and had lost his wife. Now he'd had the guts to enter a new relationship, to risk his fragile heart, and Miranda wasn't doing her part. He'd done his best to understand her issues, to support her, to help her heal. He'd been patient, but she seemed to want to stay stuck in the past and not acknowledge the strong woman she'd become.

"When I met you," he said, "I thought of you as a rose-bud surrounded by thorns. Well, I was right. You're prickly and moody. I guess you're insecure and, given your past, I can see how that would happen. I've tried to reassure you. But Miranda, all the stuff I've said and done, well, it still hasn't made you believe in your own self-worth. And it's finally sunk in that I can't make you believe in yourself." In fact, it seemed like she was determined not to, for whatever perverse reason. "It has to come from you."

Out of the corner of his eye, he saw Glory and Brent approaching. Glory must have seen that something intense was going on because she steered her partner away again.

He swallowed, a deep sorrow making it difficult to go on. "Miranda, the boys and I don't need to be involved with a woman who's insecure and self-defeating."

She fisted her hands on her hips. "That's exactly what I said! You deserve someone better than me."

"Jesus, that's not what I—" He shook his head. "You don't get it." He tried to find the right words, to somehow make her understand that she had so much strength and love and wonderfulness inside her if she could only let herself see it. But she didn't give him a chance.

"Oh, I get it perfectly." She turned and stalked away.

Luke stared after her. Well, just *fuck*.

Chapter Nineteen

"I have screwed up my life so royally," Miranda said gloomily to Iris as they had coffee in the Dreamspinner coffee shop the Friday after Aaron and Eden's wedding. It was a workday for Miranda, and she was on her afternoon break.

She gestured to the poster stuck on the bulletin board. "Julian Blake, one of my favorite musicians, is in town playing with B-B-Zee tonight and tomorrow night." The yellow thumbtack holding up the poster felt like the final nail in the coffin that had been her crappy life for the past week.

"Yes, he's usually here sometime in May or June, and at Christmas."

She sighed. "Somehow I missed the fact that he was here at Christmas." She'd been distracted by all the Blaine and SkySong family goings-on: baking, ornament-making, tree-trimming, consuming huge meals, carol singing, and gift-giving. It had been the kind of holiday she'd never experienced before and it had intimidated her. She'd hung back, enjoying it from the fringes. "Now he's here again, and I don't dare go."

Iris's smooth brow creased. "What are you afraid of?"

Miranda slugged back a mouthful of her mocha latté, not tasting it. "Oh, let me see. That Forbes and Sonia will say nasty things to me."

"Forbes will be onstage, playing. Sonia's going to be watching her husband and stepson."

"I guess. But Luke might be there, to see Julian, and, and . . ."

"And what? Do you think he'd say something mean?"

She sighed. "No, I think he's had his say and has washed his hands of me. But it would hurt too much, seeing him." She'd been rejected before, and by men she'd thought she was crazy in love with. But *crazy* must have been the operative word, because losing Luke hurt even worse than those breakups had. She realized now that she'd never truly, one hundred percent, invested emotionally in those guys. With Luke, things had happened more slowly, kind of snuck up on her, until she'd realized she seriously cared about him. Then she'd honestly begun to hope, to even believe, that she might finally have the life she'd always dreamed of.

Among all the men she'd known, Luke was special. He'd been the nice guy, the one who'd seemed to really see her and care about her. *Seeing* her, of course, had been the problem. He'd seen her too damned clearly.

Ruefully, she told Iris, "I've been doing a good job of avoiding Luke, and I guess he has, too. Not that his vet work brings him into the village much anyhow."

"I still have trouble believing you broke up with him. Miranda, I have a wall calendar with wise sayings, and each month I muse on them. This month, it's about being patient, and how you often need to go through difficult times before things become easy."

Miranda huffed. "Things are never going to be *easy* with Luke and me. And I didn't break up with him. He broke up with me. Remember how, at the reception, I was gushing to you about how Luke accepted all of me, even my imperfections? Well, hah, stupid me. Just an hour or so later, there he was, saying he and the boys deserve someone better." And the truth hurt. Bad boys were no good for her and Ariana, and she wasn't good enough for the good guys. So what did that mean for her future? Whenever she thought about that, which was only all the time, that pessimistic dark spot in her soul, the one that told her she was worthless, threatened to take over again.

In the depths of one dark night, when she'd craved something, anything, to banish that defeated, hollow feeling, she'd had an insight. Did her mother used to feel this way? Was that why she'd turned to alcohol and drugs? Just as the adolescent Miranda had taken a silver blade to her wrist? Was a tendency toward depression something Miranda had inherited from her mom?

Her mother hadn't had an Aaron to stop her, to support and encourage her. To tell her she was a dragon. But Miranda had, and her tattoo was a constant reminder. And so, each day, each hour, each minute, she struggled to forge ahead. To focus on the positives in her life—and, objectively speaking, there were so many more than ever before—rather than let pain and depression drag her into that horribly dark place.

Iris had been studying her, her unpainted lips pressed together in a thin line. "I have trouble imagining Luke saying something like that. But, well, that's your business, not mine. If things really are over between you, what are you going to do? Spend the rest of your life steering clear of him? And his family? And his friends? That's most of Destiny Island, you know."

Miranda groaned. "I was right in the beginning. Ariana and I should move back to Vancouver."

"Do you really want that?" Iris studied her over the rim of her mug. She was drinking jasmine tea that smelled wonderful. "I mean, don't let your situation with Luke force you into doing something that's not right for you. There've been lots and lots of breakups here, and mostly people do get over them and move on. You kind of have to, on an island this small."

"I hated the whole idea of living here, but it's grown on me. I really enjoyed that one-day shopping trip to Vancouver, but I realized that city life doesn't seem all that appealing anymore." Not to mention, she'd hate leaving Aaron, Eden and her family, and her new friends, Iris and Glory.

"Then buck up and move on."

Jolted out of her misery for a moment, Miranda snorted. "Buck up? What books have you been reading lately?"

"Stop agonizing over Luke and your love life. Focus on the immediate future. Do you want to hear Julian Blake or not? He really is wonderful."

Now that was a more pleasant topic than her unlovable-ness. "You like him, too?"

Iris nodded enthusiastically.

"Hey, do you know him?" Iris was two or three years younger than her, so she wouldn't have known Julian at school. But a lot of years had passed since then. "Does he come into Dreamspinner?"

"No, I don't know him, and I haven't seen him in the village. I think that, other than playing with B-B-Zee, when he's here he just hangs out with his family."

"Probably doesn't want fans mobbing him when he's on holiday," Miranda mused. She glanced at the poster again. The photo must have been taken on one of Julian's previous trips to the island. He was at a mic in front of the B-B-Zee band members, singing, guitar in hand, looking soulful. Yes, he was truly hot, and his music was wonderful. She'd seen the Julian Blake Band perform once, in her pre-Ariana days, and had loved every moment. If there was one thing that might make her forget, maybe even for an hour or two, how crappy she felt, it was watching Julian onstage. She rested a hand on her dragon. If Luke showed up at the community hall, she'd suck it up and deal. "Okay then." Chin up, she spoke with resolve. "We'll go together. You and me."

"Oh! But I don't, you know, really go out much."

"You've never gone to see Julian perform here?"

Iris shook her head.

"Wow. Okay, you say I need to move on? Well, Iris, I say you need to get out more."

"I know, but I'm so shy. It's really hard for me, Miranda."

"And the thought of seeing Luke is hard for me. So why don't we both *buck up*, put on some pretty clothes, and have a night out?"

She read temptation in her friend's dark eyes, but Iris's mouth tightened in a "no" line.

Before the word could escape, Miranda said, "I'm sorry about the shyness thing, but this is at the community hall on an island where you've lived all your life. Almost everyone there has been into the bookstore at some point, and you've talked to them."

"Well, maybe about books."

"It's not a cocktail party. I don't want to socialize either. We're going to hear Julian. We'll sit at a table together, listen, and leave as soon as the band finishes."

Iris stared at her doubtfully.

"Julian Blake," Miranda reminded her.

Ah, there it was, a smile.

"Good morning, ladies," a genial male voice said, and Miranda glanced up to see Bart Jelinek, the Realtor.

"Hi," she said grudgingly. The man had a talent for interrupting.

"Hello, Bart," Iris said softly, curling her hands around her tea mug and not meeting his eyes.

"Iris, you're as lovely as ever. A flower, just like your name."

Miranda wanted to wrinkle her nose, but resisted. At least the man's smile looked more like that of a jovial uncle than an old creep hitting on a beautiful young woman. She forced a small smile of her own when the man turned to her.

"And Miranda Gabriel. How nice to see you. Do tell your brother and Eden congratulations from me and Cathy. I hear they got married last weekend."

"They did. They're on their honeymoon now, but I'll tell them when they get back."

"Excellent. By the way, ladies, both of you should be seeing Cathy tomorrow. A niece has a birthday coming up, and of course we'd never shop online. We believe in patronizing our Blue Moon Harbor businesses."

"Thank you for that," Iris said in that same quiet tone.

"Yes," Miranda said. "Kara's so grateful to her store's loyal customers."

Bart nodded, and then raised a hand to wave at another man who'd just come in. "I must take my leave. I'm having coffee with Herb Warren."

Miranda noted that Jelinek had a friendly word to offer to everyone he passed on his way to join Mr. Warren.

Now she did allow herself that nose-wrinkle. "Is it just me, or is there something slimy about that man?"

"Bart?" Iris said, more animated now that he had gone. "He's a salesman, but I wouldn't say he's slimy. *Hearty* is the word I'd use. He's well respected here."

"You acted kind of, uh, subdued with him."

Iris's shoulders tightened and lifted, and then dropped. "That's me, not him. The stupid shyness thing."

"Okay, then I guess it's just me. I've never been great at character judgment." Look at all the losers she'd managed to fall for. Before Luke.

And now she was getting depressed again. "Julian Blake," she reminded herself and Iris. "Hopefully, I can arrange a sitter for Ariana. She's been cranky this week and keeps asking for Luke."

"This was a good idea," Iris said, leaning toward Miranda and speaking loudly enough to be heard over the audience's enthusiastic clapping. Triple-B-Zee, as they were tonight, had just finished their second song.

"I take full credit." Grinning, she hoisted her beer bottle in a toast to herself, her friend, and the fantastic music. She was enjoying herself for the first time in a week, and part of it was due to relief that Luke hadn't come and no one was shooting her censorious looks.

"You deserve it." Iris gently clicked her glass of white wine against Miranda's bottle.

The band had started with a cover of Alan Jackson's "Good Time," which got a bunch of people up and line dancing. They'd followed it with George Strait's "Give It All We Got Tonight," and as couples swayed on the dance floor, Miranda did her best not to wish she was there in Luke's arms. She had to admit, Julian Blake helped with that.

While she enjoyed B-B-Zee's music, Forbes's son added a whole new energy. First, of course, there was his appearance. There weren't too many guys with blond hair who gave off a bad-boy vibe, but Julian sure did. That hair was shaggy and the shade of burnished gold, almost matching the color of his guitar. His lean body—all muscle and sinew—was clad in ripped black: jeans and a tattered tee. A tat twined around his right arm and she knew, from the Internet, that it was notes from one of his early compositions.

And then there was his voice. Even when he sang a classic

country song in a duet with his father, the rasp of his low, husky voice added a raw edge to the band's normal sound.

Forbes announced the next song, one of Julian's and a favorite of hers, called "Mocking." The dad stepped back with his guitar, and the son took center stage to solo. She was enraptured as he sang about feeling like an outcast, being mocked by others, but then putting on a magic cloak that deflected the jeers and turned them back on those who taunted him. The lyrics spoke directly to her, and his soulful tone and inwardly focused expression made her feel as if he was singing from personal experience. Might his music be his magic cloak?

When the clapping died down, she whispered to Iris, "I think I'm in love."

Her friend gave a soft laugh. "You and every other woman in this room."

Iris looked stunning tonight, though her elegantly coiled black hair and screen-printed silk top with an iris motif would have fit better at C-Shell than the community hall.

"I love that blouse," Miranda told her. "That's one of your aunt's, isn't it? I've seen some in Island Treasures, but the price tags made me scared to even touch them."

"Yes, it's Aunt Lily's. I can get you a deal."

And then the band was launching into the next number, this one an old folk song, "Blowin' in the Wind," with Forbes and Julian singing together.

As she and Iris listened to song after song, a few people dropped by their table to say hi or ask them to dance. The women barely glanced away from the stage, and quickly dispatched them.

When the band took a break, she and Iris went to the bar to get fresh drinks. They agreed to switch to club soda and lime, because Miranda was honoring her one-drink limit and Iris was driving. They stopped to say hi to Mr. and Mrs. Nelson, who'd been on the dance floor earlier for the slow songs, him in a wheelchair and his wife on his lap. Proof that it was possible to find the love of your life, and to keep that love alive. Or at least it was possible for some people. It sure didn't seem to be her freaking *destiny*.

But tonight wasn't for angst. With Julian onstage, there was magic in the air.

Across the room, she exchanged waves with a smiling Glory, and then she and Iris paused by the table where Di, Seal, Helen, and Jim sat with several friends. Kelsey was babysitting Ariana tonight, planning to attend Saturday night's show with a group of friends.

When Miranda and Iris resumed their path to the bar, Iris said, "Eden's parents are nice, aren't they? And Di and Seal are such an asset to this island."

"Pretty good for two runaway hippies, right?" Two people who had covered up a murder. Well, actually, Helen and Jim were covering it up as well. And so was she. That was probably a crime, and a worse one than petty shop-lifting. She gave a surprised laugh, not having thought of it that way before.

"What's so funny?" Iris asked.

Miranda shook her head. "Just, the things you'll do for family." The Blaines and the SkySongs had taken her in, her and Ariana, and she would do anything for them. If she moved back to Vancouver, her life, and her daughter's, would feel awfully empty.

"Yes, family is a huge influence in one's life," Iris said, sounding as if, for her, it was a mixed blessing.

Miranda wondered about that, but before she could probe, another islander said hello, and then she and Iris needed to scramble to get their drinks and make a quick run to the ladies' room before the next set started.

When the band struck the first note, she settled back in the dimly lit room beside her friend for another hour or so of pure enjoyment. And that was exactly what she got.

Though she was aware of people dancing, her attention focused on the band. And particularly on Julian Blake. He was exactly the kind of man she'd always been drawn to, and what was wrong with indulging in a little fantasizing about the hot musician?

Such as imagining, when he sang a heartbreaking ballad of his own composition and gazed in the direction of her table, that he was singing to her. Though she supposed, to be more accurate, it would be to her and Iris.

A threesome, maybe? Quickly she raised a hand to smother the splutter of laughter that rose in her throat. Best not to share that bizarre notion with Iris. Instead, she leaned over and whispered, "He's looking at us."

"At you," her friend said quickly.

"Why not at you? You're gorgeous. You love his music, Iris. You think he's hot. Why not talk to him after their set? See if anything, you know, develops."

Iris's snort didn't match up with her elegant appearance. "If I even thought about doing that, I'd be sick to my stomach from nerves. Besides, Julian Blake wouldn't be interested in a relationship with a woman like me."

It figured that Iris's mind would go to "relationship" while Miranda's was chanting "hook up!" Not that she'd do it. Or would she? At least she could fantasize, and so she did as the music pulsed around them.

By the time the band finished its final set, Miranda was pleasantly buzzed. She'd gone out to see one of her favorite musicians, indulged in some yummy daydreams, and spent the evening with a friend. Luke hadn't shown up, nothing terrible had happened, and she no longer felt so heartachingly depressed. She could do this. Get on with her life. "Glad I persuaded you to come?" she asked Iris.

"I truly am."

"If you're not going to talk to Julian, are you at least

going home with a sexy fantasy or two to keep you warm tonight?"

Her friend's smooth, pale cheeks flushed. And then, surprisingly, she gave a cheeky grin. "Now that would be telling."

Miranda laughed, stretched luxuriously, and really wished for a second drink. But that way led to the danger of turning into her mom, and she wasn't going there.

"It's time to go," Iris said, retrieving her purse from under the table. "Are you ready?"

No, she wasn't. Back home, alone in her bed, even dreams of Julian wouldn't be enough to hold misery at bay. Here, though, with warmth and lights and music, she could perhaps stave it off a little longer. "You know, I think I'll stay awhile. Indulge in another decadent soda and lime. Feed the jukebox." With some Julian Blake tunes, since anything else would be a letdown. "You go on without me."

"But I'm your ride home." Iris frowned and touched her forehead, as if a headache was brewing. "I guess I could stay awhile longer."

"Not unless you want to. Honestly, I'll be fine. I can hitch a ride back with Di and Seal." She gestured toward the table where the SkySongs and the Blaines sat with their friends.

"You're sure?"

"Absolutely." Miranda grabbed her own purse. "I'll walk you out, then get myself that drink."

Together they crossed the room, joining a number of others who were heading for the door. Outside, Miranda stood on the porch of the community hall and breathed in the fresh, cool night air as she watched Iris walk to her car. Almost, she was tempted to call out and run down the steps to join her. But that would mean bringing this wonderful night to an end, and the longer she could postpone that, the better.

As Iris pulled out of her parking spot, Miranda raised a hand in a farewell wave. Back inside, she put coins in the jukebox, selecting Julian Blake tunes the band hadn't played tonight, and then made a trip to the ladies' room. Washing her hands, she peered at her reflection. Objectively, she thought she looked pretty good for someone who'd been dumped, yet again. All week, her eyes had been dull and faded, sometimes puffy and bloodshot, but now they were bright. *Thank you, Julian Blake!* She brushed her hair until it shone and freshened her lip gloss.

Just because a girl had a broken heart, it didn't have to mean she looked like crap.

Shoulders back in her snug-fitting black tank top and hips swinging in her denim mini, she sauntered back into the main room and across to the bar. She climbed onto a stool and ordered a soda and lime. When the bartender, an older woman, gave her the drink and her change, Miranda slid a toonie across the bar. She took a long swallow of her drink and let her eyes drift closed, sinking into the music.

"Haven't got tired of that guy yet?" a husky voice asked. A voice that reminded her of . . .

Her eyes flared open. "Julian!"

"You have the advantage," he said with one of those slow smiles that was guaranteed to melt a girl's panties. He didn't recognize her, and that wasn't a surprise. Though they'd been in school together, both had skipped more classes than they'd attended, and besides she'd looked totally different back then.

Had he heard about his stepbrother's ill-fated dating experience with a woman named Miranda? If so, he'd already have judged her and found her lacking. "I'm Randy," she said, giving the nickname she'd used in her clubbing days, and adding her patented suggestive tagline. "As in my name, not an adjective." Sexual awareness rippled through her, belying her words.

He chuckled. "My loss."

"Oh, I'm sure you're tired of women throwing themselves at you," she teased, widening her eyes flirtatiously.

She was single and this was a man she'd always lusted after. Here he was, so close she could breathe the musk of sweat and soap, while in the background one of his hit songs played. Why shouldn't she allow herself these moments of pleasure?

He gave a fake yawn and said, in a mock upper-class British accent, "It does get rather tedious." Gesturing to the empty stool beside her, he said, "Mind if I join you? My dad and the other guys are heading home but I could use a drink and some company before I call it a night."

"Please do. But be warned, I may gush about your music."

"And I may blush, but don't let that stop you."

His cheeks were already flushed, and his eyes, a truer blue than her own, glittered. He looked like he was high, and she hoped for his sake it was from performing, not from drugs.

He ordered a Blue Moonshine lager, clicked the bottle against her glass, and took a long swallow. "I saw you and your friend in the audience. She bailed on you?"

"Don't take it as an insult. She's shy, doesn't go out much. It's only because you were playing that I persuaded her to come tonight."

"And now I am blushing." He rested his arm on the bar so that his bare forearm, the one with the music-note tattoo, brushed her dragon. Nodding at her ink, he said, "I like your dragon. It's sexy and fierce."

She smiled at his perceptiveness. "I got it a long time ago. When I longed to be fierce, to be independent and breathe fire on my enemies."

His eyes widened slightly. "I like that. Could've used that in 'Mocking.'"

"That song's perfect as it is."

His gaze held hers. "It speaks to you."

She nodded. "It feels genuine, like it comes from a bad time in your life."

"All my songs are genuine." His face softened. "Fortunately, the real bad times seem to be behind me. For you, too, I hope?"

"Oh, except for the occasional broken heart here and there," she said dryly.

He kept studying her intently, and then his lips kinked up. "You should be a songwriter. Take a broken heart and a couple glasses of whiskey, and you've got a ballad."

"*You* do. One that millions of people can identify with."

"Millions. I like that. You're good for my ego." He ran a callused fingertip up her arm. "Maybe we could take this conversation somewhere private and figure out how I can be good to you." The husky rasp of his voice matched the rough-edged caress of his finger.

Her heart jumped. She could have sex with Julian Blake. And there was no reason in the world she shouldn't.

She glanced past him, checking out the place, realizing how quickly it had emptied out. The SkySongs and Blaines had gone. If they'd seen her, they would have assumed she had her own car or was getting a lift with Iris. "It seems I'm without a ride home," she said, thinking quickly. No way could she take him back to her cabin, and she guessed he was staying at Forbes and Sonia's house. But then, this undeveloped island had lots of scenic parking spots.

Would she really do this? Allow herself a half hour of no-strings, no-holds-barred pure pleasure? Create a steamy memory to serve as background accompaniment every time, in the future, she heard one of his songs?

"My stepmom drove over in her car and Forbes went back with her."

She noticed that he called his father by his given name.

"Leaving me the van." He skimmed his hand slowly up her bare forearm in a sensual caress that sent tingles through her entire body. Just like she was a guitar string, quivering when he plucked her. "Let's go."

She'd as soon the island rumor mill didn't gossip about this, so she slid off the bar stool, removing her arm from his touch. Rather loudly, she said, "Thank you for offering me a ride home." As they walked toward the door, she made sure there were inches of space between their bodies. Maintaining that distance in the almost empty parking lot, where a few other people were climbing into their vehicles, she felt as if electricity was zinging back and forth between their bodies.

"What about your guitar?" she asked as they approached a battered black van with "B-B-Zee" painted on the side, parked at the far end of the parking lot by the road.

"Forbes and I loaded our equipment earlier."

They walked to the driver's side, which paralleled the road. No one in the parking lot could see them now, and Julian backed her up against the van, moving close until their bodies were separated by only an inch or two. "Don't want people talking about us?"

She dropped her big purse on the ground. "It's a small island. The last thing I want is a slutty reputation."

"Fair enough. But I don't see what's slutty about having sex with someone you're attracted to. Two consenting adults and all."

"Me either. But that's not how everyone sees it."

"You're not married, right? Or seeing anyone?"

Suppressing a pang for her lost relationship, she shook her head. "Neither. You?"

"I don't *do* relationships. Just so you know."

"Thanks for that."

"Excuse me?"

"For being honest. Not all guys are. And to be honest back, I'm looking for a relationship. So we're good."

"I'm guessing we could be very good," he said in a raspy drawl that suggested the very same thing to her.

He moved forward slowly, so slowly, the cotton of his black tee and the denim of his jeans brushing her clothing. Closer still, so she felt the press of his hard body against her softer one, through the layers of fabric.

Her breath caught as his head bent and she had the thought, the utterly irrelevant thought, that he was an inch or two shorter than Luke. Leaner, though, which made him look taller than he was. Her arms went around him, her hands exploring his back, the heat of him, and the tensile strength of those rangy muscles flexing as he raised his arms and placed his hands on the side of the van above her head. He was caging her in, though she could easily move to the side and escape.

But she didn't want to. Her entire body trembled with anticipation, with wanting.

Chapter Twenty

Luke had said good night to the boys and Tiffie, the babysitter, and been on his way to Quail Ridge Community Hall to hear his stepbrother play with B-B-Zee when he'd received an emergency call.

Reenie Petrov's pregnant palomino, Butterscotch, was showing signs that labor was beginning. Two or three weeks back, Luke had diagnosed the horse with placentitis, which put her at risk for a "red bag" delivery: a premature separation of the placenta. He'd told the owner to monitor Butterscotch closely and notify him immediately when she appeared to be in labor.

On getting the call, he'd phoned Viola using hands-free, knowing not only that he could use her assistance and experience, but also that she loved a challenging case.

It had turned out to be placentitis, but he and Viola had been able to save the foal and administer oxygen to combat any oxygen deprivation. They had monitored both mare and foal long enough to feel confident they'd both be fine, but he had asked Reenie to keep an eye on them and let him know immediately if she saw any indication of problems.

Driving home near midnight after saying good night to both women, he was tired but felt the warm buzz of satisfaction that his work so often brought. Islanders weren't big on staying up late and he saw only another few cars on the country road. B-B-Zee's last set must be finished by now and he was sorry he'd missed the show, but maybe he could make it tomorrow night. Luke and his stepbrother were about as different as two people could be, and he didn't envy Julian his musical talent and fame, but he did like Julian and enjoyed hearing him perform.

As Luke approached the community hall, his headlights revealed a doe and fawn standing on the shoulder of the road. He stopped and waited as they gracefully sauntered across the pavement in front of him. Locals were careful on the roads here, but deer had no traffic sense and every now and then one of the lovely creatures was struck.

Slowly he drove away, rounding a bend and seeing that, sure enough, the parking lot at the community hall was almost empty. But his lights caught the front of a familiar van, parked near the road. It was Forbes's. If he and Julian were still in the hall, maybe they'd be up for a nightcap. Luke was braking when, under the impersonal light of a parking lot lamp, he saw a man and woman pressed together against the side of the van.

A lean guy in black. Julian had picked up a groupie. No big surprise. That was another way in which the two of them differed. Julian seemed to have no desire for the things Luke so treasured: the love of a soul mate, marriage and kids, building a home together. The things he'd thought he might find with Miranda. So many times this past week, when missing her was a steady ache, he'd wondered if he had overreacted. He'd heard her as saying she didn't envision their relationship heading anywhere serious, but maybe he'd misinterpreted. But even if that were true, how could a relationship work unless it was between two people who viewed themselves as equals?

Driving past, something made him glance back in the side mirror. At this angle, he could see the woman more clearly, and he almost lost his grip on the wheel. That was Miranda, with her arms wrapped around his stepbrother.

No! She's mine!

He wanted to jam on the brakes, back up, run over, and plant his fist in Julian's face.

A realization hit him like a punch in the gut: damn it, he hadn't been falling in love with Miranda. He loved her.

Which was stupid, because clearly she'd made her choice. That told him everything he needed to know. No, he hadn't misinterpreted her words. She might have hung out with Luke, but she hadn't had strong feelings for him. Not if she could get over him so quickly. And of course it figured she'd hook up with Julian. When she talked about him, it was obvious she was a total fangirl. So much for the idea that she had changed. She was the same Miranda she'd always been.

Damn her and Julian both. And himself, for letting himself fall for her.

Luke floored the gas.

Julian didn't touch her face, didn't caress her body, just maintained the full-body contact and pressed his mouth to hers. His lips were hot, talented, unfamiliar. Sexy, wicked.

Wrong.

Damn, this was wrong. Miranda groaned, wrenched her mouth from his, and ducked under his outstretched arms to step to the side, away from temptation. Suddenly it hit her how chilly it was outside. She hadn't put on her sweater when they left the community hall, and now she shivered, bare-armed and bare-legged in her tank top and brief skirt.

"What the hell?" Julian asked.

She bent to retrieve her sweater from her bag and pulled it on. "I'm sorry. So sorry. Believe me."

He scowled. "You didn't seem like that kind of woman. A tease."

"I'm not. I wanted this, but . . ." She could have made an excuse, but Julian deserved better, and maybe she owed it to herself, too, to do the mature thing and be honest. "Has anyone in your family mentioned the woman Luke was dating? The one he broke up with?"

"Yeah. Uh, Miranda, was it?" He whacked his palm against his forehead. "Randy. Shit."

"I'm sorry. Again. Still. Whatever. I gave you that name because, because . . ."

Looking disgusted, he said, "Because you knew I wouldn't betray my stepbrother."

"It's not a betrayal," she defended herself. "We broke up. He can date—or sleep with—anyone he wants"—though the thought was a knife in her heart—"and so can I. I just wanted, tonight, to . . . to be *me*, without any, you know, backstory. Without you already thinking bad things about me."

"Can't say I'm thinking good things about you right now." Then, grudgingly, he said, "I appreciate that you decided to tell the truth." He cocked his head. "Out of curiosity, why did you? Why call a stop?"

"Because it didn't feel right." She twisted her mouth. "Good, but not right."

"Huh. Yeah, well it wasn't right. So I'm glad that sank in before we took it too far." He shook his head. "Fucking Destiny Island. This place is no good for me."

She knew from Luke that Julian shunned the island, but it seemed kind of an odd thing to say, that the place was no good for him. "I used to hate it, but it's grown on me."

"Not gonna happen." He shook his head, and then said, "Why'd you and Luke break up?"

"He said he and the boys deserve better than me." She wasn't about to add that Luke had also told her to grow up. Julian would no doubt agree.

"What? That doesn't sound like Luke."

"He's right. I know I'm not good enough for him."

Julian frowned and then sighed and said, "I'm guessing you're better than you think." Under the scattered artificial lights of the parking lot, his blue eyes got a glittery, glazed expression. "You're better than you think. Song title. Song concept."

Seriously? She'd inspired a song?

"Need to go home and write," he said, opening the door of the van and jumping in. The engine started.

He was going to strand her in this parking lot? Ah well, creative genius. At least she had her phone and could call someone and get them to come pick her up.

The window opened. "Sorry. You need a ride. Hop in."

She hurried around to the passenger door and climbed in. "I'm at SkySong. And I'll shut up if you want to, uh, compose or whatever."

"Thanks."

Well, this is a first, she thought as the battered black van drove the night-quiet road. She could've been parking somewhere having sex with a superhot musician whom she'd lusted after forever. Instead, he didn't even seem aware of her existence. Yet, despite her general state of misery, she felt content. For once in her life, she'd maybe done the mature thing.

Too bad Luke would never know. Or care.

Luke spent most of the night awake, fuming. The next morning, standing at his bedroom window and scowling out at a spring shower, he debated whether to follow his normal routine. He worked Saturdays. His mom, the teacher, didn't. Forbes did his woodwork and music at home anyhow—the two-car garage had been converted, with a studio on one side and a workshop on the other—and set his own work hours. Since the grandparents welcomed any opportunity to spend time with their grandsons, Luke and the twins usually went over for Saturday breakfast and then he left the boys there for the day.

But Julian would be at the house, in his old bedroom. Or, rather, the room he'd once occupied, which he had years ago insisted on Sonia converting to a home office with a sofa bed. Luke's old bedroom had been refurbed, too, with twin beds for grandson sleepovers.

One thing Luke was fairly sure of: Julian wouldn't have spent the night at Miranda's. Unless, of course, she'd sent Ariana to spend the night with a sitter, but she'd never done that before. She said that just imagining it gave her separation anxiety. He'd understood, remembering how he'd felt the first time the boys had been away from home overnight.

He and Miranda had seemed so compatible when it came to parenting. And sex. And other things, too. He'd thought he knew her pretty well by now. Damn it, the truth was that he'd nursed a secret hope that she would come to her senses, grow up, and return to him.

Seeing her last night, realizing in that moment that he loved her and that she didn't give a damn about him, had shattered that idiotic notion. Obviously, he'd been deluding himself from the beginning, picturing Miranda as the woman he wanted her to be, not the one she really was.

Flexing his shoulders, he tried to work out the ache of tension. Whatever he was going to do this morning, he needed to get on with it.

Arranging a sitter at six-thirty on a Saturday morning would be problematic. Besides, he'd have to explain to his mom and Forbes, and the boys. Chances were, Julian would sleep in this morning anyway—worn out from performing onstage and *elsewhere*, damn him—and Luke wouldn't have to face him.

He showered and dressed, then got Caleb and Brandon up and dressed, and collected all the paraphernalia for a day at their grandparents.

Arriving at the two-story house Forbes had renovated, he found his mom cooking banana pancakes and Forbes frying bacon and humming a cheerful tune. As Luke had hoped, Julian was absent.

After the grandparents hugged the kids, Luke said, "Sorry I never made it last night. An equine emergency."

His mom kissed his cheek. "Did it come out okay?"

"A healthy foal and mom." Texts from Reenie had confirmed it.

"That's good to hear," Forbes said. "But you did miss a great show."

"I'm sure."

"Julian was in peak form."

"Yeah, I'm sure." Forbes didn't know the half of it, but Luke wasn't going to bitch to him about his son's behavior. "Listen, I—" He'd started to say he couldn't stay for breakfast, when a male voice interrupted.

"Did I hear my name?" Julian, wearing sweatpants and pulling a ripped tee over his head, came into the kitchen. He had bags under his eyes but, on spying the twins, grinned and said, "Hey, it's my two favorite nephews. Come give your uncle Julian a big hug."

Both boys—unknowing traitors—threw themselves at him and lots of hugging, screeching, and mock wrestling ensued.

Maybe he was being irrational and immature, but too many things in Luke's life felt like betrayals.

His dad, promising he'd fight the cancer but in the end

succumbing. His mom, lost to him for years, first in her own misery and then in her new love. Candace in the hospital, in labor, learning about the complications and telling the OB-GYN that if it came down to a choice, the doctor had to save the babies. His sons, forgetting his existence in the joy of seeing Julian. All of them choosing something other than being with him. Loving him.

Miranda, shunning him, then less than a week later kissing Julian. Fucking him, most likely. "I need to go," he said abruptly.

"Oh, Luke, do you have to go into work so early?" his mom asked. "It's such a rare treat, having the whole family together."

"Yeah, man," Julian said, casting him a wary look over the heads of the boys. "Stick around."

Luke ground his teeth. But he couldn't avoid Julian for the rest of his life, and some primitive male instinct drove him to have it out with the jerk. "Can I talk to you? In private?"

Julian's eyes widened, like he knew he'd been caught out. "Sure." He detached little boy arms from his anatomy. "I'll be back, kids. We'll hang out today, okay?"

Luke led the way downstairs to the rec room and, when Julian sprawled on the battered couch, he remained standing, his hands fisted. He wouldn't punch his stepbrother no matter how good it'd feel, but he could clench his fists all he wanted. "You look tired," he said sarcastically. "Long night?"

"Yeah," his stepbrother drawled. He gave it a long pause. "Writing music."

"Yeah, like I believe that. I saw you."

Eyebrows a few shades darker than his blond hair arched. "Saw me where, doing what?"

Anger heated in Luke's body. "Kissing Miranda."

"Ah."

"That's all you've got to say?"

Julian crossed his arms over his chest, sinewy muscles rippling. No doubt Miranda would've found that incredibly sexy. "You think I owe you an explanation?"

Luke ground his teeth. "Yeah."

"The way I heard it from Sonia and Forbes, you two had broken up." Julian had always called his father Forbes, never Dad. Luke figured it was one of Forbes's hippie things.

"We broke up less than a week ago," he told his stepbrother. "Where do you get off, making the moves on my ex?"

"Why do you care? You dumped her, right?"

"That's not what happened." It was Miranda who'd implied their relationship was heading nowhere, who hadn't wanted to address her insecurities, who'd walked away from him.

Julian uncrossed his arms and leaned forward. "What did happen?"

"Did she say something?"

"Said you didn't think she was good enough for you."

"Gah! That's not what I said."

"Seems that's how she interpreted it."

"Yeah, I can imagine." His anger dulled, Luke shoved his hands in the front pockets of his jeans. "She's so damned insecure. I guess I basically told her to grow up."

Julian let out an amused whistle. "Bet that went over well. Seriously, man, do you know nothing about women?"

"How would I?" he snapped. "Candace was my one and only."

His stepbrother nodded slowly. "Miranda seems pretty different from Candace."

"You can say that again."

"And yet you were dating her. Attracted to her. You care enough about her that you're pissed off she'd be with someone else, even though you'd broken up."

Luke's shoulders slumped. "Yeah. I guess." It was hard admitting that to his stepbrother, yet it seemed he'd already figured it out. "That's why it feels like a betrayal. By both of you."

Julian rose and walked over to stand in front of Luke. "It wasn't a betrayal. I didn't know she was your ex, not until after that kiss."

"Shit. She didn't tell you? Didn't she even give you her name?"

"She said it was Randy. I don't know what she had in mind—maybe getting back at you, maybe just wanting some uncomplicated sex, but—"

"Maybe a serious case of fangirl-itis. She's crazy about your music and told me she thought you were hot."

Julian shrugged. "Anyhow, she stopped. We'd just started to kiss and she broke it off. Said it felt wrong. Told me about her relationship with you." Another shrug. "I figure you should know that."

"She did?" If that was true, it wasn't a total betrayal. Maybe Miranda really did have feelings for him.

His stepbrother ambled toward the door. "I wasn't the guy she wanted to be with," he said over his shoulder. "And maybe she does have some issues, but you care and it seems like she does, too." In the doorway, he turned to face Luke. "Why don't you go after her? See if you can work things out?"

The two of them had never been close enough to share confidences, and it rubbed Luke wrong that now his step-brother was acting like some kind of relationship counselor. He shot back with, "This advice from the guy who's never spent more than a weekend with a woman?"

Julian's features pinched briefly, almost as if his hookup record caused him pain. Which would be weird, since it was his choice to play the field rather than commit to one woman. "It's up to you," Julian said gruffly. "Me, I'm going to go eat pancakes."

As he disappeared up the stairs, Luke took a deep breath

and thought about his stepbrother's unwanted advice. Should he talk to Miranda again?

"OMG, you kissed Julian!" Glory cried, dropping the biscotti she'd been dipping. She didn't even seem to notice when it submerged in her latté.

It was Sunday morning—the Sunday after the Friday night kiss—and they were sitting on the couch in Miranda's cabin while their daughters played on the rug with a couple of Ariana's fairy dolls. Both moms had encouraged them to share, and so far they were doing it amiably, which was kind of miraculous given the bad mood Ariana'd been in since Luke had gone missing from their lives. The moms were sharing, too, with the biscotti Glory'd brought and the lemon bars Miranda had made, both plated on the coffee table Forbes Blake had crafted.

"Yeah," Miranda said, gloomily crumbling her own biscotti. Yes, it was chocolate-almond, but even chocolate didn't appeal to her these days. "And then I stopped. Not because it wasn't good but, well, I couldn't get past Luke."

"The guy who dumped you. Girl, you're entitled to hook up with someone else."

"And if it had been anyone other than his stepbrother, I might have." Or not. "I mean, I know I need to move on and all."

"But you don't want to because you're hung up on Luke. Seems to me like you're in love with him."

If their little girls could share, she ought to be able to as well, and be honest with her friend. "Maybe. It doesn't feel like the times I've been in love before."

"How's it different?" Glory reached for one of the lemon bars.

Miranda sipped her latté as she hunted for words. "It's

quieter. I mean, he's really sexy and great in bed. It's better than any sex I've ever had. But the whole thing, the relationship, it's more comfortable." She snorted and corrected herself. "I mean, it *was* more comfortable until he started telling me how immature I am." She put her mug down on the coffee table with a thump.

"Guys can be so stupid. I hope you told him that."

Shaking her head, she said, "What would be the point? He thinks he knows me, and he, well, isn't that impressed."

"He should be," Glory said loyally. "And for heaven's sakes, who in their twenties is, like, one hundred percent grown up? Yeah, maybe Luke, though I doubt that, but the rest of us are still trying to figure things out. Don't you see the news? A huge number of Millennials, all they've ever done is go to school, and they're living in their parents' basements, off their charity, not even finding jobs. But you've supported yourself forever, you're raising a wonderful daughter, and you're studying for a new career. What could be more mature than that?"

"Doing it without having to come crawling to my brother for help?"

"Now you're the one who's being stupid. Everyone needs a little help now and then. And it's *mature* to acknowledge that. Luke should know that."

"He does." And so did she, now. Glancing at her daughter playing with Gala, both of them so healthy and happy, she knew she could have made Ariana's first couple of years better. If only she'd been willing to accept Aaron's assistance from the beginning.

Turning back to her friend, she said, "No, the immaturity thing was about me being, to use his words, 'insecure and self-defeating.'" She swallowed. "And I can't argue with that."

Glory opened her mouth in what looked like was going

to be a quick protest, but then didn't utter it. She pressed her lips together and after a moment said, "Oh."

"Yeah."

Her friend finished the lemon bar and then picked up her mug and spooned up a mushy mix of biscotti and coffee. Quietly she asked, "You really think he's right?"

She shrugged. "If 'insecure' means thinking I'm not good enough for Luke, that I can't measure up to Candace, that he deserves someone better, then yeah."

"I think he'd be lucky to have you."

"Aw." She reached over to pat her friend's hand. "Thank you."

"I guess the point is that *you* need to believe that."

For a couple of minutes, they drank—or in Glory's case, spooned up—coffee and watched their daughters. Then Glory said, "How did this whole conversation happen anyhow? I saw you guys at the reception and you seemed super happy together. Dancing, all romantic. How did it suddenly go sideways?"

Miranda hunched her shoulders. "You know that big-haired brunette in the sausage-casing pink dress?"

"Winnie Bender, divorced and on the prowl?"

"I guess. Anyhow, I overheard her and a friend trash-talking, saying how Luke was just with me for the sex and how he deserved way better."

"Shit!" Glory cast a quick look in the girls' direction and lowered her voice. "Didn't you see her with Luke? She wants him for husband number two and she's jealous. Besides, she's a total bitch. She says bad stuff about every-one. I think Aaron only invited her because he was inviting everyone else from our high school class."

"She was being kind of mean about Iris, too. But, what-ever. The point isn't what she said, it's what Luke did."

"So, like, what?" Frowning, Glory said, "You overheard

Queen Bitch, went back to Luke, and asked him if he figured
he deserved better than you, and he agreed?"

"Kind of." She rotated her shoulders and reached for her
mug again. "I came back and I guess I was in a bad mood.
It seemed like everything he said reinforced my fears and I
was, well, kind of bitchy myself. So he asked what was
wrong and I told him what I'd overheard. He didn't rush in
to tell me I was terrific, he asked if *I* thought I was good
enough for him. Well, I could hardly say yes, could I? I
mean, not when he'd be comparing me to Candace. So I
said no, and then he said he and the boys didn't need to be
involved with someone like me."

"Ouch."

Miranda scowled. "And okay, it's true, but he should've
realized that in the beginning! He shouldn't have asked me
out, got our kids playing together, or introduced me to his
folks. Shouldn't have made me care, and hope, and—" She
broke off, shaking her head, near tears.

"You really do love him," Glory said quietly.

"Oh, shit." She hung her head. "I don't know. Is it possible that it feels different from other relationships because
this time it's the real thing?" Was that why she'd been so
utterly miserable for the past week? More miserable than
when any other man in her past, even Ariana's father, had
dumped her.

"If it's the real thing, isn't it worth fighting for?"

Feeling pathetic again, Miranda stared across at her,
eyes swimming with unshed tears. "I haven't a clue how
to do that."

Glory smiled sympathetically. "Yeah, you try to tell a
guy how you're feeling and most of the time he just doesn't
get it. But girlfriend, you're tough like your dragon. You
can figure this out."

The supportive words were sweet to hear, but Miranda

was afraid her friend's confidence in her was unfounded. And yet . . .

Gala gave an angry squeal and tossed a fairy doll across the floor.

"Too good to last," Glory said, and rose to intervene.

Miranda remained on the couch, deliberating. She thought about her dark, pessimistic side, the pathetic one that told her she was worthless and powerless, that seduced her toward depression. Once, her only tool for fighting it had been a shiny silver razor blade.

She gazed down at her left forearm and ran a finger over her dragon's scales. Strong and smart and fierce. Aaron had called her that, way back when she was thirteen. Glory had reminded her that she was tough.

"Okay, dragon-girl," she murmured. "What's your next step?"

Chapter Twenty-One

Luke had been debating whether to try getting in touch with Miranda, when she had phoned him and asked if they could talk. The sound of her voice made his heart jerk and he'd almost dropped the phone. Now, waiting at his house for her to arrive, that same unreliable organ was racing so fast he felt like he was going to hyperventilate.

It was late on Friday afternoon, almost two weeks since the wedding. The boys were over at Annie and Randall's for their monthly dinner-and-sleepover, so Luke was alone in the house, but for the dogs whom he'd confined out in the backyard. He'd also checked with Viola to see if she was willing to cover for him if he got any vet emergency calls.

Even though Miranda wasn't due yet, he'd been looking out the front window every few minutes and this time it took a moment to register that the driveway wasn't, as it had been each time before, empty. Her Toyota was there.

The driver door opened and she stepped out. She stood, unmoving, a slim figure in a sleeveless blue top, tan capris, and sandals. A lonely figure, he thought, her aloneness somehow made even more poignant by the mid-May sunshine.

Now his heart—the heart that loved her, the heart that

wanted to heal the wounded—urged him to rush out to her. But he honestly believed what he'd said at the wedding reception. Maybe, like his mother-in-law, he hadn't phrased it as tactfully as he might, but that "I'm not good enough for you" attitude grated on him. He was willing to keep helping Miranda deal with her issues, but only if she had enough self-esteem to commit to their relationship as an equal partner.

And God, he hoped that was why she'd come.

He opened the front door. Though it didn't make any noise, her head came up and she gazed across the top of her car at him. She dipped her head in a nod, but didn't smile.

She leaned into the vehicle, pulled out her big purse, looped the strap over her shoulder, and closed the car door. Then, slowly but steadily, she walked toward him. Her shoulders were back, he noticed, and her chin high.

"Hey, Luke," she said as she mounted the steps.

"Hey, Miranda. Want to go out on the deck to talk?" It was sunny, warm enough for her clothing and his tee and khaki shorts.

"Sounds good."

He let her precede him through the house. In the kitchen, he offered her a drink and she accepted a bottle of iced tea. He seriously craved a beer, but didn't want even the slightest impairment of his faculties so settled for iced tea as well.

Outside again, she exchanged restrained greetings with the tail-wagging dogs who rushed up the steps of the deck to greet her. Then she walked to the railing and gazed out at the ocean.

Glancing past her, Luke saw that a slight breeze ruffled the dark, blue-green surface of the sea. That breeze brought a hint of wood smoke and the sound of voices from the beach below. He knew without looking that some of his neighbors had a beach fire going. Probably they'd roast hot dogs for dinner, and marshmallows later.

He studied Miranda's back, wondering what she was thinking, what she'd come to say. She turned and seated herself on one side of the picnic-style table, this time facing away from the ocean, toward the house.

The dogs trailed her and he gestured them to the shady corner of the deck that was designated as theirs and said a quiet, "Down. Stay." Then he sat across from her. "Why did you come, Miranda?"

She put down the bottle of iced tea, untasted. "You said some harsh things to me."

"I guess I didn't phrase it very well, and I'm sorry if I hurt you, but I was speaking what I see as the truth. And I need to look out for my kids."

"And for yourself. I understand. Yes, I was hurt. That was my first reaction, to just be hurt and also pissed off that you'd even started a relationship with me if you were only going to end it. I thought I'd been honest with you about who I was."

He'd seen her as the one who ended it, but he'd come to realize she might have a different perspective. "Maybe I was wrong to ask you out. I knew you had thorns but I thought . . ." That she would change from a wild rose with thorns and a lovely scent to a bland hothouse flower? No, that wasn't what he'd wanted.

"You said you kind of liked the thorns, that you were up for a challenge. That I shouldn't make things too easy on you."

Wincing, he did recall saying those words. "You'd gone through some bad stuff and I figured that when you felt more comfortable with me, you'd relax. Be the woman I thought I saw inside you." One with prickles and character, but also with the confidence of a lovely rose.

"I did feel comfortable with you, but there were also

things that made me uncomfortable. I don't know if you truly appreciate how different we are. I know you had a tough time when your dad died, but you at least had one and he loved you. Your mom went through her own issues, but I bet you still knew she loved you. You had a comfortable roof over your head, food in the cupboards. You went to one school; you had friends to hang out with. You had this one special girl who became the love of your life, and you married her."

"I'm sorry you didn't have those things, but—"

"I'm not making excuses. I realize that, as an adult, it's up to me to get past all the bad stuff. But that's been hard." She pressed her lips together, and then went on. "I kept comparing myself to you, and I always came out second-class. I only finished high school last year and you've got a professional degree. You're respected by everyone on the island, and I'm this weird former Goth girl whose mom was an addict and whore. You've always given your sons a stable home, and I've often had to scramble to even give Ariana decent food. You said I was special but, comparing myself to you, I felt inadequate." Finally she raised her bottle and swallowed some of the cold drink.

"I don't understand why you feel the need to compare."

"Maybe that's because you grew up in a stable environment. People knew you and accepted you, and I bet you never had to prove your worth."

"I guess not," he admitted. "Yeah, I guess self-esteem has never been an issue for me."

"Nor for Candace, who was beautiful and popular and rich. And generous and loving. The two of you fit together so perfectly." She shrugged. "You and me, not so much."

"But we did. Like the day we went kayaking. You, Ariana, me, the boys. It felt right."

"It did. But here's the thing." Elbows on the picnic table, the bottle held between both hands, she leaned forward.

"You could let it be. Just feel the rightness. For me, when things are going well, I question. There's got to be something wrong. It can't last. Because for almost all my life that's how things have gone."

A woodpecker had taken up drilling on a nearby tree, its hammering forming a steady percussion backbeat to her words.

"I guess that's what I meant about being self-defeating," he said. "You take something good and poke away until you destroy it."

She winced, but then firmed her jaw again. "I guess I do. That's what I did at the wedding reception. The mean girls hit all my triggers and rather than be mature and let it roll off my back, I struck out. Not at them, who deserved it, but at you. At our relationship."

She'd laid some heavy stuff on him, but none of it was a big surprise so he didn't have to reflect long before nodding in agreement. "But what were you thinking? What did you want me to do? Reassure you all over again? I started to, but if it never worked before, why would you suddenly then, when you were in that mood, let it sink in?"

"You're right, I wouldn't have." She lifted the bottle and took a long swallow. "I have a thick head. Ask Aaron and Eden. People can hammer away at it, like that woodpecker's doing to the tree, saying the same thing over and over, but it doesn't always sink in because there's a barrier in place. The barrier you identified. Low self-esteem."

He drank from his own bottle and waited for her to go on.

"You know what you did?" she said. "You stopped repeating the same message, the one I couldn't let myself believe. You poked back at me, and stabbed right through the barrier. After I got over being hurt and mad, I thought about the things you said. You called me self-defeating and you were right. A while back, Eden suggested that I was self-sabotaging."

He nodded slowly. If it was true, could Miranda ever move past it? Did she want to?

"A few minutes ago," she went on, "I said that I thought I'd been honest with you about who I was. But the truth was, I hadn't been honest with myself. I hadn't dug deep."

The woodpecker was silent now, and the only sound came from the distant voices on the beach below. Luke waited for Miranda to go on.

She tipped her head back slightly and took a deep breath. "Mom was self-destructive. Falling for losers, doing drugs, selling her body. I think my grandparents' coldness, their rejection of her, turned her in that direction. I also think she might have suffered from depression, and would try anything to escape the black moods. In the end, she did destroy herself."

"You're not her," he said quietly.

"I was always determined that I wouldn't be. I'm the dragon, right?" She rested her hand on her tattoo. "But, sadly, a part of me isn't at all strong or smart or fierce. That part tends toward depression. It's weak, vulnerable, self-sabotaging. Drawn to the wrong kind of men."

"Go on."

"Guys I thought were larger than life, with exciting lives. Except, as Eden pointed out, they had something else in common. They were emotionally unavailable."

He frowned, trying to understand. "But you told me you believed in love, you were looking for love, so why would you go for guys who weren't available?"

"Doesn't make sense, right? Except it kind of does. As a kid and a teen, everyone I looked to for love, with the exception of Aaron, let me down. Subconsciously, I learned not to trust in love, and came to believe I wasn't worthy of being loved."

Luke swallowed, and thought of his own irrational feeling that the people he loved had betrayed and abandoned him. The moment he and Miranda had a major spat, he'd leaped to the conclusion that she didn't really care about him or their relationship. Maybe the two of them weren't so different.

"If I picked a good guy," she said, "and truly gave my heart to him, then in the end he'd leave me and it would be, like, the ultimate destruction of my heart. My soul." She took a deep breath.

After letting it out slowly, she went on. "So instead of real love, I gave . . . well, infatuation, and to guys who would never love me back. So yeah, when they dumped me, it hurt, but subconsciously that's what I'd expected all along so it didn't totally destroy me. But it did reinforce my low self-worth."

"You set yourself up for rejection?"

She nodded. "Sounds totally dumb, doesn't it?"

"I guess the subconscious has its own weird kind of logic," he mused, thinking again of his own abandonment issue. "Based on the stuff we internalize as we grow up."

"Yes. I'm reading about that kind of thing in my courses about early childhood development."

His mind sidetracked, thinking about his boys. Growing up with him and no mother. He was doing his best, but each decision involved soul-searching. There were almost always cons as well as pros. What weird things were making their way into the hidden depths of his kids' psyches? Parenting was tough, even for the most loving, conscientious parent. He'd been so lucky, having two of those—and even then he had some issues. Miranda'd never had anyone who cared for her except a two-years-older brother who'd been damaged by the same disastrous life circumstances.

"I'm sorry about all of that," he said, wanting to reach over and take her hand, but instead gripping his tea bottle. "I truly am." He appreciated her self-analysis and her honesty, but where did this leave them, as a couple? Wasn't she confirming his fear that she wasn't capable of entering into an equal, healthy relationship with him?

"It's where my independence comes from, too," she said. "I'm afraid to trust anyone other than Aaron, because I learned that everyone else would let me down. When we were kids, we said it was the two of us against the world. But as I got older, I decided that even if he'd always be there, it wasn't fair to keep leaning on him. I had to be able to look after myself. And then look after myself and Ariana."

"Thank you for telling me all of this. It helps me understand what was going on. I'm sorry I wasn't sensitive enough to all you'd gone through."

"I guess I'd have liked you to be, but I'm not sure it would have helped." She shrugged. "Anyhow, so I thought, okay, that's what I'm like. I've been stuck in that pattern forever. Was there any way of breaking out?"

He leaned forward, wondering if he dared hope. "And?"

A smile trembled. "I realized I'd already started. I've accepted Eden as the sister of my heart. I'm part of her family, a real, true part and not just because I'm Aaron's sister."

"That's encouraging to hear." But what about him, and their relationship?

"I thought about what it meant, that I was dating you."

Throat dry, he croaked, "And?" and drank some more iced tea. The liquid, not so icy now, slid down his throat as he waited for her answer.

"On the surface, you're way different from the kind of

guy I've chosen before. Men who are more like your step-brother."

He grimaced slightly, wondering if he should confess that he'd believed she might have slept with Julian.

"But in other ways you are like them."

Offended, he reared back. "In what ways?"

"You're impressive. Successful. Believe me, the way you are with those animals is just as sexy as seeing Chef Emile create magic in the kitchen, or Julian sing those heart-breaking songs he writes."

"Uh, thanks." Being a vet was sexy?

"But more than that, I wonder if you're emotionally un-available."

"Me? Huh?" Hadn't he been ready to hand over his heart at that wedding reception?

"Because of Candace. Everyone, including you, told me how you were a perfect couple. You'd basically loved her from the moment you met her. Could you ever truly open your heart to another woman, especially one as flawed as me?"

He already had. But he needed to protect that heart, be-cause he still didn't know where she was going with this. "So I was another example of the self-fulfilling prophecy? Your subconscious chose me so you could have a super-ficial infatuation and not get too torn up if it ended?" If that was how she felt, surely she wouldn't have come here.

"I wondered," she said. Her lips pressed together.

The woodpecker was at it again. Normally, Luke en-joyed the sounds of nature, but now that hammering beat was annoying.

"But I realized that wasn't what had happened," she went on. "I was never infatuated with you—well, except maybe while you were treating that poor bunny. What I felt for you was different."

His heart gave the oddest bounce. "Different?"

"Slower to develop. Quieter. Deeper. It had to do with more than just your skill as a vet, your physical attractiveness, and great sex." She gave a quick laugh, her face almost relaxing for the first time since she'd arrived. "Correction: knock-my-socks-off sex. But it's also about popcorn and videos and wet dogs. It's about the kids, how you are with Ariana and with the twins, how we all are together, like we're starting to feel like . . . okay, I'm going to say it. Like a family."

His heart was now bouncing in time with the woodpecker's hammering. "You care about me. It's not infatuation."

She let out a long sigh. "Yes. And the way I felt after we broke up was so much worse than anything I'd felt before."

He was on his feet, moving around the table, before she'd finished speaking. As she swung around on the picnic table bench to face him, he reached for her hands.

Pulling her to her feet, he said, "I care about you, too. I was all set to tell you at the wedding reception, and then you started to act so weird." He framed her face with his hands. "No, I'm not emotionally unavailable. And I'm far from perfect, as proved by how unperceptive and unsympathetic I've been. But here's the thing. If we're going to take this relationship somewhere, I want it to be as equal partners. Can you do that?"

Miranda gazed up at Luke. The man she wanted so badly, the one she'd fallen for. She wouldn't lie to him, though. "I'll try my damnedest to be stronger, to have better self-esteem. But I'm still a work in progress. Can you be patient?"

He closed his eyes and she trembled. He was going to

say no, that he wouldn't put himself and the twins through more uncertainty.

But then his eyes opened and flecks of gold gleamed in their greenish-gray depths. "I shouldn't have said what I did at the reception. We should have had this conversation then."

She couldn't let him believe that, because it wouldn't have worked. "I wasn't ready for it. I needed the shock. I needed to feel utterly horrible before I could start to understand what you and Eden had said, and do some serious thinking."

"Okay, maybe. But I should have had more patience and been more understanding." He grimaced. "When I first asked you out and you held back, you know what I thought?"

She shook her head.

"That you'd been with some guys who let you down, and you didn't trust me to treat you right." Voice grating, he said, "And I didn't." He took his hands from her face, leaving her skin missing his warm touch. "You know what I did when Mom married Forbes?" he asked, sitting down so he straddled the wooden bench.

Confused by the apparent change of topic, she sat, too, the same way, so that their knees touched. His strong legs looked so great in shorts. "Uh, you were unhappy, and turned to Candace?"

"Yeah, but also I didn't give Forbes a chance. He wasn't my dad. That was all I saw. It seemed like Mom was trying to find a replacement for Dad, and that was impossible. Later, when I grew up a little, I realized that wasn't what she was doing. Oh, maybe she had mixed motives for marrying Forbes, like wanting to stop grieving so much and feeling so lonely. But the two of them have something solid and wonderful."

"I've seen that."

"I wasn't prepared to see it. Nor willing to see what a terrific guy he was. I didn't give him a chance and didn't give myself a chance. Not until a lot later, once I'd gone off to university and was coming back for holidays. I had a fresh perspective then. And now he and I are really close."

She nodded, finally grasping why he was telling her this. "You're saying you shouldn't have judged him so quickly, based on your insecurities and fears and pain. And I guess you're also saying that maybe you didn't apply that lesson when it came to me. Which means"—she couldn't hold back a small teasing grin—"that you have insecurities, too, Luke."

He wrinkled his nose. "Yeah, turns out I do. Even though I wasn't looking to replace Candace—which would be impossible anyhow because each person and relationship is unique—I guess she was in my mind. How easy our relationship had always been. Whereas with you and me, it wasn't easy. But I got to know Candace day by day over years and years, and you were brand-new in my life. I thought I was open to you, letting you be yourself, finding out who you were and who I was with you. Valuing all of it. But, as that spat at the reception proved, I was being judgmental."

He scrubbed a hand across his jaw, which showed a trace of five o'clock shadow. "I overreacted because I'd thought we'd gotten further than we had. I thought you were more confident of our relationship. I wanted to, well, declare my feelings. Then, when you acted the way you did, said the things you did, I realized I didn't know you as well as I'd thought. What I heard was that you didn't care, that you were rejecting me."

She was shaking her head as he went on to say, "I got hurt and defensive, snapped at you, didn't really listen. I'm sorry."

It hurt her to know that she had the ability to cause Luke pain, and yet it warmed her heart, too, to know he cared that much. "We all do stupid things when we're upset. How about this? If you act like that again, I won't tuck my tail between my legs and run away. I'll plant my fierce little dragon feet and say that I deserve better treatment, and we need to have a good long talk." It made her feel nervous to say that, and yet she was finally coming to believe that she *did* deserve decent treatment. A decent man, a healthy relationship. Even love.

"That sounds very good to me."

"And we'll be open with each other. Yes? We won't nurse hurts and grievances, we'll talk about them." She took a deep breath. She'd been through the wringer but had to pull herself together for one more cycle. She still had to tell him about her big mistake with Julian, and it might end up being a deal-breaker.

"That," he said ruefully, "is an excellent idea."

Again, she took a breath, readying herself. A shiver pricked her skin and she glanced up to see that clouds now blocked the sun. Hopefully, that wasn't a bad omen.

He frowned. "In fact, in the interests of openness, there's something I need to tell you."

Disconcerted, she said, "Uh, okay."

"I was driving back from an emergency call and I saw you and Julian kissing."

"Damn! Luke, I was just going to tell you about that. It wasn't—"

"I know." He held up a hand. "I tackled him the next morning and he straightened me out. And basically told me I was acting like a jerk. Which was true, but I was jealous. Mad, hurt. So I accused him, just like a hormonal adolescent thinking with his, well, not his brain."

"If I saw you kissing someone else, I'd have gone nuts,

too," she confessed, folding her arms across her chest for warmth. "And Luke, I did kiss him. I wanted him, or at least I wanted to be wanted by a guy like him. I wanted one hour of feeling sexy, of having fun, rather than feeling like crap after we broke up."

"And you deceived him. Didn't tell him your real name." Though his tone was even, not accusatory, his eyes had darkened with pain.

"That's right. So none of this is on Julian. It's all my fault. But I realized, as soon as we kissed, that it was wrong."

His brow creased. "You'd been fangirling him forever and when you actually kissed, there was no chemistry?"

"Not exactly," she admitted, hugging her arms closer to her body as she shivered. She had a hoodie in her bag, but this wasn't the time to root around for it. "But it was the wrong chemistry. It wasn't you. I only want you, Luke."

When his frown deepened, she said, "It wouldn't be honest to say I'll never be attracted to another man. But I don't want to be with someone else. Does that make sense? Can you live with that?"

As she'd spoken, a grin had slowly taken over his face. The gold flecks in his eyes danced. "I get it. You know, when I was in high school, even though I was totally in love with Candace and only wanted to be with her, there was this other girl who kind of fascinated me." He bumped a bare knee against her clothed one.

He was clearly expecting her to grin, maybe tease back, but he'd raised another concern. "It's more than that now, though, right?" she asked. "More than just some teenage fascination carried forward into adulthood?"

"Yes," he said immediately, reaching forward to rest his hand on her leg, instantly transferring warmth. "You're so different, so much more than you were then. It's the woman you are today that I want. You're being proactive, taking control of your life."

Reassured, she said, "So, are we done with the secrets now? Everything's out on the table?" She was about to rise and find her purse, to get that hoodie.

But his hand twitched on her leg and he said, "I guess there's one more thing."

Feeling chilled and hollowed out, she braced herself. "Go on."

"This is hard for me to say."

A ragged laugh escaped her. "Like any of this has been easy?"

"No, but . . ." He reached for her hand and gripped it. "Okay, here it is. I love you, Miranda."

Her heart stopped. It must have, because time froze, her brain froze, she couldn't think or feel or even breathe.

"Miranda? Are you okay?"

Everything jolted back to life and she gasped for air. "Yes, I . . . wow." She blinked. Was this real? Had he really said that or was she having a stress-fueled fantasy? "Could you, uh, repeat that?"

He eyed her warily. "I'm almost afraid to."

"No, please, I just . . . I think I'm in shock."

"It's that shocking to hear that I love you?"

Oh God, he'd said it again. And in that moment, she knew for sure. For absolute sure. The revelation was another shock, but this time not one that stopped her heart. Instead, her heart pulsed firmly, and warmth flooded through her chilled body. Smiling, feeling tears of joy and certainty brimming in her eyes, she said, "I love you, too, Luke."

His own smile was a tentative one. "You do? Really?"

She nodded, blinking against the tears. "I think I was scared to let myself really believe it, because I was so afraid it wouldn't work out. But I do, Luke. I love you."

Somehow, they managed to scramble off the bench seat and then they were in each other's arms. When she kissed him, the relief and joy and amazement were almost too much to bear. Damp-cheeked, she eased back in the warm strength of his arms to gaze at him in wonder and say, "You love me."

"And you love me." He reeled her back in and kissed her until she was breathless.

This time he was the one to break the kiss. "I need you naked."

"Oh, yes. How long do we have? Do you have to pick up the boys?"

"No, they're with Annie and Randall for a sleepover. What about Ariana?"

"She's at Glory's. I could . . ." Be away from her daughter for an entire night? The thought made her heart clutch. And yet how wonderful it would be to spend an entire night alone with Luke, celebrating their newly confessed love. To wake beside him in the morning.

Glory was her friend, a responsible mother. Brent was a good dad. They had her phone number and she would leave the ringer turned on. "I could ask if Glory and Brent could keep her for the night."

"Would you be okay with that? I can't think of anything better than the luxury of going to sleep with you and waking up with you."

"Me either." Now she did claim the bag she'd dropped on the deck what seemed like hours earlier, and took her phone from a side pocket.

When Glory answered, Miranda said, "How would you and Brent and Gala feel about keeping Ariana for the night?"

Glory let out a whoop, loud enough that Miranda hastily

pulled the phone away from her ear. Luke, overhearing, grinned.

After Glory had agreed and Miranda put her phone away again, he said, "She knew you were coming to talk to me."

"She did. And she helped me find the courage to do it. She made me see that what I felt for you was worth fighting for."

"I owe her. Big-time."

"Doubly so, because now we have the whole night ahead of us." She darted him a gaze of mock innocence. "However shall we spend it?"

His response was anything but innocent. He took her hand in a firm grip and pulled. She barely had a chance to hook her purse strap over her shoulder as she let herself be towed in his determined wake, across the deck to the door into the kitchen. Through the kitchen, down the hall, up the stairs, down another hall, and then they were in the master bedroom. She hadn't even been aware that the two dogs were following them until Luke shut the door in their curious faces.

He gazed down at her, his eyes intense. Then he reached for the top button of her shirt, fumbled it, made an impatient sound, and then ripped the front of the shirt open.

Yes! She enjoyed it when his inner caveman came out. Especially when she knew that, tomorrow morning, he'd insist on buying her a new shirt. Her bra, though, a peach lace one, she quite liked. So she hurriedly undid the clasp and pulled it off rather than let him destroy it, too.

"Wait a minute," he said. "I just thought . . . You're on birth control pills, right? What happens if you miss one tonight?"

"Not pills. An implant, a progestin rod." It was so easy, one little implant. "But thanks for being responsible."

"That's me," he said a touch ruefully. "Even in the height of passion, I'm responsible."

"It's not a bad thing," she assured him. "Doesn't detract one tiny bit from your sexiness. And speaking of which, weren't you in the middle of taking off my clothes?"

"Thanks for reminding me," he said, brushing his hands over her breasts and making her nipples tighten. After that little tease, he promptly rid her of her capris and panties.

While he peeled his tee over his head, she unfastened his shorts and they dropped to the floor. Two impatient shoves of his big hands had his boxers sliding down his hips to reveal his flat belly and a rising erection.

Not giving her a chance to feast her eyes, he tumbled her down on the duvet. Their legs twined together, their bodies pressed from chest to thighs and every delicious inch in between, and their lips met. Despite the urgency of their passion, Luke's kiss was gentle and she answered in kind. Appreciating him, appreciating this moment. Love. They loved each other, and it was about so much more than slaking the physical need inside them.

The kiss seemed to go on forever. While her sex craved the feel of him, the slow build of arousal was so tantalizing that she almost didn't want to move to the next stage. Before Luke, she'd enjoyed intercourse for the sheer physical pleasure, especially the release, but with him she'd found that lovemaking had even more to offer.

He lifted himself off her and she gave him a teasing pout and a whimper of protest—teasing, because she knew that whatever he did next would bring her pleasure.

After shoving back the comforter, he sat cross-legged on the bed. How many guys could even do that? But she'd already seen demonstrations of Luke's flexibility, so she wasn't surprised. "Come sit across my lap," he said.

Eyeing the erection that rose from the nest of dark auburn curls between his legs, she was happy to accept that invitation. She straddled his thighs and lowered herself across his lap with her legs wrapped around him and her feet on the bed behind him. "Mmm." She rubbed her center against his hard shaft. "I like this." With a mischievous grin, she said, "I could get off just doing this."

"Feel free." He took her nipple between his thumb and index finger and tweaked it gently. "Let me know if I can help."

She knew he meant it. Luke was the most generous lover she'd ever been with. "Some other time. Right now, I want us to be totally together."

"Me too. That's why I chose this position. We can do this." With his free hand he cupped the back of her head, bringing her head forward to meet his kiss. "I can do this," he murmured against her lips as he tweaked her nipple.

"And I can do this." She slid her fingers up and down his shaft. "Or this." She eased back from the kiss and braced her body with a hand on the bed behind her, lifting herself up and easing him toward her opening.

When he slipped inside, it felt wonderful, but she had a hard time keeping her balance so she wrapped her arms around him. He did the same, putting his arms around her lower back, his strength supporting her.

Gazing at her, he smiled and she saw the love in that smile, in the warmth of his kaleidoscope eyes.

She returned the smile, letting her own eyes convey everything she felt for him.

Then he began to rock his hips, slowly and easily. Not only did each rock thrust his erection in and out, but because she was sitting on him her entire body went along for the ride.

Experimenting, she got into the act, rocking too as Luke smiled into her eyes and supported her back. When she tried increasing the speed, he let her, and when arousal coiled too tightly in her and she slowed down again, he cooperated.

"Like it?" he asked.

"So much." Even though they weren't kissing, something about the eye contact made this kind of lovemaking feel particularly intimate.

He removed one hand from her back and caressed her cheek. "I'm glad. How about this? Does this feel good?" He toyed with her nipple and by now her body was so sensitized that shocks of pleasure darted straight to her core.

"Very good." Her body urged her to rock faster, and so she did, all the time watching his face.

He caught his breath and his eyes flared wider and glittered.

Normally at this point, she'd have thrown her head back, closed her eyes, and ridden the sensations all the way to climax. But this time she kept her eyes open, focused on him. And rather than speed to the end, she forced herself to breathe deeply and slow down. The longer she held it off, the more intense the pleasure would be. For both of them.

"You know what else I can do?" he asked hoarsely. "This." His hand dropped and his thumb brushed her clit.

If she'd thought her nipple was supersensitized, that was nothing compared to this. Pleasure had her clenching her internal muscles, clenching and releasing, demanding more from Luke. In response, he rocked faster, accompanying each stroke with the pressure of his thumb on that swollen bud of nerve endings.

"I love you, Miranda. Are you ready to come with me?"

"Oh, yes." She would come with him, in climax and anywhere else he asked. "I love you, too."

And on those words, their bodies shattered in unison.

Saturday morning, Luke woke to the usual alarm. But, unusually, when he went to reach over and turn it off, a weight pinned his arm. A delicious, warm, feminine weight. His next realization was that he had a hard-on.

Miranda stirred and said irritably, "Turn that damn thing off."

Chuckling, he rolled toward her and used his unpinned arm to silence the alarm. "Not a morning person, I see."

Her eyes opened, she studied him for a long minute, and then she said, "Now, that's better. Waking up to you is good. To a screaming alarm, not so much."

"Waking up with me is *good*?" He nudged his erection against her hip.

A slow grin tugged at her lips. "If I say Tony-the-Tiger grrreat, will you make coffee?"

"Only if you mean it."

She turned on her side, facing him. "I mean it so much that I'll even forgo the coffee. I bet you can think of some other way of getting me going."

He was about to offer several options, when she suddenly rolled away again and slipped from between the sheets. "Give me one sec." She dashed toward the bathroom and the sight of her slim back, curvy butt, and long legs made him even harder.

While she was in there, a sound issued from the phone she'd left on the dresser after a bedtime check-in call to Glory and Ariana. When she came out, still beautifully naked, he said, "You got a text."

She grabbed the phone and whatever she read on the screen made her laugh. She brought it over and held it out to him.

It was from Glory, saying, Ariana's fine. Go back to bed with your hottie.

"That woman gives good advice," he said, placing the phone on the bedside table and opening the sheets to invite her in.

And then, with his lips and tongue, his hands and his

swollen cock, he did his very best to awaken every single cell in her body.

He was on top when they both climaxed, and for a moment he let himself flop down on top of her. But then, conscious of his substantially greater weight, he forced himself to roll off and lie on his back beside her. She lay unmoving, but when he reached for her hand, her fingers intertwined with his.

"You're a terrible alarm clock," she said with a yawn. "You woke me up all right, but now I feel like I could sleep for days."

"I love you," he said. Not that it was an apology or an answer or anything like that, just that he really liked saying it. He also hoped she'd respond with the words he couldn't get enough of hearing.

"I love you, too," she said, giving him his wish. She turned her head on the pillow and smiled at him. "I really do. And I'm happy. Really, truly happy. Like I have everything I could possibly want." Her lips quivered. "I've never felt that way before, not in my entire life."

"Oh, Jesus, Miranda." He rolled on his side and peered into her lovely eyes, which had gone teary. "You don't know how wonderful that makes me feel." Though it also made him feel terrible that her life had been filled with so much unhappiness. But he wouldn't mention that now, and spoil the mood.

"This is big," she said, blinking to hold the tears back. "It's almost too big to take in, and yet at the same time it feels so natural and right. Do you know what I mean?"

"Exactly."

"I've had men say they loved me before."

He winced.

"But," she went on, "they never meant it. Maybe I even knew that at the time, or would have if I'd been paying attention. I was too eager to find love, so I saw it where it didn't really exist."

"It does exist here. I do mean it. You know that, don't you?"

"I honestly do. I trust you."

He wanted to trust her, too, yet what she'd said made him wary. Seeking reassurance, he said, "You really mean it, too, don't you? Those things you said, about how this is different . . ."

Her head nodded on the pillow. "I do mean it. There's so much to love, Luke. Aaron has always been my hero, the greatest guy in the world. Well, you're up there with him. But it isn't just how great you are as a person, or how sexy you are, it's how I feel when I'm with you. When I even think about you. It's like a space inside me that's always been empty and hollow is filling up with something warm and wonderful. My love for you, and yours for me."

His own heart was damned full, and now he was in danger of tearing up. Gruffly he said, "I think that's the nicest thing anyone's ever said to me." He cleared his throat. "It's different for me, because I did know love before. What Candace and I had was wonderful. After she died, I was afraid I'd never know that kind of happiness again. I'd never know love again. I don't know if it's harder if you've never had it, like you, or if you had it and lost it."

Looking thoughtful, she nodded.

"But anyhow," he said, "then you came along. You're amazing and special in so many ways. You made me feel things, Miranda. Lust, frustration, tenderness, protectiveness, admiration. Anger, hurt. Tender feelings and passionate ones. You brought me to life again. I figured I was falling in love with you and that's what I was going to say at the wedding reception. But I didn't realize how powerful my feelings were until I saw you with Julian. I had this totally primitive 'she's mine!' reaction."

"And I am."

A glance at the clock had him groaning. "I have to get up and go to work. Saturdays are always busy."

"Me too. And I have to pick up Ariana and make a quick trip home to get changed."

"Back to the real world," he said wryly. "I hope we can find a way to do this again soon."

"It's not so easy when we both have kids, is it?"

"Remind me, why did we have kids?" he joked.

"To complicate our lives?" she said with a sassy grin as she shoved back the covers.

As Miranda climbed out of bed, her phone rang. She glanced at it on the bedside table. "It's Aaron." If he was taking the morning flight to Vancouver, he was probably at the Blue Moon Air office.

"Go ahead." Luke rose, too, and headed for the bathroom.

She accepted the call and said, "Hi, Aaron, hang on a sec." Quickly she picked up Luke's tee from the floor where he'd tossed it last night, and pulled it over her head. "Okay, I'm here."

"Hey, Sis." His voice sounded odd. "Uh, are you sitting down?"

Oh-oh. She swallowed and dropped to sit on the edge of the bed. *Please let everyone be okay.* "Yes. What's happened? Are you all right?"

"What? Yes, fine. Sorry, I didn't mean to worry you. It's just, I had the strangest phone call. Or, rather, I returned a call. I mean, she phoned yesterday when I was flying, left a message, and when I called back she was gone for the day. So I left voice mail, not anticipating hearing back until Monday, but she called me as I was driving to the village. It seems she works Saturdays."

"What are you talking about? Who's 'she'?" Her brother wasn't normally so unfocused, and Miranda was a little worried. "Did you pull over? You're not driving, are you?"

"No, I'm parked on the shoulder of the road. And *she* is a lawyer in Florida. She's with the retirement community where Mom's parents live. Lived. They were both killed in a car crash."

"Oh," she said on a long sigh. Seeking warmth and comfort, she slid under the covers, propping a couple of pillows behind her back. "That's, well, I don't know what to say." She shook her head. "Poor them, that their happy retirement ended this way."

"Yeah."

She sighed. "They never showed us the slightest bit of affection, and yet I feel kind of sad they're gone."

"Me too. They were our only relatives."

They were both quiet for a moment, and then she said, "It's so final. I mean, I know there was no real chance they'd ever decide they actually liked us, but now . . ." If she'd secretly nursed a tiny hope, now that hope was extinguished.

"Well, actually . . ." That odd tone was back in his voice.

"Actually what? Did they leave us some big apology letter, to be opened in the event of their death?" She said it sarcastically, not daring to let herself believe that might be true.

"No letter. But here's the thing. They didn't have wills. And we inherit."

"Oh my God." It took a moment for that to sink in. And then she gave a surprised snort of laughter. "Oh my, that'd piss them off, wouldn't it?"

"Maybe. But maybe not. The lawyer said she strongly encourages all the members of their community to make wills. The same as Eden does at Arbutus Lodge. But our grandparents refused. She explained the laws of inheritance. They had to know that if they didn't make wills, we'd inherit."

"They probably thought one of them would die before the other, and that person could then make a will and leave it to whomever they wanted. Spouses never think they'll die at the same time, right?"

"Maybe." Her brother still sounded kind of stunned. "But anyhow . . ."

Perhaps it was mercenary, but she had to ask. "Did they have much money left?" Retirees in their eighties, paying for a Florida lifestyle, chances were they'd run through whatever money they'd once had.

"A house in a mid-level retirement community," he said slowly. "Some investments and money in the bank." He paused. "Miranda, in Canadian money, after estate and administration taxes and fees, it amounts to over five hundred thousand."

"Dollars?" she squeaked.

"Split between us. Damn, little sister." His voice shook. "I think we're rich."

"Rich? Rich! Oh my God, our grandparents finally did something for us! Even if they probably didn't mean to." Or maybe they did. Perhaps she would let herself believe that.

"I know. I'm just . . . stunned."

"You sound it. Me too." Unable to sit still, she swung out of bed and paced across the room.

She couldn't get her head around that amount of money. "Aaron, I can pay you back!" In a tattered notebook, she'd recorded every penny her brother had ever loaned or given her.

"Thanks for the thought, but it's not exactly like I'll need the money." Now he sounded more like himself.

She chuckled. "No, I guess not." But she'd do it all the same. Then she'd find a small house to rent, and pay Seal and Di rent for all the time she'd spent at SkySong, when they could've had paying guests in her cabin. And then . . . and then . . . she didn't have a clue what she'd do. A college fund for Ariana. She'd tell her that her great-grandparents had gifted it to her. Then she'd buy books—glossy, brand-new books for both of them.

"I told the lawyer I'd fill you in," Aaron said. "I said we'll phone her back when our heads are on a little straighter."

"Good idea." Her head was definitely not on straight. In less than a day, her life had gone from messed up to amazing. Luke loved her, and she and Aaron were going to be rich.

"She did say it'd take some time to settle everything— like sell the place, though there's a waiting list so it won't be a problem. But as soon as we send her notarized proof of our identities, she can advance us some funds against the final distribution."

"Okay."

"I can pay off the Beaver." There was wonder in his voice.

"Awesome!" That would be such a relief for him. Blue Moon Air was his baby, and it was a constant struggle to stay in the black. He needed to make the payments on his second plane, a de Havilland Beaver, but with only two planes and two pilots, there was a limit to how much business he could take on.

"I could even buy another plane," he said. "Have more scheduled flights, take more charters and sightseeing flights. Give Jillian all the flying hours she wants, hire another pilot, too. To spell us off, and cover for her when she's on mat leave."

"Wow, Aaron. I'm sad Mom's parents died, but seriously, wow."

"I know."

"Have you told Eden?"

"Not yet. I figured you should be the first."

That was so sweet. "Thank you." Knowing what an emotional mess she was right now, she was concerned for him. "You're not going to fly, are you? You won't be able to concentrate."

"Oh man, I hadn't thought of that."

"Call Jillian right this minute. You know she'll fill in, and then you can go home and tell Eden the news. Are you okay to drive?"

"Yeah. Now I've talked to you, I feel more grounded. I'll be fine to drive. I can't wait to see Eden's face when I tell her. See you soon."

Hanging up, she wondered if she could smile any wider.

The bathroom door opened and Luke walked into the bedroom, a towel wrapped low on his hips. Yeah, maybe she could smile wider.

"You look pretty happy," he said, smiling back.

"My grandparents died." A twinge of guilt and sorrow dampened her excitement.

"Oh, gee, I'm sorry. The ones in Florida, that you hadn't heard from in forever?"

"Yeah." She took a deep breath, allowing herself to mourn them but still feel happy about her windfall. "They didn't have wills, and Aaron and I will inherit more than two hundred and fifty thousand each." Speaking the words, she realized something. "That's a quarter of a million." She shook her head. "I can't even conceive of it. I mean, I've always had trouble making the next rent payment."

"My God." His eyes widened and he looked almost as shocked as she'd felt when Aaron told her the news. He came over and hugged her. "I'm really happy for you."

And then he grinned, his beautiful eyes twinkling. "Whew. I'm so glad we got back together last night. Otherwise, you might think I only loved you for your money."

She smiled up at him. "No. I know you love me for me, rich or poor, prickles and petals."

Chapter Twenty-Two

On the last Sunday in June, down on the beach at SkySong, Miranda emailed a couple of photos to Mrs. Sharma and then put down her phone, raised her arms to the afternoon sun, and luxuriated in it. Luxuriated in everything.

Best of all was the sight of Luke trying to teach the three kids to skip stones. Ariana—her big girl who would turn three in a month, and who almost never threw a tantrum now—and the boisterous Brandon, seemed totally content to hurl stones and not have them skip. Only Caleb was devoting effort to learning the technique. As for Honey and Pigpen, they didn't seem to tire of chasing stones that sunk rather than floated like sticks.

Miranda was content to laze in the sun while Luke supervised the kids, and Eden's family prepared a feast up the hill in Di and Seal's big house. No longer did she feel compelled to always be contributing, to earn her way. Being confident in a relationship, being an equal, meant not keeping score of who owed whom. It meant being partners who shared and helped each other, and sometimes just let the other person goof off and relax.

There was a lot of relaxing going on this afternoon, as

several resort guests strolled along the beach, perched on logs, or waded in the chilly water. Di and Seal, two runaway hippies, had built an incredible place over the decades they'd lived on the island.

Luke sent a flat stone skimming the surface, skipping one, two, three, four, five times, and she cheered, "My hero!"

He turned to smile at her, brushed his hands together, and said, "Time to rest on my laurels."

Coming up the beach to where she sat on a towel with her back against a log, he said, "I'm so glad you let me buy that bikini."

They'd been strolling through Blue Moon Harbor village the previous week, on their way to dinner at C-Shell, when they spied the gorgeous bathing suit in the window of Island Treasures. Patterned in shades of blue, it was admittedly perfect for her coloring, but also outrageously expensive. She might be inheriting a small fortune—thanks to the grandparents she'd chosen to believe actually intended their estate to go to her and Aaron—but she would always be thrifty. She didn't protest too much, though, when Luke had insisted on buying it, saying he wasn't doing it for her but for himself, and she was doing him a favor by wearing it.

That night, after one of Celia's incredible feasts, he'd asked Miranda to model the bikini before bed. Thinking back on the inspired lovemaking that had ensued, she grinned with satisfaction. She was entirely happy to benefit from all the lessons Luke had learned from those sex manuals.

"Looking forward to the party?" he asked as he lowered his muscular body to sprawl beside her.

She claimed a kiss. "I can't believe Eden's family is throwing a party to celebrate the anniversary of me moving to Destiny," she marveled. "When I arrived here a year ago, I was a total bitch. Pathetic, needy. Jealous of Eden."

"You had your reasons, and you've changed. Everyone

sees that. When I watch you with them, it's clear you're part of that family. Just the same as when you're with my parents and in-laws."

Over the past weeks, since they'd confessed their love for each other in early May, it had become a regular thing to hang out with either his relatives or hers. There'd been a few awkward moments—and blunt Annie had confessed that sometimes it hurt to see Miranda in Candace's place—but everyone was getting to be comfortable together.

So comfortable that Annie, Randall, Sonia, and Forbes were invited to the party that would get underway in another hour or so. Di and Seal had asked Forbes to bring his guitar, and Miranda knew that a lot of old folk songs would get sung tonight. Hopefully, there'd be no mention of Merlin. Annie's intense focus was now on fine-tuning her commune video game, and she apparently gave no thought to the real-life stories that had inspired it.

Down by the water's edge, Caleb was showing Ariana how to pick flat stones for skipping. "He's so patient with her," Miranda commented. "It reminds me of how Aaron was with me." In fact, all three kids got along quite well now, with Brandon fueling Ariana's boisterous side and Caleb trying to teach her new skills.

A couple of white-haired men, their aging bodies clad in shorts, strolled along the beach holding hands. Miranda exchanged smiles with them and the two men paused, glancing from her and Luke to the three kids. "You have a beautiful family," one of the men said, and the two of them meandered on.

That was nice, being taken for a family. As if they all truly did belong together, which was how it felt to Miranda. Hopefully, to Luke as well.

"Hey," he said quietly. "Here's a thought."

She turned to him.

"What that guy said, about us having a lovely family . . ."

He reached for the short-sleeved shirt he'd brought down to the beach but hadn't put on. "What would you say . . ." From the pocket he took a small wooden box.

Her heart skipped, much more effectively than those stones her daughter was tossing.

"To making it official?" Luke finished. "I love you, Miranda Gabriel. Will you and Ariana join your little family with my little family? Will you come home with me and never leave?" He opened the box and there on a pad of creamy velvet was a stunning ring, an abstract pattern of diamonds and blue gemstones.

"You're asking me to marry you?" she said. Was this really happening, or was it the best dream she'd ever had?

"I sure am. Do you like the ring?" he asked, sounding nervous. "I got it made. I chose blue topaz because it's the color of your eyes, though nowhere near as pretty."

"It's fabulous." She brushed her fingers across the top of the ring—yes, it was real; all of this was real—and then eased it from the velvet pad. "I came here a year ago, having hit rock bottom," she said wonderingly. "And now I can't imagine life getting any better." She started to slip the ring on her finger.

"Hey, wait a minute." Luke caught her hand. "Aren't you forgetting something?"

Confused, she gazed at him and then it dawned on her. Didn't he know her answer, or did he just want to hear her say it? "Yes, Luke. Yes! I'll marry you and we'll become one wonderful blended family." She would have a real home for the first time in her life. "Yes, please."

He eased the ring onto her finger, lifted her hand, and kissed her finger beside the ring. "Thank you for making me the happiest man alive."

Then he kissed her lips, and as she threw her arms around him and sunk into the kiss, her heart felt full. For the first time ever, there was no hole, no ache inside it.

She wasn't perfect, and Luke knew that. But she had grown up a lot in the past year. Her heart, which had always craved love and acceptance, had finally made the right choice. It had led her to a remarkable man, a man who loved and respected her, a man who wanted to share his life with her.

She was lucky and she was blessed—and yes, she did deserve this.

Note to Readers

Blue Moon Harbor and Destiny Island are fictional, but as is so often the case with the world an author creates, they exist in my heart. So do the heroines, heroes, and secondary characters who live there. I hope the same thing happens for you when you read the stories.

When I introduced Miranda Gabriel in *Fly Away With Me*, she fascinated me. She's tough but vulnerable, and fear can turn her into—to use her words—a pathetic bitch. She'd do absolutely anything for the two people she loves: her two-year-old daughter and her older brother, Aaron, the hero of *Fly Away With Me*. You couldn't meet a more loyal, mixed-up, or flawed person than Miranda. How could I not write her story, and make her bust her butt to find her own happy ending?

So, for the young woman who's always fallen for bad boys and always had her heart broken, I sent her a true good guy. Widower Luke Chandler has known true love, with a wonderfully perfect woman, and believes he'll never love again. So what's he to do when he develops feelings for the thoroughly messed-up, mixed-up Miranda?

Oh yes, I had fun writing this book, and I also shed a few tears along the way. I do hope you enjoy Miranda and Luke's story.

You can read seaplane pilot Aaron's romance with Ottawa lawyer Eden in *Fly Away With Me*, and single mom Jillian's reunion with Michael, her son's father, in "A Blue

Moon Harbor Christmas" in *Winter Wishes*. Coming up next is shy Iris's love story—with sexy musician Julian in *Sail Away With Me*.

Blue Moon Harbor may be a fictional community, but my writing community is very real. I'm deeply grateful to all the people who have helped me with *Come Home With Me*: my always supportive agent, Emily Sylvan Kim at Prospect Agency; my terrific editor at Kensington, Martin Biro; Martin's excellent assistant, James Abbate; cheerful and helpful publicist Jane Nutter; Emily's delightful assistant, Jes Lyons; and last but definitely not least, my critiquers Rosalind Villers and Alaura Ross.

I'd also like to express my true appreciation to my readers. I love sharing my stories with you and I'm so honored that you read my books.

I'm delighted to hear from you. You can email me at susan@susanlyons.ca or contact me through my website at www.susanfox.ca, where you'll also find excerpts, behind-the-scenes notes, recipes, a monthly contest, the sign-up for my newsletter, and other goodies. You can also find me on Facebook at facebook.com/SusanLyonsFox.

If you enjoyed *Come Home With Me*,
be sure not to miss the first book in Susan Fox's
Blue Moon Harbor series,

FLY AWAY WITH ME

*Known for its rugged beauty and eccentric residents,
tiny Blue Moon Harbor is big on love . . .*

For busy lawyer Eden Blaine, a trip to a Pacific
Northwest island she's never even heard of is far from a
vacation. Eden's ailing mother has tasked her with
finding her long-lost aunt, who once had ties to a
commune on the island. Still reeling from a breakup
with her long-time boyfriend, romance is the last thing
Eden is looking for. But her gorgeous seaplane pilot
has her wondering if a carefree rebound fling
is exactly what she needs. . . .

Aaron Gabriel has no illusions about happily ever after.
His troubled childhood made sure of that.
But he does appreciate a pretty woman's company, and
Eden is the exact combination of smart and sexy that
turns him on. Still, as he helps her search for her missing
aunt, the casual relationship he imagined quickly
becomes something much more passionate—
and much harder to give up.
Can two people determined to ignore romance
recognize that their heated connection
is the kind of love destined to last?

**A Zebra mass-market paperback
and eBook on sale now.
Turn the page for a special look!**

When Eden Blaine tugged her wheeled carry-on bag off the sloped ramp from the seaplane terminal onto the wooden dock, she almost lost her balance. The surface beneath her feet looked flat, but it moved gently, disconcertingly.

Thank heavens I left my lawyer suit and heels in Ottawa. Her jeans and loafers were much better suited to this venue, even though Vancouver Harbour Flight Centre nestled along the shore of a huge, cosmopolitan city.

For a moment, she forgot all about being rushed and frazzled. The view compelled her to stop and stare. On this sunny, early June afternoon, the harbor spread out before her in a spectacular panorama. Boats bustling along, green swaths of parkland, a cruise ship terminal, the white sails of Canada Place, commercial docks, and a whole other city on the far shore, sheltering under dramatic mountains: There was too much to take in. She breathed deeply, expecting to fill her lungs with the fresh tang of ocean air, but a nose-wrinkling underlay of fuel odor reminded her why she was here, standing on this narrow, unstable dock in the middle of all this amazing scenery. The scent, the motion, and the anticipation of the upcoming flight combined to make her jittery with nerves.

Eden hadn't done much flying but had occasionally taken a smallish jet from Ottawa to Toronto or Montreal. Compared to what she'd thought of as *smallish*, the seaplanes tied up to the dock were minuscule. Add to that the fact that she'd never taken off from or landed on water . . .

Her hand rose to her mouth and her teeth closed on a fingernail. Before she could gnaw on it, she forced her hand down and curled her fingers around the handle of the briefcase that hung over one shoulder along with her purse. Nana had broken her of the nail-biting habit when she was in fourth grade, saying that not only was it unattractive and unhygienic but it was a sure giveaway of anxiety, insecurity, and lack of control. None of which were qualities Eden wanted to reveal to the outside world.

This was going to be an adventure, and adventure was definitely *not* her middle name. Still, she'd face any peril if she could restore her mom's once-bright spirit. The seaplane flight would get her to Destiny Island a day earlier than the ferry would have, and with only a week off work to find her mother's long-lost sister, every hour was important. Her mom, fragile after a double mastectomy, followed by chemotherapy and radiation, was counting on her. Eden's parents were wonderful and she never, ever let them down.

Eden refused to let herself think for one moment that her quest might end in learning that her aunt, Lucy, was dead.

Squaring her shoulders, she tugged her wheelie along the dock toward the plane with the Blue Moon Air logo. She had to admit it looked perky with its blue-and-white paint shining in the sunlight, the wings mounted from the top of the cabin, and the pontoons holding it atop the deep, bluish-green ocean. The logo was appealing too: a blue moon with a white plane flying across it.

Half a dozen people clustered beside the plane: three sixtyish men in outdoorsy clothes, two women a decade or two younger in jeans and hoodies, and a lean but broad-shouldered guy in jeans and a blue T-shirt. His back was to her as he hoisted luggage onto the plane. One of the women spotted Eden, raised a hand in a tentative wave, and said something to the others.

The broad-shouldered guy turned, straightening, and she felt a physical sensation akin to the one she'd experienced when she first saw the horrendous taxi lineup at Vancouver International Airport. *After* her flight from Ottawa had been late arriving.

Well, not exactly akin. At the airport, the legs-stopping-moving-of-their-own-accord, air-leaving-her-lungs-in-a-whoosh sensation had been nasty, whereas this one was quite pleasant.

As she forced her legs onward, she took a visual inventory. Lean and nicely muscled; narrow hips and long legs to complement those broad shoulders. Hair so dark a brown it was almost black, longish and shaggy rather than styled. Medium brown skin. Aviator sunglasses hiding his eyes, making it difficult to assess his age, though she guessed it was close to her own twenty-nine. Ruggedly handsome features lit by a smile as he strode to meet her.

That smile warmed her in a way that made her feel special. And that was silly, because of course he merely was relieved that she'd finally shown up and the flight could depart.

"I'm Aaron Gabriel, Blue Moon Air pilot. And you'd be Eden Blaine." He reached for the long handle of her wheelie.

As he shoved the handle down and hefted the bag, she confirmed, "Yes, I would be. I'm so sorry for the delay." She hated being late, hated inconveniencing people. When she'd phoned Blue Moon Air from the airport taxi lineup, she'd said she wouldn't make the flight on time and asked if she could reschedule for the next morning.

To her astonishment and delight, the man who'd answered had said they'd hold the flight for her.

"Ah, well, airlines," the pilot now said in a joking tone. "Never can rely on them being on time."

What could she possibly say to that? She firmly believed in adhering to schedules, yet the airline's flexibility had worked to her benefit today. Rather than respond, she kept quiet as she followed him to the plane.

As he loaded her carry-on into the cargo hold, she apologized to the other passengers, who all murmured variations of "No problem."

Aaron took her briefcase from her and stowed it, too, but let her keep her purse. "Climb aboard," he told her.

"But what about everyone else?" No one else had boarded.

"We have a boarding order. Your seat's first. Hop in." He offered her his hand.

Eyeing the dock, which heaved rhythmically up and down, the plane, which also bobbed up and down but to a different beat, and the insubstantial three-step metal ladder that connected the two, she gratefully put her hand into his.

Warm, firm, secure. Touching him reminded her of just how wonderful male-female contact could be. She'd missed that since she and Ray had ended their four-year relationship. In fact, she didn't remember Ray's hands ever feeling this good. He had city hands, well-groomed but not super-masculine. Hands that were efficient in operating a computer, handling legal files, and bringing her to orgasm. Competent, yet not exactly virile.

And what was she doing, thinking about sex? Embarrassed, she clambered up the ladder and then let go of Aaron's hand. "Where do I sit?"

"Up front, right-hand seat."

"But that's the copilot's seat."

"Don't need a copilot on a plane this size. That's a passenger seat."

No copilot? Aaron Gabriel looked entirely healthy, but anyone could have a stroke, a heart attack, or an aneurysm.

He shoved his sunglasses atop his head and winked. "Don't worry. I'm one hundred percent fit." His gaze rested on her for a long moment, and there was a spark in his long-lashed, bluish-gray eyes that hinted at flirtation.

That spark sent a corresponding tingle rippling through her blood, almost strong enough to combat her jittery nerves. She'd never been a highly sensual woman, so it was unsettling to feel this purely female awareness of a sexy man. She cleared her throat. "I'm glad to hear that." Her voice came out in lawyer mode, too formal for the situation. Giving herself an internal headshake, she scrambled into the right front seat and fumbled for the seat belt as the other passengers piled in behind her.

Eden liked order and predictability, situations she could control, and this one was anything but that. Taking deep breaths, she thought ruefully that up until a year ago, her life had been happy and uncomplicated. She'd had her family, her terrific job, and Ray, her life mate. Then Nana died, Mom was diagnosed, and, two months ago, Eden and Ray broke up. Now her mom was finally finished with chemo and radiation but still feeling sick and depressed—at least until a week ago, when she'd found an out-of-the-blue clue to her sister Lucy's disappearance, and nothing would do but for Eden to follow it. Immediately. And so here she was, about to put her life in the hands of the handsome pilot and his perky miniature plane.

Aaron stowed the ladder and shut the boarding hatch from the outside, then stepped onto a float and entered through the door by the pilot's seat. He gave the passengers a safety briefing that included seat belts, turning off electronic devices, emergency procedures, life preservers, exits, and so on. He advised them to read the safety card in

the seat pocket, asked if there were any questions, and then
said, "Let's fly, folks."

Buckled in, with a headset on, he started the plane's
engine and talked to air traffic control.

Eden concentrated on memorizing the safety card,
trying not to imagine crash landings or pilot heart attacks.

Aaron signalled a man on the dock, who untied the
ropes. As they motored out into the harbor, the plane
bounced over gentle waves. The motion was rather like driving over a heavily rutted road in her little Smart car. Except
that the fragile plane was soon going to fling itself into the
great blue yonder. She clasped her hands and squeezed them
together, another defense against nail-biting.

"We'll be making three stops this afternoon," Aaron told
the passengers, speaking loudly to make himself heard over
the engine noise. "First, we'll fly up the Sunshine Coast to
Texada Island for our Sylvan Retreat couple. Then west to
Campbell River to drop off the three fishers. Then south
again to Blue Moon Harbor on Destiny Island."

Eden's dad had booked the flight and she had assumed
it was a direct one from Vancouver to Blue Moon Harbor.
Her logical brain suggested that flying north, west, and then
south wasn't the most efficient way to reach Destiny Island,
but it didn't really matter. Her goals for today were to get
settled at the Once in a Blue Moon B and B, confirm the
rental car she'd reserved for tomorrow morning, and make
inquiries of the owners of the B and B.

Normally, Eden planned everything in exquisite detail,
but the past week had been crazy. She'd had to organize
files and appointments at work so she could leave her assistant in charge and make copious notes for her younger
sister Kelsey, who was home from university for the
summer and would help Dad care for Mom. There'd been
only a moment here and there to prepare for the trip. Her
dad had helped, making travel arrangements and using his

Internet skills to search for information on the island, but most of what he'd found was tourism-focused. He'd located only two mentions of the old commune, nothing that would help Eden track down a hippie girl named Lucy Nelson who'd come to Destiny Island in 1969. Eden hoped her hosts at the B and B could identify some of the island's longtime residents, whom she could interview.

The plane increased speed and its nose came up, the floats skimmed the tops of the waves, and then the small craft lifted into the air. Rather than the white-noise drone Eden was used to when flying, she heard a whiny engine roar and a rattling sound. The dashboard—or whatever they called it in a plane—sported a collection of confusing dials and gauges. The huge window in front of her made it impossible to ignore the scarily vast expanse of sky outside. To her right was another window, in a flimsy door. If that door snapped open, the only thing holding her in the plane would be the seat belt. The aircraft seemed so insubstantial and she felt vulnerable, which she hated. She gulped, took more deep breaths, clenched her hands more firmly, and glanced over at Aaron's comforting solidness and his strong brown hands on the steering yoke.

The man's been thoroughly trained, he knows what he's doing, and he must have regular medical exams. The plane's a commercial craft, owned by a reputable airline, and is inspected regularly. There's not a single thing to worry about.

"Nervous?" Aaron asked, shooting a pointed look at her tightly clasped hands.

Since her body'd already given her away, she admitted, "Trying not to be," speaking up to be heard over the noise.

"Relax and enjoy it." He gave her a smile full of warmth and enthusiasm. "It's the best thing in the world."

You must be kidding. But he wasn't. The sincerity of his tone and body language confirmed that he meant it. As he returned his attention to the plane's controls, she mulled over his words. To this man, the best thing in the world was flying. He had a job where he experienced joy every day, just as she did. Her work as program counsel for the Butterworth Foundation involved administrative and legal details, which she excelled at and took satisfaction in, but what she truly loved was helping provide funds for worthwhile charities and nonprofits.

Still, as much as she enjoyed her job, the best thing in her world was her family. She loved her mom, her dad, and her younger sister with all her heart. They were the center of her world, her top priority at all times. Idly, she wondered about the handsome pilot beside her. What people were special to him? A wife or girlfriend? Parents? Maybe a son or daughter? Had he considered them when he made that blithe statement about flying being the best thing in the world?

She was overanalyzing. That attribute was useful for a lawyer, but family and friends kept reminding her it wasn't the most comfortable trait to bring to bear in a personal relationship. Yet her musings had distracted her from her anxiety and she felt more relaxed.

"Lions Gate Bridge," Aaron announced to the passengers. "Also known as First Narrows. It connects Vancouver's Stanley Park to West Vancouver and the North Shore."

The view was a dramatic one of contrasts: the forest green of the park versus the high-rises of the city; the impressive and beautiful man-made span of the bridge versus the untamed ocean below; the industrial loading docks versus the rugged mountains behind. "Ottawa seems awfully"—she searched for the right description—"sedate and old-world in comparison."

"You're from Ottawa?" Aaron said. "How about the rest of you?"

"Vancouver," one of the other women answered. "Even so, the scenery never gets old."

"We're from Edmonton," one of the men said.

Another added, "We came out here for the fishing a few years ago and now it's an annual thing. There's something about fishing for salmon on the open ocean that gets into a man's blood. Not to mention being able to take home fish you caught yourself and lord it over all the Alberta beef-eaters."

Fishing held no appeal to Eden and she'd had no experience with the ocean. But gazing down at tankers and sailboats gave her some small notion of what an important role the sea played in some people's lives.

Ever since she'd agreed to undertake this mission for her mother, she'd been focused on practicalities, but now a tingle of excitement quickened her pulse. She was in a new place, a ruggedly scenic setting, and something about the vista of ocean and mountains invigorated her. Adventure might not be her middle name, but it seemed she was on one, and right now it didn't feel half bad.

Something had drawn Lucy, the aunt Eden had never even known about until a week before, to Destiny Island. What had Lucy experienced there—and what lay in store for Eden?

Connect with  U s

Visit us online at
KensingtonBooks.com
to read more from your favorite authors, see books
by series, view reading group guides, and more.

Join us on social media

for sneak peeks, chances to win books and prize packs,
and to share your thoughts with other readers.

facebook.com/kensingtonpublishing
twitter.com/kensingtonbooks

Tell us what you think!

To share your thoughts, submit a review,
or sign up for our eNewsletters, please visit:
KensingtonBooks.com/TellUs.